RISE
AGAIN

RISE AGAIN

A ZOMBIE THRILLER

Ben Tripp

GALLERY BOOKS
New York   London   Toronto   Sydney

Gallery Books
A Division of Simon & Schuster, Inc.
1230 Avenue of the Americas
New York, NY 10020

First Gallery Books trade paperback edition October 2010.

GALLERY BOOKS and colophon are trademarks of Simon & Schuster, Inc.

For information about special discounts for bulk purchases, please contactSimon & Schuster Special Sales at 1-866-506-1949 or business@simonandschuster.com.

The Simon & Schuster Speakers Bureau can bring authors to your live event. For more information or to book an event contact the Simon & Schuster Speakers Bureau at 1-866-248-3049 or visit our website at www.simonspeakers.com.

Designed by Jaime Putorti

Manufactured in the United States of America

10 9 8 7 6 5 4 3 2

ISBN 978-1-4391-6516-4

ISBN 978-1-4391-6518-8 (ebook)

For my son Ian.

This is one of the stories

I never told you at bedtime.

pity this busy monster, manunkind . . .
——e. e. cummings

PART ONE

FOREST PEAK

1

Kelley Adelman hadn't written this many words since the history final in senior year. Her fingers were cramping up. The buck-a-dozen ballpoint pen left globs of ink in its wake and the police notebook paper was so thin she could read the impression of her words three sheets below. These words were going to make an impression on Danny, too, Kelley figured. If they didn't, it made no difference. Kelley was gone either way. But she wanted—needed, on some level—to know that she would have Danny's undivided attention, just for once. Even if it meant not being there when it happened.

On the muted TV by the stove, news footage of foreign wars alternated with Fourth of July celebrity chef barbecue tips. The quartz clock on the wall ticked off the seconds around the printed fishing scene on its face, the mountain wind sang its lament in the trees outside, and it was a night like any other night in Forest Peak, except it was Kelley's last one.

She realized she had stopped writing. Kelley was staring at the big black revolver that lay on the plastic kitchen tablecloth, and it was staring back at her.

Dear Danny,
When you went to war, you promised me you'd come back. But you didn't. I don't know what I'm waiting for. It's over for me. I know you never much liked to read, but I wonder if you remember a play from high

school by Thornton Wilder called Our Town. *One of the characters says something big that I never forgot. He said the dead don't stay interested in the living after they're gone. "Gradually, gradually, they lose hold of the earth . . . and the ambitions they had . . . and their pleasures . . . and their suffering . . . and the people they loved."*

Kelley felt tears of self-pity pricking her eyes. Or maybe it was plain old sorrow. The end of the ballpoint was pretty chewed up, like she could gnaw the right words out of it. She thought of switching to pencil in case she got something wrong. Or she could write out a clean copy later. But high school was done. All she had to do now was tell Danny what Danny wouldn't hear. No extra points for neatness.

I guess you figured you came back alive. And seeing as you're the sheriff, who's going to tell you different? Everybody nods and smiles when you go by, but inside they're scared of you. When you get mad, that war in the desert comes out of your eyes. And everyone here has secrets they don't want you to know.

She summoned the town of Forest Peak in her mind, this place she knew so well but hardly recognized, like a once-beloved grandparent gone senile. The foremost thing was the forest, dark and shaggy, the pelt of an immense animal draped over the mountains, the trees going on and on.

Then there was Main Street, halfway down the mountainside along a flat shelf of land. It was narrow at the ends and wide in the middle, like a guitar strap. There were uneven rows of buildings on uphill and downhill sides, some with concrete sidewalks, some with the asphalt road lapping at their foundations. This holiday weekend the whole place was strung with red, white, and blue bunting and cheap Chinese-made American flags on dowels. The locals had decorated the entire street (with money left over for fireworks) out of a $1,100 city projects fund. It offset the shabbiness a little, and also emphasized it. Mostly the décor helped attract a few hundred tourists. Main Street was nothing but a wide place along Route 144, the old road that once took Model T goods trucks from the flatlands of San Bernardino to the mountain ski resorts of Big Bear and Alpine Glen.

Mentally gliding down into town, Kelley pictured one particular house along Main Street, Jack Carter's place. Mr. Carter was the local science teacher, his career spanning the ten years between Danny's and Kelley's attendance at Skyline High.

Mr. Carter owns more than a thousand pornos, did you know that? Not just your basic action. You could spend a week watching movies in his basement and never see the same act twice. He has a closet by the water heater full of rubber and leather bondage gear as well. Just for him. I guess he's lonely.

Kelley thought of old Mrs. Dennison above the Junque Shoppe next door to Mr. Carter. She was known to be an avid birdwatcher with formidable ex-military German binoculars. It was less known that the bird she most observed through the binoculars was Jack Carter, into whose basement window she could see from the corner of her upstairs bedroom. The angle wasn't very good, but she would wait for hours to catch a slice of the solo action going on down there. She kept a notebook describing what she saw. She was thoroughly scandalized and believed Carter was a pervert who should be arrested. She hadn't missed a Carter-watching session in eleven years.

If only he knew old Mrs. Dennison is always there with him.

Kelley fed Mrs. Dennison's cat when she was away; Kelley had read the notebooks, a dozen of them, filled with meticulous observations of Mr. Carter's habits. Despite herself, Kelley relished revealing the shabby dark secrets of Forest Peak to Danny the cop. God knew what Danny would do with this information. Probably try to arrest everybody in town. Kelley could almost regret that she would miss all the fun.

But wait, there's more.

Forest Peak was the same as it ever was, clinging to the shoulder of the mountain, in desperate need of new roofs and fresh paint. With her eyes shut, Kelley could see Wilson and Pine streets branching off Main Street to twist away uphill and down. The tangled ways were peppered with frame houses, trailers, and broke-down vehicles. One of the little peeling houses was Zap Owler's. The one with the Camaro parked on the verge in front. There was a rusting 1938 Ford in the ravine out back, crashed there by Zap's grandfather the same day Germany invaded Poland.

Kelley could picture the kitchen of the Owler house, conveniently located well out of sight in the back: the precision scales, the skillets, coffee machines, double-boilers, a sea of bottles and boxes and plastic packaging materials: Contac tablets, codeine, acetone, iodine, heaps of batteries. Hanging over it all a metallic smell, like rotten garlic.

Zap Owler cooks speed in his kitchen and sells it down in the flatlands at go-kart tracks. Including that place by the freeway you took me for my seventh birthday.

That would settle Zap Owler's lecherous ass. Danny was crazy for sure, but a powerful instrument of vengeance. Kelley had an insight as the ballpoint hung above the page: She was confessing the collective sins of Forest Peak to ensure she would never, ever change her mind about what she had to do. There was something religious about it. *What the hell,* Kelley thought. *While I'm at it:*

Jimmy Dietrich killed a man in 1975 and the body is under his garage.

Kelley had seen the irregular oblong patch in the oily concrete floor with her own eyes, right at the foot of the gun cabinet. She dreamed for weeks afterward of the horror festering beneath the patch, a sightless, lipless thing in the dirt with skeletal hands still raised in supplication.

Betty Mills uses roadkill down at the Wooden Spoon Café to make the hamburger go further. Wolfman Gunnar brings it to her. That's why I never ate at the Wooden Spoon. Maybe I should have told you.

She scribbled out another half-dozen samples of the unpleasant doings that went on under the skin of Forest Peak: perverts, criminals, shameful secrets, and wrongs done. Then Kelley was staring at the gun again, its muzzle a black disk like a shark's eye. With the tip of the pen, she nudged the barrel around until it pointed away from her heart. She glanced up at the clock on the wall, without absorbing what time it was. She looked over at the framed picture of Danny and Amy as teenagers, sitting together on a horse. Then she looked back at the clock. Twenty minutes past midnight. Might as well lay it all out there.

Even your best friend Amy Cutter: She's a lesbian, did she tell you? I guess she didn't. How come I know all this and you don't? Because nobody knows I'm here. I'm the invisible girl. I've seen everybody do everything, and nobody's seen me do anything, because I haven't done anything. You're the big war hero with your Purple Heart and Silver Star. Key to the Mountains and all that. I'm only the accidental kid sister. You went off to war and I spent four years in foster homes and learned all the dirty secrets.

Twenty feet away, Danielle Adelman quit pacing back and forth in her narrow bedroom and thumbed up the volume on the police scanner next to the bed. The blat of chatter between cars and dispatchers down in the flatlands could sometimes drown out the noise in her head. The scotch helped, too, and the little yellow pills. Danny shook a drift of them onto the nightstand and pulled up the button on the alarm clock. It was set for eight in the morning, which meant Danny would wake up at six to beat the bell. Or five, or four. She didn't need the alarm, but if it wasn't set, she'd stay up all night to make sure the morning didn't catch her off-guard. Tonight could be especially bad, because of the frigging holiday with its crowds of illegally parked, littering, jaywalking, shoplifting, vandalizing tourists. Not to mention the ceremony in which she was supposed to take part.

Danny pulled the tan uniform shirt off over her head, necktie and all. No need to unbutton the entire shirt, only the top two holes. She tossed it on the rocking chair, along with the side-stripe pants. She would iron the whole rig in the morning before she went into town, set some kind of an example for the trogs of Forest Peak. Especially her three shambolic deputies. Danny glanced in the tall boudoir mirror that had been her mother's. Arched an eyebrow. Dark, rusty hair, strong features, and a firm womanly figure with an ass you could cut steaks off, as Harlan used to say before he rolled over that bomb in Sadr City. Yes, indeed. Hell of a woman. Then she turned her back to the mirror, fetching a come-hither look over her shoulder. She caught sight of the scars. Someday she would turn the mirror around to face the wall.

For now, a couple of pills, washed down with the watery remains of the last whiskey of the night. Second-to-last. She slopped a little more in the glass, a finger or two, or so. Did she need more ice? Kitchen a mile away, Kelley probably sulking on the couch watching some dipshit cop show on TV—because the cop show right in front of her wasn't suitable to her tastes. Forget the ice. Knock back the shot, neat, splash it down the throat without hitting the tongue. Burn, baby, burn. Her bedroom seemed to be slipping sideways, gravity moving out of plumb. Pretty soon she could catch some sleep. Danny fell back on the bed to watch the ceiling revolve. It was her favorite show.

I thought things would change when you came back. Instead you spend your days being a cop and your nights fighting the war again, and I'm still the invisible girl. You keep that police scanner on all night, but I can hear the things you yell in your sleep. Post-traumatic stress disorder doesn't make you a bad person. But it sure makes you a crappy sister.

A fat tear plopped down on Kelley's notebook page. She shoved the wet out of her eyes with the back of her wrist. There was something deliciously tragic in writing a note of such finality. All those bottled-up feelings, all those things left unsaid, they could all come out now, just as long as she could keep writing. And always assuming Danny didn't emerge from her bedroom down the hall in one of those escalating rages, starting off with the irritable trip to the fridge for more ice, then the trip to the bathroom, then the circuit around the house to turn off the lights (muttering about the price of energy measured in blood, and so on), and finally pacing up and down the length of the place, ranting and shouting about anything there was to shout about. Often as not, Kelley.

Kelley's boyfriends (any male under the age of fifty who looked in Kelley's direction) were a favorite subject, and how soft and spoiled her generation was, as well as anyone else that had not served in combat; Danny was also fond of ranting about how nobody knew what it was like to be a cop, how hard it was, even if it wasn't as hard as serving in combat. Sometimes Danny would stand there in her plain cotton panties and olive drab tank top and yell about the horrible brown-gold upholstery on the couch or the awful nicotine-colored wood-print paneling on the walls. Anything that took her fancy. She'd wind down around two in the morning, or sooner if Kelley left right away to sleep on the pull-out bed at her friend Ashleen's house.

Why was she even writing to Danny? Because it felt good to put it on paper? There was so much else to say, so many things to slap her sister in the face with. But on some level all Kelley could blame Danny for was leaving her, who had no more choice in the matter than did Kelley. There was supposed to be some military rule regarding sole guardianship that could have gotten Danny out of the three tours she did over there. But the military machine was bending all the rules to keep boots on the ground without a draft, and in any case Kelley wondered sometimes if Danny would have waived the right, simply for another chance to get out of Forest Peak for a while. Maybe Kelley would have done the same. Danny had become a parent to her little sister far too early in life, head of the household at age eighteen. Maybe she had preferred patrolling death's door to watching over a moody kid who wouldn't eat the local hamburgers.

And yet, despite it all, Kelley felt a tug of sympathy in her heart for Danny, even pity. Losing Kelley was going to be hard for her sister. Probably. Maybe. Kelley wasn't entirely sure.

She thought about crumpling the note up and burning it to ashes out on the driveway. Where Kelley was going, there wouldn't be any satisfaction in having been cruel to her sister. But that was only part of the reason she was writing. She also needed Danny to know, going forward, that all was not right in her world.

Tomorrow on the Fourth of July, Danny would be receiving the so-called "Key to the Mountains" award, an idiotic publicity stunt dreamed up by the town council. Every year, the one person in town who accomplished anything beyond putting up the window screens was given an oversized, yellow-chromed churchkey. Congratulations, and by the way, it don't open shit. Danny was dreading the presentation, as Kelley knew, but in some way it probably validated Danny's dream-state of "okayness." She might not be *great*, but she *was* okay. She got the Key to the Mountains, didn't she?

Danny needed far more than a chrome-plated key, a prescription from the VA, and a couple of annual interviews with a shrink, though. She needed to reinvent herself from front to back. Maybe get out of Forest Peak. This house, this town, was full of ghosts: those of their parents, their ideals, their threadbare thrift-store lives. Danny might finally figure it out when even Kelley was only a ghost.

But I won't be a ghost, Kelley thought. *I'll just be free.*

So for the sake of Danny, Kelley kept writing.

She wrote more about their neighbors, what she had discovered during her years as the Invisible Girl, staying with people she hardly knew from whom Danny had extracted the favor of a few months' houseroom, putting up with being a burden and an object of pity in equal measure, hiding herself in plain sight. When she ran out of local dish, Kelley turned back to the subject of being the younger sister to a modern-day Spartan. She wrote about her yearning to have Danny back while she was on tour in the distant desert, and how sad she was when Danny returned on leave and seemed even more distant, right in front of her eyes. She wanted to write about how Danny seemed to love her stupid Candyapple Red 1968 Mustang with the 302 V-8 more than she loved her little sister. But it all seemed petty, given the matter at hand; the car was probably easier to love.

Kelley found herself staring at the clock again, watching the second hand lurch around the face. It was time to finish this. She turned her attention back to the note, searching for the right way to end it.

Kelley pushed the pen along for a few more lines, swallowing the knot of grief in her throat. Then she signed her name at the bottom, squared up the pages of the letter, and blinked back another flood of tears. Enough. Kelley reached across the table and dragged the big, ugly gun toward her.

Danny watched the ceiling turn and listened to the scanner as the highway patrol took a drunk driver into custody down on the 10 Freeway. Maybe she should call the Forest Peak Sheriff's Station to make sure everything was shipshape. Deputy Dave was on night shift tonight, and he had no problem with insomnia, on duty or not. Could be asleep at his post. But Danny didn't think she could speak without slurring her words. The empty glass bumped up and down on her chest in time to the beating of her heart. The whiskey must have evaporated. Only a splash more, and she was definitely done for the night. She reached for the bottle on the nightstand among the pills. The bottle slipped out of her fingers and hit the plywood floor—

BANG

Danny bolted upright. Hell of a loud noise.

"Kelley? Are you still up?"

She listened. Nothing. If she had to get out of bed, Kelley was going to catch hell. Then Kelley's faint voice came through the door:

"Go to sleep, Danny."

"What are you doing awake?"

"Same thing you are. Waiting for you to go to sleep."

Kelley opened the bedroom door and looked in. She had that hunted look that made Danny crazy. For fuck's sake, nobody was hunting her. Kelley had no idea what it was like to be hunted—not for real. But her eyes looked red and puffy.

Maybe Kelley had her own troubles, overblown as they might be. Danny ought to ask if everything was all right, have a little sister-to-sister time. Incoherent and stinking of booze. Maybe not.

"I can't remember if I took my pills."

"I dunno."

"I know you don't. It was one of those questions."

"You mean rhetorical."

"Yes."

Danny searched her brain for something else to say, something to move the conversation forward a few inches. Nothing occurred to her. Kelley broke the silence.

"You want some water or something? Some ice?"

Danny lay back down on the bed. Wanted to say something meaningful. Nothing volunteered itself.

"Good night, Kelley."

Kelley closed the door. Danny tried to remember whether she had taken the pills or not. She was pretty sure she had, but they were a lifeline. She found a stray pill on the nightstand, pinched it between numb fingertips, and managed to get it into her mouth. It left a dry, bitter streak down her throat. She should talk to Kelley tomorrow, find out what her plans for the future were.

The summer was coming, the season for temporary jobs cleaning rental cabins, playing lifeguard at the recreational lake. Then college. Did Kelley want to go to college? She was smart. Smarter than Danny. Maybe she could get out of this one-horse shithole of a town.

They should talk. Danny tried to follow events surrounding a burglary on the scanner, the Fontana cops dealing with a freaked-out woman speaking rapid Spanish in her backyard. Somewhere around the third time they tried to get a description of the perpetrator, who might have been the woman's nephew, Danny drifted into unconsciousness.

They followed the M1A1 Abrams tank toward the MSR—the main supply route around Al Fallujah. Second Tank Battalion was rock-solid. You couldn't relax merely because there were tanks for protection, but you knew they would pitch in fast and hard if there was a fight on. The trick was to drive straight down their tread tracks if you could, because there wouldn't be any operational ordnance buried there. Danny hadn't felt safe in months, but she figured she was with the best guys she could ask for on a regimental combat team. Harlan had her back, and Ramirez, too, even if all he did was give her shit. Spasskey and Duke were good men, but she didn't really know them—they had replaced the casualties of last week.

They found the burning mud-brick house about a mile before the appointed rendezvous. Whoever owned the house had been building a concrete addition when the war broke out, because there were three walls with rusted rebar sticking out of them, empty doorways and window sockets cast in place but without doors or windows. No roof. Just as well because the place was a write-off now. There was gunfire in the air, but they couldn't tell where it was coming from. It didn't seem to be headed their way, but nobody knew who was doing the shooting, or who was being shot at. Could have been some of the multinationals or a squabble between the locals and the so-called Iraqi security forces, a bunch of dangerous tribal gangbangers.

Whatever it was, gunfire was combat team business. They pulled around the burning house and in the flat distance, men were running. Requests and orders cracked around the radios. Air support on the way. But sometimes these incidents were intended to draw air support. The Black Hawks limped home with holes in them. Danny's team was going to have to go out there and attract some attention. Tanks first, however. But there was a woman in front of the tanks. She was standing beside the house. Danny's instincts told her it was a setup. But her instincts always told her that. Because the whole fucking war was a setup.

The woman looked like the Grim Reaper, black-veiled from head to feet. Maybe a hardcore Shia Islamist. These were still rare in Iraq, though less so now that fundamentalism was on the rise. Or maybe she was the woman of a mercenary from Iran or Saudi Arabia. Harlan flicked his eyes at Danny: Would she do the honors? Danny dropped down out of the Humvee, Spasskey covering her topside with the M249 SAW gun. Her eyes probed every shadow, her hands were wet on the grip of the Mossberg 12 gauge, but she strode almost casually across the dirt patch that served the house as a front yard. Just a friendly visit, neighbor, couldn't help notice your house was on fire. You mind stepping aside so the tanks can roll through?

The radios inside the vehicles were going crazy. Danny couldn't quite hear what they were saying, but something big was going on. Not here. She didn't see anything here. But somewhere, something was going down. The bell wouldn't stop ringing—

Danny sprang awake as if shot up from the bottom of the ocean. Her alarm clock was ringing. It was eight o'clock on Saturday morning, Fourth of July weekend, and she was an hour late for roll call at her own Sheriff's Station. Dispatcher Dave was calling for her on the radio:

"Sheriff Adelman, where the heck are you? Come in, Danny."

Danny rushed through the house, shoving her rumpled shirt into her pants, jamming feet into boots. Hat over there. Gun belt on the chair. Gun on the table. Note from Kelley. What the hell was this? Out of the official notebook, no less! Danny shoved the gun in the holster, snatched up Kelley's note, and ran out the door. She had been awake for no more than three minutes.

As she jumped in the cab of the Sheriff's Department Ford Explorer, another bell rang in the back of her mind.

Danny's blood turned cold. Something was missing besides Kelley. She blinked at the driveway.

Kelley took the Mustang.

The road descending from the Adelman place into Forest Peak was a scribble of tar a lane and a half wide through the steep woods. It curled upon itself like a rattlesnake gliding through the immense trees: heavy-browed ponderosa pine, Douglas fir with their thick scored skins, young black oaks coming up in the gulleys where the big trees let a little sunlight get through. The slope of the mountain was so steep here that the crowns of the trees on the downhill side were at the same height as the roots of the trees on the uphill side. It was a beautiful place, especially with the morning sun cutting through the mist. Danny took the hairpin turns at forty miles an hour, the Explorer's tires screaming as they skated from shoulder to shoulder. She could make town in five more minutes. One hand grasping the radio mic, one hand on the wheel, she called in an all-points bulletin on her runaway sister.

A dark shape emerged from the brush at the next hairpin bend—Danny thought for an instant it was a bear. But it was a man, a shambling, filthy man moving with uncertain gait down the steep rocks above the road.

Then he was on the pavement, and Danny's heel jammed the brake pedal to the floor.

The SUV lost purchase and stuttered over the asphalt in an increasingly sloppy arc, Danny fighting to correct the wheel. She passed within a foot of the red-eyed thing that stumbled across the roadway, and when the Explorer stopped, it was facing the wrong way up the road in an acrid cloud of scorched tires. Another two feet and it would have gone over the edge.

"Jesus *Christ*," Danny said, and threw the door open. The passing of the big vehicle had only just registered to the ragged creature now standing in the middle of the road. He blinked at Danny as she climbed down, one hand hooked behind her belt to the handcuffs she kept there, the other hand raised in front of her.

"Goddammit, Wolfman, this is it," Danny said. She grabbed the man—a foot taller and forty years older—and spun him around against the hood of the Explorer. He moved with the underwater grace of the profoundly drunk. Danny could smell the alcohol yeast coming off him in waves, even above the raw-onion stench of his armpits. Wulf Gunnar was what they called a homeless person down in Los Angeles, but a "tramp" up in Forest Peak. He lived in abandoned hunting cabins and moved around some, wintering in the low desert. Made a little money at odd jobs in town. A kind of thorn in the side of the community, Danny thought, but there was something necessary about him, too. Like an old stray dog to remind people they weren't so bad off. But today Danny was in no mood for strays, and the adrenaline in her system wanted to punish the son of a bitch clean off her mountain. She clapped the handcuffs around his dirt-varnished wrists and he slumped for support on the Explorer, cheek against the metal.

"Gunnar, I warned you last time: You can drink yourself to death, but you can't do it in public."

He squinted at her, forming his words with difficulty: "So shoot me then."

"I about ran you down. That would have done it. What the hell are you doing out here?"

Wulf looked carefully around him, as if "here" was anywhere particular. "Keepin' outta town."

"And I told you to keep out of town, didn't I."

Wulf scratched his beard on the shoulder of his grease-blackened fatigue jacket.

"Yes," he said, at length.

Danny was at an impasse. She could let him go and he might stumble on down the mountain to Ferndale. Or he might loop around until he got to Forest Peak and stink out the tourists and puke in the old horse trough. In either case, Danny was now seriously late.

To hell with it. She hooked Wulf's elbow and steered him into the backseat of the Explorer, where he lay down on the molded bench and blinked at the armored Plexiglas panel that divided front seats from back. Danny kicked his immense, rotten boots into the compartment and slammed the door. No handles on the inside, so he couldn't open the door and fall out.

Danny got back up in the driver's seat, restarted the engine, and stomped the gas pedal. There was a dense *thud* as Wulf bounced up against the back of the seat, then rolled off onto the floor.

2

Danny took the alley along back of the downhill side of Main Street, and parked behind the Sheriff's Station, a red-brick block with a glass front entirely out of keeping with the local architecture. It had been the new Post Office in 1954, but there wasn't enough mail to justify keeping the lights on. The building had been requisitioned for the library after that, but nobody went in for reading much around Forest Peak and the librarian was suspected of being a Red. So in 1971, the Sheriff's Station was moved out from behind the firehouse on Sawyer Road, and into the refurbished Post Office building. The place hadn't seen any improvements since then, but the roof was sound and the back room was air-conditioned.

Danny had been a deputy for a couple of years before she went off to Iraq. When she came back and needed a job, she ran for the office of sheriff against Stanley Curtiss Booth, the twenty-year incumbent. He figured she didn't have a chance, so he didn't campaign very hard, but referred to his red-haired opponent as "that little carrot-top Adelman girl," until it became clear Danny's house-to-house canvassing with her Veterans' Administration–issue cane was eating away at his advantage. By the time the vote was three days away, he was calling Danny "that gun-crazy bull dyke," and on election day he called her "a high-toned cripple bitch" to her face, and that was that. Danny had never painted Booth's name out of the placard that marked the sheriff's parking space—every time she pulled up into it was a little like kicking his ass out of the job all over again.

There wasn't any relish in parking the Explorer today, however. Danny leaped out of the driver's seat and sprinted for the back door of the station, twisting her midlength hair up under her hat. *Way to go,* she thought, and entered her domain. Deputy Dave Thurin was in the back room at the communications desk, ten minutes from the end of his shift. He lurched to his feet as Danny came in, the radio headphone cord stretching to its limit. Danny waved him back into his chair.

"Anything, Dave?"

"Mrs. Davis reported her son Barry left again—"

"He's eighteen, it's his privilege," Danny said. Clear the bullshit off the blotter. Dave scratched his ear, trying to remember what else was happening even though it was written right in front of him. Danny felt a bubble of anger rising inside her.

"There's an RV illegal parked out by the gym," Dave continued, as Danny was about to bark at him, "and some kids with firecrackers—"

"Dave? Kelley. Anything about Kelley."

Dave shook his head. Danny usually wanted the shift incident reports in detail, but now her thoughts were on her sister. Not to mention the midday ceremony. And she was late. Danny would have to make up for lost time and get her shit wired down tight. And even as Dave changed tracks in his slow-working brain, Danny was suddenly, monumentally hung over. All the moisture left her head at once and her brain was high and dry, resting on bony spines inside her skull.

"Sheriff?" Dave said.

Danny flapped a hand at him and headed for the water fountain on the wall. She sucked down icy draughts, and a little life flowed into her along with the chill in her stomach. The prisoner! Danny had forgotten about Wulf.

"I got Wulf Gunnar in the back of the Explorer, Dave. Process him for me, public intoxication or something. I gotta make the rounds before they do the business with the key."

Without waiting for Dave to think it over, Danny headed into the glass closet that served as her office, dropped the blinds, and did her best to rearrange her uniform so she looked a little less like the Wolfman herself.

The back room of the station contained almost everything police-related. An evidence locker with a padlock on it. The communications desk with its radio, switchboard, and the walkie-talkie charging station. A couple of desks for whoever needed to do paperwork or take a statement. There was also Danny's tiny glass-walled office, a conference table, a gun cabinet with an impressive arsenal, mostly impounded. And at the back by the outside door, a pair of cells, complete with old-fashioned iron-barred doors.

It was a trim little operation, as long as nothing went too wrong.

Danny emerged from her office as tidied up as she was going to get. Dave was half-carrying Wulf through the door of the nearest cell, grimacing as the old man's smell was transferred onto himself. Wulf was complaining in a singsong murmur, but offered no resistance.

Danny passed through to the front room of the station, emerging behind the glass partition that spanned the space, a legacy of the Post Office days. A high countertop was let into the middle of the glass for dealing with the public. Danny unlocked the partition door and stepped into the waiting area. Beyond it were a couple of old plastic loveseats, a rest room, and a potted plant that Danny had assumed was artificial for the first four months she worked at the station, until she saw Deputy Ted watering it. On the public side of the partition were taped-up official notices, FBI Most Wanted lists, and government information posters. Some of the posters had become outright bizarre since the federal government began its "Secrecy Is Strength" campaign: The latest one featured an extreme close-up of an American eagle's eye and the motto "Help Us Watch Over You."

Outside the plate glass front wall of the station, a growing crowd of out-of-towners was moving down Main Street. Looked like the usual mix of families and retirees, working class mostly, with a few upscale seekers of quaint Americana mixed in. Not many teenagers, Danny was pleased to note. Her head still felt foul although she'd swallowed a couple of Advil tablets from the bottle in her desk drawer. She probably needed to eat something. The Wooden Spoon was right across the way, but the thought of the usual fried egg breakfast sandwich was nauseating.

And Christ, another thing had slipped her mind: the chili contest. In a couple of hours—she checked her watch: three hours, at twelve-thirty—the chili cookoff would begin, and as recipient of the Key to the Mountains, Danny was expected to be the official third judge on the tasting panel. The permanent judges were Gordy Morton, who ran the True Value hardware store, and Eleanor Dennison of the Junque Shoppe. The thought of watching the three-hundred-pound Gordy Morton eating cup after cup of chili was enough to make Danny's stomach juke left.

She swallowed hard and stepped outside into the gathering warmth of Main Street, her eyes stung by the crisp sunlight and her ears set ringing by the bleating of the Skyline High Marching Brass Band. They were belting out the theme from *Rocky,* more or less. *I'd be better off dead, if this keeps up,* Danny thought.

Inside the Wooden Spoon, Weaver Sampson and Patrick Michaels watched through the window as the sheriff of Forest Peak emerged squinting into the sunlight. They had the two-seat window table. It was Weaver's RV, *The White Whale,* that was illegally parked in the gymnasium lot, not far from the bandstand at the far end of Main Street upon which the Skyline High Marching Brass Band was sacrificing musical goats. Patrick observed Weaver's eyes as they followed the sheriff on her way down the sidewalk.

"It's the heat," Patrick said.

Weaver grunted. He had an eloquent range of grunts, being a man of few words. It was one of the things Weaver did that kept Patrick guessing. Weaver looked like one of those rugged, lean men in the old photographs who built the Hoover Dam and the Chrysler Building; he had that silent sufficiency about him, in direct opposition to Patrick's incessant babbling and complaining.

Lately Patrick had been waking up alone in the master bedroom with the chocolate-colored walls and cream trim. He no longer went stomping off to the guest room to confront Weaver, whom he invariably found sitting up in bed with his hands laced together behind his head (accentuating his veined rock-climber's arms), staring thoughtfully out the balcony window at the view of the Sunset Tower Hotel, which had incidentally been renovated by that bitch Paul Fortune. But of course Paul Fortune didn't have his own show on cable television—*that* honor belonged to Patrick. Was Weaver dreaming of another man when he gazed out the window? Of course not. Weaver was simply looking out the window; he had no interest in décor or fashion or any of the refinements of life.

That was what Patrick loved about him—and also what he loathed. They had nothing tangible in common. The more distant Weaver became, the more frantic Patrick became, and Patrick knew damn well the whole thing was a vicious cycle, and if he shut up occasionally, the problem would most likely go away.

But he couldn't, not to save his life. Not even to save the relationship. *Please* shut up. Can't. Even as the thought went through his head for the millionth time, Patrick spoke.

"She looks like she's in a very poor mood. Are you *sure* we're okay to park across all those spaces like that? I mean shouldn't we just you know park along the street or something?"

Weaver disengaged his eyes from the sheriff and fixed them on Patrick. He considered carefully, and then spoke:

"I think there's something going on."

Patrick's heart bumped in his chest. Did Weaver know about the intern? Only once, and eight long months ago when Weaver was on location in Hawaii for three weeks, but maybe that's why he was slipping off to sleep alone. Patrick pursed his lips as if to ask, "what?" but no sound came out. Weaver hooked his chin at the television up above the counter.

"Something weird. They keep showing part of these disasters in other countries, and then all of a sudden they cut away to cute stuff like babies watching parades and don't go back. Something's not right."

Patrick simply couldn't understand the man. At this moment, the eggs and toast arrived.

Danny found Deputy Ted eating a churro in front of Vic's Barber Shop. He saw her emerge from the crowd a few moments after she saw him, and made the tactical mistake of trying to consume the entire thing before she reached him. Ted was probably too fat for his health and certainly too fat for his uniform, and Danny refused to order him another one because she felt to do so would be to condone a failure of personal discipline, hence a failure of team discipline. Danny was a firm believer in the "slippery slope" theory. She accelerated her pace and reached Ted while he still had so much dough in his mouth he could hardly close his lips.

"Eating on duty, Ted?" Danny said. Ted held a finger up: Hang on a second. Danny crossed her arms and waited. Gluttony was one of the Seven Deadly Sins, as she recalled. *Whereas drowning your sorrows in alcohol and pills is A-OK*, the unhelpful little voice in her head observed. Danny uncrossed her arms and pretended to watch the crowd while Ted struggled manfully to swallow the mouthful.

"Sorry, ma'am. No breakfast this morning 'cause we had to split our shifts."

Danny's late arrival this morning must have created chaos at the station. The fact that things were running smoothly was due to successful improvisation by her deputies. She would have to acknowledge that when things quieted down. Tomorrow, after the fireworks and the drunk drivers.

"Any word on Kelley?"

"No, ma'am, but this isn't the first time she ran away, neither."

"She . . . she took the Mustang."

Ted gasped. There were lines a person did not cross. Not even family. But Danny was already on to the next thing:

"I'm going to be tied down from at least noon to one with this key thing and the chili contest afterward. I want you to be the point man if anything happens while I'm up there. Okay? Nick will be at the radio, but if you need extra hands, he can jump in."

There was a highway patrol interceptor parked at the curb down by the barber shop. Danny hadn't been notified there would be a state presence in town. She didn't see the uniform that went with it; maybe somebody was moonlighting, or had to drop off a subpoena or something. Still . . . professional courtesy said you tipped your hat to the local fuzz.

There was something bothering her, a sense of off-balance. It was probably only the raging hangover, but Danny never wrote off "one of those feelings." Ted was noisily clearing his throat. Some sugar had gone down the wrong way. He gave Danny the thumbs-up, unable to speak. Danny thumped him on the back and turned toward the Wooden Spoon, because the churro and the throbbing in her head had reminded her of something: the prisoner in cell one would need to eat. And in Forest Peak, the jailhouse kitchen and the local café were the same place.

The big woman who delivered the breakfast had aluminum-colored hair and a smiley-face nametag on her blouse that read *Betty.* Weaver asked for Tabasco. Patrick tried to change the subject, whatever that had been. Anything to take his mind off the squalor of this rustic little flypit in the mountains.

"It's like *Deliverance* without the river," he whispered.

"Just eat," Weaver said, accepting the Tabasco from Betty with a gracious John Wayne inclination of the head. "I want to see the news."

Then a red-eyed fellow turned around to face Weaver. *He looks like that singer from that band*, Patrick thought. *Or a drug addict.*

"You see it coming, right?" Red-Eye said. He was sitting at the next table, submerging a plate of pancakes in syrup and ketchup. He tapped the air with a finger. His nails were bitten down until the tips of his fingers looked like raw steak.

Weaver stabbed his eggs in the eyes with a sharp piece of toast. "What's that, brother?"

Patrick could see Red-Eye thought he maybe had a sympathetic ear. Emphasis on the *pathetic* part. His teeth were awful.

"Something," the man said. "War on D-R-U-G-Z, war on poverty, unliteracy, cancer, dietary supplements, and terror? One in a hundred Americans is behind bars, and people keep celebrating the Fourth like 'freedom' meant something. It's bullshit. They're up to something."

At the counter directly behind Red-Eye, an old-timer in Caterpillar cap and suspenders turned from his hash browns to inspect the author of these treasonous words.

"Zap Owler, you communist asshole, we stop celebrating Independence Day, the terrorists win," the old-timer reasoned. His name was Eugene, or at least his coveralls had a patch that said *Eugene* on the breast pocket.

Zap Owler turned in his chair as if Eugene had flashed a badge at him.

"What terrorists?"

"They could be anybody. Could be you." Eugene obviously figured he had Owler trumped.

Patrick ate elaborately, hoping to demonstrate he wasn't part of the conversation. But Weaver turned to face the clashing locals:

"Day like today means whatever you bring to it."

Eugene nodded in agreement. "You got that right." But Weaver wasn't done.

"Then again, can't mix patriotism with going along to get along, either. That's what happened to the Germans a while back."

"But you can't say there are no terrorists," Eugene protested.

"I'm not. But we better damn well stop using them as an excuse for what we do to people."

Zap Owler was about to add something when Betty interposed her massive behind between the men to cut off any further argument, pouring coffee refills.

Eugene's eyes drifted saintlike to the taxidermied deer head up above the front door: "I didn't slaughter all them Koreans just so I could sit here and watch some dingleberry piss on the flag. Nosir. We get into a war on terror, we finish the job."

Patrick pinched the bridge of his nose as if to clear his mind of suffering, a gesture he'd perfected on television. Zap Owler muttered under his breath and went back to his short stack.

Weaver was pissed off. He slapped the table hard enough to make the coffee slop out of his mug. He was composing a statement and it was going to be short and to the point. At which moment, a merry jingle sounded: The front door swung open and Danny Adelman walked in. Zap Owler shrank himself until he was hidden behind the rest of the patrons.

Betty appeared to take Danny's arrival as her cue, addressing Danny but speaking to Weaver: "Okay, mister, here's one of our local heroes right now, Sheriff Danielle Adelman: She done three tours of Iraq, got wounded but she won't say where. You tell 'em, Danny, you think America ought to walk away from all the sacrifice we made or you think we oughtta finish the job?"

Danny took in the room, scanning the faces that turned in her direction. She moved a lot like Weaver, Patrick thought. Same way of speaking slowly. She took off her hat and leaned on the counter.

"Sacrifice? It doesn't look like anybody here is suffering much."

Betty squeezed herself in behind the counter.

"You know what I mean. The usual?"

"One egg sandwich. However Wolfman likes it."

"He finally in the lockup?"

"Lemme know when it's ready." Danny strolled on over to Patrick and Weaver.

"Sorry to barge in on you like this. I saw that land yacht outside and I figured it belonged to one of you gents."

"It's ours." Patrick looked extremely guilty. Weaver gave her the Lone Ranger smile. Patrick blurted: "How did you guess?"

The sheriff considered this.

"That's an expensive bus, and you got the most expensive clothes in town. Thing is, you're taking up too many spaces. Got to park it up the road well off the shoulder. But take your time. Up here the shoulder goes down five hundred feet in some places."

Betty called up Danny's order. Danny put her hat back on. "You all have a great day," she said, and walked to the door with the go-bag. Then a string of firecrackers went off in the street, and Danny flinched involuntarily, half-ducking back through the open door. *Wounded on the inside*, Patrick thought. Maybe that was Weaver's problem, too.

Back in the station, Danny strapped on her walkie-talkie with the shoulder microphone, told Dave to get some rack time and be back on second shift at 8:00 P.M. (he welcomed the overtime), and pushed the sandwich in its paper bag through the bars of Wulf Gunnar's cell. The man was still heavily asleep on the narrow cot bolted to the wall. To hell with him. Nick was supposed to take radio duty at the communications center now, but he was on his way back from his tour of the neighborhood. Danny resisted the urge to look in the bathroom mirror, contenting herself with a glance in the reflection on her office window. Then she went outside again.

Forest Peak was only an hour from downtown Los Angeles, traffic permitting, and might as well have been in another country, it was so small-town and quaint—so it made for a convenient day-trip getaway from everything L.A. No palm trees, only evergreens. Snow in the winter. The hip, ironic Angelenos enjoyed Forest Peak for its guileless Americana; for others, the town was a reminder of where they came from—other small towns in other places, left behind for the biggest big city. Then again, many folks simply liked the fresh mountain air.

The crowd was picking up: babies on fathers' shoulders, kids with balloons, Los Angeles bottle-blondes with their Gucci shades and fifty-dollar tubes of sunscreen, lots of Latino families from the flatlands, some with five or six kids. There was a guy on stilts dressed as Uncle Sam, probably hired by Gordy to attract business to the hardware store. The band played on. It might have been "Lady Marmalade" they were playing, or a polka; it was hard to tell. An intense, vinegar smell of bubbling chili wafted across Main Street from the dozen or so cooking stations set up in front of the Quik-Mart. Danny saw a "For Unlawful Carnal Knowledge" T-shirt, the initial letters far larger than the rest, but she didn't have time to issue a citation to some mullet-wearing tool who couldn't dress himself for public occasions. Past the crowd was the official ceremonial flatbed truck, parked up under the shade of the town's lone ash tree.

Danny's belly tightened with anticipation. She didn't love public speaking. Gordy Morton and Eleanor Dennison were already sitting up on the back in folding chairs above the richly draped red, white, and blue bunting that hid the truck's chassis. Also up on the flatbed was Zach Greer, the fire chief, Hillman Jones, who ran the public works department, and Mayor Sy Crocker, checking his notes at the podium they'd requisitioned from the gymnasium. Sy was dressed in the ill-fitting George Washington outfit he'd originally put together in 1976 for the Bicentennial. Danny walked toward them through the crowd, muttering a last checkup on her deputies over the radio.

The noon bell on the firehouse was ringing as Danny stepped up onto the flatbed and stood with legs apart and arms behind her back in the "at ease" drill stance. Sy tipped his braid-trimmed tricorn hat to Danny and waved down the street at Julius Argandoña, the music teacher. Julius made a throat-cutting gesture and the student band abruptly stopped playing, precisely as the last ring of the bell sounded out. Now there was only crowd noise, laughter and murmuring voices. Most of these folks couldn't care less about the ceremonials, but at least they turned in the correct direction. Danny's heart was racing. She did her breathing and brought it down.

Sy tapped the microphone, then launched into his speech. "Ladies and gentlemen, and local folks, welcome to Forest Peak's Fourth of July celebration. Every year we get together to cheer on what's great about our nation and our community. And by way of raising money for the fire department, we also sling a mean chili."

People cheered at this. They'd cheer for anything edible, Danny thought. Part of the eternal holiday spirit.

"And every year we celebrate somebody who made a difference in our community, who gave more than they took, with our annual Key to the Mountains award. This year we honor somebody real special. She was born and raised here in Forest Peak, and before she took the job of sheriff, she took the job of serving with the U.S. Marine Corps. That job sent her overseas to a place very different from here. Like going from a birthday party to a fistfight is how she put it one time."

Laughter was followed by more cheers. Danny could feel a hot blush crawling up her skin, making her back prickle. For starters, she'd never said any such thing. Sy was making it up.

"Let me introduce Sheriff Danielle Adelman: She won a Purple Heart and a Silver Star, got wounded but she won't say where . . ."

Cheering, rebel yells, a "hell yeah" from the guy in the FUCK shirt. Sy patted the air down, indicating the crowd should let him finish his speech.

". . . And as you can see, she came back alive, and she is still serving our community today as sheriff of our small but capable peacekeeping force. So here's to you, Danny—it's not fancy but it is the thirty-fifth annual Forest Peak Key to the Mountains, our award to an outstanding member of the community and a great American."

Sy flipped open the official key-presenting box, revealing within its red velvet lining the gold-colored, five-inch key on a ribbon. He took the thing out and held it up for the crowd to see, then attempted to lower the ribbon over Danny's head. Her Smokey hat was too big. So she took it off, and her hair fell heavily around her neck, to the tremendous delight of the crowd. People were cheering and hollering and it was about as embarrassing as anything Danny had been through, except maybe the moment S. Curtiss Booth called her a high-toned cripple bitch in front of the locals.

At last, Sy got the ribbon on her and the key hung there on her chest across the radio handset cable. From this elevated vantage point, Danny estimated the crowd at eight or nine hundred, about half the usual attendance for the holiday. Blame hard times for that. But enough of such matters. It was time for her speech. She stepped up to the podium and her walkie-talkie squealed feedback through the microphone. The crowd fell silent, genuinely interested in this local hero.

"Thank you," Danny said, her voice painfully amplified, and held the key up, and sat down on the chair between Gordy and Eleanor. That was it. The crowd went wild. A woman of few words between them and the chili, what a great American indeed! The cheering and clapping went on and on, and Danny gratefully accepted a bottle of water from Hillman Jones. Her throat was as dry as cardboard. It was finally time to judge the chili.

3

The man ran through the trees, his mind a cyclone of fear. He ran as if hell itself had opened up to swallow him alive. He ran, screaming until his throat bled, until his legs were on fire with the pain of oxygen-starved muscles and branch-whipped skin.

And then, in midstride, he was dead.

4

Danny was on the fifth Dixie cup of chili and the world seemed to be growing dim, but she figured it wasn't as bad as a Baghdad sandstorm. So she kept on eating. The water helped. She'd probably swallowed a gallon of it, by now. The chili from Rosarita's down in City of Industry was best, she thought. Spicy, but you could still taste the ingredients. But honestly it could have been Chef Boyardee and she wouldn't have known the difference. The Key to the Mountains was heavy on her neck.

"Spicy, but you can still taste the ingredients," Danny said to Eleanor.

Three thirteen-year-old boys, the Bixby twins and their cousin Cub Maas, were running for their lives.

They had propped the stick of an immense, illegal rocket firework (*Sky Penetrator*, it promised, in gaudy orange letters on the side) in a two-liter Mountain Dew bottle. The fuse was fizzing away at terrifying speed. The boys hurled themselves behind the recycling dumpster in the alley back of the hardware store just as the rocket lit up, a pillar of white sparks blasting out from among its tailfins. The two-liter bottle crumpled and caught fire, and a carbonized star was permanently scored into the concrete yard.

The rocket took off. Not ponderously like a space shuttle or an Apollo rocket, but more like something from a cartoon: One moment it was blasting away at the pavement, and the next it was gone into the sky on a crooked pillar of smoke. The twins saw it go but Cub was too afraid to break cover until it was well up in the air. They all saw it reach its zenith and hang there; then it exploded with a mighty roar they could feel on their cheeks.

Danny hit the deck—in this case the deck of the flatbed truck. Her gun was in her hand before the thought occurred to her, and then she was up on one knee with the firearm out in front of her, watching the red, white, and blue firework blossoming overhead in a drum roll of explosions. Zach Greer leaned over, folded his enormous mitt over the gun, and pushed it down, but a number of people in the crowd had already seen. A ripple of concerned remarks mingled with the laughter and cheers at the early incendiary display. Even a war hero should think twice about waving a gun around. Danny heard the concern beneath the crowd noise. Even as she shoved the gun back in the holster, the blush of humiliation was back, roasting her face. She had an egg-shaped chili stain on her knee.

"It's the Fourth of July, Sheriff," Zach Greer whispered. He'd been in the Army during a rare lull in the endless national war program. "Lot of bang-bang gonna happen today."

"You guys go ahead and finish the chili. I gotta find out who did that and skin him alive," Danny said, and hopped down off the flatbed. "I vote for the Rosarita's," she said, and hurried away.

Danny called the station to see if anybody was on to the perps yet. Nick answered the radio: Someone said it came from behind the hardware store. But he had more important news, if Danny could come to the station right away. When she asked him what the news was, he said he didn't think it was an open radio kind of thing.

"Kelley?" Danny said.

"Something else."

"There's not a 10-code for it?"

"Let's say you have a visitor," Nick said.

Danny wanted to ask him if it was Kelley, knew she already had the answer to that question—there was no way Kelley would dare return—and bit back further remark. She signed off.

There was nothing for it: She had to get over to the station, and the dickhead with the fireworks could meanwhile make his escape.

Danny was weaving through the crowd when Amy Cutter called her name. Over by the barber shop there was a petting zoo, as there was every year, with miniature goats and giant rabbits, several weird varieties of chicken, and Diggler, the pot-bellied pig that would (if you knew the magic words) shit on command. Amy, being the local veterinarian, was called upon to officiate over the squealing kids who chased the animals around the wire pens. Danny didn't want to stop, but she also wanted very much to get some buddy time with Amy—a reassuring word would help a lot right now.

"You look like you just died," Amy observed. "Love the key, though. It matches the gold in your teeth."

Danny shrugged. "Kelley ran off, did you hear? With the Mustang."

Bless her, Amy was immediately dismayed.

"She took the *Mustang*? It must be serious. Did she say anything? Or leave a note?"

Danny had forgotten about the note, too, in all the activity.

"Yeah, a long note. I haven't read it yet."

"Maybe she said where she went in it."

"Not if she took the Mustang. She knows I'd hunt her down without remorse."

Amy separated a kid from a struggling rabbit: "Okay, honey, bunnies can't breathe if you squeeze their necks. Try this nice piggy, they don't have necks. Danny, here. Now smile."

Amy handed the rabbit to Danny, who didn't smile, and there was a bright flash and the regional newspaper had its photo of the heroic sheriff with her Key to the Mountains and a cute bunny for the Fourth of July wrap-up edition next week. They could Photoshop the chili stain off Danny's knee.

People congratulated Danny on the way down Main Street. It might have been gratifying, except by now she had been through too much to imagine any of these civilians had enough experience in life to qualify their opinions. A small boy pointed his finger at her and said, "peew, peew," in imitation of gunfire. Danny was grateful to have made it past the gauntlet when she stepped through the doors of the Sheriff's Station—and then she came up against a tan uniform of the highway patrol. A big trooper was at that moment ducking his head into his hat, so he didn't see Danny until they collided.

"Pardon. Oh, are you Adelman?" he said.

He didn't offer his name but it was on his chest tag, one of the five-year safety award pins: *Jordan Park*.

Although they moved apart, Danny's nose was still full of his cologne. He kept close and dropped his voice to a whisper.

"Glad I ran into you, Sheriff. We got a situation I wanted to run by you. I drove up here to keep it off the radio."

"I guess it's important if you went half an hour out of your way."

"It's important."

Danny nodded.

"Follow me," she said, went through the partition into the back room, and held open the door to the ladies' room.

"That's who I told you about," Nick volunteered from the radio desk.

"Thanks, Nick," Danny said, meaning sarcasm, but instead coming off as uncharacteristically polite. "This is the one place I can get any privacy around here," she said, and Park stepped past her into the inner sanctum. He needed to talk, and he didn't care where he did it.

Anybody who has been in police work for more than a week is accustomed to the necessity of barging into the most private realms of strangers; without the slightest display of awkwardness at being in the women's toilet, Park took up a position by the sink with his elbow resting on the top of the tampon-vending machine. He was a big man, Asian, with hair buzzed short. He tapped the knuckle of his forefinger against his chin, unable to be still. Danny could feel the energy fizzing off him. She leaned against the door and gestured for Park to speak. He took a breath and held it a moment, as if trying to determine where to begin.

"You haven't had any weird incidents up here," he said.

"No," Danny replied. "I mean, weird how?"

"Started yesterday. My grandparents are in Korea. They called to tell me there was some kind of incident in Busan where they live, and there was all kinds of problems in Japan and China as well. In the cities. When I say yesterday I mean it was very early this morning for us, and now I can't get through to them."

"Is this a personal matter?" Danny couldn't figure out why he was telling her these details.

"Haven't you seen the news? Heard on the radio?"

Danny was ashamed to admit she'd been in a self-induced coma and hadn't caught up with events. "The holiday keeps us pretty busy around here," she said.

"Okay," Park said, in the same way a man speaks before he jumps off a high diving board. "Okay. Well you know as much as anybody, probably. Fact is it's all rumors now. If you haven't seen the news, you haven't missed much. They're not reporting it. I mean they keep going to their reporter in New Delhi or wherever and there's what looks like rioting and then they cut to something low-key, you follow? It's like there's a news blackout, but nobody told us about it."

"Everything seems pretty cool around this area, though," Danny said. "No more activity on the radio than usual. Maybe it's only in Asia. Are you worried about your family?"

"If that was all I was worried about I sure as hell wouldn't come crawling up this damn mountain," Park said, irritated. Then he relented. "Nothing personal, obviously. My boss told me to come up here. This community is on the Eisenmann Plan."

"I don't know what the Eisenmann Plan is." Danny was already feeling off-kilter; this conversation was rapidly making it worse. She felt sick. She sat on the lid of the toilet, her elbows on her knees. Park wiped sweat from his upper lip.

"Me neither, until this morning," he said. "It's some kind of Cold War nuke evacuation plan, okay? Based on the idea of radio communications being disabled. Anyways, according to the plan, individual officers are supposed to spread out to any designated evacuation community and tell you all about it."

"All about what?" Danny muttered. "Tell me what's going on." She wanted to take a nap. Or have another drink.

"If something like what's happening overseas happens in Los Angeles," Park said, "you're going to inherit a hundred thousand displaced persons. Forest Peak is on the designated community list."

Forest Peak was at maximum capacity with a thousand or so tourists in the street, and they would almost all be gone by midnight. A hundred thousand people, stuck in town indefinitely during an emergency? There wasn't enough shelter to house them. Not even if thirty people moved into every structure in town. But that wasn't what had shut down Danny's mind. It was the broader implications of the thing.

Was there actually an emergency, and the powers that be had decided not to mention it? And the emergency plan was what, fifty years old? Did nobody learn a thing from New Orleans? And how could Park and his superiors possibly think a break in the 24/7 news cycle from someplace on the other side of the world meant impending disaster in the local area? Or did it?

Park was clearly working with an incomplete set of facts. He was low-ranking, so he got this kind of assignment without being told much. Danny's temper was heating up rapidly.

"So they sent you up here with next to no information except what your Grampy said? What the hell do they expect me to do about it?"

Park was perspiring freely. Danny waited for an answer, although the answer was obvious: Nobody knew what the Eisenmann Plan meant anymore. Or at least, certainly not Park.

"You can call my supervisor—"

"Will it help?"

"Maybe with specific stuff once there's more information from the government. There's three regions. We're the Western Region. Information gets relayed somehow."

Danny was fully awake now. "What I mean," she said, clipping her words, "is not how the plan works, but what are we supposed to do? Are we on terror alert status? Is this a security emergency? A safety emergency? Bad weather? Did Iran launch nukes at us? They didn't activate this plan thing just because your grandparents called."

"I don't know anything else, and neither does my command," Park said. "I'm here telling you what I can, because that's the first part of the plan. After that none of it works anyway. Used to be they'd drive a fleet of trucks up here in advance of the situation, loads of blankets and canned ravioli, right? No such trucks anymore. So it's just me, telling you."

Danny twisted the golden key on its ribbon. "Can you tell me anything about what happened in Korea? Or why it could happen here?

"No," Park said. "That's what rattled my cage. The lieutenant tells me, 'Drive up to Forest Peak and tell them to be aware there might be a need to shift populations around per Eisenmann,' and that was it. I had to look up what Eisenmann was. Connected that with what my grandparents said. My grandmother told me people were running and screaming down the street like *Gwoemul* was on the block, but there wasn't anything there. There wasn't an explosion or people with guns or anything. It was simple panic, for no apparent reason. If that's what's been happening everywhere . . ."

He ran out of words and his shoulders drooped. He picked at the decal on the front of the tampon machine, unaware he was doing it.

"Okay," Danny said. "I guess you did your duty. You told me there might be a situation, and if there is, there used to be a plan to deal with it, and good luck. Well I got a situation here, as it happens. I don't have enough deputies to handle the crowd as it is. So unless you're in a hurry to get back, I could sure use the extra uniformed presence. Can you stick around another three-four hours? By then I can call down the hill and if I learn anything, I'll let you know right away."

Park let out a long, gusty breath. Danny had thought he would resist staying an extra minute after he discharged his duty in this remote corner of nowhere—but in fact, he was relieved.

"Please," he said.

"Welcome to Forest Peak," Danny said, and they went out together into the back room, where Nick glanced up from some paperwork at the radio desk. He seemed intensely interested to know what was going on, but knew better than to ask. At this moment, a boy charged into the waiting area.

He hollered, "There's a dead guy!" bent double, and threw up in the potted plant by the door.

Weaver was eating soft serve ice cream. Patrick never touched the stuff. Weaver seemed to be happy, and the watchfulness he'd developed earlier had faded away.

For once, in this reassuringly hick town with its simple pleasures, Patrick was content. They'd both seen the lady sheriff go Rambo up there on the back of the flatbed truck, and this had furnished them with conversation for several minutes. Nothing relaxed Patrick more than someone he didn't know making a fool of themselves. It diverted his self-ridicule. He even felt like Weaver was his old approachable self again.

"I should get Rachael Ray up here next year," Patrick said.

"Do you know her?"

"She was the little bitty brunette I introduced you to at the party."

"Who was the tall guy, again?"

"Nathan Fillion."

"He's hot."

Patrick, his insecurity rushing back, immediately craved soft serve ice cream and the comfort only sugar and fat can provide.

Then he realized there was something else nibbling at his fleeting sense of contentment.

There seemed to be a lot of upset people on mobile phones, asking for repetition of information, asking for someone else to be put on the line, demanding their auditors calm down. The reception was terrible up in the mountains, but it was more than that. It vaguely reminded Patrick of the day Princess Diana died, and the shocking news rippled out into the world accompanied by an equal measure of disbelief. It hadn't been the same with Michael Jackson.

It was probably nothing important, just a coincidence. Patrick was finely tuned to pick up discord in his environment, that was all. Weaver was generally far more impassive, and consequently happier. Patrick wished he was like that himself.

"People acting weird," Weaver remarked, and Patrick began to per-spire.

He lay face-down in the woods, a quarter of a mile downhill from Main Street where the mountain was too steep to build on but ideal for dumping hard-to-discard trash like window glass, bald tires, washing machines, and scrap drywall. There was junk strewn all down the slope, with various arti-cles of rubbish fetched up against the roots of the trees that clung to the stony ground. Danny remembered being cautioned not to play around there when she was a girl, and how, consequently, they played in that area almost exclusively. In childhood, garbage is a kind of treasure, a discovery. The stuff that adults just want to get rid of turns into spacecraft, forts, and the raw materials of a hundred unfinished ideas. What were a few stitches and tetanus shots to the value of such riches?

Danny hadn't been down this way in years, and whatever magic she'd found there as a child was gone now. But the new generation hadn't aban-doned the place: She saw a large fort made of rusting sheet metal and lumber built up between two trees, and there was some sort of shelter made of tires and plywood as well. A little way below these projects, Danny saw a couple of kids lurking behind a tree, their attention focused downhill. Officer Park was at her side, Mike Bixby (the twin born one minute after his brother Carl) trailing along behind them.

Danny followed the boys' line of sight and saw something sprawled on a passage of naked rock that jutted out from the steepest part of the slope. She knew immediately that it was a corpse. Any combat veteran can recognize a dead body without hesitation, regardless of its pose or condition. There's a certain slack gravity to the dead that is absent from anything else, whether it is a realistic shop mannequin, a fallen-over scarecrow, or a sack of leaves.

Two questions immediately sprang to Danny's mind: First, who was it? And second, how did these kids stumble upon the body? Because Danny had noticed, even with the sour smell of puke, that Mike Bixby stank of gunpowder. If these boys had been fleeing town in a straight line from behind the hardware store—

"That's a body," Park said. It wasn't a question, but Danny heard the un-certainty in his voice. They had called an ambulance from the station before they set out after the Bixby twin, with directions for it to come along the State Forest Trail at the bottom of the mountain—not as direct a route as

Main Street, but with the crowds and unwanted attention, Danny thought it would be easier for the paramedics to hike up from below.

"Keep these kids under control, will you?" Danny said, and made her way past the other boys and down onto the rocky ledge where the corpse was tumbled. Based on Park's body language, she didn't think he'd be offended at a great big state policeman being told what to do by a mere local cop. He probably saw his share of road fatalities. The woods were spookier, however, than the 210 Freeway. Or maybe he wasn't sure how to secure a scene halfway up a cliff.

Danny had to descend toward the remains sideways, as if snowboarding, and several yards to the left so she wouldn't send cascades of leaves and dirt over the corpse. This was probably a simple case of someone falling in exactly the wrong way while taking a leak, but you never knew.

Danny got parallel to the scene, then worked her way closer over what certainly appeared to be evidence-free rock. It could be a body dump, she realized. Someone could have rolled it down the slope, hoping it would make it another couple of yards to the edge and flop down the steepest part of the mountain, where it would be well out of sight.

She knelt low and examined the body. Male, late twenties, Hispanic. Eyes open, face twisted as if with fright. Probably rigor mortis, not fear: The human face generally goes slack upon death and its expression means as little as the apparent smile of a dog. This wasn't a body dump. The corpse wasn't covered in leaves or dirt. Its arms weren't tangled around the torso, as with a rolling descent, but bent beside the head. The man looked like he'd fallen headlong, right where he lay.

"What's the story?" Officer Park asked, his voice raised. The three boys were talking among themselves behind the tree, possibly getting their story straight. Danny wished her colleague would keep a closer watch over them, but it was too late now.

"Male, deceased. COD not apparent." It was nobody she knew. Danny reached out and laid the backs of her fingers against the cheek of the dead man. She felt razor stubble there. The skin was still warm, as if alive. But he was certainly a corpse, his open eyes as lifeless as boiled eggs. "Not dead long," she added.

"We saw him fall down," Mike Bixby said, his voice hitching. He was almost done crying—his curiosity had largely overcome the shock.

"How so?" Danny asked. She wanted to sound casual, like they were discussing a television show. Keep him talking. Cub Maas spoke up next, excited by the chance to be part of a police investigation.

"He was running right at us and yelling," Cub said. "We thought he was chasing us."

"Chasing you why?" Danny asked, casually.

"Just because," Carl Bixby said, evasively, by way of warning to his cousin.

"We were running," Cub said, and knew that wouldn't be the end of it.

Danny wanted him to keep talking, however, so she relented: "Okay, he was chasing you along here and what happened? He fell and hit his head?"

"He fell over," Cub said, at a loss for words.

Carl pitched in now, apparently the ringleader of the boys, looking more confident since the dangerous part of the story had been gotten past. "I saw when he fell, Cub didn't. Cub was too busy running away like a *girl*. That dude was motoring, and like screaming as well, like this, with his hands on his head. Screaming. I thought he seen a bear or something. Then he like went down, right?"

"He fell right here, he didn't roll down the hill?" Danny said, indicating the corpse.

"Yeah, I seen him go like—" here, Carl grabbed his own head at the temples, then jerked and pitched forward, catching himself on one leg before he fell all the way, hands still on his head. "Like that, you know?"

"So he tripped on something," Park said.

"No," Carl said. "I can't explain it. He just fell, boom, like he got cold-cocked."

Danny studied the dead face resting against the rock. Certainly there were no major injuries on the part of the face she could see. He was missing one shoe, though, and his white sock was filthy, tattered, and dappled with blood. So he hadn't lost the shoe at the moment he fell. He'd been running through the trees like that for some time.

"Did he throw his hands out in front of him?" she asked.

"No. That's exactly why it looked weird." Carl was relieved somebody figured it out—he hadn't articulated it clearly to himself.

"He fell with his hands still on his head," Danny said. "Huh."

It didn't make sense. Maybe he'd been drunk and his reflexes were shut off. Or he could have been on amphetamines or something like that—somebody was dealing in the local area, but Danny hadn't figured out who—

which would also make his reflexes go haywire, and would explain why he hadn't stopped to retrieve his shoe. It was probably good old-fashioned death by misadventure. Danny very much doubted the man was chasing these boys, in any case.

Whatever the circumstances that led to this, she was going to have to spend the rest of an already busy day dealing with a dead person, and that meant whatever else went down, her deputies would be dealing with it. The thought made her despair. She wanted a drink now, more than ever.

Her radio clicked and deputy Ted's voice came over the speaker: "Sheriff, come in? We got a report from down to the Chevron station."

"Shoot," Danny said. "Kids present here, FYI," she added, in case there was anything unsavory to report, like the time a man was gassing up his car and set his pants on fire. *That* made the papers, all the way down in the flatlands.

Ted had to think about it—he wasn't fluent with the 10-signals, and Danny hadn't demanded he learn them as they were becoming obsolete. "10–53," he said at last.

Drunk and disorderly, Danny thought. It was hardly past noon and the drunks were already on the move.

"You're going to have to deal with it," she replied. "I got a 10–105 here. Misadventure."

Danny was entirely sober for once, so this was her chance to feel superior. Her radio came back to life.

"You still there?" Ted asked, and continued without waiting for a reply. "The thing is, he was running and screaming like crazy, he got away from me, and I don't think I can get to him in time. He's headed northwest."

Same direction as this one, Danny thought. "Nick, do you copy?" she said.

"Ten-four," Nick promptly replied, caught up in the radio game himself.

"Intercept this one for me, will you? I can't leave the body unattended."

Nick, in the station, was at the correct end of Main Street. But it would leave the station itself unattended.

"Sheriff?" Officer Park came downhill a few feet, and said, confidentially, "I can stay here if you need to get back." Danny was grateful. She flicked a salute off the edge of her hat and started up the mountainside.

"You gentlemen come with me," she said to the boys. They fell into line behind her. Halfway back to Main Street, Danny looked over her shoulder and saw Park speaking into his radio mic, probably reporting the situation to the brass back at his home base. Whatever was going on, it had gotten Danny what amounted to an extra deputy, and that was a big advantage. The way things were going, she thought she would need it.

What worried her most about the 10–53, as described by Ted, was the running and screaming. Second case of running and screaming that day, if the boys were to be believed.

He was inside the Forest Peak patrol car, a Crown Victoria that should have been auctioned off to a taxi company long ago. He had shoulder-length brown hair and no shirt, his skin covered in abrasions and cuts. The backseat of the Vic, like that of the Explorer, was a seamless plastic form, similar to the benches in a fast-food restaurant. It was spattered with blood. The man was completely out of control, shrieking and flailing his limbs—it looked as if he was trying to keep on running, even inside the vehicle. His wrists were cut through the skin from the zip-tie handcuffs that bound them together.

Danny was sweating profusely and so out of breath she could hardly see through the dark purple fireworks behind her eyes. She could smell herself: the sweet, yeasty stink of an alcohol binge.

". . . Three times before he stopped swinging long enough to get the cuffs on him," Nick was saying. He had an ice pack pressed to his cheekbone.

Danny had arrived after a brisk ten-minute slog along the mountainside to the Chevron station, and she was still doubled up with her hands on her knees, trying to get her wind back. The police car was parked around behind the gas station, next to the LP tank for filling barbecue cylinders. The deputies had shown some good sense, getting the perp out of sight of the general public before a crowd gathered. Highway Patrolman Park was posted by the corpse. The Bixby twins and their cousin Cub were in the hands of a neighbor. The situation was stabilized, Danny estimated. Now she had to figure out what to do with this maniac who was beating himself to a pulp in the back of the cruiser.

"You tasered him three times?" Danny said, because she hadn't been listening.

"I had to," Nick said, defensive. In fact, Danny didn't care if he'd beaten the man senseless with a shovel. Not today. But Nick was conditioned to expect disapproval if any situation escalated out of his control, as this one certainly had. "What are we gonna do?" he added, when Danny failed to reprimand him.

"I don't know," she said, and this was such a rare admission that both Nick and Ted were startled into looking closely at Danny's blotchy, sweating face. "Quit staring at me," she said. "Think of something yourselves."

All three of them stood there and pretended to think. The manager of the Chevron station, Artie Moys, was leaning against his old Toyota by the trash cans, waiting for them to get the nutcase off his property; until then, it didn't seem decent somehow to leave the police standing around alone. A couple of tourists were peeking around the hurricane fence, but from their perspective there wasn't much to see: Through the back window of the cruiser, the perp looked more like laundry bouncing around in a commercial dryer than anything else. But everybody within thirty meters could hear his discordant screams, muffled by the glass but still excruciatingly sharp.

Danny drew a normal breath for the first time since she'd left the corpse on the hill. She could think. She'd have the deputies hogtie this individual in the free cell back at the Sheriff's Station, then get the paramedics to have a look at him when they were done fucking around with the dead man in the woods. Maybe they could take the wild man away with them alongside the corpse, or Patrolman Park could drive him down the mountain after them in his slick late-model vehicle. Then somebody was going to have to clean the back of the Crown Victoria with bleach and paper towels. She wiped the sweat off her face with her hands and stood upright, ignoring the pain in her side. Time to make a statement to her minions, outlining the plan. She drew another breath to speak.

At that moment, the man in the back of the patrol car went limp and collapsed.

"What the fuck," Danny said, instead of her prepared statement. She strode over to the car, her legs sore from the hike, and examined the now-still man through the window. He was dead. He had to be. His naked ribcage wasn't moving. Nobody could scream for half an hour and flail around like he did without gasping for air.

Danny waited. If the captive was somehow holding his breath as a ruse, she wasn't going to let what was left of her humane impulses put her in harm's way. The deputies were exclaiming loudly to her left and right.

"Shut up," she barked, and popped the door latch. They all stood well back, and the weight of the man's legs was enough to push the door open a few inches. One of his sneakered feet fell through the gap. Danny saw the shoes were chewed up—he must have run a long way over some pretty rough terrain. She remembered the shoeless foot of the corpse in the woods, bloody and matted with dirt. Danny swung the door all the way open and stepped back again. If he was going to try to kick somebody, she didn't want to make it easy.

But he didn't kick. He didn't breathe. He lay there on the hard plastic seat, unmistakably dead.

"Ted, put on some gloves and check his vitals, but I think he's gone," Danny said. "Artie, you got a tarp or a sheet or something we can put over him for the drive down Main Street? I don't want any lookie-loos. They'll think we beat him to death."

"Rabies," said Artie.

Nick drove the body back toward the Sheriff's Station. It was concealed beneath a vinyl advertising banner that proclaimed *Cleanest Gas in Town,* a gift from the Chevron corporation. "*Only* Gas in Town" would have sufficed. Danny rode shotgun; Ted could walk back once he was done taking statements. Do him some good. They were halfway there, along where the first houses sprouted up to signal a human settlement was ahead, when the radio went crazy. Park had patched through the transmissions coming from the flatlands so he could explain what they were hearing.

"This is happening everywhere," the highway patrolman said, his voice cutting in over the rest. "People are running around and falling down dead, like up here. But a lot *more* of them."

Beneath Park's words, a continuous din of voices crossed and recrossed as law and order attempted to get a handle on the situation. At first it was confusion, the formless back-and-forth of a vast network of individual radios and incidents that could only be followed once you could separate one conversation from the rest. It took Danny twenty seconds before she could sort out any of it.

"We got ten or more down here on Crenshaw," someone said.

"More like fifty," the same voice amended a few seconds later.

Then another voice:

"They're running straight up Highland, must be a thousand. Lot of them falling. Something's in pursuit—can't see what. We're driving by."

"The Costco parking lot looks like a battlefield, there's hundreds," said another.

And then:

"Jesus, it's coming this way."

Officer Park interjected: "This situation is happening from L.A. to at least Claremont. I should get back down there, please advise, over."

Danny was about to reply, the handset at her lips, when a woman in bra and panties ran past the police car, screaming.

A lanky man with a beard, dressed as if for a hike, charged after the woman. He was also screaming.

"Hit the gas," Danny said. They had to cut these people off before they got to the crowded part of Main Street, or there could be a panic.

Patrick and Weaver were about ready to give up pretending to look at the crafts booths. The atmosphere had gotten very weird—the most distinct case of "bad vibes" Patrick had ever experienced, with the exception of one evening at a nightclub in Idaho. The phone calls had continued, and then people bundling their families into cars and driving away too fast through the one lane open along Main Street.

Two-thirds of the crowd was oblivious to this undercurrent of alarm, but more people were figuring out something was wrong by the second. And the number was expanding exponentially because now people were honking their horns and cutting each other off with their vehicles.

"Let's go," Patrick said. Typically, Weaver would have taken his time to respond, putting on a show of unflappable cool, but this time he simply nodded and set out through the crowd. By the time they were near the motor home, half the crowd was in on the excitement, those who hadn't gotten phone calls now overhearing what the others were saying, or assuming there was a fire or something like that—otherwise, why were people screaming?

The screams weren't coming from the crowd on Main Street. They were in the woods, it sounded like. People running and crashing through the undergrowth up behind the buildings. The band had stopped playing, and within a minute, almost the entire crowd had stopped speaking. They were all listening, trying to make sense of the cries off in the distance.

Then people were dropping their beer coolers, their shopping bags, abandoning empty strollers on the curb.

Panic spreads as fast as sound.

The voices of the crowd rose up in a roar of confusion, everyone trying to develop a reaction at the same time. Weaver took Patrick's hand and towed him straight through the remaining ranks of open-mouthed holiday-goers to the railing around the parking lot, and from there—nearly getting hit by a florid man in a station wagon—they forged on toward the White Whale.

They locked themselves inside and sat up front. The exit to the parking lot was pandemonium. Patrick was all for joining the motorized exodus.

"We don't know what's wrong yet," Weaver said, reasonably.

Patrick folded his arms. "I don't want to be stuck in this place when we find out."

"Patrick," Weaver said, again with that irritating lack of panic, "we're sitting in a thirty-six-foot rolling hotel room. We don't have to go anywhere. Unless it's a forest fire, we're probably better off sitting still in here than joining rush hour over a cliff."

"As soon as traffic lets up, though," Patrick said, going for a threatening tone.

They stayed parked where they were and listened to the talk on the CB radio and sat very still while the smaller vehicles surged and honked all around them.

People were using their cars like rams. A couple of fender-benders happened right in front of the RV. Only the first one excited any interest; the second didn't even get the drivers out of their vehicles. They just kept on going. Patrick watched a couple shove their screaming kids into a minivan. The kids had balloons tied to their wrists. The back door slammed on a string and the balloon was cut loose to drift into the sky.

"I'm not going to suggest we try to do something about this," Weaver said. "This isn't a crowd control situation." It hadn't occurred to Patrick to do anything, so this came as a relief. The CB radio seemed to be mostly occupied with truck drivers describing an immense traffic jam to each other, people trying desperately to get into the city in one direction and out of it in the other. The drivers with police scanners reported the authorities were on it, but overwhelmed. It was all happening with bewildering speed. Hundreds of accidents and stalled cars in-lane from Downtown to Santa Monica, and the roads were getting impassable to the east, as well, in the direction of Forest Peak. Then one of the truckers described thousands of people streaming past his rig on the 405 Freeway, on foot, moving through the standstill traffic. He said people were abandoning their vehicles. He said:

"I can see right down the hill at the top of the pass between Hollywood and Studio City, and there are people swarming up the hill here, goddamn, it's like bugs, the cars can't do nothing. I ain't moved ten feet in ten minutes. Folks are going past the truck right now, scared shitless. I dunno what's going on but it's bad, I don't see no smoking gun of a mushroom cloud but it's bad . . .

"Christ, they're running now, people running up this big damn hill through the cars, people getting out of their cars and they're running, too."

The squelched sounds of screaming could be heard in the background as the unknown trucker lowered his window.

"I can't make it out, they're yelling about something coming but I'm a good nine feet off the ground, I don't see shit coming. But some folks are falling down. I can see down the hill they're falling all over the place. Jesus. They're falling all around—"

That was the last thing the trucker said.

In the silence that followed, Patrick realized he was holding his breath. Weaver was watching the radio as if it had a picture. After a few seconds, the rest of the voices on the CB radio started up again, all going crazy trying to figure out what happened to their good buddy. Someone with an open microphone started to sing loud psalms, and Weaver switched the radio over to FM band, where the Emergency Broadcast System had just kicked in.

Some stations continued to play preprogrammed music. On the rest, the weird faxlike tones of the EBS screeched out, then a recorded voice said, "Stand by for an important bulletin."

In the police cruiser, Nick and Danny caught up with the bearded hiker— he'd fallen on the yellow lines a little way outside town, dead like the others. Cars were creeping past him on the way out, pale faces pressed to the windows. The screaming woman in her skivvies had run off behind the houses into the woods. They couldn't hear her cries anymore, but there were others coming now, charging through the trees and hollering like banshees. A mass of traffic was quickly tangling up where the road widened at the end of town—too many vehicles trying to get around each other, clogging the street.

The situation was devolving with the speed of a wildfire.

"Find out where Dave is," Danny said to Nick. "Get him out here. We need all hands, now. Tell Ted to haul ass back here. I want these people to stay right here in town until we know what's going on."

Danny hopped out of the car and jogged the rest of the way into town— it was faster than driving, at this point. The Sheriff's Station was only a few hundred yards away, but with the confusion reigning in the street, it took Danny twice the time she could afford. A lot of people were shouting at her from their vehicles, even climbing out to make demands she couldn't possibly meet: Get us out of here, take control, do something. Danny ignored them and kept on going until she was through the station doors, where Highway Patrolman Park was trying to organize a crowd of some thirty people jammed into the front room—standing room only, the air rancid with fear and anger.

Danny forced her way through the crowd, took a position next to Park, and banged the flat of her hand on the counter until most eyes were turned her way.

"Listen up!" she shouted. "You all need to get to your vehicles or find a quiet place to wait until we have things calmed down, you hear me?" Danny's voice sounded harsh and ragged to her ears. It sounded the way it did back in the foreign desert. "We do not have the personnel to deal with individual situations. Please leave in an orderly manner and I'll get back with everyone as soon as possible."

This last detail was patent nonsense, but it helped. The people nearest the door, complaining loudly and bitterly, went back outside. The others filed out after them with the heavy, headshaking tread common to all thwarted taxpayers. *They can write their representatives,* Danny thought. *I'm about ready to cap the fuckers.*

"I can't keep you here," Danny said to Park, as the last of the civilians slammed the door on the way out. "But you'd better get going, because traffic isn't getting any better, even if you light up the bubblegums."

Park drew a long breath and let it out at the same slow rate. "I'll . . . I guess I'll stay here. I haven't heard anything from my department in fifteen or twenty minutes. Be an hour at least before I got back there. I might as well stick around and be useful as get myself caught in rush hour on the mountain."

"Thanks," Danny said, and meant it.

Park went outside after a brief conference about Danny's objectives, which were at this point limited to keeping injuries to a minimum and maintaining general order, until the nature of the situation was clear.

Danny took a few moments at the radio desk to call around to other police and fire departments, but didn't get much useful information—they were all in the same boat, trying to catch up with events.

Wulf Gunnar was complaining from his cell, demanding to know what was going on outside, and it gave Danny a small pleasure to ignore him. Forest Peak was lucky to be on the margin. Down in the thickly settled areas, if the radio chatter was to be believed, circumstances were devolving at a pace not even a military presence could slow down. This thing was going to have to play itself out overnight, at least.

Danny was trying to find somebody at the federal level who could tell her what the hell was going on, but the FBI was not answering any of its phones and the civilian government's snarl of automated touch-tone phone assistants sent her around in ever-decreasing circles. She was setting the handset of the phone back on the cradle when Nick came in, dragging the dead man from the back of the cruiser. The body was wrapped in the vinyl banner from the Chevron station.

"Somebody gotta tell me what the fuck is happening," Wulf growled when he saw the corpse. Nick left it on the floor alongside a desk. Danny relented: Wulf *did* have a right to know, especially if she was going to keep him locked up. She couldn't remember if he'd been charged yet. She turned to speak to him.

They all heard glass breaking on Main Street, and screams—not the screams of those crazy people running through the woods, but screams of fear, anger.

Danny rushed out the front doors of the station onto the sidewalk, heard an engine racing, and an instant later got clipped by the wing mirror of a BMW with a "Trojans" frame on the license plate. She stumbled back into the wall and gritted her teeth, feeling the big muscles of her thigh contract with pain. Nick came rushing out and thumped into a woman holding a small dog. The dog leaped to the ground and ran off beneath the idling cars. The woman spat at Nick: *"Asshole!"* and threaded her way between the cars after the dog, shouting "Puff! Puff, stay!"

The BMW, meanwhile, was tearing down the broad sidewalk space between the old-fashioned wooden telephone poles and the doorsteps of the businesses on Main, leaving behind it a strew of upended trash barrels, the town's lone post box, a cardboard display of Whiffleballs and bats, and a couple of knocked-over crafts booths—and there were several other cars coming after it. Almost at the end of Main Street, the Beemer hit an abandoned chili cart and slewed to a halt, the windshield covered in beans. The driver jumped out and started scraping the chili off the glass with his bare hands. An irrelevant voice flickered through Danny's mind: *I hope that's not Rosarita's.* Danny considered for a split second making an example of the driver, hauling him out and handcuffing him, but the real crisis wasn't this one driver.

The entire town appeared to have gone insane.

From end to end, Main Street was jammed with vehicles, all heading south toward the flatlands. Before, it had been a mess, like getting out of the parking lot after a football game. Now it was impassable, and people were flipping out—there was a shouting match across the street that looked like it might escalate into a brawl. The crawling vehicles spanned both lanes of the road, incoming and outgoing, with more nosing out of lanes, daring to attempt the shortcut down what passed for a sidewalk in Forest Peak. Horns and engines and voices rose in an unholy din. Dogs were barking through back windows.

The same as she did in the Marines, Danny gathered what she knew and assembled a quick working hypothesis, subject to constant revision. Some kind of disaster had happened, as far as she could tell; what it was, nobody knew, but it seemed to be spreading fast. People were fleeing the major urban centers (or trying to return), and there were others running and dying, like the ones they'd seen here in Forest Peak, but in huge numbers. All over the place. *Out there in the wide world where Kelley is*, said the voice in her head.

It had been less than fifteen seconds since the mirror hit Danny's thigh, and she could almost move the leg again. As she had learned when she threw away the cane after the town elections, you don't heal an injury by treating it like a friend.

"You hurt, Sheriff?" Nick said.

Danny didn't have anything useful to say—this was not the time to bark at the minions—so she drew her sidearm and gestured with the weapon: *Follow me.* Nick did so. Danny fed orders into her radio mic, summoning the remainder of her tiny peacekeeping force: Highway Patrolman Park would do what he could in town; Danny wanted Dave, Nick, and Ted to assemble down on Route 114. What they needed was a roadblock, something she knew a great deal about.

Patrick thought traffic was light enough so they could start moving. Weaver switched on the video screen that showed the view to the rear, as seen by an all-weather camera mounted on the roof. There was an overturned baby stroller behind them but the cars were cleared out, room enough to back up. Weaver switched the screen off again.

"All those cars are going to be stuck on Main Street for another hour," Weaver said. "We'll only be stuck behind them."

"But Weaver!"

"Panic is panic. You think it's gonna help?"

"When do I not panic?" Patrick said.

"Patrick?"

"Okay. I know. I'm shutting up."

They waited as a few stray cars that had been parked up the hill on Sawyer Road drove past to join the fray, then they were almost alone except for the few locals who stood at the end of the parking lot to watch the pandemonium on Main Street. The locals weren't freaking out because they were already where they belonged. Patrick knew dislocation was a powerful feeling and it drove as much mindless fear as did the threat of bodily harm. He watched through the tall windshield of the motor home, but Weaver was examining his Geological Survey map, one of those outdoorsy charts that were more geared to topographical details than useful features like restaurants and outlet malls. To Patrick, the map was a mass of meaningless wavy lines, like an Op-Art painting.

"Check it out," Weaver said. "Everybody's heading downhill, right? That's here." Weaver indicated the road with his finger. Then he tapped the other end of town, where they were now parked.

"But if you go the other way—"

Here he followed a line that twisted up deeper into the mountains— "You get up to Big Bear, and from there you can go down the other side to Scobie Tree and hook up with Route 66 again. It's a bitch of a drive and it's probably three hours extra, but I guess it will put us back in civilization before any of them even make it past the Forest Peak Chevron station."

Patrick nodded. Weaver was right. Then something else occurred to him.

"What if there's trouble down there, too?"

Weaver gave him that slow cowboy smile.

"Light dawns on Marble Head. We got caviar, crackers, and beer. We got a queen-size bed and a flush toilet. While everybody is losing their minds, I suggest we wait things out right here in Forest Peak."

Officer Park, responding to Danny's urgent inquiry, thought he could hold things together on Main Street, although the sheriff told him not to hesitate to call down some of Greer's firemen if things got out of hand—anybody in a uniform would help, especially if they happened to be carrying fire axes.

Danny tried to put her priorities in order. What mattered the most: public order? Keeping the town safe? Getting everybody out? Preparing for whatever was coming from down below? There ought to be a huddle with Mayor Crocker, and anybody else in a position of authority, too. It seemed like she had to make all of it happen at once.

Danny had Dave take the Crown Victoria along the disused logging road down the hill, the one that came up on Route 144 about a half-mile outside Forest Peak, behind the Chevron station. He wouldn't get there any faster than Danny and Nick could do on foot, because the road was dirt, and mostly washed out. Not ideal terrain for a sedan. It was the way the locals took to dump their trash in the woods below town, down where the first corpse had been discovered by those boys.

"There's no hurry," Ted said over the radio. He was at the gas station. "Things have gotten pretty hectic here. People going feral for a chance at the gas pumps, and there's more of those screamers in the woods, too."

Danny turned to the deputy at her side. "Nick, I think I want you here on Main Street," Danny said. She had a feeling things were going to get worse before they got better, and if that happened, Danny was going to have to fall back—and town was the only place they could fall back *to*.

Dave at last reached the station in the Crown Vic and radioed back to Danny with a slightly better description of the situation than Ted could provide. Nobody was going anywhere, according to Dave: The road was jammed in *both* directions. The two lanes of southbound travelers were head-to-head with two lanes of northbound traffic coming up from the flatlands.

There was a fistfight winding down at the Chevron pumps, two angry fathers duking it out while their kids shrieked inside the cars. And there were people on foot coming up the mountain, exhausted by the steep grade, leaning forward as if into a high wind to ease their aching legs. A few SUVs were trying their luck along the steep verge above the road, pushing the limits of what gravity would allow. One of them had already overturned, cutting off the breakdown lane on the uphill side.

Ted almost wept with relief when Dave showed up. He got into the police car and Dave switched on the lights and the siren and used the nose of the vehicle to push a space through the traffic. Even in this extremity, people still responded to the presence of the law. Ted jumped out in midroad and set up the collapsible sawhorses they kept in the trunk. Between them, the deputies were able to block the road completely, although people were shouting death threats before they were finished.

The line between law and anarchy was stretching thinner and thinner by the moment.

Danny went back into the station, ignoring the ongoing complaints from Wulf's cell, and liberated some hardware from the gun cabinet. The dead man was a lumpy shape beneath the banner. Danny went out through the front room and locked the door behind her. Then she pressed her way up Main Street, making a presence out of her guns, uniform, and hard stare. She turned off between two buildings, reached the alley behind them, and found Amy's white cube van with *Cutter Veterinary Ranch* on the side, parked at the back of the Junque Shoppe.

Danny had a Remington 1100 tactical shotgun in her hands and an old Ruger rifle slung over her shoulder. Amy was busy cramming the last of the pygmy goats into the back of the van. Her white veterinary coat was smeared with animal dung. Danny put her hand on Amy's shoulder.

"I got a situation. You remember how to use the police radio?"

Amy nodded. Danny knew Amy had a similar unit in her veterinary barn; her work often involved angry bears, wounded deer, and rabid coyotes, animals that required the intervention of the law. A rabbit saw she was distracted, leaped out of the van, and zigzagged away down the alley. Amy started after it, but Danny grabbed her arm.

"Amy, this is more important. I know you prefer animals, but it's people time. My deputies are all out there trying to keep the peace. I need somebody with a working brain to stick with the radio and figure out what the fuck is going on. Are you with me?"

"I can't leave all these little guys stuck in the van—they'll roast."

Danny did a slow burn. This was Amy's thing. When it got too crazy in human world, she retreated into sacred animal world where nothing could get between her and her fuzzy little charges. Danny, who used to enjoy hunting deer before she went overseas to hunt men, found this self-indulgence unspeakably irritating.

"Then open the van," Danny clipped.

Amy shook her head *no* like a child.

Danny tried one more time: "They'll get hungry later and come back."

Amy stared at Danny. This was too much to ask. But someone on the Main Street side of the Junque Shoppe chose this exact moment to smash into another vehicle: Plastic crumpled and horns blared, then hysterical voices rose up over the rooftops.

"Amy," Danny said, "something is happening. Something big. I don't know what it is, but I can't handle it alone."

Danny didn't normally admit any obstacle was too big for her to handle. Amy started to protest, but there wasn't any meaning in it. She opened and closed her mouth. A chorus of horns blared over the rooftops. *I can't handle it.*

"You owe me," Amy said.

She opened the rear doors of the van, and all the animals inside stood where they were, watching her. So far, so good. Danny told Amy which radio frequencies to call in on, and how to identify the Forest Peak transmitter so other police units would know she was the real thing. She wondered how much she should tell Amy, how much would be overwhelming, or would sound plain crazy. What about this Eisenmann Plan? Was that why there were so many people coming up the hill? Or was this mass hysteria, animals scrambling to high ground before a flood?

Danny's thoughts were tumbling too fast for her to catch them and put them in order. She found she was concluding her instructions to Amy, but couldn't remember the last ten things she'd said.

"So listen," Danny continued, winding down, "keep out of Main Street. Stay inside the station until I come back. Door locked. I wish I could tell you more—"

Amy held up her hand.

"Nobody knows anything. I heard something from some woman who thought I was a doctor. She told me her sister called and people were dying. Dying, okay? Then a bunch of people were asking me what to do. Which is why I'm back here with the goats, because I have no idea. I told them I was a podiatrist. What about the Mountain Rescue or something?"

Danny realized she was squeezing Amy's arm. She relaxed her grip and patted the arm instead, in the least reassuring way possible. But she tried.

"They don't exist anymore, remember? Budget cuts. See if you can raise the highway patrol or Fire and Rescue to send us a chopper. We might need an airlift. There was an ambulance on its way at least an hour ago, but there's no way it can get here. And . . . and keep your head down. That's all I can tell you."

"And you?"

"I'll be okay," Danny said, and felt like more was required. "I got a fancy police hat."

With that, Danny started back down the alley. She considered covering the distance to the roadblock on foot, but her thigh was stiffening up. So she slung herself up into the Explorer behind the Sheriff's Station and turned it down the alley toward Pine Street, from which the logging road extended. Thank God it wasn't on the tourist maps or that would be clogged with cars, too.

It was now three in the afternoon, but it felt like ten days later as Danny reached the roadblock manned by her deputies. They were scared nearly witless; there were now at least two hundred people shouting at them from across the hoods of the foremost cars in both directions and some hot-bloods were racing their engines as if to charge. Beyond this locus of the standstill, the traffic stretched out of sight, uphill and down. A cloud of exhaust fumes was boiling up out of the legion of vehicles.

Danny couldn't hear the distant screams in the woods anymore, but she didn't know if it was because they were drowned out by the revving motors and horns and angry voices, or because the scattering of wild people had passed this location by. She hoped they were gone. Or they might all be dead now. Once the rest of this was dealt with, they might still be finding corpses in the woods for the next ten years.

More and more of the refugees from the flatlands were abandoning their rides and walking up the slopes past the barricade, and now a few of the cars that had been heading downhill were trying to reverse course and head back up to Forest Peak. But anything with an engine, including the motorcycles, was stuck in gridlock.

Danny whistled under her breath. Time to come up with a new plan, even if it was meaningless. Otherwise there would be violence.

She dropped the Explorer into low gear and rolled it up to her deputies, the roof lights flashing. She stepped out and handed the rifle to Dave, but kept the shotgun for herself.

"Is the bullhorn in the Crown Vic?" she asked.

Ted pulled the horn from the police sedan's trunk and handed it to Danny. His thick face was pale and wet. She worried he was going to have a stroke. Maybe say something reassuring? Nothing came to mind. Danny stepped up on the fender of the Explorer and from there onto the hood and the roof, placing her high enough to get a long descending view of the file of traffic twisting down the mountainside. It extended as far as she could see. Being exposed in a high place like this was something she would never, ever have done in Iraq. Even here she could feel the snipers watching. But high visibility was part of this. She raised the bullhorn in one hand and cradled the shotgun in the other, and knew what to say.

"Ladies and gentlemen, your attention, please. We are going to open up a lane of traffic and I want two vehicles at a time to come forward *real slow*, and we will give you instructions on where to go. *Two vehicles at a time.* Anybody who does not comply will be stopped. We will begin with the southbound vehicles and proceed with the northbound."

In a few minutes, the nearest cars had been organized until a narrow escape lane had been established, leading to the logging road. Deputy Dave was walking back down the deeply rutted path to establish a waiting area: They could hold a couple dozen vehicles along the logging road and then walk them back into town in an orderly fashion, meanwhile staging the next group. It was probably pointless, as there had to be several thousand cars on the road, but unless people saw something being done, there would soon be chaos.

Danny knelt on the roof of the Explorer, keeping her presence felt with the shotgun propped up against her hip, watching the more aggressive personalities on the downhill side of the situation.

Refugees, Danny thought. *These people are refugees.*

The thought hit her with palpable force. These people were basically fleeing something, driven from the course of their lives. *Refugees in California.* A cascade of facts fell into place. Danny knew how crazy refugees could get in other parts of the world. These were Americans, who had never experienced refugee status before, unless they were from New Orleans. Things could get a lot uglier.

The motorists who had been in Forest Peak earlier and were attempting to leave had begun to realize that rushing down into what could be a fatal situation wasn't going to help their loved ones, alive or dead, so the traffic pointed downhill remained orderly. Deputy Ted was letting some of them go first, to be followed by a group of the northbound refugees. Danny stood tall and tried to look like a show of force. Amy called in every few minutes and kept Danny posted with results from her efforts on the station's radio:

". . . No word from L.A. Pomona PD says the traffic on the 210 is at a standstill and there are thousands of cars with dead folks in them, dead all over the road. There are fires in El Monte and Riverside and nobody can put them out because they can't even get close except on foot but nobody wants to go near the bodies. Nobody knows what's happening but it sounds like this dying thing has run itself out on the West Side and it's moving this way."

"Amy? Let's not speculate on the open radio."

"Am I a deputy, by the way?"

"Yes. Deputy Cutter."

"Cool. Okay, I'm going to keep looking for news."

Danny never ceased to wonder at Amy's ability to find irrelevant things interesting—like being deputized—even as their world was turned upside down. She started her next transmission: "Come in, Nick. What's your situation? Over."

"Uh, lot of 11–24s—that's abandoned vehicles, right?—on Main Street. People on foot are uh gathered around the TVs at the Wooden Spoon and the Quik-Mart, they're crowding into lanes. But nothing's moving. It's a standstill. Over."

"Anything on the news?" Danny asked.

"Worse than useless, Sheriff. Crying relatives and car accidents. A bunch of talking heads in Washington blaming the Muslims. Lots of detail stuff but no big picture. It's happening all over the place, is all I know."

Nick explained he had three of Greer's firemen in full firefighting regalia to help him organize things, so Danny felt Main Street was reasonably secure. "Hey, Danny," Amy said. "Come in, I mean. I found out some stuff. On your computer. I checked all the twits and status updates and whatnot—people are going *crazy*. But nobody knows what's going on."

Danny watched a couple of excited dogs run by, most likely escaped from cars. She watched another group of vehicles file past the roadblock toward the logging road, frightened faces peering up at her from the backseats. She remembered the roadblocks in the Iraq desert, those volatile, beleaguered people huddled in their beat-up cars and pickup trucks for hours in the blazing heat, twice as hot as it was today in the mountains of Southern California. It was another world over there, every face the mask of an enemy. And yet it was exactly the same.

She was the alien, the figure with the gun and the rules that stood unwanted between them and their goals. People in crisis preferred, Danny realized, individual action over imposed order—even if the price was bloodshed and confusion. Maybe that was the primary freedom they were celebrating every Fourth of July: the right to act like fuckups now and then. She hoped there was more to it than that. It was a pity the sheriff's department of Forest Peak didn't have a .50 caliber machine gun. Danny remembered those rattling bursts of gunfire that answered a rush on one of their roadblocks in the war zones, the high, thin scream of an engine, the higher screams of those inside the vehicle as the heavy weapons opened fire. She could almost hear the screams now, though distant with time.

She *could* hear the screams now.

Her mind whipped back to the present and she stood fully upright, leg protesting. Her view included glimpses of almost five miles of road as it curved down the ruffled flank of the mountain, a glittering coil of motionless vehicles. There were tiny figures running among the vehicles almost at the limit of her vision. The screams must have been coming from there, transmitted through all that air across the ravines—they weren't the ones who had been in the woods before.

Maybe Danny was the only one who could hear them from here, high up on her perch atop the Explorer. Her heart was kicking into high gear.

Until this moment she had hoped the weird disaster that was sweeping the lowland world would mostly pass her small community by, as everything else did. Apparently not. She might have a couple of minutes before the nearby civilians caught on to the screaming, and then there was going to be pandemonium. Unless she was very much mistaken, Forest Peak was about to enter a world of shit.

There were demanding voices out in the waiting room of the Sheriff's Station, but Amy didn't think she was qualified to address the public. She was still at her post at the communications desk, headphones jauntily set over one ear so she could hear if the phone rang—which it was doing every few seconds. She answered those calls as best she could. Mostly locals were calling. Out-of-towners dialed the 911 system, which put them on hold for a couple of minutes and then hung up.

Forest Peak residents wanted to know what was happening and what was the sheriff doing about it.

"Something is going on down in the flatlands," Jim Rummint said, his voice shaky on the other end of the line. Amy doctored Jim's horses. He didn't worry easily, so that tremble in his voice unnerved her considerably. "Where's the sheriff? There's people all over the place and nobody to keep order."

"The sheriff is taking care of it," Amy said, keeping her own voice level, if high-pitched. "Like you say, there's a lot of people out there right now, and not a lot of police. In an hour or two everything will be hunky-dory, okay? No danger here, except people acting like big dopes. So don't do that."

"It's that I'm worried about," Jim said. "People go crazy. That's why I live all the hell and gone up here in the mountains. People in large numbers are dangerous."

"I have a lot more calls to answer," Amy said. "Hang in there." She hung up on Jim before he could reply and took the next call.

Meanwhile, over the headphone on her other ear, she was hearing reports that entire police forces were going silent in distant towns. As if they had abandoned their posts. And now Amy was hearing something else, too: Wulf was awake in his cell, and he was making his opinions known.

"I got rights, too, Cutter. I been in here since morning and nobody processed me or nothing. Alls I got to eat today was some egg crap. And what the hell is going on? You ain't a cop, you're the vet. They got a sick cat in here? Jesus H. Christ, come on over and let me out, I'm no danger to anybody. I got *rights*. Come on, lemme out."

Wulf eventually ran out of things to complain about, although it occurred to him to ask the vet if she knew anything about itchy scalp. His head was raging with worn-out drink, there was a taste in his mouth like vampire piss, and he was confined and bored, the two things he hated most. That big-boots, little-tits sheriff Adelman was a goddamned fool and he'd known her since she was a baby girl and she was a goddamned fool then, too, and so was Amy Cutter, and so was he for getting liquored up so late in the evening that he was still hammered come the morning of the Fourth of July. But of all the holidays, that one left him the most bitter. Adelman would start feeling that way, too, before long. Wulf guessed the sheriff was on the same road to ruin that he'd traveled down. After all, the only difference between the inside and the outside of a drunk tank was an inch of door. Wasn't that far to go.

The screaming, though still distant, was unmistakable now. Like the sound of an arena rock concert from the far side of the parking lot. Some civilians were getting out of their cars to better hear the noise, and others were getting back into their cars because it was about time to do something drastic, and the people on foot were starting to close in around the roadblock, as if a couple of cops could do anything about the entire population of the San Gabriel Valley running in their direction. Deputy Dave, too, looked up at Danny for orders—and for some kind of information as to what he was hearing. He couldn't see as Danny could from on top of the Explorer that the running people were no more than a mile away.

Her mind was blank. Their vehicle-organizing plan didn't really go anywhere in the first place; it was simply a way to clear the road so this immense file of refugees could move on through to Big Bear or wherever. Now they needed to move a lot of people very quickly, and then deal with several thousand more who were in a blind panic, if those oncoming screams meant what she thought they did. There were the dead men, the one in the woods and the one who had died in custody. They'd been screaming, too.

Again Danny thought how much easier things would be if she had a high-caliber machine gun. Or one of those M1A1 Abrams tanks. Not to shoot anybody, but to reassert authority with a few rounds over the crowd. These thoughts went through Danny's mind in an instant, and in the next the bullhorn was at her lips:

"Your attention, please! I need you all to get into your vehicles, lock the doors, and roll the windows up. Turn your engines off. Pass the word down the line. I don't want to see anybody outside a vehicle. We got some people coming, and it is imperative that we separate you from them. That means you inside your vehicles, doors locked, windows up, engines off. *Now.*"

And God bless them, most people did exactly what Danny said. Even Dave. He headed straight for the Crown Vic.

"Dave, not you. You stand tall."

He resumed his post at the barricade. At this moment Deputy Ted came trotting up from behind the Chevron station, massaging a stitch in his side. "Sheriff," he panted, "Zach Greer's guys in the fire observation post say there's thousands of people . . ." Ted had to stop for breath at the side of the Explorer, hands on thighs. Danny discreetly held a finger to her lips: Keep your voice down. Ted continued at a stage whisper:

". . . Thousands of people running up Route 144."

He cocked his head, hearing the approaching screams for the first time. Danny opened the magazine on the shotgun. It was fully loaded.

"Ted, Dave, I want you two up on top of the Crown Vic, don't worry about the paint job. I want you both up there with long arms in your hands. We need to stop all those people running. The three of us need to make a human firewall and stop this thing in its tracks before it hits town."

The screams were distinct now, so close Danny had to raise her voice. The deputies looked as if they might lose control of themselves. Danny thought it was time to get serious. She racked a shell into the chamber of the shotgun one-handed and let the barrel swing out over the river of stopped traffic, sweeping across all those terrified faces watching her through windshields. Not everybody had listened to her orders; a steady trickle of people was running along the roadside toward town. It couldn't be helped. The consensus on the police band was that this thing was some kind of contagion. Danny figured if a person was running, she had to assume he or she was exposed.

And she was about to get exposed herself.

5

The first of the runners came charging between the cars on the left-hand side, a thin woman in a tank top, with dusty colored hair and a face mottled from the exertion of running up the hill. Her mouth was a red O as she ran. There were a few people standing outside their cars to watch the action; they jumped back as she approached, then dived for their vehicles.

Danny knew she was at a turning point. Whatever happened in the next few minutes would determine whether Forest Peak joined the historic disaster that was unfolding down below. There were a dozen runners behind the first, and from the almost continuous screams coming up the road, Danny knew there were hundreds more around the next bend. She discovered the shotgun in her hands was aimed at the woman. Shoot her down, it might stop the rest of them. She tried the bullhorn one more time:

"Stop where you are. This is a police barricade. We will use force."

The woman kept on running. Now Danny could see her eyes, and there was no recognition behind them, no mind. Time to make an example. Stop one, maybe stop a thousand. But that was crazy—this was an American, not some cipher from another world. Yet no different, not really. Danny ought to be able to kill this woman as easily as she had killed others in that previous lifetime beneath a crueler sun. Or had it ever been easy?

Danny never got to find out whether she could pull the trigger or not. Instead, the woman with the dusty colored hair dropped in her tracks.

One instant she was running full-out between the cars, no more than a hundred feet from Danny's perch; the next she was tumbling limp against the trunk of a maroon Honda Accord. Her face bounced off the sheet metal and she dropped out of sight. There was a girl screaming in the car directly behind the Accord. Then two young men sprinted into range, waving their arms around their heads as if the air were full of bees. The legs of the one in front buckled under him and he fell on his back. The other man kept running. And now more people were coming through the cars, running at full tilt. It was too late to use force.

Deputy Ted hollered: "Sheriff, what do we do!"

Danny figured on Deputy Dave to hold his ground. She was wrong. As the surviving young man ran around the end of the Crown Vic and charged through the roadblock into the south-facing cars, Dave jumped down to the pavement and threw his gun at Ted.

"I'm outta here," was all he said. And he ran after the young man in the direction of town.

That did the trick. Suddenly everyone was starting their engines, cars were surging forward into the one or two feet of space between them and the car in front, and a human stampede was pouring around the vehicles, screaming and waving their arms and some of them falling, always some of them falling everywhere Danny looked. It was as if a tide of human beings was washing up the mountainside, and now the foamy crest of the wave was swirling past Danny's position on top of the Explorer.

She saw a late eighties Buick leap forward from its position at the front of the northbound cars, attempting to make it around the barricade. Instead, the long nose of the car pinned a young woman—*Kelley's age,* the voice said—against the fender of a pickup truck. Danny heard the long bones crack in the woman's legs, and her wild screams went up three octaves. The Buick lurched backward and the woman collapsed, both legs shattered, but kept crawling on; then another car smashed into the back of the Buick, and more runners were tumbling over the obstacles. A couple of them stayed where they fell, and the others leaped up and scrambled onward.

Deputy Ted held his position, rifle pointed downhill but not at anyone specific. He stayed there until a knot of runners smashed into the Vic, rocking it on its shocks, and several of them clawed their way over the hood. When Ted tried to shove them off it, they swarmed over him and he went down heavily beneath the churning limbs. Danny's instincts kicked in and she fired the shotgun into the air. A few of the faces behind their steering wheels ducked, but nobody in the scrum paid any attention at all. It was as if they'd gone crazy. And then it occurred to Danny that maybe they *had* gone crazy, maybe they'd been exposed to a nerve gas that made them run until their hearts failed. She thought of the woman with her mangled legs crawling away between the cars.

Ted emerged from the crowd, bleeding from the nose. He looked up at Danny and she reached down to pull him up, but there was nobody home inside his head. His mouth fell open and he screamed like the others, then bolted away into the crowd of runners with his hands thrown out in front of him. The Explorer rocked on its shock absorbers as a big man slammed into the driver's side door and flopped to the asphalt with his head twisted around. Danny almost fell. The ground trembled with the pounding of human feet. There was a solid mass of people swarming past now, like a marathon, and with these numbers the Explorer might even end up over-turned, parked across lanes as it was. But it wasn't the runners that she needed to worry about.

Above the screaming and the arrhythmic thump of bodies hitting metal, she heard the sharp, blatting roar of an illegally muffled exhaust stack, then a cloud of black smoke leaped up from among the northbound vehicles. A huge jacked-up Toyota pickup with vertical exhaust pipes, a winch, and tires like millwheels lurched out of lanes and ground its way up the shoulder, scraping against lesser cars, peeling off side mirrors. There was a rebel flag decal in the back window of the primer-brown cab. Maybe Danny was going to have to shoot someone after all. But a shotgun wasn't worth shit against an angled safety-glass windshield. Not the first round, anyway.

She kept one eye on the screaming mass of bodies rushing below her and one eye on the Toyota. He wouldn't be able to make it past the Buick, she estimated. She was mistaken. The Toyota belched smoke, the bark of the exhausts as loud as the shotgun—and the silhouette at the wheel floored the accelerator. The truck rose up on its quad shocks and plowed through a mess of running figures, even as Danny brought the shotgun around. There was no aim. Runners were hammering full-body against the Explorer, causing it to sway and bounce.

Someone's face made a crimson rosette on the Toyota's matte brown hood as it bounced off the panel, then the truck T-boned the Buick, shoving it sideways across the pavement. The driver's side door collapsed as the truck bit deep into it. Danny saw the airbags fill up the passenger compartment, then deflate, and then the Buick was obscured because it was slamming into the Explorer, crushing bodies against it so that grape-sized globs of blood and tissue spewed out. Screams became banshee howls. Danny got a bead on the truck at last. She fired the shotgun and a giant snowflake appeared on the Toyota's windshield.

The Explorer lurched beneath her, two feet, four feet back, and her hat flew off—Danny was on her belly sliding along the roof, squeezing the trigger again, but the pellets flew wild, off into the trees on the uphill slope. Then the Explorer was mashed up against the guardrail and tipping over it in a cloud of sooty exhaust, the Toyota climbing the hood like some kind of imbecile metal-eating beast. Danny wanted to leap onto the hood and punch the driver in the face, the red meaty reverse-baseball-cap-wearing face she glimpsed behind the shattered windshield—

But Danny wasn't on the roof anymore, she was flying, her guts turned to feathers inside her as she tumbled, and now trees were going past her, and the Explorer, with its bubble lights still flashing red, white, and blue (*patriotic,* the voice said), was looming end-over-end above her. There was a shower of sparks, followed by a message that said *pain*, but Danny never got it. The last thing she saw was the Forest Peak Sheriff's Department medallion stenciled on the door of the Explorer, coming at her from above, upside-down.

Danny was posing for a picture with a couple of gap-toothed Iraqi kids. They wore grimy shirts much too big for them so you couldn't see their shorts, only their skinny brown legs. Both of the boys were holding plastic bottles of water given to them by Harlan. Danny was holding her rifle across her body, away from the kids.

Then she was watching a camel spider crawl away from its tormentor, a herring-bellied puppy they weren't supposed to have on base. The spider was all jaws, but too heavy for its own good. It didn't have the speed it needed to get away from the puppy. Danny was nauseated by the sight of the spider, a pale, corpse-colored thing with crablike limbs and those immense jaws, a pair of razor hooks so big that its eyes were mounted at the root of them.

The woman in black from head to toe stood next to the burning farm-house. Danny walked toward her as casually as she could manage, as if it was just another day in the life of the occupying army. Which it was. But there was no such thing as just another day. Only another day survived. Danny could see the horizon rippling like water in the heat from the struc-ture fire, and the same shivering heat coming off the exhaust grilles on the tanks idling not far from the woman. Then the woman was moving. Moving toward the foremost tank. Danny saw that her arms were folded protec-tively around her belly, as if she was cradling a child. But it wasn't a child. Danny began to run, her boots slipping against the grit of the yard. Hands wet on the shotgun. She began to run, not knowing—

It was fully dark, but there was a moon riding over the mountaintop. She was up against a tree root, and a few yards away the Explorer with the Forest Peak Sheriff's Department medallion stenciled on the door was up-side-down against a tree at the base of the retaining wall below Route 144. It was quiet up above on the road. As the initial blast of pain dialed back to a loud throb, details of her situation were coming back to Danny. Confusion and pain made her mind ripple like the heat from the burning farmhouse.

She had been on the roof of the Explorer with a gun. Where was the gun? Somewhere around. Never lose track of a weapon. She groped for the four-cell flashlight on her belt. Didn't carry the preferred eight-cell because it pulled her pants down. Her fingers were unresponsive but she got the light on and shone it around. Carpet of rusty tree needles. No shotgun. The Explorer totaled. Blood all over it. The town council was going to love that. There was a plowed path through the tree litter that showed why she hadn't been crushed underneath the big Ford: She had kept on sliding after she hit the ground. Fetched up against this root. See? Detective abilities working fine. Body found some yards from scene of accident, ejected from roof of vehicle. Clear as day, Your Honor. But Danny couldn't for the life of her imagine why she'd been holding a gun on the roof of the Explorer. Good way to get shot by a sniper.

A small hatchback was over the side some distance away through the trees. Nobody hanging out of the windows. Good. There was another vehi-cle at the end of the flashlight's power to reveal, hanging halfway over the guardrail. What the hell had been going on? She was on the roof of the Ex-plorer, she knew that much. Everything else was gone from her mind.

Danny was still in the position she'd awakened in, lying on her back. Time to get up and find out what she had missed.

There were fireworks lighting up the night after all—inside her skull. Danny must have hit her head on the root pretty good. She felt a massive knob on her skull that hadn't been there before. It was wet. Fingers in the flashlight beam: yes, blood. Awesome. Was she concussed? What was the approved procedure for concussion? She didn't recall, but she knew it wasn't climbing up a man-made stone wall fifteen feet high. However, that's where the road was. Unless she wanted to hike over to the logging road. But Danny wasn't feeling entirely certain she could find the way without getting lost, and if she'd been on the roof of her vehicle the reason would be right up above. She needed to see.

She didn't end up climbing the wall. Her sense of balance was nowhere to be found. Instead, Danny groped her way along the dry-laid stone, keeping herself steady against it. There was a loud bagpipelike droning in her ears that never stopped. The ground sloped up toward town, so she eventually reached a point she could climb over on her hands and knees. Then she inspected the situation up on the road. It all started to come back as she swept the flashlight back and forth over the frozen scene of chaos around her. Danny was glad she wasn't standing up, or she might have fallen down. The droning noise in her ears was deafening.

There were cars everywhere, cars and trucks and motorcycles and rubbish like foam party coolers and sweatshirts and McDonald's sacks and broken glass. Accidents had stopped in midcourse: vehicles with bumpers tangled together, front ends pushed up on trunks, motorcycles spilled under the wheels. But the vehicles weren't the main thing. That would be the blood. There was blood everywhere. And dead people. Heaps of them. Danny's mind was reeling as she swallowed these huge chunks of information. Danny remembered all the people running. She couldn't remember why. There weren't many children among the dead here, probably because children simply couldn't run as far before they fell down dead.

She made her way to her feet and approached the nearest car, a station wagon. Shone the flashlight inside. Nobody there. In the next car she could see the outline of a driver, head tipped forward against the steering wheel. And there was the Toyota truck with the giant tires. Danny struggled to remember why it angered her, then she remembered it had something to do with the upside-down Explorer. This was as much deduction as anything else; the truck was climbed up onto the bent-over guardrail right about where the Explorer went down. She approached the truck on unsteady legs, stepping over dead limbs sprawled on the pavement.

The Toyota driver was slumped against the B pillar, wedged between the door and the seat. Somebody had shot him through the windshield. Lucky shot. Not much penetration on those angled safety-glass windshields. A lot of people had died in their vehicles, but not from gunshot wounds. Danny's light found them in almost every other car, usually slumped forward or flopped across the backseats. Then Danny realized the loud droning sound she heard in her ears wasn't from the blow to the head. It was the sound of thousands of dead people slumped against the horn buttons on their steering wheels. If the horns were still going, that meant it could only be a few hours since Danny lost consciousness. Otherwise the batteries would have died. But it had been afternoon, last Danny could remember. Maybe around five o'clock. She'd been out of commission for at least five hours . . . Why she was alive when so many others were dead, Danny could not imagine. But she was not grateful for it. It was high time she got back to Forest Peak and found out what the hell she'd missed.

6

By the time Danny made it halfway to town, she was pretty sure she was the only living human being left on earth. The dead lay three deep on the roadway. Not far from the beginning of Main Street, she saw the tan shirt and brown pants of a deputy among the corpses littering the road. She turned him over with her toe. It was Deputy Dave. His face was slack, one eye wide open, the other half-closed. He hadn't made it far before he died, unlike some of the other victims.

If this thing was a disease, Danny thought, maybe she shouldn't be touching the corpses. Or be anywhere near them. But she wasn't up to a hike through the woods. And if she wasn't dead yet, the worst was probably over. Danny passed the first couple of houses in town without seeing them, dark and silent under the trees. No auto horns blaring in town. Maybe nobody had died in their cars here. Maybe someone had moved the corpses off the steering wheels.

Danny passed the first commercial building in town, the one with the real estate office and the VFW she'd never been into, although she was eligible. The whole place was dark, even the apartments upstairs. The street lights were working, so it wasn't a blackout. Nobody had turned on the lights. All the way down the street there was darkness in the windows, except for a couple of shops and the gymnasium way down at the far end: Danny could see the side door was open, a rectangle of greenish fluorescent light.

Beneath the street lights there were more cars parked helter-skelter or abandoned where they stood, doors hanging open. And on the ground, everywhere she looked, more bodies. They lay under the lights and in the shadows, most of them face-down, most of them with their heads pointed to the north. They had died running. Danny switched off her flashlight and thought her boots had never sounded so loud on Main Street.

She was too late. She wondered what she could have done differently. It seemed to Danny these people were dead because of her, on some level— and not a level very far below the surface. If she had taken the Eisenmann thing seriously, or come up with a better plan of her own, could some of this disaster have been averted? These thoughts she stowed away in a compartment in her mind. Forget them for now. Maybe forever, if she was lucky.

She saw smoke billowing from the top of the doorway of the Wooden Spoon. The last thing this town needed was a structure fire. Danny climbed up on the hood of a car and crossed from one vehicle to the next to avoid the heaps of corpses, then jumped down in front of the café. Her bruised leg almost gave out, but she propped herself against the doorway until the pain dulled down.

It was dark inside the Wooden Spoon except for the exit sign at the back and the television over the counter, blank and glowing. There was an almost-delicious smell coming from the galley kitchen, but there was something else with it, too, that reminded Danny of something she would rather forget. She stepped over what looked like an entire family that had died on the threshold. More bodies under tables. There was a dead man slumped over the counter, arms flung forward. Danny moved to the counter and found Betty at her feet, the big woman's face a mask of shock, a weird parody of the smiley face on her plastic nametag. The smoke was coming from behind the counter, where the cook, Mitchell Woodie, had collapsed on the grill.

Danny didn't want to get any nearer the source of the cooking-flesh smell—or the hissing sound. Her stomach was leaping already, and her back prickled intolerably. But she couldn't leave Mitchell there. She went around behind the counter, stepping over a number-ten can of jalapeños that had spilled on the floor. The stench of pickled peppers, burning meat, and scorched hair and fabric sent stinging bile into Danny's throat, but she reached out and pulled hard on Mitchell's apron strings. He was stuck firmly to the grill. Danny's reason caught up with her gut reaction, and she realized the first thing to do was turn off the heat. This meant reaching around Mitchell, which meant she could see his face: It was blackened, with rivulets of melted fat running out and sizzling on the steel plate of the grill. His hair was reduced to tightly curled fluff. The eye nearest the heat was a hard, red knuckle protruding from blistered eyelids.

With profound misgivings, Danny reached down and tugged the spatula from the dead man's hand. Then she grasped his shoulder, which was hot to the touch, and started scraping his face off the stove. It took something like thirty hard strokes before the weight of the body pulled the remaining skin away, and Mitchell flopped heavily to the floor. When his charred, smoking face hit the pepper juice, a puff of steam rose up into Danny's nostrils and she had to run outside. She vomited on the curb in a small space not occupied by corpses. For a long minute she stood there with her head down, a headache pounding behind her eyes, watching a long string of bile stretch from her lip to the ground. Tears leaked from her eyes. What a crappy evening, all told. Then she forced herself to get moving again.

Danny crossed to the Sheriff's Station, where there was faint light from inside. She stepped over a woman and two kids sprawling down the front steps. Several corpses in the dark front room. There was a light in the back, the partition door standing open, another couple of strangers dead on the floor in there. Danny wondered if Amy had run, or if she had held her post. If she was lying under the communications desk where the single light was burning. *Something* was under the desk. There wasn't any reason Danny could come up with to suggest Amy should be alive, when so many others had died. Danny moved through her silent domain past the corpses, stopped breathing, and looked under the desk. It was the chair overturned beneath it. Amy wasn't there, but she could be anywhere, growing cold on the ground with the blood settling into the lowest parts of her body, stiff in death.

Danny drew a long, stuttering breath. The voice in her head was working overtime: She could remember the first runner now, a woman. Maybe she should have fired the shotgun at that woman, scared some sense into the rest of the runners. But it was impossible. And it wouldn't have worked. There were too many of them. Thousands. And these people were crazy, running like maniacs. Maybe it was one of the symptoms or side effects. They wouldn't have stopped even if she shot every second one.

Then again, she could have formed a defensive line with some vehicles, created a physical barrier. Or even set some fires across the road. There were all kinds of ways to shape panicked people's behavior, and Route 144 was a natural bottleneck. If only there had been time to think.

Now that there *was* time, though, beating herself up wasn't going to help. If she was alive, other people were alive. She had to find them, organize them, and see about cutting any further losses. Then take a little rest. Her head hurt. And her leg. And the scars were prickling. Danny looked around at the station, probably the only living member of her force, and tried not to feel the grief and remorse that were coming at her out of the shadows. It was so quiet she could hear the ticking clock on the wall.

And then a voice like crushed gravel came from the darkness:

"Lemme out."

It was Wulf Gunnar, forgotten in the back cell. Danny jumped, but controlled the reflex to go for her gun. Wulf saw it, though.

"Don't like surprises, right? I know the feeling. And loud noises, and people raising their voices."

All true, but Danny wasn't in the mood to chat about the personal legacy of combat. She flipped the switch for the ceiling fixtures, rows of sickly tubes pinging and flickering before they flooded the interior with cheap government-issue light. Her eyes contracted painfully.

"You're the only other person I seen alive since this afternoon," Danny said, and found her keys in their snap-down pouch. She unlocked the cell and threw the door open. "How come you're not dead?"

Wulf scratched his chin, considering the question as he strolled out of the cell. He looked around at the corpses.

"Lemme have one of them rifles you got. The Winchester Model 70."

"No."

"I heard a whole shitload of screaming and running around. Then your buddy the dog doctor said she had to go find you. She run off out the back. That was when it was still daylight, sun over that way. These ones run in and fell down a minute later. It got real quiet after that. What the hell happened?"

"Come on."

Danny led the way toward the back door. Wulf crossed over to the communications desk and picked up a pile of loose paper.

"Your buddy said this here was yours. She read it, and she said you better ought to read it yourself."

He handed the paper to Danny. It was Kelley's note. Danny's eyes unexpectedly stung with tears. Her lip trembled. This wasn't the time. Not now. She took a few hard breaths, stuffed the feelings down, and carefully folded the pages until they would fit in her breast pocket. She buttoned the pocket, careful not to look at the note, careful not to see the looping Kelley handwriting. She went straight out the back door, where the exterior area light was blazing down on the dumpster and the parking spaces. Nick's motorcycle was there, and some civilian's car with the door open. No bodies. Danny was holding her breath again. She focused on breathing, on denying the madness of the situation.

It was like a raging river. She had to stay on the shore. If she went in past her ankles, it would sweep her away. Wulf trod along behind her, impassive. With the bush of hair and beard and his barrel chest with drooping, crooked shoulders, he did look like a bear. And smelled like one. She'd smelled worse on occasion, though, and Danny would take his company over a carpet of corpses any time. So she welcomed the old ruin of a man that followed her down the alley, then up Pine Street past a heap of bodies that had accumulated at the corner. The whine of distant horns was fainter. Maybe the batteries were dying. Danny noticed there were no dogs barking. You could always hear a dog or two in Forest Peak. They must have fled earlier in the day. She remembered seeing dogs running up Route 144.

In silence the two survivors continued toward the gymnasium, picking their way through the carnage on Main Street. How could *nobody* else have survived?

Hours earlier, Patrick and Weaver had been arguing in the motor home about whether to stay in Forest Peak or try the back road. Then the screaming began. They stopped bickering to watch a very tall man sprint past the windows, his arms held up almost straight over his head. The locals scattered at his approach. The tall man ran full-tilt into the low fence at the far end of the parking lot and did a spectacular forward flip, landing on his back. Then he lay there motionless. Patrick almost laughed, but it would have been a laugh of hysteria.

The screams were coming closer. Weaver went for the door of the motor home to see what was going on, but Patrick had, for once, held him back by sheer force of will—and by the sleeve, which he pulled on until the stitches began to pop. Weaver stayed where he was, and they watched the terrified people rush past in ever-greater numbers, charging nowhere at top speed, then falling. Many of them didn't fall, but ran into the woods or down the road. But again and again someone would flash by, full of life and animation, then abruptly crash to the ground like a cast-aside rag doll, where he or she would lie twisted and motionless.

Patrick at first thought they were being shot, maybe by a gunman on one of those flat Old West–style roofs on Main Street. But there wasn't any blood, no jerk of impact—these people simply *dropped*. There was no human expression in their faces as they ran, only animal terror, mouths stretched open. A man in jeans that hung almost to his knees ran for the side door of the RV, yanking on the handle as if to tear it off the hinges. But his mind was gone. He didn't even attempt to work the latch, but clawed at the door until he fell dead. Patrick thought that he personally was going to have a seizure and die himself: His heart was racing and sweat poured freely down his back and sides. His mouth was so dry he could hear his tongue rasp against his teeth.

"It's like there's an invisible hammer hitting them on the heads," Weaver said. He locked the door and set the chain and went around securing all the RV's windows and the front cab doors. Then he pulled all the curtains except the windshield and suggested they move back to the lounge area and wait for the screaming to stop. They waited there in the over-stuffed captain's chairs, in the dark, with the air hot and still inside the motor home. There was a fly buzzing around, making a circuit from the windshield to the back bedroom in long looping courses. Its outboard-motor hum could be heard when there was a lull in the cries outside.

Every few minutes someone would run right into the RV, clapping against the aluminum skin. The glassware in the bar racks would jingle. Patrick didn't know if these runners were falling dead or scrambling back up to keep on going. A million thoughts swarmed through his mind, none of them about Weaver, which was rare. Maybe all he'd needed was a *real* crisis to stop him fretting about the petty insecurities in his life. This would make a great movie of the week, he found himself thinking. Talk to the people he knew at Lifetime, maybe.

Weaver was sitting there looking timeless and rugged and strong, eyes reflecting the light. He could have been watching a bluejay instead of the end of the world. Patrick was determined not to think out loud, just in case Weaver snapped and left to join the running and screaming and Patrick was left alone in the dark motor home. So he studied the custom baseball stitching that ran along the arms of the captain's chair. The sun was slanting toward the trees on the mountain ridge above them when Patrick fell asleep.

It was dark when he awoke, and the side door of the RV was standing open. Patrick could see the dim blue rectangle of moonlight on pavement. He got rushed by panic; his heart went through the roof. He clattered down the steps and out into the world, forgetting his fear of the dead, the maniacal running people.

But it was so quiet. There was no screaming, no thunder of feet slapping the asphalt. Nobody except him.

This is it. This is really alone, he thought.

There were dark blotches on the ground all around the parking lot. The dead. It was like one of those dim Civil War photographs of the aftermath of battle they used in Ken Burns documentaries.

"Weaver?" Patrick called, but so softly he could barely hear his own voice. Then he heard a scraping sound. Held his breath. It was the sound the Mummy's feet would make, dragging across the stone floor of his tomb. Patrick backed away from the RV. The sound was coming from behind it.

Weaver's silhouette emerged from the dark bulk of the vehicle, hunched over. He was dragging a corpse away from it.

"Weaver," Patrick whispered. Weaver heard him this time. He let the corpse's arms drop and stood up, wiping his brow with his palm. "Hey," he said.

"What are you doing?"

"Moving these bodies so we can get the bus out of here."

"Good idea."

"You want to help?"

"Not really."

"There's gloves under the sink."

"You okay?"

"You?"

It wasn't a question that required an answer.

A moment later another voice rang out in the night air: "Hi, are you alive?"

It was the woman in the white doctor's coat Patrick had seen earlier, the one who had been wrangling the baby goats. He recognized her at a distance by the faint moonglow of the coat against the shadows and the way she picked her way among the corpses, arms held up in a sort of "jazz hands" position—it was precisely the way she moved through the pen full of animals.

"I guess," Weaver said.

"Have you by any chance seen the sheriff?" she asked.

"Not since the chili contest," Patrick said. "Like ten years ago."

"Oh," the woman said, slumping inside her coat. But as quickly as she registered sorrow, she came back:

"I'm Amy Cutter. Local vet. If I was the coroner I'd be rich right now."

Patrick didn't know whether to laugh or vomit. In fact he could have gone either way. But Weaver smiled, and that was enough. The living were all members of an exclusive fraternity, it seemed.

After that they started to make progress of a kind. Amy knew where to find the big knife switches that turned on the parking lot lights, and how to light up the inside of the gym, and that there was a phone in the coaching office in the gym. The phone didn't work, to nobody's surprise. But the light was a tremendous relief. Amy opened the double doors at the side of the gym, then returned to Patrick and Weaver.

"I think we better set up some kind of relief station. That's what Danny would do. She's the sheriff. A friend of mine. There's a lot of people wandering around out there, a lot of people didn't die. But I'm worried some of them will if we don't get them inside where there's no cliffs to fall off in the dark. That's what Danny would do."

So they went down Main Street with keychain flashlights and called for people to come down to the gym. It was difficult to raise their voices above speaking volume in the presence of so many dead: Maybe it was some ancient human instinct. But out there in the dark there were people alive, climbing warily out of cars, emerging from doorways, stirring in the street where they had been cradling the heads of the people who had died in front of them, their loved ones, faces they knew in life. Amy took charge of them all. There was reeking meat-scented smoke coming out of the Wooden Spoon. Nobody wanted to go inside to find out what it was. Nobody did.

Inside the Quik-Mart, Weaver gathered a trash bag full of junk food from around the cash register, while Patrick filled a Graco double stroller with cases of bottled water. He didn't know where the babies from the stroller had ended up. *What happened to the ones that couldn't run?* He pushed the thought aside.

At the back of the store, concealed by the shelves of brightly packaged rubbish he wasn't supposed to eat, Patrick found a teenage girl with blue-streaked hair and a boy of around ten, both clutching the corpse of a woman who must have been their mother. It smelled as if she had soiled herself upon death. Patrick simply reached out and took the girl's hand and she followed him, meek and glassy-eyed. The boy followed her, looking back once at the dead woman as if to be sure she was going to stay where she was.

"You push this water cart, okay?" Patrick said, and the boy took command of the stroller. It would have been faster to push it himself, but Patrick didn't want the boy looking back at his mother again. These young survivors were probably even more shell-shocked than Patrick was, having lost someone before their eyes, but they couldn't kneel there mourning all night while the dead cooled. They had to live.

So the living had gathered in the gymnasium. Patrick and Weaver sat in the gymnasium bleachers on either side of the blue-haired girl and the ten-year-old boy, and passed a bag of M&Ms back and forth, eating one at a time by unspoken treaty. The girl emerged from her trance very briefly and said to Patrick, "I seen your TV show."

She didn't say if she liked it or not, but lapsed back into brooding silence. They had probably been sitting there for half an hour when the sheriff walked in with a big, shaggy derelict at her side.

The basketball court was lit up bright as midday on the moon. There were several dozen living people in there, locals and outsiders, shoes squeaking on the waxed wood floor as they paced around, waiting out the long night watches. There was a portable shortwave radio with a crowd around it, like an illustration from a vintage phonograph advertisement. It found ethereal voices speaking urgently in foreign languages. Elsewhere in the room, someone was sobbing, someone weeping softly, someone praying to *hayzu-creesto.*

A few people conversed in low voices. A baby cried once, then went back to sleep. The sounds echoed in the rafters. Amy was refilling a coffee urn set up on the floor, flanked by heaps of junk food from the convenience store. There were rows of water bottles and two-liter fizzy drinks and a tower of white Styrofoam cups. It could have been a town meeting without the furniture. Even with the poor state of her brain, Danny could see the survival rate wasn't good, if this was everybody who had made it through the disaster. Wulf, interested as always in the immediate need, headed straight for the food.

Amy turned around when she saw Wulf go by. Her face lit up when she recognized Danny, and she beamed that big immodest Amy smile. She was even going to holler her delight, then recalled the gravity of the situation. Instead she waved and trotted over to Danny and threw her arms around her and squashed her in a desperate embrace. Danny put her arms around Amy, and the human contact reminded her how tired she was, how bone-tired and worn out.

"You look even worse than before," Amy whispered.

"Slept in my clothes," Danny said, and headed for the water. She drank an entire bottle in ten loud swallows, the cold liquid spreading through her belly. She needed to pee and she needed to wash the filth and blood off herself. Having Amy there gave Danny a little permission to think of her own needs, at last.

Amy was right beside her, serious: "Your head is covered in blood. I didn't see it at first. Are you okay?"

"No," Danny said. Amy prodded the gash in Danny's scalp and it flared pain. Danny swiped the offending fingers away. She could hear the ocean.

"Sorry," Amy said. "Between the glassy eyes and the ostrich egg on your head, I think you might have a concussion. Maybe you should sit down."

"In a minute," Danny replied, and limped toward the restrooms.

"I'm so glad you're not dead," Amy called after her. Danny shrugged as if to say, "Of course," but there wasn't any feeling behind the nonchalance. There wasn't anything but being alive. *Just like the old days,* the little voice said. She remembered being presented with the Key to the Mountains, and wondered where it was. Not around her neck anymore. Somewhere in the woods, probably. Ten thousand years from now some archaeologist could dig it up and wonder what the hell the thing was for.

By the time Danny had limped out of the darkness, the majority of the survivors had already left town: some on foot, some in vehicles, on up Route

144 toward Big Bear. Weaver had shown them on his topographical chart how to get up over the crest of the mountains and down toward Scobie Tree, after which they were on their own. They took cars and trucks from the northern end of town, away from the massive jam of cars on the way to Los Angeles. Lots of survivors in each vehicle, crammed in as if they were on a school field trip.

All of the stray children they could find went with the convoy; only Blue Hair and her brother remained behind in town. The rest just wanted out of there. Since the main convoy left, more groups followed them in vehicles to which they had located the keys, regardless of provenance.

Danny's return found fewer than 150 living strangers in town, and very few locals seemed to have emerged from their burrows. It was this latter consideration, as well as a desire to stem the flow of people into a completely unknown situation in the outside world, that drove Danny's plan of action when she returned from the ladies' room and heard Amy's narrative of earlier events in town. Danny huddled with Amy and one of the local firemen, Troy Huppert, and explained her idea.

"There's no point," Amy said. "Let's all just sleep on the floor for a few hours."

Danny shook her head.

"We can't let these people have time to think. Amy, it was okay earlier, you did the right thing letting people leave. We couldn't have handled hundreds of them. There's not enough food in town. But now it's late. These people are wired, but they're exhausted. They'll fall asleep at the wheel. They'll run over people on the road. So we need to keep them here. Wear them out. They can sleep in the morning, and by then we can figure out what to do next. But we can't let any more of them leave tonight."

"The more of them that leave, the more capability we have to cope, though," Troy said. "Remember that snowstorm in '07? Fewer than thirty people stranded in town for four days, and we were about ready to throw a Donner Party by the time the snowplows finally got here."

Danny looked around at the survivors in the gym. Some of them were drifting closer, wanting to listen in. Others most emphatically didn't want to know. But with Troy's huge boots and yellow fireproof pants, Danny's ruinous sheriff's uniform, and Amy's doctor coat, they were the center of gravity in the room. Rescue, law, and medicine, all in one place. Danny wondered if they'd have as much pull if these people knew they were actually looking, respectively, at a probationary trainee from East Los Angeles, an alcoholic, and a horse doctor. Troy was a diligent guy, but he was also the newest firefighter in town and the most recent resident. It occurred to Danny that since the disaster, Troy might now be the *only* firefighter in town.

Danny dropped her voice, almost whispering: "Troy, I lost hundreds of people out there. My job is to keep people safe, and I lost hundreds. And Christ only knows how many died on the way up here. You know what I heard on the radio?"

"What."

"Nothing. We have no idea what happened to cause this, or how big it is. It could be they're picking up the pieces and in a couple days it will be right back to business. But I heard a couple of things that make me think it's the Gulf Hurricane, times ten, everywhere in the entire country."

Troy fell silent, considering the possible scale of the disaster beyond the mountains. Now Amy was pleading with Danny—not her best mode of expression, in Danny's opinion:

"Danielle Adelman," Amy interjected, "you are injured and this can wait until morning. I'm totally okay with the macho bit, it's kind of cute, but this isn't the time."

Wulf Gunnar ambled up, crumbs of what looked like Sun Chips in his beard. Danny had never noticed before that the old man's long nose changed direction three times along its length.

"I'll go with you if I can carry that nice little Winchester," Wulf said.

Danny smiled. "My old man's sixty-three: custom twenty-six-inch barrel, squared receiver face, lapped bolt lugs. Field true for five hundred yards. That thing is a legend. You can't have it."

Amy was fuming. She tried one more time: "Do not ignore me! It would take the two of you a week to search this place, by which time the National Guard will have come and gone."

Danny turned back, and now her face was serious and cold. The bravado was gone. "The National Guard is in a desert seven thousand miles away."

With that, Danny called for the attention of all present and began to outline her plan.

Those who could sleep, let them. Those who could not, let them work. Danny chose the workers from those who least appeared to have lost their minds. Very few to select from. Danny picked Wulf. They would work in pairs to search the outlying neighborhoods while the rest of the survivors organized the dead into rows along the sides of the street. Amy could keep that bunch going while Danny was gone, with Troy to assist. She didn't expect much from Amy's work detail, but the survivors couldn't be allowed to spiral into complete shock and become incapable of caring for them-selves—or worse, start looting. There were too many, few as they were. Danny started to introduce herself to Patrick and Weaver, but they already knew her name.

"We met at the greasy spoon," Patrick interrupted. "You're Danielle Adelman. I'm Patrick Michaels—" Here he paused, as if expecting Danny to recognize the name, but there was no flicker of recognition. "And this is my partner, Weaver Sampson. We never moved the RV."

Danny shook his hand.

"Consider yourselves deputies of the Forest Peak Sheriff's Department. We'll skip the oath of duty for now."

Danny deputized Wulf as well, refused once more to give him a gun, and the four of them picked their way around the corpses down Main Street to the Sheriff's Station.

They would need radios, flashlights, gloves, and some cans of spray paint, of which Danny always had a supply, confiscated from the local graf-fiti artists. Mostly friends of Kelley. Weaver and Wulf dragged the people who had died inside the station out to the sidewalk, arranging them in a rough line along the foundation. Patrick wasn't any help with the corpses, so Danny had him collect the materiel while she checked the radio again. There were a couple of units down in the valley that still had someone on radio duty, but they didn't know any more than she did.

"Only that the dead outnumber the living," a shaky-voiced cop in Artesia told her.

There was some small comfort in the fraternity of law enforcement, knowing she wasn't the only one in the world on point. With regret, Danny signed off.

"He said 'good luck' and you said '9–10.' What does that mean?" Patrick asked, arms loaded with big rechargeable box flashlights.

"It means, 'I can handle the situation on my own,'" Danny said.

"Can you?" Patrick asked. It was a sincere question.

Danny palmed her fist. "Let's find out."

As Danny's search teams headed up Wilson Street, Amy led the larger work party into Main Street to start shifting the dead out of the roadway. Amy knew it was make-work as well as Danny did, but it was better to be doing something. She saw Danny limping away into the darkness, a rumpled outline in the glow of their flashlights. Amy thought she knew the real reason Danny wanted to do a house-to-house search. Not to determine who among her community had died. But to make sure Kelley wasn't among them. *Just as well,* thought Amy, *that Kelley wasn't here. At least Danny can hope.*

Dawn was coming. The sky was a shade lighter than the pitch-black world below. Danny and Patrick approached a low-slung bungalow with aluminum siding, one of several in a row: cheaply built weekend cabins that got pressed into service as full-time homes over the years. There was a corpse flopped over the wire fence in front of the house. Danny crouched beside the body and shone her light in its downturned face. One of the corpulent Doone brothers, she couldn't tell which. They were identical twins. Danny went to the house and tried the door. Unlocked. Called inside. No answer. Danny sprayed a red stroke on the siding by the door, then Patrick followed her inside. The place was so small they had it searched in less than two minutes. Danny handed Patrick the can of spray paint and headed for the next house.

When she looked back, he was still staring at the wall of the first house, his light shining up into his eyes like Bela Lugosi. He hadn't finished the marking.

"Patrick, are you still with me? Because I actually can't do this alone."

"Yeah. I'm just kind of . . . you know?"

"I feel ya."

She returned to his side and took the can, shook it. Crossed the first stroke of paint with another one, making an X.

"One more time. This is how they did it in New Orleans. One line means we went inside. Second line means we came out. Date and time in the top quadrant . . ."

She checked her watch and sprayed in the numbers—

". . . Over here, T1 for Team One . . ."

Patrick held out his hand for the paint.

"I know, and at the bottom, zero for no bodies found."

Patrick carefully drew a circle at the bottom of the symbol. Danny folded her arms.

"You don't have to write neat."

"I can't help it—I'm an interior designer."

"This here is the exterior."

Wulf and Weaver emerged from a house a few doors down on the opposite side of the street. Weaver sprayed a 1 at the bottom of their symbol in green paint. The theory was that when a cleanup crew eventually came to remove the dead, they would mark their information in the last remaining quadrant. Wulf shambled up the road toward Danny.

"Sheriff? Old Gladys Miller's dead."

Weaver walked past the corpse hanging over the fence and waved his light at it.

"What about this one?"

"We'll come back for him later."

Danny's ears were ringing, and it wasn't automobile horns. She hadn't slept in twenty hours, unless you counted unconsciousness, which contains no rest. She hadn't slept *well* in a year and a half, to begin with. The back of her head felt like a blacksmith had been working on it. She'd gotten pretty good at ignoring discomfort—if you're hurting, you're not dead—but the present situation was something more than an ordinary bad day. It was getting to her, just as it was getting to Patrick. She marched up to the next house in the row, one of the places where Kelley had bunked for a few months when she was a sophomore in high school. Danny peered through the screen door, but it was entirely dark inside.

"Marlon, Frances, you in there? Sheriff Adelman here. Hey, if you're there, holler . . . Okay, I'm coming in."

The door was unlocked and Danny went through. Patrick made the first stroke of paint outside, then followed her. The place was small and low and gloomy, smelling of cigarettes and cats. Patrick shone his light into the kitchen.

"Oh, my God, it's a nightmare."

Danny was immediately at his side.

"Did you find them?"

"The décor, I mean. Sorry."

Danny saw nothing out of the ordinary. "Everybody's place looks like this."

Patrick crossed to the television, an old-style box with a digital signal converter on top. There was "Please Stand By" or a test card on every channel that hadn't gone to static. It seemed there were fewer working signals by the hour. On top of the box was a ghastly porcelain sculpture of kittens holding up a gold-plated basket containing plastic violets.

"Please tell me you don't live this way."

"It's only a place to sleep. I have this kid sister, been kind of raising her since our folks died . . . I inherited the family house but I got called up for duty, and the place—well, it kind of ran down—she lived here for a while, one time while I was overseas . . . Her name is . . . was . . ."

Danny's voice cracked and she choked on it and the tears came to her eyes. When Patrick turned around, the indomitable sheriff was sitting on the arm of the sofa, her face in her hands, shoulders hunched as she fought to stop the grief from coming. No luck. It had her. Patrick stepped around the coffee table and rubbed Danny's bowed back between the shoulder blades, trying to think of some way to comfort her. Nothing suggested itself.

"Did you find her?"

"She ran away a couple days ago. No, wait . . . Jesus, it was only last night. She was out there somewhere when all this happened."

"I'm sorry."

Danny felt Patrick's hand on her back hesitate. She knew what he was feeling, something strange under her easy-wash shirt. She wanted to shrug off his touch. Her back wasn't for touching. But she kept herself still. His hands moved up to the smoother surface of her neck and shoulders, and he did what he could to knead some of the tension out.

"When this is all over," he said, "cross my heart, I will hook you up with a home makeover."

Danny sniffed back snot and wiped her face with her hands. She tried to smile for him, and almost made it. Then her walkie-talkie spoke, and it was back to business.

Back in town, Amy's work crew had done better than she'd expected. Going slowly, because the unhappy laborers treated the fallen with reverence, and a couple of True Believers insisted on improvising a sketch of last rites for every body they slung up onto the flatbed truck. But except for some tears and a few individual retreats back to the gym as loved ones were discovered, real work had been accomplished. Maybe Danny was more cunning than Amy credited her for. She was getting the most difficult job done while there were still a lot of hands to help.

Everyone wore a double layer of latex examination gloves. Most of them wore paper dust masks. They had sped up the collection process by commandeering the flatbed truck, which had belonged to Eugene, who knew the tree business better than anybody. His corpse was among those already lined up on the sidewalk. The jolly tricolor bunting still hung on the sides of the truck, which lent a macabre touch to the proceedings. But with the flatbed they didn't have to carry every individual corpse the full distance out of the street. As they cleared the corpses from a section of the pavement, a couple of men led by Troy Huppert would move all the cars that still had keys in them. In this way they'd created a crooked but passable traffic lane halfway down the street. Heck, in two years they'd have the road cleared all the way down the mountain.

Partway through the work, Amy radioed Danny on the walkie-talkie with a piece of good news.

"There's a lady here, name's Maria, she's a part-time taxi dispatcher and she knows all about radios. She can work a police set."

"Get her in there right away," Danny said. "Right to the communications desk. Have her make a wider search for correspondents. Get some information. Try the military bands as well as the police bands, and make sure to write everything down." Danny reeled off some frequencies she could remember, Maria said "thank you" into the radio, and then Amy watched as Maria gratefully left the death detail for the relative comfort of the Sheriff's Station, which had already been cleared. Now, as several of Amy's party struggled to get an obese woman's corpse onto the truck, Maria emerged from the station with a scrap of paper held over her head.

"Doctor," Maria called, and waved Amy over. Everyone there was operating under the misapprehension that Amy was a medical doctor, and Danny had warned her not to suggest otherwise. Amy met Maria halfway across the street. The work party had stopped to listen. Maria touched a finger to her lips and hooked her eyes at the station. Amy beckoned the crew to keep going.

"I'll be right back. Take five. There's water in the cab, and change into fresh gloves. We don't know what this is, yet."

Inside the station, Maria showed Amy the piece of paper. She had written the bandwidth and the message in square capitals. Amy raised Danny on the walkie-talkie.

"Danny, are you there? Over and out. We got a pretty weird message off what Maria says is the weather band. It's a recording that repeats every ten seconds."

Danny's voice sounded hoarse when she answered:

"You're supposed to say 'over,' then when we're done talking say 'out.' How's it going? Over."

"You've been crying," Amy said.

"Allergies," Danny replied. "What's the transmission say?"

Amy cleared her throat as if for a recital. But she didn't read the message aloud.

"Actually, Danny, I think I'd better check this in case Maria misheard it. Hold on. Stay on the line." Maria was shaking her head in protest, but Amy went into the back room and set the walkie-talkie on the communications desk with the frequency open. Then she turned the radio from headphone to speaker mode and punched the preset button for the weather band. The message was in midrepetition, a computer-generated voice based on keyboard input, like the voice of that physicist in the wheelchair, Stephen Hawking. It was an eerie sound, distant but clear:

" . . . Will rise again. Repeat: The infected dead will rise again. Repeat: The infected dead will rise again. Repeat: The infected dead will—"

Danny was saying something on the walkie-talkie. Amy picked it up while Maria switched the radio back to headphone mode, nodding her vindication.

" . . . Some kind of a joke?"

One of the things that Amy found charming about Danny was her extremely rudimentary sense of humor. Danny found the Three Stooges funny, and that was about it. Hitting over the head, caveman stuff. She could hear the funniest thing in the world and just stand there looking suspicious of anybody who laughed. This meant, however, that she sometimes thought things were jokes that a wittier person would recognize could not be. Given what she'd witnessed over the last several hours, Amy was pretty sure this transmission was not a joke. A mistake, maybe, but not a joke.

"It's a real message on the real weather band," Amy replied. "But I don't know what it means. The dead people up here haven't shown any signs of activity."

"*Goddammit!*" Danny barked. "Okay, I'm coming down there and figure out what the hell they're playing at in San Pedro at the weather bureau."

Maria resumed scanning the radio's bandwidth.

"Did you lose people?" Amy asked, almost shyly.

"My husband," Maria said, sighing heavily. "He went crazy and ran away. Not the first time he ran away, but never like *that* before."

Amy left her there in the station, searching the radio for signs of life.

In the Marlon Jackson residence, Danny had splashed some water on her face and mastered the grief. Patrick was standing in the living room, still gazing about him with wonder as the predawn light increased, revealing more and more heinous interior detail. He had an idea for a new decorating show, to be called *How Can You Live This Way?* But he thought it would be extremely tacky to mention it under the present circumstances.

"Feeling any better?" he asked.

Danny was about to reply when a holler came through the front door. It was Wulf.

"Holy fucking *shit,* get out here, Sheriff!"

Danny blew right past Patrick even though he was closest to the door. He followed her outside. It had grown lighter in the quarter-hour since they ventured inside the little house, the sky glowing pale and opaque, drowning the stars. The shadows of night were retreating from the street, curling up under the trees. The world still lacked color but it would come with the sunrise. Wulf was standing nearest to Danny, across the street at the edge of the house lot opposite. Weaver was behind him at the door, halfway through marking the wall: team two, one dead inside. Both men were standing stock-still, eyes fixed on an object down the street. Danny saw it, too, and blinked, and still saw it.

It was one of the Doone twins, standing slack-jawed beside the wire fence. He was a heavy man in life, and now his flesh sagged over his bones, mottled and yellow. He looked around him with filmy eyes, as if trying to remember something. It sure looked like the twin who had been hanging dead over the fence not twenty minutes before.

Danny knew what death looked like. There could be no mistake. Yet the body was no longer on the fence, and this one, if it was the second twin, was dressed exactly the same way as the missing corpse: plaid shirt, brown Dickie work pants. The Doone twins didn't go in for identical outfits. But this *had* to be the other one. There was no way Danny had mistaken unconscious for dead.

"He was dead, Sheriff. That guy was dead." It was Weaver, now pointing with the spray can at the figure down the street.

"They're twins," Danny said. It *must* be the other one. She walked out onto the street, but didn't get close. Her instincts were screaming at her that something was very wrong.

"Are you Mikey or Geoff?" she asked. The Doone twin turned to look at her, his motions halting. Like a paralytic drunk, Danny thought. *Like Wulf yesterday morning.* "You been drinking?"

But the fat, jaundiced thing in front of her didn't respond. It didn't understand. Maybe he was in shock, or maybe he'd been in a coma and he wasn't all the way out of it. Danny knew people down at Walter Reed Hospital, buddies of hers like Harlan, who were going to spend the rest of their lives in that condition. If they were still alive. Danny realized Patrick was almost pressed up behind her.

"What are you doing?" she asked.

"Don't go any closer. I'm totally creeped out."

Weaver came up the yard and crossed the street to Patrick. Wulf approached the Doone twin warily, as if evaluating a potentially rabid animal. "This cocksucker was deader'n disco, Adelman. I swear it."

"He's not dead now."

"I don't know about that."

Wulf got to within fifteen feet and waved his hands in front of the swaying fat man. The eyes, cloudy like poached eggs, followed the motion with difficulty. Danny was unaware that her hand had slipped to her sidearm and unsnapped the holster flap. She wasn't going to make the town derelict deal with this. So she stepped right up to whichever Doone it was. He turned to face her like a drunk in a game of blind man's bluff. There was a small fly walking across his cheek.

"Can you hear me? Do you understand what I'm saying?" Danny asked. The twin's tongue was rolling around in his mouth like a big, meaty grub, but there was no attempt to form words.

Weaver took his arm from around Patrick's shoulders and stepped closer for a better look: "If he's not dead, Sheriff, he's pretty damn ill."

Wulf backed away, making a noise of exasperation. Of *course* the thing was dead. Danny wasn't listening. She was staring at the round Doone face, getting close enough to smell the urine that stained the brown work pants.

"Look at his eye," she said.

The small fly had wandered up the cheek and over the pouchy lower eyelid. Now it was walking across the man's eyeball. It stopped on the dome of the cornea to clean its forelegs. The eye never blinked.

The one certainty in the universe for Danny was death. It was absolute. There was no breaking the rules. Until now. Time for a new working hypothesis.

Something flashed into Danny's field of view and there was a solid *clang* and the Doone twin dropped to the road, brown fluid spilling out of his nostrils. The fly skidded away through the air. Wulf was standing behind the corpse with a shovel in his hands. There was hair on the blade. Danny leaped back. Before her boots hit the ground, the gun was in her hand.

"Jumping Jesus Christ! What the *hell* do you think you're doing?" she yelled.

Weaver ran up to Wulf and pulled the shovel out of his gnarled fists. "You killed him," he said.

Wulf shook his head, unrepentant. "He was already dead."

Danny holstered her piece and knelt beside the body. It was as dead as before. But now unquestionably: a deep cleft was chopped into the back of the skull right through the bald spot. The edges of the bone showed like teeth under the ruptured skin. Weaver whistled low and long. "He was dead, but he got up again."

Wulf took this as an opening to present his ironclad defense: "Anybody born after 1940 knows when a zombie shows up, you gotta smash its head. Destroy the brain."

"Don't call him a zombie," Danny said. "That's bullshit."

Wulf spat on the ground. "There's living and dying. You can't have both."

Wulf was in a staring contest with the angry sheriff. The old man snarled, "We gotta destroy the brain."

Danny realized what could be happening, right now, while they argued: "We gotta get back to town."

7

The living wept on Main Street.

Danny and her search teams arrived at the base of Wilson Street. There were a dozen of the risen here, wandering among the cars, faces vacant. They were absolutely silent. The survivors who made up Amy's work crew had gotten back against the walls of the buildings, keeping well clear of the now-animated corpses. But they didn't run away from them, either. It seemed like there was some kind of possibility, some kind of hope. Maybe they hadn't been dead, after all.

The sky was bright now, dawn only minutes away, and despite the fresh horrors below them, the songbirds were enjoying their morning shouting contest. For a long minute Danny, Patrick, Weaver, and Wulf stood where they were at the intersection of Wilson and Main, watching the once-neat rows of corpses along the sidewalk stir and twist, begin to rise. Not all of them showed signs of animation. Maybe half or two-thirds, Danny thought. The rest behaved like proper dead bodies, lying still.

Nobody knew what to say until Wulf found the words.

"This situation," he announced, "is shittier than an asshole sandwich."

One of the ambulatory corpses had spotted the quartet and was now staring at them, mouth drooping. After an interval, it took a few uncertain steps in their direction. Wulf pulled down the spear-tipped flagpole from the front of the notary's office and held it out before him, ready to thrust. Danny stomped the shaft with her boot, snapping it in half.

"Forget the brain," she said.

Wulf muttered obscenities and backed away. Amy was down the street from the station, giving the walking dead as wide a berth as possible. Several of them followed, swaying in her wake.

Danny kept close to the buildings as she made her way to the nearest civilians, a group sheltering on the steps of the barber shop. It was the place nearest to the flatbed truck, upon which a couple of the things were struggling to their feet, tangled in overturned folding chairs. One of them wore the uniform of a highway patrolman. It was Jordan Park, dead like the rest.

Hours before, Danny had been sitting on one of those folding chairs, eating chili and nursing a hangover, thinking things couldn't get much worse. Danny thought she should probably take the radio and sidearm off Park's corpse—she didn't like the idea of the thing having a weapon on it, and the radio might be useful.

She noticed that several of the reanimated dead were attracted to the motion of her moving down the street. They shuffled toward her.

Danny was trying to decide between hope and horror. To lose someone to death was to come up against a great, hateful mystery, a thing that would claim everyone some day. To see that person return from death, if only halfway—was that some kind of mercy, or was it the worst possible outcome?

Several of the things were coming down the Wilson Street grade. Earlier, on the way down the hill, Danny's search teams had seen some of them standing inside the windows of paint-marked houses, heads turning slowly to follow the living as they passed by. Maybe these were the same ones, following her.

Danny felt dizzy. Her eyes burned when she blinked. Was this the onset of the poison or contagion or whatever it was? And then she realized what she was feeling was probably something simpler: exhaustion. It had been twenty-four hours since the alarm clock beat her to the punch.

She glanced at Amy as she arrived. Amy's forehead was wrinkled in the middle with the concerned look that usually meant Danny was falling apart and didn't know it.

"I'm going to have a look inside a couple of places here and see if anybody's alive and hiding," Danny said.

"Just don't kill yourself," Amy said. "I need you around." She hurried away to talk with a couple of men who were escorting a sobbing woman down the street. Danny opened the unlocked door of Mr. Carter's house. It was as much for something to do as because she wanted to see if anybody was alive inside. Maybe she could find some Excedrin. Painkiller and caffeine all in one convenient pill. Mr. Carter had been Danny's science teacher, and maybe Kelley's, too, if she remembered correctly. "Mr. Carter?" she called down the front hallway. No response.

Danny considered the situation of the dead things walking around outside. They had the limbs and faces and hair of human beings, wore the clothing in which human beings had dressed them the previous day, but there was something fundamental missing, the absence of which marked them as not-human. Danny felt a need to identify what that was. It seemed important. If she knew what was wrong, maybe she would know what to do about it—or at least how to feel. Maybe she was overthinking it. They were dead. She was sure of that much. Her mind wasn't set up to analyze the semantics of mortality. The actual words she thought were: *The lights are on, but nobody's home.* But she was thinking in shorthand, and understood there were bigger questions underpinning the ones she was framing for herself.

Danny looked out the front window and watched one of them, a child no more than five years old, as it shuffled down the street, its head swiveling slowly from side to side like an oscillating fan. Hell, that kid barely even got started. Danny wondered if there were babies lying around, undead like this, lying there staring at the sky. She wanted to shake off the questions that swarmed in her mind, but they wouldn't go away. She needed to approach the thing systematically or she was going to end up like the other survivors she could see along the edge of the street, locked in a useless staring contest with the walking dead.

Danny moved out of the living room past the stairs to the kitchen, and saw nothing except a relentlessly ordinary house. There was a newspaper open on the footstool in front of Mr. Carter's favorite chair. A half-cup of coffee standing beside the kitchen stove. No sign of a world-changing crisis, not even in the paper. Maybe his shambling remains were wandering around on one of the other floors. She could search upstairs, look in the basement. But there was no point. He was dead, regardless of whether he could move.

The power was still working, and there was a notebook computer open on the dining room table. Danny checked the internet. It looked normal. There was the search page. She could tap in a news query.

Danny treated computers like telephones. They were conveniences for staying in touch with Kelley during deployments, more than anything. The internet was for headlines, and navigating the VA health care bureaucracy. She didn't know how to dig much deeper than major news outlets and a couple of social media sites. Danny's area of expertise was rooted in the analog world: guns, vehicles, and tactics.

dead rising again, she typed.

Answers came back, and Danny's heart leaped. But then she saw it was all monster movies and Christian websites. Not news. She navigated over to the Fox News page. It was down for repairs. CNN had stories a day old on it. Danny clicked through a couple of them: They described the early stages of the panic overseas, with fears it could reach the United States, but there wasn't anything recent. There seemed to be some early consensus that it was a disease, a biological agent. Maybe a virulent flu. But it was all speculation, leading nowhere.

She spent a few frantic minutes clicking around a variety of sites, and it was the same thing everywhere, as if the entire internet had turned its attention to the strange malady spreading through the world, then abruptly ceased to be updated at some point during the previous day. Which, she reflected, was probably the case, if the death toll was the same everywhere. It seemed strange, though. Surely there were shut-ins and people hiding in their bedrooms who had survived this long. They ought to be twatting or chirping or whatever they called it, sending out bulletins. Maybe there were, and she didn't know how to find them.

Or maybe they froze those government servers, she thought. After all, nearly everything on the internet passed through federally operated American hubs. Maybe they just flipped a switch and suspended the entire system in time. But that kind of paranoid thinking wasn't going to get her anywhere. Instead of informing her, the internet was making Danny crazier, panicky. She folded the computer shut.

In the back of her mind, the part that analyzed the available data and built plans upon it, Danny was organizing the chaos of questions into some kind of usable form. She knew that some deadly agent had killed millions of people. It was transmitted somehow—an aerosol dropped from aircraft, or a gas, or terrorists running around with Hudson sprayers.

She had to choose a starting point. Danny's working hypothesis required it. So she decided to assume the agent was a disease. It made enough sense to get on with. The resulting wave of death had traveled rapidly because the victims, once infected, would run as fast and as far as they could, until they fell down dead. She didn't know if the disease killed them or if they simply ran until their hearts gave out. But many of the people they came in contact with also became infected. Then those people ran. The thing didn't stop spreading until there were no more people to infect. It was like a fatal relay race. Danny was either immune or hadn't come into close enough range to get sick. She thought of her deputies, how she had ordered them to remain in an exposed position. But at the time, exposure wasn't a part of the equation. Maybe it still wasn't. Regrettably, she didn't know dick.

She went halfway down Mr. Carter's basement stairs and called for him again. No response. If he was down there, back from the dead, let him stay there. If the Army or someone could spare a few units to clear the town, so be it, they could take Mr. Carter away.

Danny returned to the living room and sat on the couch, but her back was to the door. So she moved to the easy chair. But it commanded the view out onto the street, and she could see the infected wandering around. She needed something else to look at. She took Kelley's note out of her breast pocket and turned the tightly folded pages in her hands. She was afraid to read it, but wondered what it contained. She wondered if Kelley was alive. She imagined a conversation she could have with Kelley, explaining how she didn't have any choice, how she was sorry to be such a hard-ass but that was what life had handed them both. But Kelley wouldn't stop talking back. She wasn't listening. Danny wanted to shake her or something, get the damn kid's attention. *Don't turn your back on me.* But then

Kelley twisted around, one hand extended, a rat-eaten finger pointing at Danny: She was dead, her jaw hanging loose, eyes like blisters.

"You," she croaked.

Danny woke up.

It had been only a few minutes since she dozed off in Mr. Carter's easy chair. Not refreshing, but it would help. She put the note back in her pocket. As she headed up the front hall, Danny continued summarizing what she understood. Had millions really died? And a few hours later, they got up again? Some hadn't gotten back up. But even the ones that rose again were cold to the touch, and didn't have heartbeats. They were not alive, but did that mean they were truly dead? This was where Danny's hypothesis fell apart. A tree didn't have a heartbeat, either, and it probably didn't feel if bugs were eating its leaves. But a tree was alive. *So why aren't these things alive?* she thought. *Why am I so sure? Does it matter?*

She went outside, her head throbbing, and almost walked into one of the things. It was standing at the foot of Mr. Carter's front stoop, looking up at Danny with those empty eyes and the mouth hanging open. It was a soft-faced boy, fourteen or fifteen, wearing a Dodgers T-shirt. His skin was pale as candle wax except for lips that were almost black, and the inside of his mouth was gray. Danny recoiled. The boy had no reaction. She wondered if it could respond to anything, maybe simple commands.

"Shoo," Danny said, and whisked her hands at him. The boy's eyes fixed on her hands. He stared at them even when she dropped them to her sides. Stupid, but more than stupid. He knew nothing. The boy was a robot made out of meat. Danny swung herself over the stoop railing and went around the dead teenager.

She needed a plan.

Some of the more intrepid survivors had begun unfolding a plan of their own while Danny was inside Mr. Carter's house. They were herding the infected (as Danny now thought of them) together. It could have been sheep or pigs they were gathering: Some of the survivors stood with their arms outstretched in a pose Danny associated with basketball defense, keeping themselves in front of the nearest infected and shucking side-to-side. With their gloves and masks they looked like Japanese traffic cops. Others would enter this ring of arms, towing one of the infected along behind them. They would leave it, and go off to find another. It was a human corral. Danny had to admire the expeditious spirit that drove them to do it—survivors keep themselves busy as a way to stave off shock and despair—but she wasn't sure if they knew what to do once the herd had swelled beyond their ability to keep its members in. There were at least forty or fifty in there now. Maybe half the infected population of Main Street. Danny was also concerned about the potential for transmission of the disease. If it *was* a disease, had it burned itself out? She didn't think so. If those things could walk, she had a feeling the infectious agent was still at work. Maybe they shouldn't be getting close. She still didn't know.

Danny watched for a minute. Sometimes one of the living would recognize a friend or relative and start crying or babbling, trying to tell the others *this* one was different, but in general it was a good effort. Then one of the men who seemed to be in charge of fetching the infected came near her, to collect the Dodgers boy in front of Mr. Carter's stoop.

"Where do you plan to put them?" Danny said.

"There's a fellow there named Troy who says we can run them through the Quik-Mart and out the back into the alley. It's like a ready-made jail-yard."

"Is Troy around?"

Danny found the fireman in the alley behind the downhill side of Main Street. He was overseeing the construction of barricades at each end of the six-car parking lot behind the Quik-Mart. His team consisted of several survivors, including the boy and the blue-haired girl she'd seen in the gym. They'd been eating candy with Weaver and Patrick, Danny remembered. Now they were using convenience-food display racks to fill the gaps between cars parked side to side in the alley, forming a fence. If the risen dead stayed as numb-nutted as they were now, she thought, this primitive containment would probably do the trick.

The next question was how many of these things would they have to deal with? There were fifty at the beginning, and in the last hour that number had doubled. There could be several thousand of them within a few miles. So far, the survivors were behaving with admirable calm. It was mostly shock, Danny knew from experience, and when it wore off they were all going to be useless basket cases. Then she would have to deal with hysterics, fights, looting, and God only knew what. And if the walking corpses started to decay . . .

For the first time, it occurred to Danny that the living would probably have to get out of Forest Peak. All the years she kept crawling back, swearing they'd get out of there, her and Kelley—this wasn't how she'd envisioned it happening.

Troy met Danny a few yards down the alley. "I had to get people doing something," he explained, sounding apologetic. "There was some woman all up in Amy Cutter's face because she wouldn't try to revive her husband. Now he was already revived, right? I mean he was walking around. But she wanted a heartbeat to go with the walk. And Cutter didn't know what to tell her. So I got in there and broke it up and followed your advice: Keep 'em busy. They seem to like having something to do. But I don't have any idea what we do after we got the victims locked down."

"Victims?"

"The dead people. I don't know what to call them. Wolfman said they were—"

He made a face. Didn't want to say it. Danny almost whispered: "Zombies, I know."

"Well it don't seem right."

"I been thinking of them as 'infected,' but that's not much better. Here's the thing, though. There's a shitload more of them out there. I mean a hundred to one. I'm not sure we can hold our position in town. There doesn't seem to be any danger, but what if it's still contagious? What if they start to . . . you know, to rot? We may need to go somewhere further up the line. Forest Peak got hit pretty hard, but the wave stopped here, I think. Up the line in Big Bear or Alpine Glen, it could be a lot better."

Troy watched the survivors examining their corral-making handiwork around the parking lot. Almost time for the roundup. Herd those dead suckers into the pen. He looked back at Danny, nodding.

"You said 'the wave stopped here.' That's what it was, a wave. Meaning we're at the high tide line."

"Meanwhile," Danny resumed, "get your people back to the gymnasium. See if Amy can get that woman to allow her to examine the dead husband. I'd like to know what we're dealing with, if there's anything she can figure out. Amy can do that."

As Danny walked toward the back of the Sheriff's Station to check on Maria, another piece fell into place in her working hypothesis. If Forest Peak represented the end of a theoretical Los Angeles outbreak zone, and assuming downtown L.A. was the epicenter of the disease, that meant you could probably draw a big, ragged circle around the city—beyond which there would be a vast uninfected zone, until the perimeter of the next epicenter. She needed to look at the map on the wall in the station.

Danny was sick of making half-plans that went nowhere. But there didn't seem to be much else she could do. She couldn't get out in front of this situation. She raised Amy on her radio.

"Have you begun the examination? Over."

"No, out. I mean over."

"Is the victim's wife cooperating?"

"That's a big negatory, sir."

"Keep trying. Or grab another one of the infected. I want to know what we're dealing with, over."

"Rooty-toot," Amy said, and the radio went silent.

Inside the Sheriff's Station, Maria was still at the communications desk. She had a couple of candy bar wrappers and a Diet Coke at her elbow. Danny felt a pang of guilt: She wasn't attending to her people's needs any better than she was attending to herself. Maria should have some real food, if they could find any. "How are you doing?" Danny asked.

"Okay," Maria said. But she didn't sound like she meant it. "You haven't seen a man with a mustache and a Coors T-shirt? He was wearing a denim jacket. And low-heel cowboy boots. Light brown ones, I think. Maybe your height."

Danny smiled. "No, but you would make a good cop. Good powers of observation and recall."

Maria smiled back, but her eyes were blurred by tears. She hitched a sigh and tapped the radio set with a pencil. "No news anywhere. The internet isn't showing anything new. There's still six police places on the radio that I know about. There were nine before, but now there are six. None of them know squat." She put her hand primly over her mouth, as if squat was a rude word. Her accent suggested Spanish was her first language, so she might not be sure if it was.

"But they said everybody got up again, like here," Maria went on. "All the living people brought their dead relatives to the hospitals and the police stations and fire stations and now there are these huge crowds of those . . . those *muertas vivas* all filling up the places. One of the policemen asked if we could come down and help them. I said I would ask you."

Danny snorted. First responders swamped by walking corpses. She wished Forest Peak had a hospital, right about now. Danny took a look at Maria's block-print notes on the remaining radio conversations. "What's this one?"

"The weather station went off the air twenty minutes ago."

"Any new messages from there?"

"The same thing over and over about the infected dead rising again, until it shut off."

"And nothing from any of the military bands?" Danny already knew the answer would be *no*. Aside from the general military proscription against loose radio talk, these days all branches were using digital satellite transmissions for most communication, not radio. Digital you couldn't listen in on. And Danny didn't even know how many units were in-country. They routinely lied about troop levels in every theater of war. The real number of personnel on American soil was far lower than most people imagined. They were probably all crammed in C-5B Galaxy cargo planes on the way to clear the streets of Washington, D.C. So the leadership wouldn't be troubled by unsightly dead people.

Danny placed her hand on Maria's shoulder and suggested she take a break. Maria shook her head. What was she going to do, go for a walk? Danny could understand that. "Lemme know if you hear anything new."

Amy examined the dead man while Weaver and Troy held him down.

The man struggled feebly like a turtle flipped over on its back. He was stretched out on one of the folding tables in the gym, the only one of the infected they'd brought inside. They had kept him in the anteroom at one end of the building, not wanting to risk spreading whatever it was into the area where people were sleeping and eating, although it might have been just as much a desire to keep somewhere in town death-free as any medical consideration. The gym had become a sort of sacred space for the living. Patrick stood a few feet away, next to the dead man's wife by the door. She had never given anyone her name, but called the walking corpse Larry, and she insisted someone figure out what was wrong with him. As Amy had decided to perform an examination on one of the dead, he would do as well as any other. He did not recognize his wife.

Amy's veterinary tools were mostly identical to the instruments used on humans. She'd brought a selection from the van, which was now parked by the gymnasium. All of her furry friends had escaped during the morning. She hoped Diggler was all right. He was some pig. Amy's instruments were in a scalpel roll, not her veterinary bag, because the bag had her business name in gilt letters on the side, and she didn't think Mrs. Larry would respond well to a veterinarian examining her husband—even if he was dead. Some people were so sensitive. Among other instruments there was the penlight for eyes, an otoscope for ears, a stethoscope, and an ultrasonic Doppler veterinary sphygmomanometer, which didn't look anything like the human version with the inflatable cuff, but measured blood pressure just as well. She listened to Larry's cold, spongy chest. There was plenty of sloshing around in there, but no heartbeat. And no pulse at the wrists or neck. Patrick wrote down her observations on the blank pages of a math class notebook he'd found under the bleachers.

"I'm not getting any pulse at the neck, either," Amy said. "So no circulation, no dilation of pupils, and body temperature has remained around eighty degrees for the last twenty minutes. The, uh . . . remains . . . or the ill person, anyway," Amy corrected herself as Mrs. Larry gave her a sharp look, "is fairly active, so that may be why the temperature has stayed constant. Muscular activity produces heat. Okay."

The infected thing opened his mouth and a faint hiss came from the throat. Amy made an involuntary noise of disgust. "Moving right along. There seems to be some respiration, but it's not involuntary or whatever. Autonomic I mean."

Larry's distraught wife broke in:

"How can you not know the right words? You're a doctor."

"Doctors are notoriously forgetful," Amy explained. "Anyway, we were thinking of changing the terms around. Autonomic sounds so cold, doesn't it?" She returned to her examination. "I'd like to take a liver core temperature but the spouse of the party probably won't go for that . . ." Amy looked at Mrs. Larry, who shook her head. She'd seen enough episodes of *CSI* to know that's what you did to dead people, and her Larry was not dead.

"So," Amy went on, "I guess then let's do a little prick test."

"That's disgusting!" the nerve-wracked wife started to object.

"She means prick test with a needle," Patrick offered.

"Don't you hurt him," the woman said, and covered her eyes. Amy used an ordinary sewing pin of the type used to keep the holiday bunting together.

She poked the dead man's fingers, gave a jab to the corpse's ankle, and tried the side of his face. No flinching at all. "No reaction to pinpricks. No sensation. Like a diabetic or something."

The examination continued for another fifteen minutes. By the end of it, Weaver and Troy were sweating from the effort of holding the body down. There was no apparent strength in its limbs, but the arms and legs had a way of twisting around in the grip, the skin loose over the muscles, that made it extremely difficult to hang on.

And Larry never got tired; he never stopped moving.

During the exam, Weaver was initially paying close attention, studying the corpse wriggling under his hands. He could see razor stubble on the face. The skin was ash-colored, almost metallic. There were tiny dark veins under the surface that caused this appearance, he could see that much. The mouth didn't seem to be wet, the tongue the color of day-old fried steak. The teeth looked unnaturally yellow, almost like kernels of corn, probably because the cold blue-tinged flesh made them look that way by contrast, not because they'd changed color. Patrick often delivered long sermons on how color worked. Weaver would grunt in response, although it was all actually kind of interesting. He simply didn't feel like he was qualified to remark.

And the eyes—Weaver couldn't look into them, although even when he made eye contact with the thing, there wasn't any real recognition. It was as if someone had injected watered-down skim milk inside the eyeball. But the most disturbing part was the way the eyes would roam around the space, almost blindly, but then fix upon a human face and stare intently.

Weaver looked away, and found himself staring at Patrick, standing there with the notebook and pen in a strange pose with his shoulders halfway up to his ears and his knees pressed together. Weaver was worried about him. Patrick had far more strength than he himself suspected, but he was so invested in *reacting* to everything, so into the drama, that you couldn't tell where the real feelings started and the theatricality ended. Then again, that was one of the things Weaver liked about him.

Weaver thought of himself as inhibited, bottled up. Patrick was practically inside-out. Right now the poor guy looked like he couldn't decide whether to puke or faint, although at present the corpse's wife was out-matching him in the histrionics department. *Out-Hecuba Hecuba,* Weaver remembered. From the Shakespeare play *Hamlet.* Patrick (who had designed the sets for a production of the play, not long after they first met) had explained who Hecuba was to Weaver, although Weaver promptly forgot. Patrick had a wide range of subjects he was intelligent in, including classical theater. Alan Rickman was playing Polonius in that show, and Weaver dug Rickman a lot, he remembered that, too. They shook hands at one of the after-parties. Hecuba was a lot like Larry's wife.

It popped into Weaver's head that gay marriage was no longer going to be the hot-button relationship issue in society. Marriages between living and dead people, like what they were witnessing now, would be the new crisis. The Catholic Church was going to have a field day with this. Was Alan Rickman still alive? Weaver cleared his mind. *I'm babbling,* he thought.

When Amy was done, despite the protestations of Mrs. Larry, Troy and Weaver got her husband back on his feet and pushed him outside, into the parking lot. They closed the doors as the corpse lumbered toward the living again. "You can't do this, it's a free country!" the woman protested.

"Dead people don't have human rights," Troy said, and went off to the men's room to wash his hands. Mrs. Larry didn't volunteer to be out there alone with her husband, Amy observed.

In the Sheriff's Station, Danny told Maria everything was under control and went out the back way. This made Maria think everything was not under control, because it was the same thing *she* said when the taxi dispatching went to pieces at work. She wondered if her husband was out there, and if he was, how were they going to get through this? He was always in some kind of situation. Now he was probably dead and even then she couldn't rely on him to behave. She swallowed her grief and rolled the radio band selector along the frequencies, searching for life. The red-haired sheriff was doing her best.

Moving down the alley, Danny felt the same flutter of panic she'd experienced the previous night when she walked toward Main Street in the dark and wondered if anyone else in the world was alive.

Right after her parents died she'd had a series of dreams like that, people leaving without telling her, finding herself lost in places like schools and hospitals, empty except for her.

Then she saw the girl with blue hair.

She was crouched between two of the cars that formed the nearest side of the barricade, her arms folded around her bony knees. She was watching the trapped infecteds jostling each other. Danny crossed to the girl and the smell of the stale bodies in the midday sun was stifling. "Which one are you looking at?" Danny asked, because the girl's eyes were following one of the things.

"My mom," she said, and pointed to a dumpy middle-aged woman with a perm. The dead woman stared into the middle distance, unaware of her child.

"Where did the others go?"

"To the school gym, the black guy said."

"The fireman?"

The girl fell back into silence. Danny knew she ought to make introductions, find out the girl's name, but she didn't want to personalize anybody. They were generic civilians until further notice. Until, if she was honest with herself, she was sure people would stop dying. Danny glanced up and found the girl's mother was facing them, although the dead eyes still didn't seem to have registered the presence of the living women. Danny needed to give this girl a project, and fast. It wasn't any good for her to fixate on a dead person, regardless of who it was. Danny said, "You have a brother, right?"

"Jimmy James."

"I'm going to need your help. Somebody has to look out for him, and I'm too busy."

The girl focused her eyes on Danny for the first time. She was naturally fair, with pale eyelashes and tiny, even freckles. She appeared to be assessing whether Danny was bullshitting her so she would move along, which Danny was. The girl didn't answer, but returned to watching her mother. Danny tried again.

"Look, I'm real sorry about your mom. This situation blows for everybody. But I can't leave you here, understand? I can't. And in a couple of days when the rest of us are down at the rescue center in the valley and you're all out of potato chips and these folks start to rot, I think you're going to wish you had come with me."

The girl looked as if Danny had slapped her face. Her eyes watered, then tears began to spill down her cheeks and her chin puckered up and she started to bawl. Danny grabbed her and held her head against her chest, and wished it was Kelley she was holding. The girl wept until Danny's shirt was wet through. Danny felt the sting of tears she had yet to cry herself, but there was an ocean of those inside her somewhere.

Then they got moving, scrambling over the alley fence into the bushes, then along through the brush until they crossed Pine Street.

The dead were everywhere, swarming.

They seemed to be moving a little faster than before. Maybe the heat of the sun activated them, like lizards. But they also seemed to take a greater interest in the pair of living beings who were now tacking through them, back and forth, looking for the clearest path.

Danny led the blue-haired girl along behind the houses on the other side of Pine Street, then they emerged from cover into a fenced yard. The yard formed a clearing in a forest of terrible swaying bodies. Beyond it was the north end of Main Street, and across the intersection was the gymnasium. The street and the parking lot were both crowded with the undead. Almost all of them were facing the gymnasium. Danny got Troy on the radio.

"Troy, gimme a 10–66."

Troy answered in a low, confidential voice, slightly muffled as if he had his hand over his mouth.

"We're okay here, we have the doors locked, the place is secure. But we're outnumbered, as you probably noticed. And there's a woman here flipping out because her husband is outside."

"Is he alive?"

"No."

"I'm across Main Street. The situation looks like it might be devolving. We need to get the survivors out of town. That big motor home, it's not far from the door. That guy Weaver has the keys. I'm guessing it will hold thirty people, packed in pretty good. How many have you got?"

"That's the good news," Troy said. "A bunch of folks bugged out not five minutes ago, they took some trucks and a van and went up 144. So I got a dozen or so, and Amy just came in with five. They're freaked out. I can understand the feeling. What's your situation, Sheriff?"

My situation is fucked, she wanted to say. *Thanks for asking.* But she replied, "I have a girl here—"

"Michelle," the blue-haired girl supplied.

"Named Michelle," Danny continued, "and Maria back at the station. I don't know where the Wolfman is, unless you have him." Danny suddenly had a rough idea what to do next. "Okay, here's what I want to do. We get everybody we can into that motor home, maybe put anybody extra onto Eugene the Treeman's flatbed, and we bug out of here ourselves. Get on up to Big Bear. They're going to have thousands of refugees on their hands, but with our uniforms we might be able to get some love. Any objections? Over."

Troy didn't answer for a few seconds. Then: "Refugees . . . Damn. Yeah, I'm ready to split town. We can put up a sign so whoever's hiding in their basement around here can follow us up when they get the balls. Ah hell, 10-6, over."

Ten-six: *stand by*. Danny heard some noise in the background over the radio, then the channel went silent. Seconds later, she could hear shouting, and one of the doors of the gymnasium flew open. A woman ran out, crying, "Larry! Larry, where are you?" The woman rushed into the thick of the walking dead and Danny lost sight of her. A moment later, Troy emerged. When he saw the increase in the number of the infected, he stopped moving and backed up against the building. Danny waved over the heads of the walking dead. "Troy, over here." He waved back and pressed the radio to his face.

"Sheriff, you want me to get her or leave her? Out."

"I got her, you keep the rest from panicking, out." Danny turned to Michelle. "Follow me close," she said.

They went back the way they came.

Danny pushed through the front door of the sheriff's station into Main Street where the dead were milling around, drugged eyes following her as she bounded down the steps and into the mass of bodies. The girl Michelle stayed behind, and Danny could hear Maria speaking to her, probably glad to have someone around who was a little warmer than Danny. She could hear Larry's woman calling for her husband in the crowd; she hadn't found him yet, and predictably he wasn't responding. Danny shoved her way among the repulsive things, their stink of excrement and old fish making her throat close. She had smelled terrible things in her life, foremost of all the savory stench of burning flesh, but this smell wasn't only disgusting, it was alien. She'd never experienced anything like it before. Her stomach roiled. Then another voice joined the frantic cries of Larry's wife.

"Danny, where the heck are you?" It was Amy.

Danny shoved through the corpses as through immense slugs, repulsed by the touch of them but unwilling to allow herself any squeamishness. Touch them and be damned. Get to Amy. It was slow going, though: The dead were more active than before, groping, clutching at her uniform, as if wanting her to stay.

They met in the street in front of the Junque Shoppe. Danny saw the reanimated highway patrolman shamble past, and behind him the now-dead mullet man with the FUCK T-shirt. Somehow his lower lip had been torn off, hanging now by a scrap of flesh at one side. His teeth showed through.

Then there was Amy, emerging through the crowd behind him, trying not to touch the infected but getting squeezed anyway as they lurched into each other.

"Nice to see someone alive," Amy said. "Have you seen another live woman in a yellow polo shirt?"

"She's over there," Danny said, and hooked her chin down the street. "Let's get her. I want everybody out of town in half an hour."

The two women moved away through the silent, shuffling crowd, Danny in the lead, Amy following with her hands up at her shoulders as if she'd seen a mouse, not a thousand reanimated corpses.

"He's not dead!"

There was Larry's wife, pointing accusatorily between Amy and dead Lawrence, as if she'd caught them in an affair.

"I know he's moving, but he's not alive. We can't leave him in the gym." Amy was pleading, something that never worked, in Danny's experience.

So Danny stepped in between husband and wife. She took a deep breath. One more try. Her patience was all dried up. She took hold of the wife's arm.

"It's not her fault, ma'am. State regulations. Let's get back—"

"There's no such regulation!"

Amy took the woman's other arm, and she and Danny began to gently propel her toward the gym. The zombies—*hell, that's what they are,* Danny thought—were coming uncomfortably close to them as they argued. Others were following the survivors toward the gym, and still more were emerging from the trees, from doorways, from behind the buildings. Hundreds of them. Amy continued to reason with the woman, who was gibbering with upset, tears flowing down her cheeks.

Then she lunged forward, teeth bared, an inch from Amy's startled face: "If he isn't alive, why is he walking down the street? What kind of doctor are you, anyway, if you can't tell the difference between alive and dead?"

Danny pulled the woman back, but she shook Danny off and chugged straight down the street toward her Larry, calling out his name. Danny caught Amy's wrist: *Let her go.* She didn't want a hysteric in the gymnasium anyway, if she was going to stir up the others. Just as Danny was about to suggest they start the move out of town, Danny's radio squawked.

"There is a new message recording. I think it is urgent," Maria said.

"Not something for the open radio?" Danny asked, speaking into her shoulder mic.

"No," Maria said. She sounded afraid.

"We'll be right there," Danny said. "We're pulling out of town, get ready to move."

She didn't care where they went, as long as it was free of dead people. Then Patrick and Weaver appeared behind them.

"We're here to help with the crazy lady," Patrick said, and Weaver grunted.

"Forget about her," Danny said.

They skirted their way toward the Sheriff's Station, keeping well away from the ever-increasing number of zombies. Danny had now lost two living people to the confusion, by her reckoning: Larry's wife, and Wulf. The old man had melted into the scenery at least a couple of hours back, in that polecat way of his. Danny had no idea where he was. They passed Mrs. Larry, now with her arms thrown around the neck of her husband's stumbling corpse, her head pressed to his chest and his un-beating heart. Danny observed the zombies were starting to move a little faster.

"It's like the death is wearing off," Amy said, reflecting Danny's thoughts. "They seem to be speeding up."

They stepped inside the station and locked the door.

"Listen." Maria was crying. She twisted the volume knob on the radio. It was the synthesized voice again, programmed by some anonymous soul out there at a communications station somewhere:

"—Eat living flesh. Repeat: The dead eat living flesh. Repeat: The dead eat living flesh. Repeat: The dead eat—"

Danny reached out and snapped the volume down. Weaver scratched the back of his neck as if trying to think out a chess problem. Then an ancient voice grated out: "I told you and told you. We gotta smash 'em in the head."

It was Wulf. He must have come around the back way, the alley being free at present of zombies except for those still trapped in Troy's corral. Now he was sitting back inside his cell with the door open, stuffing a back-pack with foraged supplies.

"I'm not staying," he said. "This here is the only safe place in town, but not for long."

Maria gripped Danny's wrist. "What do we do about this message? Is it true?"

Danny scratched her neck in the same way Weaver had. The engine of her mind was racing, but she couldn't get it in gear. This new information was too much. If the message was even possible, if it was true—

A shrill scream rippled through the air from out on Main Street.

8

Danny rushed through the station door, then stopped in her tracks on the step.

The dead shuffled past, some stopping to look at her like she was an animal escaped from its cage. A mass of bodies from one side of the street to the other.

Mrs. Larry was holding her right hand against her chest and pressing it with her left, but she couldn't stanch the blood streaming through her fingers. She was standing a few feet from Larry himself, down whose chin a quantity of blood had spilled.

He was chewing.

Zombie.

Danny clattered down the station steps, followed by Weaver. Danny's gun was aimed at Larry, but she tried to keep aware of the other zombies drawing closer to them. In the few minutes since they'd left the street, the number of them appeared to have doubled.

Like the crows, she thought.

Vividly, from nowhere, Danny remembered a scene from an Alfred Hitchcock movie, the one with the seagulls. And the crows. The scene she remembered had crows. The blonde was outside a school, having a smoke. There was a crow on the jungle gym. Puff. Then there was another crow. Puff. And a few more after that. And by the end of the cigarette, the blonde looked up, and there were two hundred crows sitting on the jungle gym, ready to attack. Scared the shit out of Danny, age eight, when she saw it with her father. Kelley never got the chance to watch movies with him.

"Step away from it," Danny said, her voice tight as a tripwire. Mrs. Larry didn't move, so Weaver took a chance, moved past Danny, and got right up under Larry's nose to pull the bleeding woman out of range.

Dead, chewing Larry took a couple of steps after them.

Danny thumbed back the hammer of the revolver, took two-handed aim.

Mrs. Larry struggled out of Weaver's grip, leaving a crimson smear across his shirt. She ran straight back to her husband and planted herself in front of him. Danny couldn't fire.

"What happened, ma'am." Danny said. Maybe she could talk her away from the thing that had bitten her.

"It's only a scratch. An accident. There's no need to shove your gun in his face, you *fascist*!"

Weaver circled around closer to the woman, but there were two other zombies—a teenaged male and a short white-haired woman—taking exceptional interest in him. Weaver had seen the same movies as Wulf. It did not escape him that these things might sense the blood. *My God,* he thought. *Man-eating zombies. I shoulda taken notes.*

Up on the steps, Patrick was hunkered behind Wulf, and Amy couldn't get past either of them. Wulf was holding a steel office chair out in front of him, legs first.

"Amy," Danny said, "we're going to get this individual back inside and I want you to be ready with the first aid, okay?"

Mrs. Larry fairly hissed at Danny. "I'm not—"

Just then Larry lunged, jaws gaping, and sank his teeth into her neck. Danny saw the flesh compress, his teeth too blunt to slice—but the human jaw can produce two thousand pounds of crushing pressure. Her face registered agony, then the woman's skin broke, snapping back away from the wound, and the tissue beneath was not as resilient. The zombie's yellow teeth sheared through the big muscle under the ear, dug deep into a dense network of glands and vessels, and met around the thumb-sized artery below.

Mrs. Larry screamed as her husband twisted his head. A jet of blood spurted ten feet in the air from the crater in her throat as he tore out a fist-sized chunk of meat. Danny could see the end of the artery: The blood looked like long red scarves shooting from it, some kind of magician's trick. Then the blood came raining down, spattering the faces of the dozen nearest zombies.

Danny saw everything that followed with the perfect clarity of adrenaline, almost in slow motion. Those dull, dead faces felt the blood upon them, and its effect was galvanic. They became alert. The eyes were milky but active. And their mouths changed. The slack lips pulled back, exposing teeth.

Before the third jet of blood had spewed into the sky, Danny heard a sound that would never leave her again, a sound as primal as the howl of wolves.

The zombies moaned.

First the bloodied ones, then more and more until it was like the wind in the trees, a sobbing, mournful wail. It was a call stained with yearning and loss and desire, the davening of the dead.

Yet it was none of those things. In truth, it was only the call to the feast.

Mrs. Larry hit the pavement and the moaning creatures surged forward. From all sides, reaching for the living with writhing fingers, they lurched to the kill.

Danny fired a single shot through Larry's jaw as his wife slumped down him, clutching at his belt. The bullet slammed his head back and his wife's flesh was dislodged from his mouth. He stumbled backward, stiff-legged. Behind Danny, Wulf said, matter-of-factly:

"Headshot."

Danny squeezed the trigger and blew the top of Larry's head off. A mass of sepia-dark brain spat from the skull. He collapsed on his wife. Weaver darted in to shove the twice-dead thing off the woman, but she was so wet with her own gore that he couldn't get a grip to drag her toward the station. The short white-haired zombie was fumbling at his back, jaws stretched open.

"Weaver, don't move," Danny said.

The pistol cracked and dark stew vomited from the white hair and the old woman flew backward. *Zombies bleed black,* the impartial voice inside Danny's head observed, as if watching events on television.

"Behind you, Sheriff," Wulf said.

Danny turned, keeping her weapon level, and fired it into the open mouth of a zombie that was barely arm's length away. In her hyperaware state, she saw the inside of its mouth light up with the muzzle flash. There was a kick of brick dust on the building façade behind the creature as the bullet passed through its head and ricocheted away. Danny turned back to Weaver, who was trying to pull the injured woman along by the collar of her shirt. Several zombies were falling to their knees around the bloody victim, clawing for purchase on the prey.

The calculus of survival was clear. "Leave her," Danny said.

Weaver looked back at her with disbelief, and so saw that he was surrounded. His face registered confusion. Danny knew the look, had seen it in combat: He was caught between action and reaction.

"Leave her," she repeated, but Weaver only shoved the nearest zombie away and reached for the bleeding woman again. Danny stepped forward to pull Weaver out of the fray, knowing that she was making the same mistake he was: throwing one life after another.

"Weaver! Get over here *now*!" Patrick shouted, and Weaver snapped out of his trance. He got his legs under him and shoved for an opening between a couple of the shambling things, but they collapsed onto him.

Weaver twisted and kicked and threw his fists, blindly trying to keep the teeth away. But he was fighting against bodies that might as well have been made of clay. They had no speed, no nerves—only implacable purpose, their dark mouths yawning toward him.

Danny grabbed the uppermost of them and shoved with all her strength. It seemed to turn halfway around inside its skin, like a fighting dog. But it fell against the legs of another one, which toppled without any attempt to break its fall, face splatting richly on the pavement.

In the struggle, Danny lost her gun. It skidded away past Weaver. On his back, he hitched his feet up under the second zombie and kicked it away from himself. It toppled across the others that were tearing Larry's wife apart. She was still alive, legs churning. Weaver rolled and fell on his elbows. Danny felt cold fingers skidding across her spine, then a crushing weight, and she knew there were jaws coming at her from behind to rip her skin. The thing reeked of aftershave. She thrust herself away and the zombie fell to its knees, teeth snapping. There was another one coming at her with the speed of a living man—

It was Wulf. He brought the office chair down on the head of the nearest zombie, parting the vertebrae in its neck. The head sagged across the thing's shoulder and swung down on its chest and the zombie staggered sideways and fell. Danny recognized Sy Crocker, still in his George Washington costume. Wulf threw the chair indiscriminately into the advancing horde, scooped up Danny's pistol, and aimed it straight at her.

This was more than Danny could respond to. She was at that place where you died simply because a better idea didn't occur to you.

The gun barked, and Danny saw the pale pink core of the flame spit from the muzzle, something she'd never seen before. She felt the heat of the explosion. Liquid squirted into her face, and another zombie—one she had not known was there—collapsed against her arm, its teeth bared. The teeth skated over the fabric of her sleeve. Filth spilled from a hole in its temple. It fell and stayed down.

Fresh adrenaline blasted into Danny's nervous system. Her limbs felt like clouds of electricity. She grabbed Weaver's hand. They both scrambled to their feet, shoving straight-armed against the undead things that were coming at them. Patrick was now screaming at the top of his lungs, and Amy was shouting instructions that Danny couldn't understand.

Wulf struck one of the things across the nose with the revolver, then shot it point-blank. The kick of the discharge against the skull knocked the gun out of Wulf's hand. Danny saw one of the undead grab Wulf by the sleeve of his foul fatigue jacket. Its eyes glittered with something like desire as it stretched its neck to bite.

Wulf reached up under the jacket at the small of his back and his hand came out clutching a combat knife, one of the old-style ones with a grip made of stacked leather washers. He caught the creature by the hair and shoved the knife into its eye socket, all the way to the hilt, and twisted the blade as if opening a lock. The zombie went limp. Wulf wiped the blade on his sleeve and hopped over to Danny and Weaver.

"Let's go inside," he said.

It sounded like a good idea to Danny. Without any particular method, the three of them charged toward the station doors, pushing and kicking, and Patrick and Amy were on the steps blocking the doorway in their eagerness to pull their friends inside. "Get the *fuck* out of the way," Danny barked, and in seconds they were all sprawling inside the station.

Patrick grabbed Weaver and embraced him, then recoiled as he realized Weaver was soaked in organic fluids: blood and the brown-black ichor of the zombies. "Are you bleeding?" he said to Weaver.

"Everybody's doing it," Weaver replied, and a high, strained laugh escaped him, as if this was the wittiest remark he'd ever made. As Danny locked the station door behind them, she could see a dozen of the things coming up the steps, uncertain of how to ascend.

They were having to learn how to move again. *Zombies.* The word still slammed against the gates of Danny's mind. But that's what they were. If they were this dangerous now, in the infancy of their new existence, how much worse would it get? How clever could they become? *How did this begin, and how was it going to end?*

Beyond the things struggling to negotiate the steps, Danny glimpsed twenty or more of them falling upon Larry's wife. She was dead.

Danny shoved everybody through the partition to the back room. She didn't know if the back door was unlocked or if any of the windows were open but it was sure as hell time to secure the building. Her legs were already turning to jelly. The problem with sudden, massive infusions of adrenaline is the letdown afterward. Merely to return to normal would be bad enough; adrenaline was essentially Superman juice. But you didn't return to normal. You crashed, and your hands shook and your legs went useless and you often enough puked for half an hour. Danny had spent plenty of time like that after bad patrols. They didn't have time for symptoms, not now. Danny kept moving, hoping her body wouldn't let her down just yet. The things outside might not need rest. Danny couldn't guess. But she was nearing the limits of her own endurance.

The things hammered on the glass wall of the station with their fists. They were moaning. Danny kept everyone out of sight in the back room, keeping watch herself by peeking through the posters taped to the partition glass inside the waiting area. Her mind was in chaos. Her limbs felt like balloons.

Marla had gone around closing all the blinds in the station. Danny followed Maria, rechecking the locks, trying to get her sizzling nervous system to flatten out. She saw Patrick take Weaver into the men's restroom, where he tried to scour the blood off him with granular pink soap powder and paper towels. Weaver was stomping around yelling about "The fucking zombies, man, this is it." Amy headed Danny off at the doorway between the two rooms of the station.

"Danny? I need to check you for injuries," Amy said.

"Of course I'm injured," Danny snapped. "You should see my back."

"I mean if you got bitten, you could get infected," Amy said, and Danny shivered. She thought of camel spiders and scorpions and rancid infections from wading through hot sewage on patrol in Baghdad.

For now, the zombies didn't look like they could get through the shatterproof glass of the wall. The place was secure for at least a few minutes. Danny saw bloody hand prints on the glass and realized that even the zombies that had been devouring the woman were distracted by fresh prey. *They like it bleeding,* Danny thought, tucking the data away for later use. *A fresh kill doesn't buy you much time.*

Danny crouch-walked behind the partition counter and ducked into the back room. Amy's hands flew over her skin, her eyes searching for bites. She roughly turned Danny around and checked her back, her arms. Then she breathed out, and Danny realized they had both been more or less holding their breath since they got inside the station. "You look okay," Amy said. "Remember, I got bitten by Tucker Pease in second grade? It was a big deal. This is probably worse. Don't get bitten."

"New rule: Nobody get bitten," Danny said to the room at large.

Wulf stormed up to her, waving his arms. His face was veined and purple with anger, beard bristling. "I ain't gonna die unarmed, Sheriff," he said.

"You have that knife," Danny replied. "Guess I should have searched you better, but you were so drunk it didn't seem decent."

Wulf spat on the floor. "Knife, hell." But he sat heavily on the nearest desk and started gnawing one of his black-rimmed fingernails. Danny thought to tell him to keep his hands out of his mouth until he washed the zombie blood off them, but she said nothing. Any zombie that bit Wulf would die of bellyache. If she was going to choose her team for surviving a zombie apocalypse, it probably wouldn't include a paranoid old homeless guy, a veterinarian (not even Amy), or a couple of Hollywood pretty boys. Then again, it probably wouldn't include an alcoholic sheriff, either. Christ, she needed a drink. A whole row of drinks. There was a thirst on her that she was going to have to satisfy at the earliest possible opportunity.

To distract herself, she checked in with Troy by radio.

"I heard some yelling," he said.

"That was down here," Danny replied. "The dead have got a new thing going on."

"They learned how to dance?"

"They attacked and killed somebody."

Troy was silent for so long Danny was about to ask if he was still on the radio. But as she opened her mouth, he spoke.

"Killed? Like *Night of the Living*—"

"Just like that."

"Sheriff, if I didn't know you for a completely humorless individual . . ."

Danny cut him off. "No time to talk you into it. Double-check every door in that place, make sure they're all locked, and don't let any of the civilians make a run for it," she said. "We're on a raft in an ocean of sharks. I'll tell you the plan soon as we have one, okay? Out."

"Good luck with that," Troy said, and signed off. Danny felt like going to sleep, her eyelids dragging. That was the adrenaline wearing off. She yawned, and she kept on yawning as she listened to the moaning and scratching at the glass of the station.

Patrick got Weaver mostly cleaned up, although now they were both soaking wet and smelled like cheap perfume, due to the soap. Weaver had a scratch on his wrist but no apparent bites. The scratch didn't look too bad but it would need watching. The Cutter woman had dressed it expertly with some kind of ointment and a bandage from the station's duffel bag first-aid kit. That thing had it all: There was even a portable defibrillator in there. Patrick found its presence comforting, as well as the veterinarian's observation (mostly to herself, he thought) that there wasn't any difference between people and animals except fur and buttocks, and you could find humans with the former and without the latter. She was nuts, but funny.

He studied Weaver's face. Pale under the tan. Those creases around the eyes that came and went with his smile hadn't gone away. He looked downright wrinkled. The sheriff, too. She was exhausted. Yawning, despite everything. It was contagious—Patrick also yawned.

It was five o'clock. The second day of the crisis was flying past. The summer sun had another few hours to move across the sky before it went behind the mountain, and another hour after that before it sank below the horizon in the flatlands. Darkness was coming, a darkness infected with nightmare.

Danny and Troy stayed in contact by radio, but there wasn't much to do except hope the zombies didn't figure out how to jimmy a lock. All of the known living were accounted for, and anyone who hadn't emerged yet was in for a nasty shock. There wasn't anything Danny could do about that, either. Larry's wife was a red scarecrow sprawled out in front of the station, one zombie still picking at the remains; the rest seemed to have lost interest. What was left of her corpse was still recognizable, blonde hair matted to her bitten face.

The dead had settled down again after the attack, and appeared to have forgotten there were living people inside the station and the gymnasium. Danny watched Main Street from the concealment of the partition, and over the course of the last half-hour, several of the zombies had actually lain down on the ground. She couldn't tell if they had died again, or if they were sleeping, or possibly even playing possum. Subtle tricks didn't seem to be the way of the things, but then again, they were full of surprises. One or two had fallen like puppets with their strings cut, and Danny suspected those were truly dead—done for good. Maybe the disease didn't take with all of them. Maybe it would wear off. That was a beautiful thought. Maybe tomorrow morning they would all just stay dead and Danny would only have lost one of her flock to the undead wolves. Maybe not.

But Danny wasn't going to wait for dark before taking action. It was the gymnasium she was worried about. The place must have had ten sets of double doors, and they were designed to stop a couple of teenagers getting in, not a thousand zombies. The sheer weight of the things could break a set of doors open, and then there was really nowhere to run. The gym was a big, rectangular box with a foyer and bathrooms. She'd spoken to Troy about this, wording her remarks very carefully in case one of Troy's group of survivors should overhear.

"I hear what you're saying," he said. "And you're about right. There's a lot of them against the doors on the Main Street side. They're out there moaning."

"You got a plan?"

Troy explained what they had to work with. The basketball hoops were the type that lower from the ceiling, so maybe some people could cling to those, out of reach. Maybe they could hide under the bleachers. The bathrooms could hold all the survivors, but the doors were only interior-grade hollow-core. He didn't think they would stop anything.

"In fact," he concluded, "they're not even fire-rated for their present application."

"Spoken like a fire chief," Danny said. "So if a barricade isn't going to work, and you're pretty sure the exterior doors aren't up to the job, we still gotta figure out how to get out of town. It's just that there's this new aspect to it, over."

"Yeah—the 'getting eaten' aspect," Troy whispered. "Over."

Danny watched the zombies sliding along the glass wall outside, leaving oatmeal-like smears in their wake. They couldn't see her, she was sure of it. But they could sense her somehow. Maybe they could remember that living people had gone inside. But she didn't think so. The things didn't seem to be able to retain information, or they might have reacted defensively when she started shooting them. Could they smell the living? Smell their blood? Did they recognize people they'd known in life?

She realized her train of thought was leading her into a place of sadness and horror, a place she couldn't afford to go. Not yet. She spoke into the radio again.

"How are the survivors holding up over there? Over."

"They're flipping out," Troy said. "It's like one of those old disaster movies. You say 'keep calm' and they know they're fucked. They're trying to be cool, but it don't play."

"Okay, Troy, let's pull ourselves together. I have half an idea," Danny said, ". . . and the rest will come to me."

Danny felt as if she was looking over the brow of a cliff. The world seemed to be tilting away, and she was going to fall. The injuries, the exhaustion, the sheer horror of the situation was dragging her over the edge. But most of all, it was what she realized she now had to do, if she were going to get those people to safety. She took a deep breath. Waited while the pulse rushed in her ears three times. Then she continued:

"What we need is a decoy." As she spoke, the entire plan of action came into her mind.

"If those things are coming my way, you'll have some room to get your people onto the RV. There's going to be some shouting and some shooting. That will be me. Keep an eye on the crack in the door, be ready with the keys, and when you see an opening, get everybody to the motor home. Out."

"Hang on, Sheriff," Troy said.

"Come back," Danny replied. She had a sinking feeling.

"One problem. Weaver has the keys. He's with you."

9

Danny had a system for dealing with despair. The first thing to do was to acknowledge that your situation sucked more than seemed fair. The second thing was to remember that "fair" was an imaginary idea that had no basis in reality. The third thing was to identify a simple long-term goal, something beyond the world of shit, and make that your purpose in life.

So Danny pictured herself sinking into a deep, hot bath, soaking until the water cooled off. That was the long-term goal. For now, all she had to do was get a thousand man-eating zombies to chase her down the street while two groups of survivors, between whom the thousand zombies were currently situated, joined up in a motor home at the far end of the street and drove away through an obstacle course of abandoned vehicles and yet more zombies.

There were some obvious difficulties with this scenario. It meant Danny would be going in the opposite direction from her ride, for one thing. In addition, her group of survivors had to somehow make it past all the undead. They might earlier have used the relative safety of the alley, but now it was no good, because Troy had carefully herded a hundred of the zombies into it. The woods were likely swarming with the undead, too, so taking the long way wouldn't help. And even if they all got to the far end of town and reached the RV, Troy had his hands full, so if there were any complications down there, Danny wouldn't be able to help. Somehow the despair kept creeping back.

Danny drank more water at the cooler and ate a Snickers bar out of the vending machine by the conference table. She watched her companions, the team she was going to be working with. Amy stuffed a backpack with first-aid supplies. Patrick was complaining to Weaver about how they should have gone to Hawaii like he wanted to do. It was probably an ordinary day in Hawaii. Weaver was grunting in response, Maria was listening to the radio with her chin in her hand, Wulf was circling around the back room like a caged tiger, muttering under his breath, and Michelle had fallen asleep in the second of the two cells, lying in the fetal position on the hard cot bolted to the wall.

Outside, the zombies were moaning. There was a faint thudding sound as they collided with the glass wall of the station.

Danny couldn't come up with a way to make her plan workable, and meanwhile the sun was sinking toward the toothy ridge of the mountain above them. The situation was not improving with delay. She wondered how much ammunition they had in the gun safe. A thousand mixed rounds? More like two thousand, including what they'd confiscated over the last year. Fuck, she could go up on the roof and shoot the damn things in the head, one by one.

The roof.

A rush of inspiration hit Danny.

The roof of the station was lower than that of the building next door, but only by a few feet. And then, all along this side of Main Street, the roofs were flat. Different heights, but easy to cross, and there were only narrow passages between the buildings that didn't share common walls. Three or four feet apart.

They could get as far as Vic's Barber Shop, then slide down that pitched roof and it was only nine or ten feet from the eaves to the ground. Which would put them at the intersection of Pine and Main. Danny could get her people close to the motor home—within sprinting distance—without touching the pavement once. She didn't think the mindless, hungry things outside would be able to figure out how to climb a drainpipe or operate a foldaway fire escape. They could *make* it.

Then Danny recalled that still left her running for her life in the opposite direction.

No plan was perfect.

She walked to the gun safe and unlocked it.

"Here's what we're going to do," Danny began. She was about to issue orders when the glass wall at the front of the station shattered and collapsed.

The enormous windowpanes that made up the station frontage were set into steel frames. The frames were screwed into the brick footing and columns that supported the roof. The glass was held in the steel frames by narrow strips of channel molding on the inside. These moldings were made of aluminum, not steel, so they were easy to cut and bend during on-site installation. The moldings were set in place not by screws, but with fat beads of silicone caulk. This arrangement had served the community well for over fifty years. But it was never intended to be particularly secure. The original glazing had been untempered and not the least bit shatterproof; during the renovations in 1971 the entire wall was replaced with safety glass, which gave it a greenish tint and made the place earthquake-ready.

The safety glass was one-sixteenth of an inch thicker than the original glass, so screws had not been used to replace the moldings. The relatively new synthetic caulk was used instead, and it had gamely held the heavy sheets of glass in place for decades. The 1970s renovations committee had not considered the possibility that scores of living dead bodies would be throwing themselves against the glass. Decades later, it hadn't occurred to Danny to check that the windows were properly anchored in their frames. Nobody broke into police stations, after all.

Danny rushed into the space behind the partition. From there she could see two dozen zombies struggling beneath a sagging blanket of broken glass, the top still suspended in the frame. Even as she watched, the pane fell entirely, spilling a million glittering crumbs across the floor. It was the central one of three large panels that had given way, pushed out of the frame at the bottom by sheer biomass. The glazing was composed of sandwiched layers of glass and plastic, so it formed a pendulous sheet like a broken windshield. The zombies tore it apart in their struggle to get into the station. Although the brick footing of the wall was thigh-high, two of the things had already made it onto the station floor and were dragging themselves to their feet, fragments of glass falling from them like droplets of water.

Their eyes were on Danny. Already, they were on the hunt again.

For an instant, Danny thought the partition might stop them. But she knew better. It was only two-by-fours and plywood with Plexiglas above, not one of those serious bulletproof screens found in banks. She had sixty seconds, assuming the partition door even held that long.

Now there were ten zombies on their feet, lurching across the waiting area. The window had collapsed less than thirty seconds earlier. The rooftop escape was not going to happen. Danny's fingers were clawing at the holster on her belt. There was no gun. She stepped backward out of the front room, closed the door, and turned to her companions.

"Wulf, you still want the Winchester?" she called out. But Wulf wasn't there.

"He already took it," Maria said. She was no longer at the radio. She stood against the wall, her hands crossed over her collarbones in a posture of supplication.

"And left," added Weaver. He was locking the back door.

"That old sack of shit," Danny said, wishing Wulf luck after her own fashion. She was in constant motion now, wasting no instant of time. *Delegate,* she thought, but she couldn't think of a task it wouldn't be quicker to do herself.

Except: "I want everybody to grab a weapon. You, Blue Hair! You ever shot a gun? No? Grab anything you can use as a club. Patrick, you make sure she gets moving, but she's not your problem. Amy, you can shoot, we both know you can."

Danny tossed a rifle to Amy. It had a banana clip. Amy grabbed a box of bullets and started thumbing them into the clip. Danny knew Amy hated guns, and hated hunting more—many of her patients were wild animals wounded by idiots who just shot at things for the sheer hell of it. Danny's own love of hunting sprang from her desire to spend any quality time with her father, but Danny hadn't been hunting since she returned from the war.

Danny knew something else about Amy and guns, though: Despite her antipathy toward firearms in general, Amy had been born with the deadeye gift; she could hit damn near anything she aimed at.

Danny stuffed shotgun shells from the gun cabinet into her pockets, then hefted out the Remington pump shotgun, the last of their Mossbergs, and an ugly sawed-off lever-action she didn't know the make of. They had confiscated it from that lunatic Jimmy Dietrich in February. Danny turned and threw a box of shells at Weaver.

"Load this thing up. You know how to shoot?" He nodded. "Good." She tossed him the short-barreled gun. It looked like a Marlin 410, she realized, and then felt a flash of anger. Her mind was not on the job. Guns weren't going to solve this problem. Rapid improvisation was the ticket to the rest of their lives.

Danny had locked the door between the front and back rooms, and after a crash on the other side of the wall, they could all hear the fingers clawing over the surface. And the moan. They were swarming in there, moaning with hunger. Pressing against that door. A thump on the *back* door. More of them outside. Maria screeched involuntarily and pointed at the window beside her. A flood of pale faces was swirling past, moving toward the alley. *They can think a little,* Danny saw. *They knew enough to look for a door.*

"Patrick, Maria? This button is the safety. Leave it off. This here is the trigger. Aim for the head, and hang on because these things kick." Danny crossed to Maria and slapped an LAPD-issue Beretta into her tiny hand, then pulled Patrick and Michelle out of the cell. She took Patrick's hand and closed it around a Saturday night special Danny had personally liberated from an unregistered gardening truck two weeks earlier. He shrank away from the thing, but Danny kept her hands around his until he relaxed a little. Everyone was standing around her now, at the door to the cell. Quick summary, then it was time for all hell to break loose.

"Those things don't move fast. They're not strong. We're going outside. I'll clear a space at the back door. Then you go right, you understand me? Come out behind me and *go right.* There's a chain-link fence, get behind it and run toward Main Street. Do not stop under any circumstances. You're going to hear some shouting and screaming from me. Ignore that. It's for those things. You all get it?"

The others nodded. Weaver was slipping shells into his shotgun with practiced skill. Maria was holding her automatic by the barrel like a dead fish.

Weaver spoke: "This decoy thing won't work. It's suicide."

As if to punctuate his statement, there was a loud impact on the other side of the door between front and back rooms.

"What?" Patrick said. He didn't look like he was going to last very long. Weaver put an arm around Patrick's shoulders and pulled him in tight.

"She's going to try and get those things to go one way and we go the other," Weaver said.

"But that's *crazy*," Amy said. "Absolutely not, Adelman. I forbid it."

Danny didn't have time for this shit. Weaver unhooked his arm from around Patrick and extended his hand to Danny.

"You're a hell of a guy," he said. They shook hands.

"No, this isn't going to happen," Amy said, and broke the handclasp by stepping between them, her face an inch from Danny's. Danny said nothing, but pushed Amy away with the barrel of the shotgun across her chest.

"You have one advantage, and it's not firepower," Danny said, turning her back on Amy. She didn't want any more hesitation. It sent the wrong message. She crossed to the back door. "Your advantage is speed. You need to keep close to the buildings so you're protected on one side, understand? And *run.* Run for the motor home. Here's the hard part. If somebody falls, leave them. If somebody gets bit, don't stop. Just run. Run like all the devils of hell were after you."

"They will be," Patrick whispered.

"We're on the same page, then," Danny said.

"Danny," Amy said. Danny shook her head. No more. There wasn't another second to waste, because if one person in the world could talk Danny out of doing what she had to do, it was Amy. Danny would have loved to hear why they could do something differently, but none of it would be true. They would end up fighting an army of the undead inside the station, and all of them would be torn apart like Mrs. Larry. Out in the open, there was a chance somebody would get through.

"Please!" Amy cried.

Danny couldn't look her in the eye. She turned to the door, threw back the lock, and yanked the door open.

Danny racked a shell into the chamber, and it sounded like the apocalypse when she fired it into the mass of exposed teeth in gray faces that surged toward her. A geyser of meat and bone and zombie blood sprayed into the air. The stuff looked like used motor oil. Danny could see the shape of the blast as it carved a channel among the zombies' heads.

An instant later she fired again, to her right, and then again, to her left. Six or seven of the things were crumpling, falling away. There was a gap now. Danny fired again and again until the gun was empty, then swung it like a club. She had two more guns across her back, but somehow she didn't think she was going to get the time to deploy either one.

"Go!" she barked, and threw herself full-body into the writhing night-mare of limbs and teeth.

There had been about twenty zombies in the alley when Danny opened the door, and out of the corner of her eye she saw more of them coming from both sides of the building. Only around the door were they packed in tight.

There was a hair-thin chance.

But Danny had to break through this first swarm if she was going to get anywhere near Main Street—or anybody else was, for that matter.

She wasn't thinking now. Not since she threw the door open. She was only responding to the shape of the situation in front of her, looking for the next action to take.

The shotgun had plowed huge ruts through the zombies, creating space. Danny hurled herself into it. The zombies went for her. Danny was already moving, rolling on knees and elbows, keeping every part of herself in motion so that the monsters would have to work hard to get a piece of her between their teeth. But she couldn't move away from where she was, not quickly, or the things would become distracted by the other survivors. They had to keep responding to the easy meat in front of them.

Danny hadn't warned her companions to keep quiet. Amy was shouting. If these things hunted by sound, she was ruining everything. Danny felt an excruciating pinch on her leg and brought the shotgun down across the neck of a dead child that had a fold of her skin in its teeth. Danny used twice the force necessary and the small head almost broke free of the neck, but the biting stopped.

She couldn't tell if her own skin was broken. She was already back on her feet, whirling the gun to knock back the reaching hands that clawed at her. Whether the others were clear or not, Danny had to start moving fast.

She broke into a run, and immediately discovered she didn't have much use of the leg that had been struck by a wing mirror so long ago. She'd let it get stiff. The knots would have to come out the hard way. She forced the sluggish limb to pump alongside the other. Rammed the butt of the shotgun into a gaping mouth, then reversed the thrust into an eye socket directly behind. She left the gun there, the zombie groping to pull the weapon free. The second shotgun, the Mossberg, was already in her hands.

She heard shots. Somebody else, at least, had gotten outside. She didn't know how far away the shots were or what direction they came from. She blew the head off a big zombie in her path and the entire cranium flew off the neck and spiraled into the sky. She leaped at the body as it fell and almost surfed the thing into the zombies behind it, then threw herself through the thicket of legs below.

Danny felt like there was no strength in her body. The repeated doses of adrenaline, the lack of sleep were catching up fast, and there were parts of the reptile brain that wanted to cut their losses and die. It was a wall, the same one athletes hit. The body ceases to cooperate and willpower takes over. When the willpower is out of bargaining chips, there is nothing else left but to keep moving, somehow. Any way possible. Danny kept moving, but she knew there was nothing but luck between her and a hundred mouths ripping spurting chunks out of her until she died of shock and blood loss.

Another mouth crushed into the skin of her shoulder, but she twisted away and the teeth only tore her shirt. She ran blindly forward, ramming into the undead, shoving them away with boneless limbs. More gunfire from somewhere, and screaming. Then Danny hit the chain-link fence, so hard it almost knocked her out. She tumbled backward, dazed, and as she hit the pavement, the hands and teeth seemed to pour out of the sunset sky, rushing down to rip her apart.

There was a deafening bang, and fountains of blackened meat and streams of blood sprayed out and the whole corpse tableau jerked sideways and Weaver was there, firing again with one hand and reaching down for Danny with the other. He dragged her a few feet, Danny using her legs to kick rather than walk, because the zombies were trying to bite her in earnest now, six at a time trying to get a purchase on her flesh. She rolled and came up beside Weaver and they shot their way out like Butch Cassidy and the Sundance Kid.

They got free of the almost solid mass of things that had converged on Danny's position, and were now in a narrow channel between those that were turning to follow Danny's group of survivors, and those that had gone after Danny herself. The things were slow—that was what saved their lives. Danny saw but did not absorb that Patrick, Amy, Maria, and Blue Hair had all made it to the end of the station and were rushing out into Main Street as she and Weaver reached the driveway that led away from the alley.

Danny and Weaver sprinted after them, the stink of cordite and spilled guts rank in their nostrils.

The zombies had a tendency to bunch up, because they had no regard for anything but their immediate desire to rip into living flesh. Somewhere in Danny's mind this fact was filed away and added to the hypothesis. It was already of some use. There was a big gap in the crowd where the zombies had staggered away after the others. Danny rushed into it.

"Weaver, go after them," she said.

"I'm with you," he replied.

"You have the keys, asshole!" Danny said.

Weaver clubbed a zombie to the ground, once a short, stout man with a bald head. The butt of Weaver's shotgun was covered in scraps of hair and skin.

"Gave 'em to Patrick," he said, and ran toward the junction of 144 and Main. And with that, Danny was no longer out in front of her own plan.

She ran as fast as her stiff leg would carry her, shouting at the top of her lungs and waving her arms to draw as much attention as possible.

"Come and get it!" she yelled, wishing she could come up with something cleverer. She fired a shot from the hip that blew a zombie's pelvis open twenty feet away. Its bowels dumped out of its body, coiled intestines bulging through a membranous oyster-colored bag.

The zombie horde turned about to follow her.

There was a mass mind in the way the undead responded. When one of them turned to move, the next would turn to look. And so they would focus on prey. The fastest-moving prey they ignored, if there was something slower to be had. There was, if not logic behind it, at least a dim sense of the shortest odds. Some vestige of analysis still echoed inside the blackened, diseased brains of the things. Danny did not think this so much as she *knew* it as it was happening, so she forced herself to slow down.

Of Amy and the others there was no sign. As much as half of the zombies had come after Danny, a horde so immense she could not see past the first couple of ranks. How many had continued after the others, she could not guess. The most frightening thing to her was the silence of the zombies. They would break into that moan all at once, and then fall silent, and all she could hear was the scraping of feet and the slap of thick limbs one against the other as they jostled to get close. She could hear Weaver panting for breath.

There were no more gunshots from the direction of Main Street. Her other companions might be struggling under the teeth of a hundred zombies right now, throats torn out so they couldn't scream. Danny saw that there wasn't much room left behind her and Weaver, or in front of them, or anywhere. They had been zigzagging toward Route 144 through gaps in the enemy, but it was a box canyon: The gaps got narrower and narrower.

"Follow me, quick," she said to Weaver, and climbed up onto the roof of a vintage Chevy Suburban. It was no kind of place to make a stand, but they might be able to see an escape route from up there. Weaver was right behind her, gasping for breath. He was soaked with sweat and zombie gore. Danny assumed she looked the same. There was a chromed roof rack at their feet; they stamped hard on the hands that reached for them. But already a zombie had crawled onto the hood of the vehicle, following their lead, groping across the metal with fingerless, half-eaten arms. The thing looked up at her. Danny recognized its face, or what was left of it beneath the bloody yellow hair.

It was Mrs. Larry. She was back from the dead.

Danny blew the woman's head all over the brush guards, then methodically reloaded, although her hands were shaking so much she dropped every third shell.

Amy tried to go after Danny when she hurled herself into the press of zombies. Patrick threw his arm around Amy's neck and pulled her back as the clutching hands and bared teeth closed around Danny and she disappeared under the things. Weaver moved forward as a space appeared to their right, alongside the back wall of the station.

"Now," he had said, and fired his weapon. The roar of the gun snapped Amy out of it. She had to move, or Danny, whether she was injured or not, would stay where she was and be torn apart in front of Amy's eyes. But in hesitating, Amy had been the last to get out of the station doorway. The zombies that couldn't get close to Danny had already turned to find the others, leaving Amy a narrow passage that was closing up fast. Patrick was several yards in front of her. His gun went off, once, entirely by mistake, and blew the fingers off a hand that was reaching his way. Then Amy lost sight of him and she was cut off from the others. Cloudy eyes were upon her, a dozen zombies closing the gap. She was pressed up against the cool brick of the station wall, sliding along.

Then she was at the corner of the station at the driveway and she was as alone as Danny. Someone was screaming and crying very nearby, but Amy couldn't tell who it was.

If she'd been on a horse, everything would be different. She could handle a horse better than most, especially on the unsure mountain trails. Ride out of here cowboy style. She even had the hat. But these things would rip the horse apart, too. *My horses,* Amy thought. She had two of her own, Gladys and Spiro, and they were in the corral. Maybe they'd kicked their way out by now. There were soft but insistent fingers closing around her arms, twining into her hair. Yellow teeth in cheese-colored faces.

Somewhere there were more gunshots. The screaming was endless.

Weaver was at her side, pulling her so hard the sleeve tore halfway off her white doctor's coat. He was yelling at her: "Stop screaming!" He drove the barrel of his gun into the mouth of a zombie that was leaning in to bite Amy, not two feet from her throat, and then he fired the gun, and that zombie's head did a somersault in the air and the face of the one behind it vanished like a popped balloon, leaving behind a complicated structure of exposed nasal passages and bone, overhung with rags of brown meat. Amy recoiled as atomized blood and tissue hit her in the face. But her screaming stopped. She followed Weaver, and it was okay, because there was a way out. Weaver was making a path through the zombies. He was covered in black slime, smashing into the zombies, plowing them over. Amy remembered she had a gun, and she thought she should do her bit. More gunshots away up ahead somewhere, and behind her. So she made sure everybody around her was dead, and then aimed at the leg of an old male zombie with a chin beard. The thing showed no response, but Amy couldn't just shoot it in the head.

That was the whole *problem.* People kept shooting each other, or bashing each other with rocks, or whatever they could do to cause pain. Amy didn't fire. She kept going, the chin-bearded zombie lost from sight, his thin arms outstretched in a pose almost like yearning before the others crowded in between them. Weaver was still there in front of her. Amy hooked her hand in Weaver's belt so she wouldn't lose him. He brought the butt of his gun around, but checked the swing.

"Lemme know it's you," he said, in a voice hoarse with fear.

They made it to Main Street, and they could see right away where the others were. The zombies formed a dense pack in their footsteps, creating gaps in the crowd on either side. They were so stupid, but so dedicated. *Like Republicans,* Amy thought. She wished irrelevant things wouldn't come into her head so much. Danny was so focused. Danny was probably dead. Maybe the zombies would not be able to get their teeth into her. Danny was tough as rawhide. *Keep those dead guys rollin', Rawhide!* A scrap of the old song popped into Amy's head. She was losing it.

Weaver kicked a little kid in the chest, a zombie maybe four years old, then shot a slightly bigger one. Its arm flew off but no blood sprayed out. An adult zombie's thigh burst apart behind it. Amy heard the screaming again, and she thought it might be her, so she stopped, and the screaming stopped.

"Follow them," Weaver commanded.

He was pointing down the space the zombies had made when they bunched up in the path of the others. There were more turning toward Amy and Weaver every instant that went by. Amy was going to say something, but Weaver was already gone. She was alone in a world of the hungry dead. There was nothing to do but run.

Patrick lost his mind. He didn't know what was happening until they turned the corner onto Main Street. The little Mexican woman couldn't run for anything, and Patrick kept crashing into her back. Ahead of her was the girl with the blue hair, which was completely the wrong shade for her complexion.

This was the worst nightmare ever. Patrick thought a lot of things were the worst nightmare ever, but this was the real deal. This one was for the record books. The Mexican woman had a snouty pistol in her hands and she was firing it with real proficiency, picking her shots even as she ran. *She can't hit dick,* the cool, calculating voice in Patrick's head observed. But she knew what she was doing. Patrick was about to be devoured by monsters, and somewhere in his mind he could still spare the resources to be jealous of someone else.

It was the adrenaline. Every second was a long, complex thing to be examined and considered, even as events unfolded. But his mind was not trained to this heightened state of awareness. It was much better off ad-libbing snarky comments in front of the cameras; give him a press conference and he could outquip anybody. *This isn't a press conference,* the voice remarked, and Patrick realized that on top of everything else he was babbling inside his head again. Weaver wouldn't do that. Weaver was up in front, leading them to safety.

Then Weaver was going past Patrick in the wrong direction.

"Run!" Weaver shouted, and hammered his way through the zombies that were closing in behind them. Patrick saw that Maria was almost out of sight ahead, the zombies closing in like the spectators closing in around the winning cyclist of the Tour De France.

He did what Weaver said, and ran.

Danny thought they could possibly jump from roof to roof of the vehicles still parked all over Main Street and Route 144. From up on the Suburban she could see the cars like low islands in the undead river. If they could jump far enough and not slide off upon landing, and if the hands didn't close around their limbs before they were able to jump to the next one. Weaver reloaded while Danny fired into the crowd, and they both stomped the fingers that snagged at their feet.

"Fuck," Weaver mumbled. He was standing there looking at one of the zombies. Danny turned and sighted down the barrel of the shotgun on its head. Charred flesh, boiled eyeball. It was Mitchell Woodie, the cook from the Wooden Spoon. It didn't look like he felt any pain—only hunger, pushing through the crowd around the Suburban, unaware of the appalling damage to his flesh. Danny knew how much that should hurt. Despite all the horrors Weaver had seen in the last ten minutes, he appeared mesmerized. The adrenaline was wearing off, Danny realized. They were in a temporary place of refuge, and he was crashing.

But Danny had an idea.

It was the blackened remains of Mitchell Woodie that clued her in. She should have thought of it before. But it wasn't too late. She adjusted her aim.

"Gas tank," Danny called out, and squeezed the trigger.

The explosion made the pavement vibrate under Michelle's feet. She was running fleet as a deer through the zombies, blue hair flying. They couldn't touch her. She didn't know or care who was around her or behind her or anything except she knew she had to run, as fast and as far as she could. She knew how to run. She had been on the track team at school for an entire season before she realized how stupid competitive sports were and how it was just another way for the Adults in Charge to keep the more interesting kids occupied and tired so they couldn't cause trouble.

She didn't stop running when the explosion came, but she felt the heat on her back and the bounce in the asphalt, and a moment later there was a strange slapping sound among the zombies that were lurching up the street toward her. Not so many zombies here—she could handle it. Until a severed arm and part of a head came down and hit her and she fell and scoured the skin off both her knees. She got up again and it stung like fire, and now she was facing the wrong way and she could see the slapping sound was chunks of dead bodies raining down from the sky.

A big, greasy torus of black smoke rose into the fading sky, and below it huge orange flames jumped up from the zombie crowd.

The woman named Maria was coming up right behind her, huffing and puffing, her face blotchy. Michelle had lost her lead in the race. Maria took her by the arm and said, "Let's go." The gay man with the bleached hair was right behind Maria now. That was Patrick Michaels, the famous guy with a TV show about how to live in attractive and inviting spaces, just like the rich and famous, without spending a fortune.

The zombies were starting to turn in their direction, though Michelle had only fallen for a couple of seconds. Time to run again, even if her knees really, really hurt. There was another explosion, louder than the first, and something metal clanged off the building to their left. Michelle put her hands over her head. More chunks of meat were thudding down on them.

"There it is!" Maria shouted, and sure enough, the motor home was ahead of them, only a few zombies in the way. Michelle didn't see anybody else there. She didn't see her brother. Maybe they were all inside. She saw people behind the big windshield, waving and pointing. Troy, the nice fireman, came down out of the driver's door with an axe in his hands and ran toward them and Michelle felt her legs turn to rubber. She fell down again and a very thin, tall zombie woman with her hair in a knot on top of her head was reaching to bite her. Her crooked smoker's teeth were tanned pegs in a bloodless face.

Maria tried to shoot the woman, but her gun was empty. Then the woman crashed to the ground beside Michelle, the fireman's axe sticking out of her back. She was still reaching for Michelle with the arm that wasn't immobilized by severed muscles. Troy scooped Michelle up and carried her away from the zombie, and Patrick and Maria ran past them. Patrick had the keys. He had to make it no matter what, or they were all dead.

He did make it. Eager hands pulled them both into the RV, and Michelle felt herself lifted up, too. Her bloody knees smeared the upholstery as people set her down inside in the back, where she saw her kid brother coming through the people to throw his arms around her. Next, Troy was up front in the driver's seat, slamming the door on the gray, clutching fingers that wanted so badly to grasp the warm flesh packed inside the vehicle, to pull it down to snapping jaws.

Patrick clambered through the crowd to the passenger's seat beside Troy. Michelle saw that Patrick's hands shook with such violence he couldn't get the keys out of his pocket.

"Pardon me," Troy said, and dug the keys out himself. He selected the ignition key, and a moment later the enormous diesel engine rumbled to life.

The first blast knocked Weaver off the roof of the Suburban.

Danny had not expected such an explosion. She'd seen plenty of vehicles burn, and she knew they seldom blew up. And it wasn't the car she shot that went up—it was the one right next to it. So the whole effect of the thing was ten times what she had intended. She only wanted to set fire to the zombies. They might respond to fire, that most primal fear of human beings. But even if they didn't fear it, they would burn. Danny had a hunch that zombies on fire wouldn't be quite as single-minded. It's hard to go after prey with eyeballs that are melting out of your skull.

The roar of the blast continued, and Weaver flew through the air. Danny didn't see where he landed; she was flung off her feet and smashed down on her back across the roof rack. It hurt as if her spine was broken, which meant it wasn't.

A zombie immediately hooked its fingers into her ear, and she tore painfully out of its grasp. She got on her knees, craning to look for Weaver, but he'd already disappeared beneath the undead, wherever he was. Danny's ears were ringing, half-deafened. She could hear a bell-like note sustained above the faint sound of roaring flames and the zombie moan that rippled through the swarm. If Weaver was down, she couldn't even find him. He might have been knocked out by the explosion, or killed by the fall, or he might be right as rain, crawling through a forest of cold legs.

A zombie was pulling her down by the belt. She aimed over its head and fired another shot at the nearest car, a low maroon sedan.

This one didn't explode. The shot punched a big hole through the rear quarter panel, low by the wheel well, where the gas tank would most likely be. She could smell it now, the gasoline and the burning rubber and that rich, sweet stink of roasting human flesh. Danny fired again, and the gasoline spilling from the maroon sedan caught fire with a *whump* she could barely hear, although she felt the heat on her blistered face. The zombies shuffling through the gasoline went up like torches. Danny chopped with the shotgun at the hands that were pulling her down. She struggled to her feet. The Suburban was standing in a sea of burning, crackling bodies, their slow limbs flailing, the flames spreading from one to the next. The smoke stank obscenely and made Danny's eyes stream.

If Weaver was lying senseless on the ground, he was going to burn. It was the worst way to go, but there was nothing else Danny could do. She wasn't going to throw her life away without taking a bunch of these things with her, and if Weaver was already dying, she didn't want him coming back like Larry's wife. Danny had to move from her position; the paint on the Suburban was rising in fat blisters from the heat of the fires.

She jumped down on the hood and kept her momentum as she leaped for the car in front, a hatchback. It was a messy landing because of the blazing arms that flailed at her in midair, and she hit the hatchback badly and broke the rear window, then fell sprawling on the ground. Immediately the things were coming after her, even the burning ones. Gobbets of blazing fat and clothing were dropping all around her, and through the legs she could see the hungry flames turning the asphalt into boiling syrup. Danny crawled on her belly underneath the hatchback and kept on going, ignoring the scrape of bolts and fittings that projected beneath the vehicle. Hands reached for her, and some of the things were even down on their knees, looking for her, their eyes glittering in the firelight.

A ribbon of flaming gasoline meandered toward her from under the sedan. *She* was going to burn, too, unless she moved quickly. There had to be some avenue of escape in all this chaos. She hoped to God that Weaver had found it.

She should have given Weaver more warning before she shot the tank on that car. She didn't expect there to be an explosion. No excuse, but she just didn't know. Now it was time to move. One of the hatchback's tires was burning. The panic was hitting Danny like a million tiny knives all at once.

I'm going to burn.

A dozen cold hands had gotten hold of Danny's legs and they were pulling her backward. In a matter of moments she would be exposed again, and the biting would begin and her legs would be eaten first so she had plenty of time to experience some serious agony before she was ripped apart or caught fire.

From her position a couple of inches above the ground, she could see the undersides of several vehicles. Through gaps in the maddened zombies, she could see the axles, the suspensions, the gas tanks. It was worth one more try, and if she was lucky the explosion would blow her head off.

If not, she had a couple more shells in the gun. She would do it to herself.

Danny could not remember what happened next, just as she could not remember what happened when she got knocked over the side of Route 144 with the Explorer. She took aim, and suddenly the claws grabbing her legs dragged her back a foot or more, and she fired the shotgun. Her hearing cut out on detonation, that much she knew.

Then there was a jump in the chronology.

Suddenly she was standing in the middle of what looked like a butcher's shop hit by a missile. One of her eyes was closed and she was still holding the shotgun, but the stock had broken off, leaving a sharp stump like a broken bone. Several cars were overturned within a dozen yards, and the hatchback under which she had been lying was now standing on its side behind her, resting up against the burning sedan. Huge clouds of black smoke filled the sky and the red flames were brighter than the fading daylight: The sun might not have been all the way down in the flatlands, but evening comes early in the mountains.

It was absolutely silent: no ringing in the ears, no screams, no crackle of flames. Fire was everywhere, and the grotesque shapes of bodies with no limbs and limbs with no bodies. Strewn in the wreckage were heads, black and red, with the ears and hair burnt off them so they looked like huge roasted thumbs. Danny tried to walk, but her feet wouldn't move, and she looked down and discovered she was ankle deep in human intestines. She looked at her own body and didn't see any big holes. The intestines belonged to somebody else.

Outside the ring of twisted metal and fire there were still hundreds of zombies, although the first few rows of them were scorched and torn up to such a degree that they were impeding the forward motion of the ones behind. They couldn't see or hear or smell. Some of them couldn't bite, either, because their faces were torn off. Danny wondered briefly what she had done to cause all this destruction. *It worked pretty good,* the voice observed. But Danny seemed to recall she was supposed to be dead. Maybe she was. Maybe she was one of the zombies now.

Then she saw Weaver.

He was dragging his left leg, and it looked like the knee might be broken. The foot faced almost backward. He was moving away through the zombies. They ignored him. He was pretty beat-up looking and Danny thought maybe she, too, was in such bad shape they'd mistake her for one of their kind.

Weaver, she tried to say, but no words came out. She didn't know if it was because she couldn't hear or because she couldn't talk. But he was headed toward the gymnasium, so she followed after him, marveling on some level that her legs continued to work at all. The zombies couldn't catch her. She was a superstar, and so was he, and they were going to *make it*—all the way back down Main Street, together, after which she could explain to Weaver why she'd risked setting him alight.

Danny reached him in front of the Quik-Mart and tried to call his name again but could only croak. Still, Weaver turned around. And Danny saw the milky eyes and the waxen skin and the windshield wiper arm protruding from his chest with a waterfall of blood spilled down below it and she knew that Weaver was dead before he hit the ground after that first, surprise explosion. So whatever brought people back, it was accelerating. There wasn't any down time, any more. She fired the shotgun almost casually—after all, she knew him a little, no need for ceremony—and Weaver's head blew apart.

Danny made it halfway down Main before the zombies came for her. But when they did, they were as enthusiastic as ever, while Danny had lost her zest for everything: life, hope, love, even the sacred absolution of death. Still, force of habit—she fought back.

A couple of zombies reeled back with smashed faces, one she definitely killed, because she hit it clean on the temple and the broken butt of the shotgun went in like a cake knife, and a couple she shot the legs out from under. But the last shell, the one she knew was there for sure, was for her. She didn't figure it would hurt, and if it did, it would only be for a moment, and even then, would she know it? Pain traveled through the nervous system at three hundred feet per second. All those pea-sized nuggets of metal (number four buckshot, twenty-seven balls) would pass through her brain at *thirteen* hundred feet per second. It wouldn't hurt, but it would permanently change her hat size. *Sucks to be me,* Danny thought. She was concussed now, that was for fucking sure.

The only thing intruding on her perfect well of self-pity was Amy. Her friend's voice was coming in high and fast, cutting through the deafness, shrill as always when she was worked up. *Incoming!* But Danny could definitely hear Amy calling from somewhere. From right about here, Danny realized.

Amy was beside her.

"Jesus, Danny, you look awful."

They were surrounded.

"Why are you here?" Danny asked, although she couldn't hear if it came out of her mouth. For that matter, she couldn't hear Amy. But she could read the shape of her mouth.

"I told them to go," Amy said. "The motor home is leaving."

"Why?" Danny croaked. She wanted to understand how, despite all this effort, she had failed to get Amy, of all people, out of this nightmare.

"You," Amy replied.

Danny fired that last precious shot and blew a zombie down. It was coming at Amy. Instinct took over. Danny cursed. Last shot wasted. Now what was she going to do, stab herself to death? Then she saw the highway patrolman, Officer Park, the corpse shambling along toward them, arms half-outstretched as if it didn't quite believe it had found prey. Danny strode forward as well as she could with a pair of half-working legs and pulled the automatic out of the highway patrolman's holster. He didn't mind. He wasn't interested in guns anymore. He was all about the teeth.

Danny pulled the patrolman's Smokey hat down over his eyes and fired the automatic through his head. The hat caught fire at the muzzle point and the trooper fell down, a curlicue of smoke following him to the ground. Sound was returning. A horn was honking somewhere. Amy had her fingers in her ears and her eyes shut.

"What are you doing?" Danny said.

"What?" said Amy.

Danny grabbed Amy's arm and pulled her finger out of her ear.

"I said . . ." Danny couldn't remember what she had said. The world was falling upward, very slowly. She could stay on her feet, but she was eventually going to fall into the sky. Amy took Danny's gun.

"You take the gun," Danny said. That way she was still in charge. Danny pointed at a zombie. "Shoot that one quick."

Amy fumbled around with the weapon. Danny swiped the gun away from Amy, who was obviously not going to manage such a simple task, and shot the zombie. Its teeth shattered on the pavement an inch from Danny's boot. Lord, were they ever about to get bitten to death, eaten alive. All *kinds* of zombies coming in. There was a high, gassy lightness to Danny's state of mind, a shakerful of hysteria and blows to the head.

"Danny? You got another plan?"

"There's too many."

"Two bullets," said Amy, "is all we need."

Amy took Danny's gun hand and guided it to the middle of her forehead, the end of the barrel pressed into the skin. She looked into Danny's eyes, and Danny understood why Amy was beside her, instead of tooling up 144 toward Big Bear. Because, even after she was gone so long in the desert at war, or maybe for that reason, Amy needed her more than she needed herself. If not Kelley, there was Amy. If not Danny, Amy didn't want to live.

Danny was touched. She pulled back the action on the pistol. Amy closed her eyes.

Bang

Danny looked around. She hadn't even pulled the trigger. What was the gunshot? Amy opened her eyes, staring at the zombie behind Danny that had just puked its brains out of its ear.

Bang

It happened again, and a zombie went down with its head emptied out like a piñata, close behind Amy.

Bang

Sniper.

Danny almost hit the deck, but then she remembered: They were in America. No snipers here; not many, at least.

Bang.

Another zombie flew off its feet, and Danny swiveled around to look in the opposite direction from where the zombie's brains had gone.

"Run, you dumb shitheads!" Wulf bellowed.

He was up on the roof of the Quik-Mart with the Winchester 70, working the bolt action and firing again. The zombie that clutched Danny's shoulder snapped clear out of her field of view with a hole in its head.

"You old son of a bitch," Danny said, and grabbed Amy's arm.

"Danny? Let's boogie," Amy said. Amy had to help her stay upright, but Danny ran as best she could.

Wulf kept up a steady fire for at least a minute and a half. He was slipping those shells into the gun like a lover: pop the trigger smooth as silk, another zombie in the scope gets its card pulled. Squirt of black oatmeal and down. Nothing to it. Reload. Pop. Down. Wulf's eyes stung with perspiration. He experienced the rush that he'd not felt since he left Vietnam, all those years ago. Decades. He'd been asleep, drunk, pissed off, ruining marriages, half-raising crooked kids who didn't give a shit about him, kids who told their lovers he was dead. Maybe grandkids by now. All he knew was the old fighting machinery—that infernal engine with only one use on this godforsaken earth, given him by the U.S. government in return for anything else he ever could have been—was running again like he'd last topped up the battery and oiled the cylinders with Marvel Mystery Oil this very morning, not forty years earlier.

He rocked the bolt back and chambered another slim, sharp round and there was the head in the scope and he blew the skull open, another zombie out of the sheriff's way. Wulf was going to see that tough little gal lived. He'd seen everything she did, from up on the rooftops. He'd watched her draw the enemy out, take stupid risks, and he'd even thought about popping her through the head a couple of times, to save her the trouble of dying underneath all those bloody teeth. But she kept on going, outmaneuvering death at every turn, so he kept on letting her, and when he saw that crazy veterinary come along, Wulf could have thrown up it was so damn touching. But he figured the time had arrived. He sighted on the sheriff's scorched, half-scalped head, crosshairs intersecting at the vein jumping in her temple.

Yet when it had come to the moment to shoot the high-toned cripple bitch, as that old peckerwood Sheriff Booth had called her, Wulf couldn't do it. Not even as a mercy killing. Any more than he could kill himself for the same reason. She'd be like Wulf, soon enough. Couple-few years. Pass the baton and die in a ditch, that was plan enough for an old man.

Meanwhile, he laid down fire. One after another the zombies dropped, and it was like a scythe swinging through the undead. They were at a tough angle now, though, so Wulf got himself up and ran and threw himself across the narrow space between this roof and the next and went down on his knee again, sucking wind because he was too damn old, and twitched off a couple more rounds that cleared the way pretty damn good for an old ass-hole, as he thought to himself. Now two more, then reload, and keep on shooting. Hadn't missed a single one yet.

They came to the sleek interceptor left behind by the late highway patrol-man Park, and Danny realized she had the answer to the whole damn thing. Troy was pulling the motor home around in a wide, messy arc in the broad intersection of Pine and Main, crunching abandoned cars out of the way, and he wasn't going to be able to reverse to Danny and Amy. But neither were they going to make it on foot to the motor home's present position. Not if he hit the gas before the sheer mass of zombies blocked them in on all sides, which he had damn well better do in the next few seconds.

The daylight was beginning to fade.

"Danny, no!" Amy shouted, but she didn't even sound all that sure of why she was saying it. It was almost a question. Danny was running back into the legion of zombies that were right behind them, half their number hideously burned black and red and crackled fat-white by the gasoline fire, but not the least bit deterred.

"We can *make* it!" Amy cried. She was pressed up against the highway patrol interceptor and there was another bang and Wulf had taken the near-est zombie down again, and bang, another one.

Then Danny was running straight back at Amy with keys in her hand.

"Get in the goddamn car," Danny rapped, and threw the keys to Amy. Amy got in. Out of the corner of her eye Danny saw Wulf, a misshapen hulk leaping apelike to the roof of the barber shop. There was a rifle in his fist. The old man slid down the far side of the roof, hurled himself out into space, and Danny lost sight of him; Amy found the ignition and shoved the key in and Danny was in the seat beside her and Amy got the engine going and she floored the gas pedal.

Four zombies flew over the hood, legs bent at crazy angles from where they'd hit the fender rams on the front of the car. Then there was a space, and Amy took it and whacked a couple of zombies aside. Danny hung on to the shotgun mount on the dashboard as Amy slalomed through the next opening and kept on driving after the RV that was now powering up Route 114 into the last glow of the sunset, shoving abandoned cars out of its way.

Just before they passed out of the end of Main Street and under the boughs of the tall, dark trees, Danny saw Wulf on the roof of the motor home. He was clinging to the luggage rack, looking back into town, the rifle in his hands. The wind blew his long, matted hair around. His eyes looked like chips of stone under shaggy brows. It could have been twenty thousand years ago. The original man, with his weapon and his filth and his will to live, watching the unknown world that swarmed with enemies, and death. And yet the master of it all. Might be the master no more.

Then the shade of the trees flew up around him, and he was gone from sight, and Danny closed her eyes. Amy kept driving into the darkness.

PART TWO
THE UNCANNY VALLEY

1

Danny wanted to drive.

The night was a hallucination. Danny slept through most of it, although she drifted awake for a few seconds now and then. They traveled at a crawl: There were roadblocks and checkpoints set up mostly by civilians, and the night was lit up in places by flares, whirling emergency lights, even fires. There was gunfire. Radios blared in fire trucks. The Forest Peak convoy idled in long lines of other vehicles escaping through the resort communities, creeping past crashes and dead bodies and teams of men with guns. At one point there was an argument between Amy and several men.

Danny was so groggy she couldn't join in, although it had something to do with her. Amy was insisting Danny was living and breathing, and some kid with a flashlight was shining it in Danny's face and someone asking, "Is she alive?" Then, what felt like weeks later, there was an argument at a checkpoint concerning the RV. Somebody wanted to take it for some reason. Another argument, this time with Troy pitching in. Danny saw him shaking a rifle by way of emphasis. After a while, they moved on.

Danny remembered the tree shadows outside Forest Peak, and pale, misshapen bodies looming out of the darkness into the headlights. Their eyes had reflected yellow. Later, Danny had come out of a doze, and saw Amy with thick rivulets of tears spilling down her dirty face, mouth bent down in grief, knuckles white on the steering wheel. But she was silent, and kept her eyes on the road. Danny went back to sleep.

The woman, veiled in black from head to toe, was not holding a baby. It was a bomb. Danny was sure of it. The rippling desert horizon was a burnt orange line between brown sky and yellow sand.

Danny brought the Mossberg up waist-high. "Drop it," she called. "Drop it." The tanks were idling with their snoring rumble behind the farmhouse—she was all alone, until the rest of the patrol trotted around to her position. All alone with the woman in black.

The woman looked at Danny with eyes like obsidian. She raised the thing in her hands, as if offering it to God. Danny could see it now. A satchel mine of Chinese manufacture. A gunshot split the baking air. Somewhere to the left—

Danny awoke with her head against the doorframe and watched the pavement unspool beyond the windshield. It got quieter on their route, and after a few turnoffs the convoy had the entire road pretty much to itself. Most people were going the opposite direction, headed for Lancaster or Bakersfield. She had gotten plenty of sleep by her standards, six and a half hours according to the dashboard clock. Better than average. She needed to pee and stretch and drink a very large amount of water, eat a huge, fatty breakfast at a booth in a big chain restaurant, then sit in the shade and drain a bottle of something crazy expensive like Chinaco Anejo. Maybe get the dreamed-of soak in a deep, hot bathtub after that. Then pass out on the bed for three days.

For now, it was time for Amy to let Danny drive, because they were going to go the wrong way.

It was dark but the sky at the horizon was glowing rose-gray with dawn, and when Danny saw that there was a horizon she realized they'd made it all the way down out of the mountains. She could still remember vague passages of the night, but her impressions were jumbled and fading.

Now they were heading downhill, but on a gentle grade, with the black bulk of the mountains on their left and a broad, flat landscape to the right, unmarked by streetlights or neon, even in the far distance. The sun would rise straight ahead of them; they were driving almost due east. Scobie Tree would be somewhere up ahead.

There were decisions to be made.

Danny twisted around to look out the rear window, and her body protested with audible creaks. The motor home was directly in back, and behind that were several other, smaller vehicles with their headlights on.

"You awake?" Amy said.

"I guess," Danny said, and turned carefully to face the front again.

One of Danny's front teeth was chipped. There was a rough edge she couldn't stop rubbing with her tongue. She held up her hands and examined them. Her skin was uniformly filthy, blackened, smeared with ash and dark blood. Her palms were scraped up, her right knuckles skinned, and both hands were shiny-hairless and blistered from the heat of the gasoline fires. Her left ring finger was missing part of the nail. The nail bed had bled until it formed a black crust. Her left sleeve was gone and there were three perfectly legible human bite marks on the upper arm. None of them had broken the skin. They looked like red tattoos. She checked her aching calf and found a similar mark, the skin there also intact.

There were hand-print bruises on both her wrists and a long, jagged cut ran up her right forearm. There was a piece of metal protruding from the end of the cut. She pulled it out. The thing didn't want to come, tugging a pyramid of skin with it until at last it slipped free. It was a splinter of chromed steel, three-quarters of an inch long. Blood rose up in a ball where she'd removed the splinter, then ran down her skin.

Danny thought of Weaver with the dead eyes and the windshield wiper arm sticking out of his chest. Her own chest was half-exposed, or at least the sports bra was. Her shirt was in tatters. She felt the pocket and Kelley's note was still inside. It might not be legible, but she still had it.

Kelley.

Oh, dear Lord, Kelley.

"We need to talk about where we're going," Danny said.

"To civilization," Amy replied, not looking over at Danny.

"Civilization? We don't know where that is. We got to keep away from any large human population until we know how many zombies there are. This wasn't a local thing, Amy."

"You need a hospital."

"There probably aren't any hospitals anymore. Trust me. That's where everybody took the dead."

Danny considered their enemy. The disease, if that's what it was, had a brilliant strategy for self-promotion. The running and screaming was a great start. But then human nature became its best ally, as untold numbers of the dead (walking or otherwise) were brought to first responders: police, fire stations, emergency rooms. Then, after a little break in the festivities, they turned cannibal. So there wouldn't be an intact emergency facility of any kind for a hundred miles, Danny suspected. You were more likely to be eaten than treated.

Danny got on the radio, and Patrick answered her call.

"Glad you're alive," he said. "Is Weaver with you?"

Danny took a long time to answer. The silence told Patrick what she couldn't put into words.

"Oh," Patrick said.

Troy took over the conversation. "Sheriff, we should stop for a break soon. This bus is getting crowded."

They pulled over into a rest stop surrounded by acres of dry grass and gravel. Troy led a couple of expeditious men on a scouting sortie, inside and behind the toilet building, and around the dumpsters parked off to the side of the paved area.

"Have them keep a lookout," Danny said. She was sitting in the passenger seat of the interceptor with her legs out the door, boot heels resting on the ground. She should get up, but she'd been overcome with drugged torpor. In the absence of an urgent, life-or-death call to action, she couldn't lift a finger.

She watched the survivors stand in line for the toilets. The men who just needed to take a leak were going around the back of the building. People were trying their cell phones, getting nothing. Danny thought of Kelley's cell phone, the contract too expensive to keep. It was in a kitchen drawer back at the house.

Dawn was a few minutes away, the sky a pale eggshell green shot with pink. The fields of grass were dim, the color of cardboard. In daylight they would be golden brown. Patrick emerged from the men's room with an aluminum flask containing water and carried it over to the interceptor.

"Thanks," Danny said, and tried to take the water, but her fingers wouldn't close on the container. Patrick tipped the mouth of the flask against Danny's lower lip; she drank hungrily, water spilling down her chin. Then she looked at Patrick. His face was grave, his eyes sad like some saint in an old painting.

"We should talk," Danny said.

"Was it quick?" Patrick was holding back a flood of grief, his chin quaking.

"He never knew," Danny said. "We're here 'cause of him."

"Did he say anything before it happened?"

"The last thing he said was I should take care of you," Danny said. It wasn't true. The last thing he'd said was *fuck*. Danny was a terrible liar, and even as she spoke, it sounded like week-old bullshit.

Patrick smiled, although tears spilled from his eyes. "He never would have said that. He would have said I'm supposed to take care of *you*."

"That was it," Danny nodded.

Bless his heart, Patrick believed it. He took a gulp of air and walked back to the RV with his shoulders squared, and Danny felt as if she had just made some kind of blood vow that could never be broken. Her heart ached along with the rest of her. She owed Patrick more than she had to give. Weaver might still be alive, if she'd done things differently. Still—she crammed the remorse down into the hole where all the untimely feelings went. She could grieve over her own failings some other time. There was plenty enough grieving to do as it was.

They had been at the rest stop about fifteen minutes. The sun rose, splendid and hot, gilding the mountains that marched off into the purple distance. Danny hauled herself out of the interceptor and took a brief walk around it, careful not to move farther away than she could reach, in case she collapsed. Amy was busy dealing with Michelle's knees on the steps of the RV, pouring something over the scrapes.

People were coming out of the toilets looking tidier than before. Danny knew she would have to clean herself up, as impossible as the effort sounded to her at this moment. But right now, before these civilians started arguing about what to do next, it was time for a quick come-to-Jesus meeting. Danny put two fingers in her mouth and blew a piercing whistle. Her lower lip split. Heads turned. For an instant she saw the zombies turning, too, but then it was gone. Just a phantom in her mind.

"Listen up," she whispered. "Listen up," she tried again, and this time people heard and they walked toward her. Soon the entire group of survivors had emptied out of the toilets and was gathered around the interceptor, except Amy and Michelle, still at the RV. And Wulf. He had just disappeared again, and that seemed to be his way, so Danny put him out of her mind. The survivors she didn't know personally all had fear of her in their eyes, same as the Iraqis: acutely alert, pulled-back, as if confronting a growling dog. Anger spat through Danny's mind. *You owe me, shitheads, show me a smile,* she thought, but only cleared her throat.

Amy joined the group, in the back row. There were around twenty-five or thirty survivors in the bunch. Danny could see Patrick and Maria and Michelle with her arm around her brother. Troy was standing in the back near Amy. Familiar faces. At least she'd helped keep *them* alive.

The two kids made Danny think of Kelley. She needed to start talking, or she might lose it.

"You all must be pretty tired and some of you may have injuries, but we're in a difficult position. I know I'd like to get to a land line and find out if some folks made it through all this okay. And I'm guessing there are people thinking the same thing about you. Anybody made phone contact since last night? Email?"

People were shaking their heads.

"Lost contact with everybody not long after things went bad," a man said.

Kelley came into Danny's mind again; she dismissed the image, and continued, "So we don't have any way to find out what's in front of us. And we got a kind of a big problem. See that cloud back there on the western horizon?"

Danny pointed off past the foothills, beyond which a dark thunderhead rose up. Its leading edge was touched with salmon highlights from the sunrise, but its depths were black as tar. People looked at it, then back at her.

"It doesn't rain out here from June to October. That's smoke. That's Los Angeles."

A woman turned away, and a man put his arm around her. Everybody started talking. Danny cleared her throat again and tried to run her hand through her hair. But there was some kind of lumpy, gnarled stuff all over her head. She dragged some off with her fingers and looked at it. Burnt hair. No wonder they were staring at her. She must have looked worse than most of the zombies. This was one of the very rare occasions when Danny felt the need to look in a mirror.

"I guess I'm not looking my best," Danny said, and a couple of people laughed out loud. Good. Keep moving while there was a little sympathy. "Anyway, we better not go back toward the highly settled areas. We have to keep moving up along the edge of the desert."

Now they were talking over her, stirred up like hornets. Consternation, objection, alarm. Danny waved it all away.

"Listen. Listen! Maria there was on the emergency bands for hours yesterday. That's the only communications system still online." Danny hesitated. Was it only *yesterday*? "She talked to law enforcement and emergency personnel all over the Southland. They were swamped. I mean they were knocked out of commission before those things even got back up. If anybody here thinks they can just drive on home, you need to face a hard reality."

Maria raised her hand.

"I think I lost everybody," she said.

Now the survivors were looking ill and miserable. Better to get this over with, have everybody fall apart at once. It would help consolidate their need for leadership, as well, which would relieve Danny of the need to engage in any pissing matches with the more macho types.

"I'm going to tell you why else we're not going back to Los Angeles," Danny continued, "and why we're not necessarily going to San Diego or any of the other big cities around here, not for a while. There were ten million people in Los Angeles County, two days ago. Whatever killed all these people in Forest Peak, from what I heard yesterday, it spread out from a center not too far from downtown L.A. I looked at the big map in the station and figured out there's a circle you could draw all the way around the city that hits Forest Peak to the east, maybe as far as Banning, then all the way to the ocean on the west, and as far south as Temecula. To the north I don't know if it made it over the mountains, but if it did, you're talking about Lancaster and Apple Valley. I don't know this for a fact, but it works on the map."

Not everybody could conjure up the map of Southern California the way Danny could, but she saw the truth dawning on some of the faces. The mountains made a natural firewall against the spread of the death-dealing agent northward, but there was nothing stopping it—or the hordes of starving, ambulatory corpses—in any other direction. Only the ocean, and that stopped the living, as well. Already Danny could see questions surfacing on a couple of faces. She needed to keep talking while the momentum was hers, although her throat felt like it had been scrubbed with bleach and a wire brush.

"So what we have is huge concentrations that are too dangerous for us to go into. If there's some kind of federal effort to deal with this, we'll hook up with that as soon as possible. Until then, I want to keep us moving northward where there are fewer people, probably less contagion, if that's what it is, and ideally we'll regroup with other survivors there. Ten more minutes, then let's pull out. We can make Scobie Tree in a couple hours. Don't wander off. We don't know what's out there."

There was more discussion than Danny liked, after she was done speaking. In the service it was considered insubordinate to openly discuss an officer's judgment. These civilians didn't try to hide their skepticism. They were expecting a vote or something, Danny thought. Fuck 'em, they could vote in November. She had to keep them moving.

Amy was standing there at the back as the huddle broke up, watching Danny with narrowed eyes. Amy was thinking about something, and her expression said it was something to do with Danny's remarks. Amy was always too smart for her own good.

"Keys," Danny said.

Amy shook her head. "You get washed up, have a look at yourself in the mirror, and come back to me for some medical attention. I got the stuff from the station, so we should be able to fix up some of the less serious damage. But you really need to look at yourself. *I'll* do the driving."

It was a long way to the toilets. Danny felt like she was walking on rubber stilts.

She stared into the steel mirror bolted over the sink of the women's room. Someone had scratched a looping graffito into the reflective surface with a key, and someone else had tried to buff it out with sandpaper, but she could still see plenty enough of her reflection. Her hair was the first thing. She had clearly been facing the blast she couldn't remember, because her hair, especially on top, was roasted into a chunky, dreadlocklike mass. She had less than two inches of hair left in front, from crown to ears. The hair that had survived in back was largely plastered down with layers of dried blood. The face below the hair was so filthy that her bloodshot eyes stood out like a cartoon character blinking in the dark. With the red around them, her irises stood out electric green. But not for long: The left eye was swelling shut.

Her face was covered in zombie and human blood. There were cuts and scrapes and heat blisters all over her exposed skin, her lips had split open in three places, and one of her ears looked like the object of a rat attack. If the zombie infection got in through fresh injuries, she was in serious trouble. But she was still alive, so maybe instead of incubating it, she was immune, or the heat of the fires killed it. Or maybe she was just lucky, if this was what qualified as luck. Maybe it wasn't an infectious disease at all.

She splashed water on her skin and it stung furiously, but she kept splashing and scrubbing, black and red droplets staining the white sink for five minutes before she had gotten herself mostly cleaned off, at least the front of her face and neck. What was going on in the back of her head didn't bear thinking about. Then she more gently cleaned off her arms up to the elbows. They were too sore to scrub, and large areas of skin began to peel away. She didn't use any soap. It seemed like it would hurt too much. Danny decided to let her skin air dry, hawked and spat, and trudged out the door to face the world again.

When she emerged into the brilliant light of a new morning, the survivors were standing near their respective vehicles, but everyone was facing her way. Somebody started clapping, and then the rest followed, some shouting thanks, even a couple of whistles. Maria ran her hand down Danny's upper arm, beaming at her.

Danny walked back to the interceptor without acknowledging the applause. She suspected Amy had a hand in this embarrassing display. And one thing Danny knew for sure: These people wouldn't be pleased with her for very long.

2

They reached Scobie Tree after three more hours of driving. Amy drove the interceptor at the front of the pack, and Danny dozed beside her. It was a hot day and the thick black cloud over Los Angeles was visible on the horizon, rising into the stratosphere, borne up on volcanic heat. There were other fires, not so far away. Probably in places like Riverside and San Bernardino.

With her first waking thought, Danny wondered what downtown L.A. would be like. There were living people there. No matter how bad things got, people always survived. And they suffered. What was happening in the city must be biblical. Sodom and Gomorrah, if she remembered her Good Book. Huge buildings devoured by coiling dragons of fire that sprang three hundred feet in the air. There would be sheets of white flame sucking the oxygen out of the streets, turning the little hiding places where people curled up into vacuums as airless and deadly as outer space. Underground gas lines would explode, turning streets into canyons of fire. Windows would melt and run down the sidewalks and the vehicles and mailboxes and trees and corpses would become stumpy, brittle skeletons.

But the flames would cook those flesh-eating zombie sons of bitches, too. The more of them that were consumed by the fire, the fewer of them would have to be taken down. Burn the fucking city to the ground, if it destroyed a few hundred thousand of those things. *But don't let Kelley be there. Pray she went the way I think she did, if she's still alive.*

"What," Amy said.

"I didn't say anything."

"You growled."

"I didn't." But Danny knew she had. The guys in Iraq used to imitate her doing it.

She realized her bandaged left hand had stolen up to the tattered breast pocket of her uniform shirt, and she was touching Kelley's note, folded within. She couldn't bring herself to read it, and yet she wanted to follow where Kelley might have gone. She knew Kelley well enough—or rather, Kelley knew her big sister well enough—to know she wouldn't tell Danny where she was going, not if she took the Mustang.

Danny didn't know what to think about Kelley. If her sister was one of those things now, did Danny wish her happy hunting? Or would she want to be the one who put a bullet through her head? The only thing Danny was sure of was that she had to *know.* She couldn't go through however much life she had left without knowing what had happened to her sister.

"It's Kelley, right?"

Danny stared at Amy, who was driving the interceptor with the AC blasting and her window down, elbow hooked over the sill. Her hair was whipping around against the acrylic divider panel behind their heads. This could have been one of their early road trips, after both girls had licenses and Danny got her *first* Mustang, a white 1981 piece of shit. This was almost relaxing. Against her better knowledge, Danny had decided to take her boots off. She knew she might not be able to get them back on, but this wasn't the war and she wasn't on patrol. Her toes almost screamed audibly upon release. She dragged off the damp drab green socks she'd been wearing since the night she passed out *the night Kelley ran away* and her feet smelled vinegary and there were blisters all around the edges. The air-conditioning felt heavenly on them. And here Amy was, reading Danny's mind again.

"Yeah, Kelley," Danny said. "How did you—"

"You're crinkling the note in your pocket."

Danny let her hand fall away from her chest.

"How do you know that I have Kelley's note in my pocket?"

"Duh. Because you wouldn't get all wet-eyed if it was parking citations."

Danny swabbed at her eyes with the soft white bandage. She could still see with both of them. It looked like the shiner wasn't going to swell all the way, which was good. She had a feeling this would be a bad time to lose the advantage of binocular vision.

"Read it, will you?" Amy said. "Danny, why the heck don't you just read it?" Amy slapped the steering wheel with her palm, which made the interceptor swerve out of the lane. Danny, irritated, looked back at the motor home rumbling along behind them. If she'd been driving that never would have happened. But she wasn't irritated with Amy. It was herself. She had come up against an obstacle in her head, and she couldn't understand it.

"What if she's dead?" Danny said.

"Reading her running-away note won't change that."

"Amy, for fuck's sake, don't make me say it." Danny felt a blush rising up her face. It burned, flaming beneath the raw skin. But she had to confess. "I'm scared shitless to read this note. I'm scared of what's in it."

Amy nodded. Then she said, brightly: "If Diggler survived, Kelley survived."

Danny felt a wave of despair pass through her, like ghosts. She needed the sane Amy with her now, not the queen of the non sequitur.

"Ah, Jesus, Amy. What are you talking about?"

"Diggler. He's a pig, right? Kelley's like ten times smarter than him."

"How is Diggler still alive?"

The smile melted off Amy's face and went all the way around the clock to misery.

"How can you say that?"

"Are we really having this conversation? Seriously, how do you know the pig's alive."

"He just is."

"That's irrational."

"So is driving in this direction. You can't fool me, Danny. I know what's up. You want to catch Kelley."

Danny made a noise of contempt and looked out the side window. "Don't be stupid. Less danger this way. Simple as that." Amy was nuts. Completely crazy.

Crazy like a fox.

Danny was silent after that, until the convoy pulled into Scobie Tree.

The town of Scobie Tree had dried up and blown away in 1958, when the military traffic along the roads into the desert settled down from the Cold War high. The place was never impressive: It had been a stagecoach stop 150 years earlier, then a silver mine opened up and kept a few hundred souls occupied for thirty or forty years until the automobile came along. A handful of folks stuck around to pump gas and change tires after the silver ran out; they made it as far as the Second World War, and prospered again briefly, then drifted away.

Now Scobie Tree consisted of a bunch of outbuildings (they always seemed to outlast the structures they were built to serve), an old brick hotel (then rooming house, and finally a good place to store whatever was scavenged from the abandoned buildings around it), a gas station, and a general store. There was a plaque bolted up on the gas station wall. A couple of scenes from the Robert Mitchum movie *Out of the Past* had been filmed there, according to the plaque.

Scobie Tree had one important thing going for it. About a mile outside the three-building town, there was a freeway interchange: The tail end of Route 114 met the 12A, and the 12A could take you to other, bigger roads anywhere you wanted to go—west to the high desert communities, north-west all the way to San Francisco, northeast past the Mojave to Las Vegas, or due east to Arizona.

It was a crossroads in the middle of nowhere. An ideal place to keep away from the living dead and still have some traveling options.

Danny was sure Kelley would have gone this way, because Kelley had privileged knowledge gleaned from her cop sister: There wasn't a dedicated police force anywhere in the area. She could run that shiny red Mustang at 120 miles per hour and not see a cop all day, unless it was a highway patrolman—and Danny had a police radio in the Mustang's glove box. Kelley would have known well ahead of time if there was a rogue Smokey in the desert.

Danny was sure she was on the trail of her wayward sister. And although she hadn't scraped up the courage to read the note, Amy had, and Amy didn't say anything to contradict Danny's thesis. Danny would read the note while they were stopped in Scobie Tree. She hoped she could handle it.

Danny got on the radio and explained how they would approach settled areas from here onward. She was going to take a tour of the town in the interceptor, and if she spotted any survivors or undead she would note their position and a party could go out and take the appropriate action.

Just outside town, Danny made Amy pull over and she hauled her boots on and got behind the wheel, body racked with stiffness. The two of them drove slowly up and down the grid of six short streets that composed Scobie Tree. There were foundation holes and the outlines of footings where buildings had been, and piles of paper-dry clapboards and framing wood where the structures had collapsed. A lot of hiding places if a zombie was prone. Danny remembered seeing some of them lie down in Forest Peak, although she didn't know if that was commonplace. They might have died for good. In any case, nothing stirred. The town was empty.

As they made the circuit back to Central Avenue (Scobie's brief claim to 114), Danny saw the motor home was no longer parked outside town. It was up at the gas station, and there were people swarming around.

"Ah shit," she said, and accelerated.

They were looting. No other word for it.

Troy was standing by the gas pumps, filling the motor home's immense tanks with diesel. The electric pumps were still getting power. He had his arms folded in an embarrassed posture as Danny pulled up. She popped the bubblegum lights on, and the survivors climbing in and out of the now-shattered front window of the general store dropped their swag and tried to look innocent. Danny was out of the car before the engine died.

"What the hell are you people doing?" she asked the nearest survivor. He was a midforties man, not tall.

He didn't answer her question, but spoke to someone in the crowd: "Shoemaker," he said, "tell her."

"I'm asking *you*," Danny said.

The one called Shoemaker stepped forward. "Let me handle this, Gluck," he said.

Like this is a fucking traffic ticket, Danny thought, and felt a spike of rage drive itself into her temple.

Shoemaker had an alert, serious face and made phony eye contact, looking very slightly not into Danny's eyes. Hawaiian shirt with a muted pattern, the only thing worse than a Hawaiian shirt with a loud pattern. *Probably a divorce lawyer,* Danny estimated. He was one of the men Danny had identified as troublemakers back at the rest area. He spoke in a low, confidential voice.

"Officer," he began.

"Sheriff."

"Sheriff, these people are hungry and they don't all eat brie and caviar, which is what's in that bus there."

Patrick emerged from the motor home with a big white plastic bag full of trash. He didn't look pleased. When he saw Danny was back, he rolled his eyes eloquently. Danny circled Shoemaker, but kept her gaze on the others ranged inside and outside the store. She raised her voice and was pleased to discover she could do so again.

"Listen up. Hungry and thirsty, I got it. You all didn't have the keys, though, so you broke in. That's a felony. We're still in America, and the law still applies. You are all guilty of breaking and entering, theft, looting, and I'm sure I can come up with more, depending on who grabbed what. We are not going to do it this way. I'm not in a position to make arrests, but if you want to roll with my group, you observe the law—"

"Sheriff," Shoemaker said, stepping slightly on Danny's speech. *Definitely a lawyer.* "You don't seem to understand the situation. I know you went through a lot back in that little town of yours, but we're not there anymore. Heck, this isn't even your jurisdiction," he added, turning to take in the crowd around him. There were nods and murmurs. "We need to stock up for what certainly looks like a long drive. Just where are we going, by the way?"

More murmurs. A couple of people picked their loot back up. Danny saw Michelle and her brother deep in the shadows inside the store. Troy, arms still folded, walked over to stand next to Danny. The big man with the goatee was standing by the motor home with his hand resting on the metal skin like he didn't want to risk getting left behind: She thought he was probably on her side as well, which was a surprise. She was grateful.

And she thought she had an answer to the question of where they were going that most of them would buy.

"I'm taking this stage by stage. We scope out an area, we move in. It could be there's none of those things out here at all. Life goes on as normal. In which case, what you have done here is even worse. But we don't know anything. The fact that you broke those windows may mean nobody has else stopped here. So the area could be clean. But we don't know. What if those things were inside? I don't see any of the people that live here. Maybe they're reanimated, right nearby. If they were in the store, you would have let them out. Those kids in there? How do we know there's not a zombie in the freezer behind them?"

Danny pointed at Michelle and Jimmy James. They involuntarily stepped forward to the window, away from the freezer with its magnetic floor-length doors. A great hiding place, in fact. Danny thought she should remember that. The kids looked scared to death, but she wasn't in a position to be delicate. It was probably the word *zombie* that got everybody on her side of the issue at last.

Now the survivors were shuffling away from the store, suddenly eager to get back to the safety of the motor home, but waiting for official permission.

"What's your first name?" Danny asked Shoemaker. There was authority in last names. She would keep him on a first-name basis.

"Ted," he replied.

"I had a deputy by that name. He's dead now."

"That sucks. Anyway, we're just grabbing some supplies and moving on, and I think you can cut everybody some slack if we're kind of in survival mode right about now, think so?"

Troy looked angry now. He stepped forward, well inside Ted's personal space, but he didn't say anything. The muscles in his jaw were jumping.

"How about the next people that come through?" Danny said.

Ted smiled. "They won't have to break a window."

Danny wanted to punch this glib cocksucker in the teeth. Her vision went red as she struggled not to lose her temper, the shadows filled with a blood-colored glow. Inside her head was a chaos of angry replies, shouting, fighting. Outside herself, she stood very still except for her fingers, which curled up into fists. But the line between inside and outside was hard for Danny to see. Then Amy was speaking from somewhere close behind her:

"Just remember, everybody: We don't have the medical facilities to deal with an infected bite wound. Nobody does. There isn't a working hospital for a hundred miles, maybe more."

That did the trick. They were back on the road within five minutes.

They motored up the 12A toward the Mojave Desert. There was no traffic, which seemed strange. Danny had expected they would run into heavy refugee populations getting away from the cities.

This time, Danny was in the driver's seat of the interceptor. She needed to project at least the illusion of control, or people were going to wander off and get killed. The radio was silent most of the time, except for the occasional lonely query from a unit somewhere out in the great, flat spaces. Danny wasn't the only cop alive. But all the living cops were alone.

"I lost five men," the first of these lonely voices told her. "One came back, and I let him in. He bit my arm. God help me, I blew his brains out. Now all I want to do is go to sleep."

Everyone she spoke to over the radio was the last of their force, having survived the initial onslaught essentially by luck. They were on an isolated call, or sick in bed, or in one case stuck on the road with a dead battery. Danny thought the cop who related this story, from the Martell division, was probably lying. Cop cars didn't get dead batteries. She tried not to blame him, but she did.

It looked like she was going to get away with her diversion into the desert. It did make sense, from a tactical standpoint, to get well clear of the population centers. She wasn't acting entirely selfishly. It was just that, given two equal alternatives, she had chosen the one that would most likely lead her to her sister. Perfectly honorable thing to do, not like sitting out the crisis in a police car on a remote side road somewhere. Not nearly as bad as that.

Danny was hating herself. She couldn't talk herself around to the idea that searching for Kelley with a bunch of fairly helpless people in tow was an okay decision. She knew damn well she was valuing one life above the rest—a life she'd failed to value enough before.

As she pulled out onto the deserted 12A, Danny looked back and saw one of the vehicles peel off from the convoy. It was a pickup truck with a camper shell on the back. The truck took the right-hand turn and headed south, the opposite direction. That meant there were now six vehicles, including the interceptor and the motor home, under her charge. If the entire Riverside contingent was in the truck, her little tribe of survivors was now six members smaller, as well.

They're dead, Danny thought, and felt a chilly curl of vindication in her belly. *Fuck it. Let them die.* The rest of her didn't feel that way, but there was a small and vocal minority voice inside her head that hadn't cared for people much, anyway, since she got back from the war. That voice was getting more airtime lately. She would have to watch that. It made the anger worse. She was starting to wonder if there was any difference at all between these people and the people she had confronted in the desert of Mesopotamia.

They had been on the 12A for twenty minutes when they saw the first zombie.

It was at least half a mile away across an expanse of dirt that had once been a cattle stockyard, back when there was water. Danny wasn't sure why she knew it was a zombie, but there could be no mistake. The figure was a short charcoal stroke on the bright, brown landscape, moving alongside a wire fence. Something about the way it moved.

Danny wondered what it was doing here. Hell, how did it get this far? She considered stopping to check the thing out, maybe neutralize it. But by that time, her charges would have had time to think again. They would have realized if there were zombies here, they could go another way where there might not be zombies at all. So Danny kept on going, hoping nobody in the motor home had seen it. The radio squawked, and Troy was speaking:

"Come in, Sheriff, you see? Over."

"Hundred-and-four, out."

She didn't want to discuss it.

A few miles later, there was a possible answer to the question of where the thing came from. The convoy passed a long pair of wheel ruts that eased over the embankment of the highway and abruptly curved down into the deep drainage ditch below. A medium-duty white stakebed truck was overturned at the bottom.

Danny hefted the shotgun out of its cradle inside the interceptor and knelt at the edge of the ditch. Three zombies down there, scrabbling uselessly at the steep dirt walls of the ditch, unable to get out. Danny stood up, then fired the weapon from her hip. The gun bucked in her hands, and one after another the monsters collapsed.

She walked back to the interceptor. Troy and Patrick were standing beside it, now, alongside Amy. Nobody had spoken a word. They stood and scuffed the ground and looked out across the huge landscape, with its arid, treeless mountains looming up above the highway on one side and the ever-expanding desert flats on the other, its far margin indicated in the distance by more mountains, a pale violet saw-blade along the horizon.

"What are we going to do?" said Troy.

"Keep moving," Danny said.

"Where?" Patrick asked.

"Away from these things," Danny replied.

"I get the feeling there's no 'away,'" Amy said. She was holding her elbows in her hands, rubbing them as if it was cold. In fact it was hot and they were starting to sweat in the sun.

Danny could feel the heat etching into her blistered scalp. She needed a hat. "If we keep on going, we will reach a point where the people that did this—" Here Danny pointed toward the overturned truck with her chin— "couldn't get to, before the change happened. I'm guessing what went down here is these things came to life and the driver wasn't expecting it. He lost control and crashed. Say there are others that didn't crash. How far did they get before the zombies started attacking? How long was it for us, five or six hours? Longer?"

Patrick looked like he was going to cry, but his voice was even and cool. "So what you're saying is this perimeter thingy of yours just got pushed out, am I right?"

Danny nodded, nudging a pebble around the edge of her shadow with her toe.

"Yeah. I gave it a hundred-kilometers radius. Sixty-odd miles from downtown. We're a hundred miles from downtown right now."

"As the crow flies?" Amy asked.

"By road," Danny said. But Amy wasn't really speaking to her; she was looking at some crows circling above their heads.

"I like crows. They're the most intelligent bird, did you know that?" Amy continued.

Irritated, Danny opened her mouth to speak, and as suddenly as she became angry, it was gone, erased by realization. There was method in Amy's madness. *The crows*, she thought. *Like that Hitchcock movie.*

"We should keep our eyes out for crows," Amy said. "They like to keep an eye out for dead things."

With that, Amy shoved the first-aid kit back into the trunk of the interceptor and went to sit in the shade of the open passenger-side door, leaving Danny to reel in her thoughts.

Patrick and Troy were squinting up into the bright sky, watching how the crows circled overhead with their sleek black heads cocked down at the scene. It was time to make a decision, Danny knew. Another decision. Always another. She could hear the hot wind keening through the desert scrub, the cry of a crow, and the idling engine of the motor home.

The whole world seemed to be waiting.

"Let's push the radius of our safe zone out another fifty miles," Danny said, calculating in her head, picturing the big map. "Joshua Tree or Twenty-nine Palms east, uh . . . Barstow north. Forget west and south. Lancaster and Palm Springs. Too many people."

"Palm Springs was full of zombies to begin with," Patrick muttered.

They were on the road again. Troy radioed to Danny a few minutes after they were rolling. "Come in, Sheriff, this is RV, over."

"Go ahead."

"There's been a lot of discussion while I was away. Thought you should know, out."

Danny's stomach knotted. *Shit.* Those stupid bastards were second-guessing her every move, of course. That slimeball Ted Shoemaker was probably the ringleader. There might need to be another come-to-Jesus moment pretty soon.

"Ten-four, out," Danny said, and hung up the handset.

Amy had her forehead against the window, almost as if asleep, but she said, "Too many control freaks, not enough Indians."

Danny didn't want to discuss it. "That was a damn good idea with the crows. Could save some lives," she said instead.

They drove in silence for a while, the mile markers flashing past on the side of the road. Signs for little desert towns that would probably be gone in ten years, zombies or no zombies. There simply wasn't anything worth staying for. The price of gas was so high, the weather that much drier.

People in remote reaches of America had started to drift back in, closer to the big places. It had happened in Forest Peak. Some families couldn't afford the commute down to the flatlands, so they moved. *Turns out not to matter,* Danny mused. Price of gas, length of commute, global warming. All wiped off the list of pressing concerns for an indefinite period of time— maybe forever. Her thoughts were churning, following no pattern. There wasn't enough information to start tinkering with a new working hypothesis yet. They would just have to see how far things went.

Instead, she tried to organize her memories of the last couple of days, to make some sense of the death and chaos. But all that came into her mind were snippets of irrelevant nonsense, like those envelopes of photo prints that accumulated at the back of a drawer when all the good ones were tucked away in an album: pictures of people's thumbs, accidental shots of shoes or the corner of a building or somebody blinking when they were supposed to say "cheese."

What the hell were the monsters that had stood up and started killing people? How could they be dead, and yet want to eat? Were they dead? Had the definition of death changed, and Danny was only slow to catch on?

That they could move, that their eyes could see, did not make them living things. They were no more alive than the closed-circuit cameras that clustered under the eaves of public buildings, craning their motorized necks to watch the passers-by. And yet, what made a man alive?

Danny struggled across this alien philosophical terrain, not knowing where to begin. What was life? Was it the intelligence within? The beat of a heart? The suck of lungs? Her comatose war buddy, Harlan, had been alive. Danny felt sure of it, even though she had sat at his bedside for a week and he'd manifested less life in a practical sense than these infected things. She had held his hand that felt nothing, looked into his eyes that saw nothing, and spoken to a mind that could not form thoughts, but it was still Harlan there on the bed with all the tubes and wires. Even though he would never come back. He was, in some way that Danny yearned to define, alive.

And these walking corpses were not.

Danny's thoughts were in shorthand, as ever. She thought all of these things, but in the minimum of words: *They're like security cameras. How come they're still dead even if they can move?* And: *Harlan's alive, even if he's not in there. So why aren't they?*

Then Danny found herself staring at Kelley's note fluttering on the dashboard. She tucked it back into her pocket, this time vowing silently to read it before the sun went down.

3

Sunset in the desert. The sky was a deep bronze bowl, molten red where the sun burned down toward its lip. Danny and her entire contingent of survivors rolled into the town of Riverton Junction.

Their progress was agonizingly slow: In the Mustang, on an ordinary afternoon, Danny could have made it here from Forest Peak in less than three hours. It had taken the convoy an entire day. Danny still hadn't looked at the note.

Another tiny place, Riverton Junction even owed its name to somewhere else: A train line passed through, running east-west with a spur line to Riverton, thirty miles north, where there was a profitable bauxite mine. This was nothing but the junction of the two lines. There were a dozen low frame houses and some trailers, spread out over a junkyard landscape that could otherwise have been on Mars. A church with a tin steeple. Some metal cow sheds from back when beef came this way by rail, headed for the several military installations in the area. And miles of barbed-wire fence. Riverton had one paved street that intersected with a road running alongside the railroad tracks. The rest of the streets were scratched into the dirt across it like the spurs on an old-fashioned television antenna.

What mattered was that Riverton had a gas station and a grocery store, although Danny wasn't holding out hope that either one would provide much selection. She had discussed their approach into town at a brief halt a few miles outside the settled area. The smaller vehicles at the back of the convoy would cruise the side streets, looking for signs of life, or zombies. Danny would ride point to the town center. The motor home would wait for the all-clear outside town.

Danny and Amy were alone as the last wafer of the brilliant orange sun slipped below the mountains to the west. The interceptor rolled to a stop in the middle of Leche Avenue, Riverton's main street. Danny took the place in at a glance. On one side there were a couple of commercial buildings—a feed and hardware store and a surveyor's office. On the other side was the general store, which wasn't any bigger than the Quik-Stop, and looked much poorer. Next to the store was the gas station with its three pumps. There was a big sheet-metal roof over the pumps, and even with the fading light the heat rippling off the roof was visible against the sky. It was ticking and groaning as it cooled. Hand-cut plywood letters on the roof spelled TEXICO, suggesting the gasoline available might be generic. What caught Danny's eye, however, was the tableau beside the pumps.

Three motorcycles were parked there, two choppers and a restored vintage Hog. There were three corpses, as well.

Danny warned Amy to stay where she was and sit low, then eased out of the interceptor, availing herself of the shotgun that came with it. She had no idea if the weapon was loaded, but regulations stipulated it should be.

Her mind slipped back in time to another desert not long ago, and she was filled with the kind of fear that borders on elation. Hide-and-go-seek with killers. She had always won the game, so far, and she thought she might be better at it than most people.

Danny scuttled crabwise from the interceptor to the recessed vestibule at the entrance to the store. No shots, no answering sound of running feet as hidden assailants ran for better cover. It occurred to Danny that she should have called Wulf to cover her. He was a badly damaged human being, but he was vigilant as hell and he could shoot.

The town radiated fading heat and emptiness. There were even tumbleweeds down by the railroad tracks. Danny slid along the façade of the store and knelt by the trash barrels at the side of the gas station lot. No signs of life. Even the dead weren't moving. She broke open the gun and checked it: It was fully loaded.

"Come out!" Danny called. Somebody had to be around. These people didn't die of mutual suicide. "My deputies and me are here to take you to safety."

No answer. Danny looked around her at the low, falling-apart buildings, the cracked pavement, the short, scrubby trees. There were a couple of old cars parked at the curb in both directions, in and out of town. Maybe the entire population was holed up in the church, or maybe they all got out of town in one school bus. Probably no more people lived in Riverton Junction than Danny had under her tender care in the convoy.

She decided to take a risk, because otherwise she could spend the rest of the night crouched by the stinking trash, and her knees were too sore for that. She rose slowly, holding the shotgun in a relaxed position, but ready to switch up if circumstances changed. Then she did her breathing for a few seconds and walked as casually as she could toward the gas pumps. It was the same casual walk she had developed in Iraq. It was bullshit, but you couldn't tell from a distance.

Two of the corpses by the scooters were dressed in dusty, worn-out ordinary clothing that had been washed too seldom, and yet too often. Locals. A man in his fifties and a woman some years older. The third corpse was a smallish man with a long mustache. He was dressed to ride, in chaps, leather jacket, and red bandanna. He had some very good boots on, and Danny found part of her mind wondering if they were her size. Her own boots were ruined, the soles melted and cracked.

All three corpses had been shot in the head. She squatted down among them, looking at the wounds. Then she heard a soft noise behind her and spun around.

Amy was out of the interceptor and strolling across the street. Danny made throat-cutting motions, but Amy just made them back. Hopeless.

"Troy wants to know if it's clear," Amy asked, in an ordinary speaking voice. Danny all but threw herself flat on the ground. This was exactly how to draw enemy fire.

"Obviously not," Danny hissed.

"That's what I told him. They say the rest of the town is empty."

"Awesome," Danny said.

"What's the problem here?" Amy asked. "We've been seeing dead people all day."

"Look at the blood," Danny said.

Two of the corpses, the locals, had bled the dark slime of the zombie. The biker had bled red blood, and plenty of it.

"Murder," Danny said, and Amy crouched down beside her.

Danny was trying to figure out what to do next. Whoever killed these three were well within their rights to shoot zombies, as far as Danny was concerned. But the biker was alive, red-blooded and aware when he went down. No matter how bad the situation was, murder was murder. Yet whoever had done this didn't seem to have a motive: The bikes were gassed up and ready to go. Didn't they want to steal them? Unless the bikes belonged to companions of the dead man. Maybe they had been attacked and were hiding somewhere. Danny absentmindedly reached over and touched the cylinder head of one of the choppers. It was hot, running hot. Now she had an idea. But at this moment, a sound was rising from the distance. She looked down Leche Street and saw the motor home rumbling toward them, the headlights like big bug eyes in the fading light. It pulled up behind the interceptor and rumbled to a stop.

Troy jumped down out of the driver's seat, and moments later several of the survivors came out of the side door.

"What the fuck," Danny said, standing up. In a target-rich environment like this there was no point in keeping low.

Troy hitched a thumb over his shoulder. "Ask him," he said, and knelt to examine the bodies. Ted in the Hawaiian shirt was coming up behind Troy, a look of vindication on his face. Patrick and Wulf, an unexpected pair, emerged together. Danny realized a few moments later that they were deep into an argument. Then Ted was standing at the curb, surveying the scene at the gas pumps.

"Did you kill them?" he asked. Danny's vision grew red again and she thought she was going to go over there and skull-fuck the son of a bitch with the shotgun. She counted to ten, breathed, and waited.

Then she said, "We have a murder on our hands here. And the murderer is probably still in town."

"Murder. As opposed to a mass epidemic of cannibal corpses."

Danny could see Ted was showing off for the bunch of survivors that were standing off to the side, listening. He must have been rehearsing his arguments during the long afternoon drive in the back of the motor home. She walked over to Ted and spoke quietly.

"What's your damage? You want to go off on your own? Go. There's nothing stopping you."

"Yeah, right," he said. "Off on my own, great idea. I have another idea: How about we all agree where we're going to go, together, in a group? Because you seem pretty determined to take us all to the middle of ass-nowhere."

"That's about right."

"And now we have to fart around here while you investigate a murder. What are you going to do, catch the guy and put him in jail?"

By this time, Wulf had disengaged himself from Patrick and was crossing the street, rifle tucked loosely under his arm. "Dude, cut the shit," he said.

"Seriously," Ted continued. Now he was facing the others, not Danny. "You gonna find the killer and put 'em in front of a judge? You know any judges that are still around? Or are you gonna pop 'em in the head like you do the zombies?"

Everybody was listening now. Troy and Amy and Wulf on Danny's side of the line. The rest in the street with the shadows gathering around them. Maria shoved her way to the front of the onlookers and pointed indignantly at Ted. "Why do you have to make so much trouble? The whole way, you make all this trouble!"

Danny turned to Troy: "How about you and Wulf go around the station and see if the lights work?"

"You want us to stick around?"

"I got this handled." She turned back to Ted as the other men walked off toward the garage office and repair shop. "There are laws. This is a country of laws. No matter what happens," she said.

Ted put his hands on his hips and laughed at the ground, bent over at the waist. A pose that reminded Danny of professional baseball players. The smile fell from his face. "Country? What country! We were trying the radio all the way down that mountain, Sheriff. You know what we found? Nothing. There's nobody *out* there. Got a nice satellite TV in that bus, too. *Nothing.* I think the country may be gone. And I think the laws are gone, too. We need new laws, even if they're temporary, like you don't get to run the show. We all do."

The floodlights under the tin canopy over the pumps popped and sizzled and lit up, and now the shadows were ten times darker in the town, but the gas station was lit up with a lurid greenish light that made the corpses look especially dead.

Danny didn't know what to say. Her arguments had run out. But she could change the subject. She picked up the shotgun, and the triumph in Ted's face went out like a shaken match. There was fear in his eyes. Then Danny shouted, unexpectedly loud in the quiet of early evening despite her cracking voice: "Okay, listen up! I know you can hear me. I got a twelve-gauge pump here. This is the sound of me shooting the Shovel Head cruiser."

Danny squeezed the trigger and a spurt of flame jumped halfway to the vintage bike. The roar of the gunshot was loud enough to make Ted throw himself to the ground, Danny was pleased to observe. The bike's instrument cluster blew apart and several holes speckled the immaculate paint of the gas tank. The bike toppled like a wounded buffalo and crashed to the tar. After about twenty seconds, the gunshot came echoing back off the mountains.

Danny could hear people running behind her, survivors deciding to get out of range of the crazy sheriff, presumably. Scrupulously not looking to see how Ted was reacting to her actions, she walked over to the nearest chopper and shouted again: "You hear that? Next I got what looks like an early seventies one-thousand Sportster Chopper with an eagle on the tank. I'm going to count to three, because I'm guessing you can't count any higher than that. One."

She could hear more people running away, and someone was crying. It sounded like Maria's voice.

"Two."

Danny cocked the shotgun. It made such a muscular sound. As she trained the barrel on the chopper, she wondered if this was a deliberate design feature. Now it was just what was needed.

"Don't shoot! For the love of God, don't shoot!" The voice came from beyond a shed out in the darkness.

An enormous biker came out of the shadows and stepped into the edge of the light. He had a huge gut, hands like catcher's mitts, and a black chin beard five inches long. His leathers were old and well-broken. Not a city biker like the dead man. This was all outlaw, as big as Wulf must have been in his prime. But he looked scared, his fingerless gloves raised to collar height. Danny turned to face him squarely, the shotgun pointed easy at the ground.

"Didn't hear us roll into town, Easy Rider?"

"Jesus, Billie Jean."

"Who's Billie Jean?"

"You blew her up."

The big man wanted to go over and look at the bike, but Danny put herself between him and the machines. Could be a weapon in one of the saddlebags. The biker slumped and rubbed his face in both hands. Pressed a finger alongside his sunburned nose and cleared a nostril with a violent snort.

"Hell, I guess it don't matter anymore."

"Down on your knees, hands behind your head," Danny said, advancing on the big man. She reached her handcuffs off the back of her belt, shotgun braced against her hip with its bore trained at the biker's waist. He dropped to his knees, hands up, but he was angry now.

"What the hell gives you the right—"

"Murder."

Danny circled around behind him and plucked a nickel-plated revolver from the back of his wide, studded belt. Skidded it away from her, toward Wulf and Troy.

"Has it been fired?" she asked, clapping the cuffs around the biker's thick wrists.

Wulf scooped up the gun and sniffed the barrel.

"Sure enough."

"You think I killed Mike?" the biker suddenly roared. Danny backed up a couple of feet, to see where this was going. "You think I done that to him?" He was enraged, his face the color of raw steak. He twisted around to look at Danny, his small eyes bright with hatred. There was spittle on his lips. "Ernie! Ernie, you jumped-up catfucker! Get over here!"

Danny turned sideways to take in both the biker and the shadows toward which he was directing his voice, out in back of the gas station where the wrecked cars were kept. Moments later a bizarre figure emerged from the darkness. It was a skeletally thin man with a long, curving body, like a weasel. He wore a beat-up beaver top hat with feathers stuck in the band, a leather cowboy-style vest, and no shirt. His thin arms were cabled with veins, he had the face of a much older man than the rest of him suggested, and he wore thick-lensed glasses that made his eyes look like twin goldfish. He held his hands up just high enough to indicate they were empty.

"Topper's all right," Ernie said, in a high, whistling voice. "You can take my word on it."

Wulf stood behind Ernie, taking him into custody simply by proximity.

"Up," Danny said. The big man called Topper heaved himself upright and walked over to the corpse of Mike without consulting her. He was muttering under his breath. He knelt beside his dead comrade and brought his cuffed hands down in front of his head, then reverently pulled back the sleeve of the corpse and slid a rag down the wrist, exposing a deep wound in which Danny could see tendons and bone. Danny had assumed it was a red handkerchief protruding from the sleeve, but the fabric had originally been white. Topper let the limb fall back and rose to his full height, towering up past Danny like an oak tree. Ernie spoke first: "See?"

Topper sighed, and the anger seemed to seep out of him. He wasn't done grieving, same as everybody else.

"He got bit back in Palmdale, where we came from," Topper said. "We rode this far but he couldn't go on, he lost too much blood. He said it was taking hold of him."

Amy knelt by the body now, shining a flashlight on the dead man's face.

"Did he show any symptoms? This would be a good thing to know."

"Not now, Amy," Danny said.

But Topper hadn't heard. He went on, lost in his thoughts: "He wouldn't have got bit at all except he went to his ex-wife's place to see if she was all right, and she wasn't. I don't know why he took care of her, she never did shit for him. But I guess you could say she took care of him after all, in a way."

"She sure did," Ernie said, shivering all over like a dog.

"So old Mike," Topper continued, "he had that piece on him, and he told us to get some beer from somewhere as a good-bye present. We turn our backs, he shot himself in the head. Sure, we shot the other two. They was already dead and lookin' for munchies. But Mike, he went and shot himself."

Ted pushed to the front of the onlookers. He spoke too loudly, probably trying to get his stolen thunder back. He'd been forgotten in all the excitement, and this was supposed to be his scene. "He did the right thing, man," he said.

Danny held out her hand to Topper, who was still glaring down at her. Topper extended his own cuffed hands, and Danny opened the bracelets with her key. She now knew what she wanted to say, how to respond to Ted's argument that the laws were gone.

"Ted here asked an important question. Until we get our country back, how can we have laws? No judge, no jury. And I'm not the executioner, whatever you people think. Lemme make this simple. Few days ago, this was a country with laws. Until we get that back, all we have is *rules. My* rules. You don't like my rules, it's a long way to run from here. Am I clear?"

Nobody spoke. Topper folded his thick, tattooed arms. Danny could see the globe and fouled anchor drawn on there among the other, mostly lewd designs. She stuck her hand out at him.

"Lance Corporal Danny Adelman. Three tours in Iraq."

Topper's surprise was almost comical. From the corner of her eye, Danny could see Ernie's glasses reflecting the lights as he looked back and forth between them, the enormous man looming over the small woman with the scorched hair. There was a long silence, broken only by the buzzing of insects around the lights.

"Semper fi," Topper said, and shook Danny's hand. Her hand hurt like hell, but she felt as much relief in that moment as she had driving out of Forest Peak. Wulf stepped up.

"Where did you do your time?" he asked Topper.

"Gulf War."

"Nam, '65 through '69. Spent the Summer of Love killing zipperheads, God love 'em." Wulf shook Topper's hand as well.

Then a petulant voice came out of the darkness in the street. It was Patrick, unimpressed: "Okay, ooh-rah everybody, we have the first in and the last out, can we get on with our lives, now?"

They slept on the rooftop of the grocery store. An old aluminum ladder provided access, and one of the survivors had dragged a charcoal barbecue up so they had light from the burning twigs heaped on the grill. The survivors had sorted themselves into vague groups, people having formed fragile alliances of one kind and another during the stressful but boring drive up the desert roads.

Danny sat up, her back against a vent pipe that jutted up through the roof. Amy was sleeping next to her, mumbling occasionally. She had her filthy doctor's coat wrapped around her like a blanket. Patrick was next to Amy, lying on cushions from one of the RV's deck chairs. The girl was sleeping under a pile of curtains with her little brother in her arms, with Maria snoring on the other side of him. The girl's name was Michelle, Danny had finally learned. She was talking a little before they dozed off, which had to be a good sign. Danny remembered seeing their mother as one of the undead: empty-eyed, mouth open, before the hunger set in. She had a perm, as Danny recalled, and her dress was soiled. Unless she was one of the things caught in the fire, she would remain like that until she rotted away. Danny hoped neither of the kids was thinking that far ahead.

That prick Ted was sprawled across the roof nearest where they had pulled the ladder up, probably so he could book out of there at the first sign of trouble. Various people were lying in between, under all manner of blankets, tarpaulins, and tablecloths. There was a young mother, a pretty woman with a small baby that never cried; Danny hoped the baby was all right. She should have Amy check it out in the morning. An undead infant wasn't something Danny wanted around.

There were a couple of college-age kids, too, boy and girl, who looked like they had been very well-cared for before all this happened. His name was Matt or Mark or something like that. Danny hadn't heard what she was called. They were not so much younger than Danny, but they were kids to her, untried by life, untempered in the hot forge of violence. There weren't many intact couples, Danny observed. Most people lost the person right next to them, somehow, and now they were all alone together. She was lucky to have Amy. What a stupid thing to do, coming back for Danny the way Amy had.

Danny silently toasted Amy's dumb courage, then took another pull on the hip flask she'd appropriated from behind the counter of the store. She chased the whiskey with a swig of beer from a warm can. Why wasn't she asleep? She'd been struggling not to fall asleep at the wheel all afternoon, going in and out of a trance that had her eyeballs spinning and her eyelids dragging down as if weighted. Now she was alert, though exhausted.

Topper and Wulf and the weasel-man Ernie were sleeping on top of the motor home. Or rather, the bikers were sleeping. Danny suspected the old derelict was probably as awake as she was, although lying down with the Winchester rifle cradled against his cheek. Troy was inside the motor home, the only person in the group who was close to the ground. But he had agreed to stay there in case something happened. If there was a situation, the driver of the huge machine should be able to take the wheel within moments. Anyway, he was safe enough, fairly high off the ground and surrounded by metal. There was no moon, but this far from mankind (*or the remains of mankind,* the voice reminded Danny), there wasn't any light clouding the sky, or smog or smoke. The stars made it down to the horizon, only blurring to the south—where, presumably, Los Angeles still burned.

The gunshot had come from the left. Danny took her eyes off the woman in black. The woman with an explosive device in her hands. In the farmhouse, at the front window, Danny saw the sand-scoured muzzle of an automatic weapon. She fired two rounds from the shotgun without an instant's thought, and the rifle jerked back into the house.

Danny whipped the shotgun around at the woman, only to see her falling. The black robes, the veil, were of much lighter-weight stuff than they appeared. They caught the thick, hot air as the woman fell, billowing up around her. The satchel mine tumbled from her fingers.

An instant later, a tank gun banged, and the farmhouse seemed to jump three feet sideways. Dust and smoke billowed out of the window in which Danny had seen the gun—

Danny awoke when she heard a squeaking sound. It was very late; she hadn't known she was falling asleep. She looked around and saw the ladder had been lowered over the side of the building. She moved carefully to the parapet and looked down. Below, in the street, Ted and a couple of others were rolling a car away from the store. Danny knew it was Ted because he wasn't on the roof anymore. Another person joined them down there, having completed the trip down the ladder. Danny looked over and saw Wulf was also awake, watching. He saw her looking at him and made an open-hands gesture: *Now what?*

Danny gave a dismissive flip of the wrist and settled back to watch the escapees roll the car away. They started it up outside town, but didn't put the lights on until they were well down the road. Danny supposed Ted was laughing at her, exhilarated to have outwitted such a formidable opponent as herself. When he was dying beneath the throat-shredding jaws of a ravenous corpse, maybe he would remember her, Danny thought, sourly.

She didn't feel like she was going to get back to sleep. Wulf was now sitting and smoking over there atop the RV. She hadn't known he was a smoker.

She opened her shirt pocket and took out Kelley's note. Threw some twigs on the barbecue. Then she hunkered down in the dim, red firelight, and read her sister's words, and when she was done reading them through for the second time, she wept silent and bitter tears until dawn.

4

It was time to get their shit wired down tight.

The following morning brought another bright, cloudless day. Three zombies were wandering the street at first light. Danny noticed Wulf waited for a while, probably so the people on the roof could catch a little more sleep, before he shot the zombies down. Several people didn't wake up even then.

Ted, Gluck, and the guy with the goatee had fled in the night, and a couple of others that Danny could only vaguely picture. She'd been too busy so far to become familiar with all of the faces around her, but she knew they'd be well-known within a day or two. And now there weren't so many of them.

The unexpected thing was that they hadn't picked up any stragglers while they were leaving the mountains of home; Danny had expected roads lined with hitchhikers and lost vehicles, but their way had been mostly deserted. If this was Kelley's route, it was a brilliant choice. Nobody knew it existed. They could make good progress on the journey ahead.

Before they pulled out, Danny arranged a foraging party, with orders to take only what they needed, and only part of what they found. She got everybody doing something. And she knew the reason she was keeping them busy: to keep herself busy. To take her mind off Kelley's note, which had slashed her soul open to the bone.

There was a whirling trail of dust behind the interceptor as it raced up the road out of Agua Rojo. Up ahead on the main road the RV was parked, less than a mile distant, with its tail of smaller vehicles strung out along the shoulder.

Agua Rojo was a fair-sized town, and Danny had told everyone to stay put while she "scouted for survivors." She didn't mention she was also looking for a red vintage Mustang. She'd seen a Mustang there, but it was the wrong color. There had been hundreds of bodies lying in the street when she arrived; Danny assumed they were ordinary corpses.

Danny looked back and saw the first of the zombies reach the pavement behind her, crawling out of their hiding places along the road. It would take them ten minutes to get within range of the survivors.

Danny raced up to the intersection, where several of her companions were standing around in a knot. She threw on the brakes and the interceptor rose up on its shocks. There was a zombie on the ground right beside the RV, with a fantail of black brains a few feet away. It must have been Wulf who shot it, based on the direction of the spatter. The grimy rifleman was at his post on the roof of the motor home, shading his eyes to look down the road Danny had come up. He raised the rifle and sighted down the scope. And whistled.

"You sure as fuck got some attention, Sheriff!" he hollered. Danny ignored him, sprinting from the interceptor to where Michelle lay on the ground, sobbing and gripping her elbow, blue hair hiding her face. Amy was bent over the girl, and Jimmy James was kneeling beside her, clutching his sister. There was a collection of frightened faces in each of the motor home's windows, looking down.

"Danny," Amy said, coolly. "Glad you could make it. Some zombies showed up while you were doing your thing."

"We need to get out of here. Did she get bit?"

"No, she fell on a rock. But it was *this* close, Danny."

Amy snapped her fingers under Danny's nose. Topper came storming around the RV, a claw hammer in his fist. "I found another one back over there and busted its head," he said. "Hey, look who's fuckin' back."

"We can talk later," Danny said. "There's a swarm coming."

"Wulf caught that one coming up out of the ditch," Topper continued, ignoring the urgency in Danny's voice. "It came after the blue kid there when she was trying to take a piss in the bushes."

"But don't leave us hanging again," Amy said, her voice low. "No matter how good you think your reason is."

So Amy hadn't told the others about Kelley. Thank God for that. It gave Danny the boost she needed to get back into leadership mode.

"We need to get out of this area," Danny said. "Lot of them coming up the road. But here's what happened. Those things, those zombies, they go dormant. You follow me? They go to sleep and *wait.* They just lie there until something comes along, and then they get up and move, okay? So no dead body is a dead body until there's a big goddamn hole in its head, do you understand? When I drove into town they were all dead bodies. When I drove out, it looked like a goddamn Halloween party. Hundreds of 'em."

She looked around at the faces inside and outside the vehicles, taking everybody in. They needed to absorb this lesson or people were going to die.

Wulf called down from above: "They're coming closer, Sheriff."

Danny ignored him. They had another couple of minutes.

Amy had Michelle on her feet. Patrick emerged from the motor home and guided the girl toward the steps. Her brother offered his shoulder to lean on. Between the bruises on her knees and the one she would soon have on her elbow, Michelle's hair wasn't her only blue feature anymore.

Danny pointed at the headshot zombie lying between her and the interceptor. "They could be anywhere. So here's the deal. The time of being private is over. I don't care if you need to take a ten-pound crap, you bring somebody with you. From now on, nobody goes anywhere alone."

"Except you," Topper noted. "You get to do whatever you want."

Danny got up close to him, fuming with annoyance. She needed everybody to get with the program, not change the subject. She had been scrupulous about avoiding any mention of Kelley until now, but Topper's accusation had lit her fuse.

She simply forgot herself.

"I'm looking for my fucking sister!" she shouted—and instantly regretted it.

Topper's pockmarked face registered surprise, then anger. He swung around and punched the side of the motor home with enough force to dimple the sheet metal. But he spoke carefully, without raising his voice: "Dammit, Sheriff, we all lost somebody. You want rules, here's one for you: None of this vigilante crap; we're all in this together."

He paused and looked up at the faces in the windows, the faces waiting to get the hell out of there. They could all see the swarm of zombies coming up the road now. People were pointing. Topper wasn't finished: "This country was built on the vote, let's have a vote."

Amy walked over to Topper. She raised her hand.

"I vote we go straight to the nearest military base. They can't shoot us—we're Americans."

Danny was boiling with shame and anger and defiance all at once. They didn't need a vote. She'd lost herself, so she'd lost control of the situation. They knew she had other plans. There was nothing for it—she would have to pretend she'd seen the light.

Maria shoved open one of the windows at the front of the motor home and pointed down the road at the horde of slow figures shambling toward them.

"Can we go now?" she asked.

They went.

5

The solid black smoke rose half a mile straight up into the afternoon sky, then blurred as if smudged by the stroke of a giant's thumb. It had taken Danny, Wulf, and Topper the better part of an hour to reach their vantage point above the base, high up on a mountain ridge. It took them less than ten seconds to realize there wasn't any refuge in Fort Irwin.

"It's on fire," Danny said to the crowd gathered around her.

"Our *safe place* is on fire?" Patrick said.

"Burning like love," Wulf said, and spat on the ground. Topper was the last one down the hill. "The ammo dump went up while we were watching," he said. "*Big* old bang, that made."

"Maybe a bunch of Army guys will come to put it out," Amy said, hopefully. Something clicked in Danny's mind. She had an idea, but she needed a name.

Danny rubbed her temples with both hands and felt hunks of brittle hair snap off. It was dawning on her that she'd been going about this all wrong.

She was desperate to find that Mustang, because if she found the car, she might find Kelley. *Might* find her, like she *might* find a giant gorilla at the local Wal-Mart. But she'd been dragging along this heavy tail of malcontents and feebles, dealing with their getting upset if she walked away for ten minutes. The whole process had become so unwieldy that Kelley could be halfway across the country by now, and Danny hadn't made it to the Nevada border.

Kelley's welfare was the dominant theme of Danny's waking hours, driving her crazier than she'd been before. Danny felt the bitter rebuke of that farewell note every time her sister's name came into her head. But there were little clues: Kelley wrote that she might decide to go to college, for example. Kelley was highly predictable, in Danny's experience. And not adventurous. She hadn't been many places. It didn't sound like Kelley planned to go anywhere new, just somewhere *away*. That narrowed the field to half a dozen places, and the only big college town she'd ever seen outside the Los Angeles area was San Francisco.

How much pain was inside that girl that Danny hadn't seen. Danny had been so wrapped up in her own crap that she failed in the single most important task of her life. Now Kelley was out there, maybe alive, maybe reanimated, maybe bloating in the sun, tangled up in one of those wrecks down on the 15.

What Danny needed to do was get these people to a safe place, as they had wanted all along. They were absolutely right—she needed to find a refuge like they wanted, with showers and beds and great big fences around it.

And then she would have some options.

"Amy, do you remember that helicopter demonstration?" Danny had changed the subject so fast, Amy was taken up short.

"What?"

"Before I went to Iraq. They brought that heavy lifter up over the mountains to demonstrate firefighting techniques."

"Yeah. And?"

"Remember where the chopper came from?"

"The sky? I don't know."

The name was flickering in the corner of her mind. She needed to check her map, but there was a real chance they could find refuge before nightfall. Danny pictured the massive helicopter with its bellyful of red firefighting dust, the white lettering on its tail, the insignia on the side, the name of its home base lettered across the cockpit door. She saw it in her memory.

"Boscombe Field."

Danny rode alone again, her thoughts turning in gloomy circles around her mind. She had already been forced to refill her flask from the bottle concealed in the trunk of the interceptor. You couldn't get a proper buzz on, in this kind of air. It wasn't the heat, it was the dryness. They were traveling on the old 379 now, a short leg that took them into the heart of the baddest badlands in a bad countryside. Then it showed a little pity and returned to the shadow of a spine of mountains in the Panamint Range that eventually led to Telescope Peak, the highest point in Death Valley. The mountain was already visible in the distance, jutting up eleven thousand feet above their present location. The convoy rolled past several accident scenes: a tractor-trailer overturned against some rocks. A motorcycle with rider, tumbled in a strew of chrome fragments around a curve. The rider's head was missing. Topper and Ernie stopped to see if it was anybody they knew.

In a place less than two miles from their destination, between two sandstone steeps where the intensity of the reflected sunlight was so bright it wrung the eyes, there was a highway patrol car. It was a Chevy Impala, a 9C1 police package model Danny had never had the opportunity to drive. It was parked on the shoulder with its driver's side door open. There was a green Buick Century a dozen yards in front of it. The Buick's front door was also open, and its hood was up. Danny slowed to a crawl. The patrol car was empty. She radioed back for the motor home to stop for a minute while she checked the scene. A coyote slunk away through the boulders—she had started seeing them everywhere.

Danny climbed out, shotgun in hand, and walked down the center of the road. Staying in the middle of the paved surface was a habit formed in Iraq, because improvised explosive devices were usually buried under the shoulders. But it was also an effective way to keep plenty of space between her and anything lurking among the rocks on either side. She found herself instinctually glancing at the ridgelines above her, looking for snipers, which was absurd. She was going to have to change her habits. Charlie don't surf. Zombies don't shoot.

There was something huddled at the front of the Buick.

Danny walked around the vehicle, giving it plenty of room. There was a cell phone lying on the ground, and beside it, turned upside-down, a dusty campaign hat, similar to the one Danny had lost. Hunched over the radiator was the highway patrolman. His body was swollen, already decaying. The back of his head had been smashed in with a rock; the rock still lay inside the engine compartment, lodged between the firewall and the plastic engine cover. There was blood spatter on the underside of the hood of the car. But whoever had killed this man hadn't taken his vehicle, which was strange. What was the motive? Danny was at once enraged to discover such a vicious crime, and analyzing the circumstances for clues. She wanted to smash the perpetrator's head with the same rock. She also wanted to know why it had happened at all.

She looked inside the Buick, and had part of the answer. There was a zombie in the backseat, lying on its back and staring at her. The thing had been hog-tied. It was still active, but appeared to be in an advanced state of decay, considering it couldn't have been dead more than three or four days. Then Danny saw it was the corpse of an old woman, with tangled silver-gray hair and skinny, wrinkled limbs. It couldn't turn its glazed eyes to follow her; rather it turned its entire head. And when Danny walked out of view toward the back of the vehicle, the zombie struggled into a sitting position and watched her through the rear window, its chin pressed against the seat back.

Danny heard scraping footsteps. Down the road, coming around the corner past a furrowed jut of stone, was an undead adult male. One of its hands had been wrapped with strips of cloth. The bandaging had been done while the thing was still alive, because the cloth was stained with red blood, not black. There were big, oily stains in the crotch of its khakis and under the arms. Now Danny thought she knew what had happened: This man had been bitten by the old woman in the backseat.

He'd tied her up and was driving down the road when the Buick broke down. The cell phone suggested he had called the police while the system still worked, or maybe he never got through and the cop rolled by serendipitously. For some reason he got paranoid, or the patrolman said something he didn't like—Danny thought the old woman was probably the subject— and the man smashed the officer's head while he was looking at the engine. But the man died of the infection before he could switch vehicles.

Danny was angry. She was in a state of near-permanent hangover. Her skin was blistered and sore, and she stank, and she hated this whole nightmare situation.

The zombie shuffled toward her. The motor home was around a bend, nobody watching. Danny considered the shotgun, but picked up the fatal rock instead.

She took a chance getting close. The zombie was secreting foul-smelling fluid from its armpits, crotch, and mouth, as if the heat was causing it to dissolve. Its eyes were nearly opaque, but the thing knew right where she was, mouth yawning open. Could it taste her? Smell her?

Whatever. Danny crushed its temple with a single hard swing of the rock, and when the thing collapsed, she threw the rock at its head with both hands. She thought of her deputies, dead because she had needed them, and she wished there was some kind of built-in justice in the world. But there wasn't. You had to make it yourself, and it was easy to get wrong.

Then Danny walked to the Buick, picked up the slain officer's hat, slipped the Beretta out of the holster on his belt, and went back to the interceptor. She saluted the dead with her hip flask and took a long, burning pull of the liquor. Then she swallowed a mouthful of stale bottled water, radioed the all-clear to the rest of the convoy, and moved on.

The convoy rolled to a stop at the gates of Boscombe Field. The sun was going down. They had left the 137 behind for an even smaller road called Ore Creek Highway. It ran in a series of straight runs joined by long curves—the old wagon route—along the edge of Death Valley. They were now at least a hundred feet below sea level. Dim crags, almost two billion years old, imprisoned a lunar plain of jagged rock and sand. Rumpled yellow hills rose out of the dust at long intervals. The landscape was inhuman, ancient. It seemed too harsh to support life. Yet there were Joshua trees and golden grass and gnarled creosote bushes, tough survivors half-buried in the grit.

Ore Creek Highway ran through a series of old flat-bottomed river washes, shaped like branched lightning on the map. It was surrounded by tan sandstone hills, worn down until they resembled the biting surfaces of immense back teeth. Beyond the hills were low mountains, lacquered with rust, and beyond those were the distant blue crags. The road was in poor repair, having long been relegated to supporting the scant local traffic of prospectors, eccentrics, and park rangers, for whom potholes and cracks were a negligible inconvenience.

But Danny's map had included the thing she was looking for: Boscombe

Field, represented by a tiny airplane silhouette, right at the edge of the valley in a place called Shoshone Springs. There was no town, only the air-field. The nearest settlements of any size were Lone Pine to the west and Pahrump to the east. There were a few tiny towns along the 190 that ran straight through Death Valley, but their populations were minuscule and Danny didn't think zombies could walk that far in the Death Valley heat. Unless a lot of other people had thought of hiding out at Boscombe Field, it would be an ideal refuge in which to spend a couple of weeks, waiting to see what happened out in the world.

Danny rolled up first, according to the system they had agreed upon, with the rest of the vehicles idling a quarter of a mile down the road. She was wearing the dead officer's hat and sidearm when she stepped out of the car. The airfield was laid out in the middle of a long, shallow slope of gravel that extended for another half mile before abruptly jutting up into fang-topped cliffs of dark dolomite. The entire installation was surrounded by a twelve-foot chain-link fence topped with accordion wire. It looked to be a couple of square miles in area. The entire near end of the place was paved, and there was a single paved runway jutting across the dirt beyond. Several helipads were painted on the tarmac at the near end, upon one of which squatted the big, red Sikorski S-61 Sea King helicopter Danny re-membered. Its five drooping rotor blades made it look as if the machine was asleep. Behind the helicopter, two large sheet-metal hangars dominated the field. A Cessna high-wing spotting plane was parked in front of the far hangar, and there were a couple of civilian aircraft visible behind the enor-mous building. Five large metal tanks were ranged along the fence at the back of the hangars.

There was a low control tower on the opposite side of the runway. Not far from the main gates, along the same axis as the runway, was a terminal building, according to the routed wood sign above the door. This was a low ranch-style structure with big, broad windows and a two-story addition at one end. Assorted sheds and outbuildings completed the infrastructure. Danny knew there would be generators and a machine shop. Because the Death Valley fire suppression arsenal was based here, there might also be emergency medical facilities. And there were probably showers.

Nobody was there. After a few attempts to raise someone on the radio and another with the interceptor's loudspeaker, Danny used the regulation bolt-cutters to lop through the chain that bound the gates shut. Then she drove through the gates over a cast-iron cattle guard, into the parking area in front of the terminal. There were no crows in the sky, but a couple of hawks circled a mile away at a tremendous height. Danny had seen no zombies and no sign of traffic on the road. This remote corner of the world appeared to be deserted.

She drove around the outsides of all the major structures at Boscombe Field, then up and down the runway, watching the surrounding landscape for the undead. Over the last couple of days they'd seen them occasionally, away in the distance, little apostrophes punctuating the empty desert. How they got where they were, and where they were going, it was impossible to guess. Danny knew that for every standing zombie she saw, there could be ten more lying prone, out of sight. She saw none here at the airfield, so she reported back by radio: "Come on in, White Whale and Minnows. There may be a few zombies, but I haven't seen them yet. Shut the gates behind you. This place could be sterile, and if it is we're going to keep it that way."

There was a collection of vehicles parked in the foremost hangar near the gates: In the front rank there was a small tanker truck for spraying firefighting chemicals, and a push-back tractor with wheels as tall as its body. Behind those was a light-duty pickup, an older sedan, a couple of golf carts, and a portable generator. In the back, hidden under a tarpaulin, was an immaculate 1957 Thunderbird with the original Starmist Blue paint.

Wulf emerged from the second hangar and gave the all-clear, at the same moment Topper got the generator going inside a big shed between the two hangars. Danny stepped out of the control tower building across the asphalt yard and raised her thumb in the air. They had already cleared the terminal building, and most of the survivors were inside it. Patrick hadn't yet joined the party; he was once again cleaning out the White Whale.

"Topper, let's do the perimeter together," Danny called. Topper sketched a salute and headed for the fence that surrounded the airfield. He took a position opposite Danny, with Ernie following after him. Wulf shambled toward the RV, one hand thrust down the back of his evil pants, scratching. Danny started walking down the fence, Topper keeping pace on the far side. All members of the search team were equipped with short-range walkie-talkies that Troy had found inside the first hangar, neatly pegged onto a charging rack over a workbench.

The paved runway surface was about three thousand feet long, and before they'd gone a quarter of that distance, Danny could feel the sun eating into her skin through the rips in her shirt. She was glad for the hat.

They all needed new clothes, except maybe Wulf. For him, four or five days in the same underwear was just the beginning. *If* he wore underwear, Danny reflected. The desert beyond the fence wobbled in the heat, the horizon lost in a salty haze. Danny could see a mirage of glittering water out there on the flat desert floor.

"I got a couple here, Sheriff," Topper said over the walkie-talkie, about halfway down the runway. "I'll drop 'em."

"No," Danny replied. "Wait for me."

She trotted across the tarmac to where Ernie and Topper were leaning against the wire, watching a pair of the undead lurch toward them over the margin of crushed gravel riprap around the fence. Topper had his dead friend Mike's automatic in his hand, but he refrained from the coup de grace according to Danny's wishes. Both bikers seemed to respect her commands, Danny was glad to observe. She'd been on her best behavior since Agua Rojo, and between that and taking most of the dangerous jobs herself, she seemed to have gotten everybody to trust her again.

Danny hooked her fingers through the fence and looked at the undead. One was a small Hispanic girl in a pink princess dress. She was missing her right arm at the shoulder, except for an elbow-length flap of skin that hung down her side. The other one was a portly adult male in boxer shorts and a wife beater T-shirt. His bare feet were in tatters. How the zombies got here, Danny could not imagine. Maybe they rolled off one of those trucks full of corpses. Maybe the things had walked all the way over the mountains. Maybe—Danny couldn't come up with anything. She looked at the little girl. She was wearing scuffed black patent leather shoes with straps across the instep. Kelley had always wanted a pair of those when she was small, but had to make do with no-name running shoes from Wal-Mart instead.

"Let's take 'em down," Topper said. He was obviously unnerved by the walking corpse of the child.

"No," Danny said.

"Is this one of your rules, or is it a law?" Topper said, turning to face Danny. Maybe her hold on them wasn't as strong as she thought.

"Let's watch them. We can see if they have any problem-solving ability. And they'll show us any gaps in the perimeter."

Ernie nodded vigorously. "She's good, Topper. You should ask her out," he said.

Topper handed Ernie the gun.

"You keep watch, Cochise."

Despite its name, the terminal building wasn't so much a waystation as a bunkhouse, loosely modeled after the live-in facilities of a fire station: There was a communal kitchen, a dining hall, and a recreation room, both leading off a broad foyer at the front door. There were large bathrooms with multiple stall showers and wall-length mirrors over counters inset with half a dozen sinks. One was marked *Aviators* and the other *Aviatrixes*; the male facilities were twice the capacity of the female ones, reflecting the demographics of the relatively male world of aviation. In the upstairs addition was a long dormitory with three small private rooms, each with two single beds, and communal sleeping quarters with bunks for another twenty people, divided into male and female rooms. This arrangement was usually altogether empty, but during an outbreak of wildfires the entire place would be crammed with pilots, firefighters, and ground crew.

Between the canned goods, the showers, and the commercial washing machine, the survivors felt like they'd landed in heaven. Danny was no longer the crazy hard-ass cop. She was their savior.

6

Amy took the second-to-last shower. Among the women, only Danny had yet to bathe. It was the fourth night of the disaster, the fifth night since Kelley ran away, and they had, at last, found a scrap of normalcy in the mad universe.

The hot water seemed to be inexhaustible and there was a gallon jug of cheap strawberry-scented shampoo. The lights were on, there was a thousand-gallon tank of diesel feeding the generator, and everybody had feasted on boiled rice, Vienna sausages from jars, and succotash from a huge tin that reminded Danny of the spilled jalapeños on the floor of the Wooden Spoon, and therefore of scorched human flesh. She had skipped the meal on the pretext of checking the perimeter one more time. But the rest of them were fed and clean and feeling a little more secure on the safe side of a twelve-foot fence.

The two zombies, the man and the girl, had wandered listlessly along the wire for a couple of hours, but showed no intelligence at all. They clutched at the fence mesh and hung their mouths open and moaned periodically, staring at the lights that burned in the buildings, but they didn't have the wits to creep toward the gate, or climb over or dig under the fence.

Danny was also keeping herself scarce because she didn't want to listen to the compliments and enthusiasms of her motley band of survivors. Some of them, like Michelle and her brother Jimmy James, remained subdued, their grief still fresh. The college-age couple, Martin and the girl, whose name Danny was not surprised to find was Pfeiffer, were also sad and kept mostly to themselves, sitting on the brown Naugahyde couch in the rec room with their backs to four shelves full of *National Geographic* and aviation magazines.

At last, however, most of them were upstairs or in the rec room and Danny was able to slip unobserved into the aviatrix's room, where Amy was luxuriating under an old-fashioned sunflower showerhead. Danny pulled off her boots and unbuttoned her shirt, but she didn't want to stand around naked in front of the big mirror on the wall over the sinks. She wanted to get straight into the shower.

"Hey, Amy," she said. Amy jumped, spun around, and wiped the suds out of her eyes.

"Don't scare me! I have this fear thing."

"Sorry," Danny said. She contemplatively picked a couple of chunks of fried hair off her head. She glanced sidelong at the mirror and saw what the others saw: She was an apparition, covered in dirty, peeling skin, the flesh red and raw underneath. Lips like fried bacon. No eyebrows, no eyelashes, her hair a mass of rusty gristle, burned to stubble in front. Her ragged uniform was so filthy it looked like camouflage cloth.

"What," Amy said.

"You read Kelley's note, right?"

Amy rinsed the shampoo out of her hair, bent double so the water ran her hair into a point that hung from her forehead. She didn't answer right away. Danny figured she was trying to second-guess which one of the five hundred points addressed in the note Danny wanted to discuss.

"Yeah," Amy said, drawing the middle of the word out into a question.

"Are you really into women?" Danny asked.

"Not if they smell like you," Amy said.

In the end, Danny had to shower with the water almost entirely cold; her skin was so thoroughly burned, scraped, cut, and bruised that the hot water felt like boiling pickle juice. Still, she stayed under the cool spray for a long time, allowing the dead skin to soak off and gently working out the worst of the burnt parts of her hair. Then she put on the clothes Amy had gathered for her: an extra-large T-shirt that went to her knees, and a pair of disposable Tyvek painter's pants from one of the hangars.

Stinging all over, but much refreshed, Danny allowed Amy to lead her to the motor home, inside which Patrick intended to stay the night now that it was safely behind a fence.

It was around 10:00 P.M., with a deep black sky frosted with stars overhead. A man named Simon, an accountant by trade, was taking first watch up in the control tower. Beyond the gates, Danny's interceptor was parked facing down the long slope of Boscombe Field Road: she had decided to leave it out there, she explained to the others, to serve as an indication that someone was in residence at the airfield. Depending on the motives of such travelers as might happen by, it would serve as a welcome—or a warning. The zombies wouldn't care.

"Look at you," Patrick said, spreading his arms and smiling. Danny was touched to realize he was genuinely pleased to see her. There were bags under his eyes and his skin was chalky. But he'd put on a clean shirt from one of the hidden closets in the bedroom, there was music playing low and soft on the seven-channel sound system, and the interior of the White Whale was invitingly clean and orderly. Danny saw a small framed picture of Weaver on the wet bar. There was a narrow black ribbon draped across one corner of the frame.

Patrick gave Danny a hug, rubbing her back. Then he held her at arm's length and looked straight into her eyes with a look of concern he'd perfected on television when revealing to hapless homeowners that they had made fatal decorating decisions.

"Sheriff D., I have to ask you something embarrassing."

"Okay," Danny said, thinking, *This is the night for embarrassing questions.* Amy was looking in the fridge of the galley kitchen.

"What," Patrick asked, "did you do to your back?"

Danny felt her face go hot and redder than ever. She looked around for help. Amy was scrupulously avoiding eye contact, head halfway into the fridge.

"I got burned," Danny said. "In Iraq."

Patrick nodded. "So that's why there's a running joke about 'you got wounded but you won't say where'?"

"Yeah. They all know I broke my leg, but they don't know what else. When I say 'they,' I mean back in Forest Peak."

"Have you ever heard of 'La Mer'? It's a skin cream."

Patrick bustled off to the bathroom and emerged with a small jar.

"This stuff is a hundred twenty bucks an ounce. Great for scars, burns, the works."

"Amy gave me this stuff called 'Bag Balm.' It's like five bucks a pound."

Amy chimed in: "It's for cow udders, but it greases up the old scorcheroos on Danny, too. I don't think that Mer stuff would last for more than a day. Show him, Danny. It's amazing."

"Uh, no," Danny said.

Patrick made a face and set the jar down in front of Danny, who was now sitting on one of the bar stools. Danny indicated the bottles locked in the cabinet behind the bar.

"You got any Black Label?"

"I can't believe it," he said, his eyes growing wet.

"What."

"The only reason I have Black Label is Weaver liked it."

"Peas in a pod," Danny said, thirsting for a drink. She watched Patrick fool around with glasses and ice cubes for what felt like a year and a half, but at last she had the drink in front of her, swizzle stick and paper napkin and everything, like in a real bar. Amy was sitting on the couch by now, head tipped back. Danny drank most of the scotch and then pretended to savor the rest.

"So what brings you estimable ladies to my humble abode?" Patrick asked, fussing around. He was getting self-conscious, Danny saw. She hated that. She wanted to relax, and he was feeling awkward.

"I'm looking to feel normal for a few minutes. You have a drink, too," Danny suggested. "These may be the last ice cubes on earth."

Two hours later, the three of them were fairly well plastered.

Troy Huppert lay on his bunk with an open window beside his head, listening to faint sounds of revelry coming from the RV. It was good to know that Danny Adelman was letting what was left of her hair down. They all needed her to take care of herself, and that included R&R. Troy liked her as a person. She'd been one of the first people to welcome him to Forest Peak and mean it. But Troy also needed Danny to keep herself alive and functional for another, more selfish reason: He was probably second in line to command the group, if Danny was out of commission.

Troy was a capable leader and an effective part of any team, but he never imposed his personality on a situation. That came from the inner-city upbringing. You could join the ever-escalating gangsta sweepstakes and walk with the most elaborate bop, wear the latest fashions, and live in a state of crippling self-consciousness at all times, or you could fade into the background and make your small plans to get out of town.

Contrary to popular imagery, life in Watts wasn't, for most people, a battle with gangs, drugs, and the lure of easy money. There *was* such a battle, and it was waged right out in front of decent folks' homes, but most of them weren't involved in the party. Most of them were living three generations to a house, putting together an income one month at a time. The problem was jobs. If you wanted to work, you spent half your time finding it and the other half doing it.

Troy had gotten out of town. Way out of town, until he was what his grandmother referred to as a "nigro pioneer." He was living up in a remote, wild place where most people were white. He was trailblazing. It wasn't intentional. He'd never even heard of Forest Peak. He had been a trainee at the fire station five blocks from the house he grew up in. There was a notice on the bulletin board: summer training program for wilderness firefighting. That was where the overtime was. Fighting blazes during the ever-worsening wildfire seasons, deep in the mountains where rich idiots built mansions. He was in.

Two years later, he was still in, and settled in Forest Peak. No mansions there. But every morning he woke up feeling free. Who gave a damn if he was the only brother in town? The other dudes at the firehouse knew he was cooler than them. They welcomed the change. And he knew somebody had helped make all that possible: The locals figured if they could have a lady sheriff, they could even have a colored fireman.

But now it was only the lady sheriff between him and leadership in a time of unprecedented crisis. He didn't feel like he was ready for it. Amy the veterinarian was Danny's understudy, but she wasn't a leader. She was the sidekick type. Troy listened to the faraway laughter and wondered how many of them would be called to lead, regardless of their qualifications, as the boldest among them continued to die.

•

Danny woke up suddenly from a dreamless sleep. The sun was slanting in through the windows. The air-conditioning hummed in the ceiling. She was disoriented for a few seconds: strange bed, strange room. Then she understood where she was: she'd passed out inside the motor home. It was morning. She was still alive, so her schedule of watches must have been kept overnight. A surge of panic hit her, but she stayed still. If something was wrong, she would have heard about it. Boscombe Field was apparently still peaceful. Danny yawned and stretched, which hurt all over. Then she rolled over and saw, on the bedside console, the empty jar of La Mer cream.

She stumbled down the short passage past the bathroom into the living area of the RV, the empty jar in her hand. Patrick was lying on the converted sofa bed, watching a movie on the big TV that flipped out of the bulkhead wall. The sound was almost inaudible. Danny ran her fingers through her hair and realized her scalp felt cool and her fingers were running through a downy layer of short fluff, not hair.

"Good morning," Patrick said, as Danny ducked back into the bathroom for a look in the triple-view mirror. Someone had cut her hair to about half an inch long, all over her head. Only in a few places was there any trace of the burning.

"Did you cut my hair?" Danny asked.

"Yes," Patrick said. "I had to wait till you passed out, though."

"And what about this?" She emerged from the bathroom and held up the cream jar in what she hoped was an accusatory manner.

"It's empty," Patrick said. The movie on the TV was in black and white and Gregory Peck was in it. He was a submarine captain. Danny had no idea what movie it was; the only thing she'd seen Gregory Peck in was *The Omen,* on television. Her father had let her stay up late to watch it.

"Yes," said Danny. "I noticed that, too. And I was wondering where all that cream went."

"On you, of course. Your arms, your face, and your back."

"So you've seen my back?"

"And more. You have no secrets from me, Sheriff D."

Danny's face turned red. She was blushing so hard her ears were hot. *Way to go, have a blackout in front of people,* the voice said. And: *Now he knows you're deformed.*

"I must have passed out."

"It was your idea to put the cream on," Patrick said. "You ate some of it, if I remember right. But the haircut was my idea. I didn't want you shedding all over the bed."

There was no judgment in his voice, he had no problem making eye contact, and if he felt any kind of revulsion for Danny's condition, he was hiding it extremely well. Which Danny knew by now he was incapable of. So, incredibly, he must have had no problem with it.

"It's disgusting," Danny said. "My back."

"It's impressive," Patrick said. "I assume you got burned in the line of duty?"

"Yeah. Hit an IED—an improvised bomb—on the side of the road in Basra. Blew our M3 Bradley upside down, with me in it. My buddy Harlan got thrown out, except for part of his brain that stayed with me. Fuckin' thing caught fire, so I crawled out and went after Harlan and I didn't even know I was on fire until one of the other guys started throwing dirt on me."

As she spoke, Danny felt an immense, almost physical weight lift inside her, like an iron plate that had been clamped down on some part of her mind. A sore, cramped, mental limb was free again that had been bent double all this time. She had never told anybody outside the military exactly what had happened that day, not even Amy. Now, in a few words, it was out. She was trusting Patrick with things she didn't trust to herself, and she didn't know why. Along with the rush of freedom inside her came a rush of fear, like parachuting for the first time.

"Don't tell anybody," she said, too quickly. It felt ridiculous to have said it, and she understood on some level that she was letting Patrick down, dishonoring him by doubting her own trust in him. "I mean I know you won't, but I never—"

Patrick raised a languid hand.

"Lie down, I'm safe," he said, and patted the bed beside him. Danny took a chair by the bed. It was the best she could do.

"What movie is that?" she said, desperate to change the subject.

"*On the Beach.* Gregory Peck, Ava Gardner, and Fred Astaire. And Anthony Perkins one year before *Psycho*, with the worst Australian accent you ever heard. It's about the end of the world, this cloud of radiation that circles the planet and kills everybody except in Australia, where they have a few extra months. And it's what they do with their time until the cloud comes."

"No shit. How can you watch that?"

"Under the circumstances? I'm looking for ideas."

"Did you ever see *The Day the World Ended*? That was awesome. I saw it when I was six. It scared the hell out of me . . . Also black and white," Danny concluded, lamely.

"Starring who?"

"It has a three-eyed mutant with extra arms."

"I see. We also have *Night of the Living Dead* here. Weaver's choice, not mine. Maybe we should watch it to see if there are any pointers we could use."

"Weird how much this situation . . ." Danny trailed off, thoughtful.

That was something that mystified her. The real plague was so similar to the made-up one in the old movies. Not in every way, of course. But the idea that it bore *any* similarity was weird. How could the dead get up again? That was strange enough. But the dead eating the living—it was as if God was having a laugh at mankind's expense. Or the other way around. The theory had been forming in Danny's head that this disease must be engineered somehow. She didn't go in much for theories that lacked practical applications, but the more you knew your enemy, the more you knew how to win.

"You know how they figured out how to splice genes to order?" Danny said.

Patrick's eyebrows went up. "Apropos of what?"

"What's 'apropos'?"

"I mean where did that come from?"

"Zombies. Real zombies. We're talking about old movies, and I'm wondering if maybe the Iranians or North Korea or somebody has a disease factory set up and made this thing to order. Especially North Korea. I hear their guy, Kim Jing Ding or whatever his name is, he's a big movie buff. Maybe they chopped up some DNA and sewed it back together for him. A little of this, a little of that, right? And made a zombie disease."

Patrick shook his head. "Jesus, I don't know. I'm still trying to get my head around everything that's happened, and you're doing detective work to figure out whodunit."

Danny stood up and ran her fingers over her short-cropped head again. Patrick was right. No point speculating on the big picture. She was thinking way ahead of where they needed to be.

"I gotta go see if my uniform is dry yet," she said.

"How does it feel?" Patrick asked, as Danny reached for the door handle. She paused.

"I guess I'm glad I told you."

"I mean how does your back feel? We rubbed two hundred bucks on it last night."

In the end it came down to this, once the supplies were counted and the rate of burn estimated: They could last a month without ever setting foot outside the airfield fence, if they lived modestly. Food was the shortest supply. But foraging parties could probably reach out into the sparse communities around Boscombe Field and put together enough sustenance for another few weeks, after which they would have to venture into the big cities.

A long-distance supply run would have been the perfect excuse for Danny to leave the airfield for a few days, but nobody liked the idea. Ultimately Danny didn't argue the point. They could wait until the supplies were low, then make the foraging run. It was all the same to Danny.

She was leaving either way.

7

There was a narrow slice of moon hung low in the starry sky. The night was hot, but a little breeze was blowing down off the mountains and it might be quite chilly by morning. The Milky Way arched up through the velvet darkness, a bridge of stars halfway to infinity, and the world below was bathed in darkness and quiet. A hermit come down from the mountains would not have known there was anything amiss. Boscombe Field showed a couple of cheerful lights in windows, the generator rumbled in its shed, and except for the evening watch patrolling the perimeter fence, it was a scene of reassuring order and calm. Danny didn't like it.

She wasn't the only one. On her patrol around the airfield, Danny found Wulf sitting in the depths of a hangar doorway. He was staring out into the darkness beyond the perimeter. Danny studied his profile. His skin was so wrinkled, each line as sharply defined as a razor cut, that he almost appeared to have been shattered and reassembled by someone unhandy. His bent, purple nose and the wilderness of yellowed whiskers beneath it caught the overhead light and seemed to glow on their own.

Danny wanted to thank Wulf for saving her life and Amy's, but she knew he'd shrug it off with a curse. He liked shooting the undead, that was all. She saw that he had a way of moving his lips as if speaking, even when he was not. She wondered if there was a voice in there, below the surface, making his lips move. She wondered if she moved her own lips when the voice was speaking inside her own head.

Then Wulf spoke aloud, surprising Danny: "You having trouble sleeping, Sheriff? Nightmares?"

"None of your business."

"I been there. Come back after three years in combat, nobody gets what you been through, so you shut them out. Can't keep a relationship going. Sent that man of yours packing, right? Don't let anybody too close. Feelings are dangerous. You even kept your little sister at arm's length."

Danny didn't like this line of reasoning at all. This old bag of shit wasn't allowed to mention Kelley.

"We were talking about you, not me."

"I'm talking about both of us. Can't trust people, don't like surprises. Always got one eye on the tree line looking for VC or the Mujahideen or whoever it is, other eye still seeing what you went through back there . . . Ain't no way to live."

"If I want a shrink," Danny said, with great dignity, "I'll find one that lives indoors, okay?"

Wulf spat on the ground and turned to confront Danny, and now the light caught only half of his face, like a close-up picture of a quarter moon, with the rims of craters and mountains lit up on one side, and darkness on the other. His one illuminated bloodshot eye glistened in its nest of ravaged skin.

"Every day it gets a little worse," he said, and spittle flecked his beard. "Right now you can bury yourself in the job, folks think you're a hard-working little girl. But ten years from now, if you're still around, the ghosts will still be crawling up on you, the enemy coming to kill you in the dark, and you'll be drowning the sons of bitches in alcohol just so's you can get out of bed. And one day you won't even go to bed. Then we can talk about *me*."

"You're not telling me anything I don't know," Danny retorted. "Post-traumatic stress disorder. Yeah, I got it. Yeah, I can handle it. Not everybody that goes through combat ends up a fuckin' derelict like you."

Wulf wasn't listening. He was looking out into the darkness again, combing his beard with his fingers.

"Every night your buddies die in the mud again, and you kill some foreign shithead right back for it, and you bury 'em all in the back of your mind. Every day, you're surrounded by civilians so goddamn useless, they couldn't pour piss out of a boot if the instructions were written on the bottom. It makes you mad, don't it? Makes you so damn mad you hate your friends for it. You get to feeling pretty alone after a while. And then, a while after that, you *are* alone."

"And what do you do about it?"

The question came out of Danny's mouth without her permission. Wulf had her full attention. She wanted to know if he had an answer, despite the shape he was in. Maybe something that would work better for her than it worked for him. He turned his old eyes back upon her, and Danny felt a dislocated sense of shame again.

"I go camping," Wulf said. "I been camping pretty steady since nineteen hundred and ninety-one."

Danny walked into the tower building. The downstairs consisted of an office and a place to park a vending machine; the rest was occupied by a flight of perforated metal stairs leading upward. She paused to inspect the contents of the vending machine—it was the usual assortment of brand-name candy and weird snack items nobody would ever eat. *Unless they were surrounded by zombies and there was nothing else,* the voice reminded her. Amy came in through the same door behind Danny, yawning. Danny waved her away and put her boot on the bottom step of the stairs. Amy put her hand over Danny's, pressing it to the handrail.

"Wait," Amy said. "I'm worried about what you've got in mind."

"I got nothing in mind," Danny said.

Amy was looking right through her. "Now that we're here, you're thinking of going off alone."

Danny turned her eyes to the window. She could see nothing there but her own reflection. "Why do you say—"

"Listen," Amy interrupted. "I read Kelley's note, and I know you. You don't like people handing you problems you can't solve. It's gotta be eating you up. But there's two ways it can go. Kelley is alive, or Kelley is not alive. In either case, your job is to keep on living. No lone wolfing it."

"Where do you get that idea?"

"Come on. You know it's true."

Danny scrubbed her face with her hands, stinging both face and hands, neither of which were fit to be scrubbed. She felt tired and itchy and stupid again. She didn't want to be questioned.

"I gotta find her, Amy. Even if she's one of them. In her letter she said I promised to come back and I never did. I gotta do better this time."

"That guy Patrick. You passed out but I stayed up with him. While you were snoring, he was crying, all last night—because of his friend Weaver."

"Yeah, but he knows Weaver is dead. Kelley's in mumbo."

Amy laughed out loud: "In limbo, you mean."

Danny was angry again, emotion flashing up. She wished it wasn't so much easier to be pissed off than to try to figure everything out and explain herself.

"Okay, limbo. Big fucking deal. You said we were in Doom Valley before. It's Death Valley. You always call things the wrong thing."

Amy was not set back by this speech. She laughed again, fondly, and that was even worse. Danny didn't want Amy to be affectionate with her. It made her plans harder to carry out.

"You got a damn weird sense of humor, you know that?" Danny said, looking for a reaction.

Amy smiled, but now her eyes were sad. "And you have no sense of humor whatsoever. It's a part of your charm. Things will get back to normal, Danny. I think they will."

Danny flailed her free hand around her head, shooing the idea away. "For who? The survivors? The zombies? Normal is gone."

Danny pulled away from Amy and walked up the perforated metal stairs to the control tower. She could hear the door below slam as Amy left, and she felt guilty and mean.

The control tower's air traffic control room was a small space, with walls of green glass that angled sharply outward from the bottom to the top to reduce glare in the daytime. Maria was at the radio. Most of the gear looked ancient and barely adequate, the technology utterly outmoded. But the satellite radio was extraordinarily good gear for such a remote outpost. Danny got the sense that they had built this place to expand, but had never expanded it. Except for the glorious communications device before which Maria now sat.

"How long have you been at it?" Danny asked. Maria carefully rotated a coffee cup on the console so that the handle made a full circuit.

"Since morning."

"Take any breaks?"

"A couple. I'll sleep up here for now." She looked exhausted, her brown face yellowish.

"Save your energy," Danny said. "We'll be here at least another week, no matter what happens, okay? If they heard you, they heard you. They know where the signal is coming from."

"Who is they?" Maria asked.

"I don't know," Danny said, and wished she had any talent for lying.

A bad liar, but perfectly capable of omission, the negative space surrounding a lie. Danny had intended to wait another night, to make sure things were entirely quiet and everyone was settled. But after tonight's unpleasant interviews, it was time. She'd had the plan in place since before Riverton Junction, but originally it was supposed to be a kind of side venture along with protecting as many living people as she could. Now, however, the people she had were safe enough. She could easily be back before they ran out of supplies. Unless she died, in which case it was a moot point. But they were only going to hold her back, and make speeches about how fucked up she was, and wander off to piss in the bushes and get attacked by zombies.

There were a couple of gallons of water stashed in the interceptor, and some energy bars. She had enough ammunition to stage the end of *The Wild Bunch,* thanks to the zeal of the California Highway Patrol purchasing department. She even had a box of Road Blocker rounds, shotgun casings with a single ball inside, capable of penetrating an engine block. And she had Kelley's note, once again tucked in her shirt pocket. She waited until one in the morning, pretending to sleep on the couch in the downstairs office of the tower. Maria was snoring upstairs. It was time.

One of the light aircraft parked on the edge of the tarmac was a high-wing Piper, and the tip of its wing was only a couple of feet from one of the pressurized fire retardant tanks. These tanks stood higher than the fence, and less than four feet away from it. The fence was there to keep people out, not in. Danny's presence around the airport at all hours was expected by the watches, so when Simon, sitting out his watch in the control tower, saw her walk across the pavement with a rucksack in her hand, he thought nothing of it. She moved off into the shadows behind the hangars. It didn't occur to him to make note of her return, so he didn't realize it never happened.

The interceptor was parked on the far side of the illuminated area beneath the single exterior light that burned above the airfield gates. That was also part of Danny's plan. A watchman's eyes would get accustomed to the darkness. From the tower he could see miles of desert. But he would have one blind spot: the glare of that single light. The light was exactly positioned between the tower and the interceptor.

When Danny pushed the car down the shallow slope of Boscombe Field Road, following the example of Ted and his fellow escapees, Simon didn't see it. Whether or not he saw the taillights when she started the engine a half-mile away, it hardly mattered. She was gone.

8

The miles swept beneath Danny's wheels.

The interceptor rode on wings of darkness through the night, its headlight beams burning a path through the shadows. She rode the center line and the road became a swiftly flowing river of stone running through a black tunnel toward a distant, unknown goal. Features whipped past: stark forms of rock, skeletons of trees and bushes, fences flashing their Morse code of posts and rails. Sometimes a sign would emerge from the dark, its reflective surface glowing like a one-eyed cat, looming large, then in a stroke of light it would be gone behind her. The roar of the engine and the thrum of the tires became a dirge for a dead civilization. The thunder of blood in her ears kept time to the growling threnody of the machine.

Danny drove until the gasoline was gone, and found more, and drove again until the sun rose, always searching, her mind analyzing the words in the note for clues to Kelley's plan.

Danny had a new working hypothesis, but it meant covering a thousand square miles. Or ten thousand. She needed something more to work on than the speculation that Kelley would head for San Francisco, because she'd been there before. She sought a clue, what the better detectives called a *tell*, some unconscious action that directed attention toward what the suspect wanted to conceal. There had to be a tell somewhere in the note. Danny had the thing almost memorized. It had to be something in the loose handful of facts she knew, or could guess. She knew, for example, that the Mustang had a driving range of between 230 and 260 miles from full to empty. It was on half a tank when Kelley stole it. So assuming she took the route Danny thought most likely, Kelley would have had to fill up the tank in Riverton Junction. Danny had surreptitiously checked the cash register of the gas station for a receipt that could have clued her to Kelley's earlier presence, but there was nothing to go on. Most cars carried sixteen or seventeen gallons of gasoline, same as the Mustang. There were fifteen receipts for that amount or less on the Fourth of July. Kelley would have used cash, so there was no telltale credit card slip with her blessed signature on it.

Then again, Kelley could have taken a different route altogether. She might have heard there was trouble on the radio and decided to hole up somewhere, or she might have kept on going straight up to the 58 to the 99 to the 5 to San Francisco. Eight hours' driving, at most, if she kept the hammer down and didn't stop to eat, which she wouldn't. It seemed like Kelley could go days without eating. If she made it to San Francisco, she was either dead or very, very lost, and Danny would not find her on her own. Danny's hypothesis stopped working about two tanks of gas away from Forest Peak. San Francisco, Las Vegas, Glendale, Arizona—even Tijuana, Mexico: A determined girl could make any of those places from Forest Peak in a single day, and still have time for a restaurant meal afterward. Hell, she could cross the entire *country* in four days.

So Danny stuck with the current hypothesis. It was that, or concede her mission was insane.

She kept on driving through the night, the white lines whipping under the interceptor like tracer rounds from a .50 caliber machine gun. She had forgotten everything behind her. Amy, the other survivors, the airfield, they were old memories. By dawn, her mouth hung open and her face was pale. Her eyes were glassy and vacant. She saw herself in the rearview mirror and for an instant she was looking at a zombie, not herself. She snapped her jaw shut and pulled off the road, to rest for a while beneath the tortured limbs of a piñon pine. It stood beside a dry creek in a plain of cheatgrass and red brome, two non-native species that had wiped out most of the local vegetation. Danny felt a certain kinship with the tree. There was another non-native species around, and it was wiping out the locals, too.

Danny woke up startled, her stomach lurching with a sensation as if she'd caught herself falling. Immediately she scanned her surroundings. No zombies in view. The interior of the car was sweltering hot. Danny had opened the windows only a couple of inches despite the heat; she didn't want anything reaching in and grabbing her while she slept. Now it was a quarter to nine in the morning—she had been asleep for two and a half hours. Time to get moving again. She started the engine and rolled back toward the road, kicking up a thick cloud of dust. And before the wheels were back on the tar, another piece of the puzzle had clicked into place.

Kelley had mentioned that social reject, Zap Owler, in her note. She wrote of how Owler sold methamphetamine at the go-kart tracks in the flatlands. And she specifically mentioned the one Danny had taken her to for her seventh birthday. That was Kartland, in Potter. Danny remembered that Kelley didn't seem to enjoy it much, but she could sure drive. That little face in the big red rental helmet, pale with big dark eyes, Kelley's expression set and grim from the moment she stepped onto the track until the end of her third race. Danny hadn't been able to beat her, even though she started ramming Kelley's kart from behind. Her theory at the time had been that Kelley didn't weigh anything, so her kart had a speed advantage. But in fact the kid was a born driver, and determined. Kelley had a grape slushie after the races, and then she was in the bathroom forever because she had to completely drape the crapper with toilet paper, forming a hygienic bird's nest around the seat.

Danny's sinuses started to ache. Tears wanted to come. She inhaled and exhaled and pushed the loss back down where it wouldn't get in the way. Her hands were locked hard around the steering wheel. They had some good times in there, Danny thought. A few. She had a terrible feeling those were the only good times Kelley ever had.

But she had to keep her mind on this clue, if it was a clue, to Kelley's plans. Danny thought Kelley was smarter than she was, by a fair amount. But she wasn't more clever. She didn't yet know the means by which people give themselves away in conversation, reveal their thoughts or motives.

Danny, however, had spent years doing it: first in Iraq, trying to second-guess those poor inscrutable bastards that had to call the place home, and second in the American police business. Nobody knows how to talk straight to a uniform.

Danny had the note out, pinned to the steering wheel with her right thumb.

Zap Owler cooks speed in his kitchen and sells it down in the flatlands at go-kart tracks. Including that place by the freeway you took me for my seventh birthday.

There was something to that. Why did Kelley mention that particular place? Why not the track in Riverside they went to a couple of years later, with Danny's then-boyfriend Kyle Williams? Or the school outing to Race-world, where Kelley won five bucks off Mr. Carter by winning two out of three kart races against her classmates? *Mr. Carter the porno king,* Kelley had written.

Danny folded the note back up and stowed it in her pocket. She couldn't see a reason why Kelley would name one track over the others, unless it was on her mind for some unstated reason. Danny had been there each time, and they'd had about the same kind of fun. If Owler sold speed at Kartland, he sold it at the other tracks, too; they were all about the same distance away. But it was Kartland she specifically mentioned.

The town of Potter, where Kartland was, connected to the big roads. It had a railway station. Amtrak came through that way. You could get to Colorado by morning. It was a fair-sized town where strangers wouldn't stick out. Three gas stations, a bunch of fast-food places with those hundred-foot-tall signs off the freeway, and an ideal place for a teenaged girl to gas up a car and take her pick of destinations.

Danny felt a terrible sense of foreboding. If Kelley *had* gone to Potter, her next step could have been toward anywhere. The trail would run cold. But Potter was the one place she had mentioned in the note besides Forest Peak and Iraq, and Kelley didn't have a passport and she wasn't nuts, so she wasn't on her way to Iraq.

The interceptor's low fuel light came on.

Danny's reasoning hit the wall with the idea of Potter. If that's where Kelley went, Danny would have to start looking along all the major routes, following the roads and the train tracks across the entire American West. She scoured her brain for some limiting factor, her right foot jammed to the floor of the interceptor as she raced the machine toward Potter.

What about money? Kelley could have stowed away any amount from two hundred dollars to a thousand, Danny guessed. She had her own account at the bank and she'd had a part-time job at the Quik-Mart since graduating high school, plus a little extra income helping Amy down at the veterinary clinic. How much? Could she afford the gas or a train ticket to New York, for example? The money had to go in the "unknown" category, and again Danny cursed herself for not knowing more about Kelley's life. She had been unforgivably incurious about her sister's daily existence. All this time, Danny had been accusing Kelley of being morbidly self-absorbed—

now Danny could see with excruciating clarity that the self-absorbed one was herself.

She remembered her own drunken harangues, the hours of browbeating and railing against what she saw as Kelley's obstinacy and selfishness, and she felt fathomless regret. Every minute of it had been nothing less than abuse.

At that moment Danny wanted a drink more than she wanted to breathe. Car needs gas, driver needs buzz. Gotta have it. But her supply had run out the previous evening, the precious fluid sloshing lower and lower in the flask tucked between her thighs. Potter was only a few miles ahead. She could recharge all fluids.

Now, what else besides money would shape Kelley's thinking? Danny couldn't come up with anything in the note, so she conjured up the map in her mind's eye, intricately detailed around Forest Peak, getting less and less informative as it extended outward. Was Kelley even on the map? If so, was she alive, or dead, or undead? Only time would tell. And maybe not even that.

Time. Undead. A set of rusty little tumblers in Danny's head turned over, and there was an idea back in there somewhere, if she could just reach it. Danny teased it out of the shadows. Time was a variable. It would shape Kelley's behavior. That was it. Kelley fled Forest Peak sometime after midnight on the Fourth of July. She could have driven all night. She probably did. That would have placed her in Potter by morning, long before the crisis began. Would Kelley have stayed in Potter for a while? Things began to break down by around two o'clock in the afternoon. If she was listening to the police radio in the Mustang, as Danny was sure Kelley would have done, she would have known of the disaster sweeping Los Angeles long before most people did. She might have decided to stay where she was until she knew what was happening.

No, Danny didn't think so. Kelley would have seen the disaster as the hand of fate trying to push her back to Forest Peak. She would have taken it personally—just as Danny had. She would have pushed on.

Danny wiped a rivulet of sweat off her face. The air-conditioning was blasting, but her skin was wet. Her heart thudded against her ribs. She was digging down to the last variables, the last possible conjectures she could make about Kelley. Soon it would be time to stop wondering and start searching, and there would be nothing to think about. Nothing she wanted to think about, at least. That's when the bottle would come in handy. Would

Kelley have gone on alone, even knowing there was a wave of death swarming the countryside? Would Kelley have gone on alone in any case?

But Kelley didn't know anybody, anywhere else. To push on in the face of an ever-mounting crisis, all alone without a cell phone or credit cards or even a vehicle that belonged to her, would seem pretty daunting to a sheltered kid from a small town. It was the kind of thing even Danny wouldn't have dared to do back at that age, unless maybe Amy was with her. But Kelley didn't have any of that kind of friends.

Friends? Maybe Kelley had a boyfriend or something, waiting somewhere for a liaison. Impossible to say. Danny simply had no idea. She always assumed every male with eyes was ogling Kelley, the gloomy Goth girlie with longer legs than her big sister and no keloidal burn scars over 30 percent of her body. It was part protective reflex and part jealousy to think that way, Danny knew. She hadn't gotten laid in the better part of a year, and she didn't remember the last time very well on account of the many rum and Cokes involved. She felt ugly. So she almost deliberately avoided knowing what Kelley was up to, and with whom she was up to it. Was Kelley a virgin? Jesus, Danny didn't know *anything*.

Danny wondered how long the fuel reserve would last before the interceptor's engine quit. She still had a big chunk of road to cover before the next gas station.

When at a dead end, go back to the last crossroads. Danny reached with her mind, back through the nightmarish week she'd just survived, to the events of Independence Day morning in Forest Peak. The last normal day in the history of the world. She had been hung over. She had just arrested Wulf, who was still drunk. She'd found Kelley's note. Ted was eating on duty, and there were firecrackers setting her teeth on edge. Was there anything else? Hadn't there been something somebody said? Something about runaways?

A bolt of ice shot down Danny's spine. The sweat on her skin turned cold, and her mouth dried up. She *knew.* She was sure of it. A kid named Barry Davis. One of the faces around town, nobody special. He faded into the scenery. The only reason Danny knew of him at all was that his mother was a pain in the ass, always calling the station to complain about Barry for things that weren't illegal. She was using the police as a surrogate to replace Barry's father, who had wisely run away, as Deputy Nick had once surmised.

Barry Davis was reported missing by his pain in the ass mother on the morning of the Fourth of July. If Kelley was going to have a friend, a boy-friend, whatever, it was going to be Barry Davis. Why? Because they both faded into the scenery. Two of a kind.

"Holy shit," Danny said aloud. If Danny was right, and she felt sure she was, Kelley would have waited in Potter. Would they have remained there while the crisis spun out of control?

Danny realized she once again had no idea. And now she was imagining the interceptor's engine was beginning to miss. Was she about to run out of gas in the desert? Danny checked her wrist for the tenth time that morning, and for the tenth time noted that her watch was gone. It had probably been pulled off by one of the undead.

Danny caught herself making plans for what she and Kelley would do after they were united again. She was dreaming. That was the worst thing she could do. Always think methodically. First, fit the facts together. Then fill in between them with the most likely hypothesis. After that, the edu-cated guess. Maybe flip a coin. But never, ever hope. Because hope clouded the whole chain of reasoning, all the way up to the top. The moment you started in with that, you were limiting the outcomes to the ones you wanted. And that very seldom happened. Not in this life.

Danny needed to remain absolutely clear about the hypothesis she was building, untainted by hopes that it might turn out better than expected, because this was probably going to go down the hard way. If Danny did find the Mustang, and Kelley was with it, she still had to face the three possible scenarios: Kelley alive . . . Kelley dead . . . Kelley undead.

The engine starved a half-mile outside Potter.

Danny walked to town in the broiling morning heat, the shotgun in one hand and the prybar in the other. This was a king-sized fuckup. If Potter had been hit by the disaster—and the total radio silence suggested it had—there could be twice as many zombies there as there had been in Forest Peak. Maybe a lot more, if a steady stream of refugees had reached it before the death got that far.

Danny's boots scuffed on the road, and she saw that sand was beginning to blow over the paved surface, softening its edges. There was no traffic to sweep the road clean. At this rate, it would be buried in a couple of months. For the first time, Danny saw trash on the side of the road and didn't think of it as litter. She saw it as evidence of life. There was a Reese's Peanut Butter Cup wrapper nestled at the foot of a creosote bush, and a plastic

Jack in the Box cup a few yards further along. The cup still had the lid on it, and there was a straw stuck through the lid. Someone ate the one, someone drank the other, and they chucked them out of a car window, and now they were probably dead.

Danny was letting her thoughts wander when she heard the crows.

And not only crows, but vultures.

She didn't need a filling station. The traffic lights were dark, so there wasn't any power in town. That meant the gas pumps wouldn't be working. She had a coil of garden hose over her shoulder and a couple of empty plastic jugs. What Danny needed now was a vehicle with gas in it.

Potter was laid out at the bottom of a hill. The edge of town was defined by railroad tracks running north and south, dividing the town from the empty landscape beyond: a baking-hot plain of white, salt ground. An ocean floor, some million years ago. Danny walked down the road into Potter, keeping to the center line, then headed down the hill toward the tracks across an area largely devoid of vegetation.

She crossed a plot of land that had once, long ago, been a miniature golf course. A little green pigment still clung to the amoeba-shaped cement islands with their crumbling windmills and castles and lawn sculptures. She could make out the foundations of the clubhouse restaurant that had once stood there. It had burned down when Danny was small, before Kelley was born. But the miniature golf course hadn't been operating in Danny's lifetime. All that remained vital of the original place were some palm trees that had once lined the parking lot. Otherwise it was difficult to tell what had ever stood there.

Would the whole town of Potter look like that in twenty years, or would humanity have moved back in? Danny didn't see why they would bother, but somebody must have loved this town.

She reached the hard, white silt of the saline valley floor. The train tracks ran along a few hundred yards away. Danny crossed to them, her boots crunching in the arid dirt.

The tracks were laid on a raised bed of clinker stone, and Danny saw that the once-bright rails were already dim with rust. She thought water was required for anything to rust, but then again, the hot rails cooling at night would probably attract dew. Danny walked along the rails, stepping between the thickly tarred wooden ties. She still felt sore from the action in Forest Peak, with Technicolor bruises all over her limbs, but felt like she could run if she had to. Like she could *fight* if she had to. She just wasn't sure how long she'd last.

The vultures circled in the blue sky. Flights of crows would abruptly leap into the air and circle from one perch to another, croaking and jockeying for position. Danny wondered if they were responding to a threat on the ground, or simply following the witless reactionary groupthink of birds, the way pigeons and geese did. But Amy had said crows were the smartest bird. In that case, they were probably playing keep-away from the zombies. She assumed zombies would eat anything they could find, not just men. *This will give the crows a break,* she thought, and then she saw the train.

It was not an ordinary train. Almost the entire thing was painted in a camouflage scheme of swarming squares in tan, black, and gray, one of the digitally generated designs calculated for maximum visual disruption. But it wasn't one of the military service patterns, at least not one with which she was familiar. The rearmost car, the one she saw first, had a crew cabin at the back and a flatcar section forward; chained to the flatcar was an M3A3 Bradley fighting vehicle. Tanklike in appearance, designed as a troop transport and a tank-killer, this one sported a medium machine gun, a 25mm chain gun capable of delivering two hundred rounds per minute, and an antitank missile launcher. Danny knew it well. She had almost died in a similar specimen.

What this thing was doing in Potter, California, instead of in one of the several theaters of war where the troops were desperately undersupplied with functional gear, Danny could not imagine. It wasn't an ideal fighting vehicle. Although armored, its skin was aluminum: It sacrificed strength for speed. But in a typical civilian environment, the thing would be unstoppable.

She wondered what had stopped it.

Danny walked away from the tracks, out into the desert, keeping well clear of the train. She didn't think anyone was aboard; there were crows sitting on the barrel of the chain gun and walking along the top of the train cars ahead. There were two camouflaged troop-transport cars in front of the flatcar, then five ordinary civilian passenger cars in assorted livery. These were the only parts of the train not freshly painted in camo. Ahead of that was another flatcar covered in a tied-down rubberized tarpaulin; Danny thought she recognized the outlines of a couple of Humvees under it. An odd detail was a machine gun mounted on the flatcar, facing the civilian cars. Ahead of that was a sealed container car, and ahead of that was the engine. There were some serial numbers stenciled on the engine, but they meant nothing to Danny.

The train had pulled up to the station, she could see that much. But she couldn't tell what had happened after that. Maybe they were on maneuvers, killing zombies, clearing the town. But if that was so, why were the fighting vehicles still on the train? Danny would sure as hell have preferred to be inside one of those against a foe armed only with jaws. Had they abandoned the train, or left it behind for some future purpose? There was a coat of dust all over the top surfaces, which suggested it had been there for at least a couple of days.

Danny felt the sun baking down on her, and Kelley's fate receding into the distance, and the urgent need for action overcame her caution in the face of such a strange discovery. It was time to get moving, whatever had happened here. Maybe there was a platoon of heavily armed men on the other side of town. Her shirt under the coil of hose was streaming with sweat, and her muscles were beginning to ache from holding the thing in place.

Danny circled around to the front of the train, crossing the tracks about fifty feet ahead of the engine. She smelled it, then, faint but unmistakable. Death. She moved along until she could see the space between the train and the platform.

There was a mass of corpses. It filled the gap like an avalanche.

She worked her way closer, trying to be silent. There was a sound, something like radio static. She kept the bulk of the train between herself and the undead, as they probably were, piled up against the bogeys. A couple of crows took flight. A vulture spread its wings on a rooftop up in town, cooling itself off. It appeared to be praying to the sun.

Nothing else moved. The noise was getting louder with each step, and now the full stench hit Danny's nostrils and poisoned her mouth.

They weren't zombies. They were corpses. And they were swarming with legions of flies.

Danny unhitched the compact binoculars from her belt and swept them over the heap of rotting bodies. There were at least two hundred, and probably considerably more. They were full of meaty craters, suggestive of gunfire.

Danny put the binoculars away and moved toward the embankment at the end of the station building, keeping low until she could see down the length of the platform. There were piles of bodies there, as well, some of them torn apart with limbs flung a dozen feet from the nearest torsos. She could see a heavy female corpse with its belly blown open. It looked very much like a hand grenade injury.

Danny moved down the platform, keeping her back to the station building until there were windows. Then she split the difference between the embankment and the building, so she wouldn't have to deal with an arm reaching through the broken panes to grab her. But nothing stirred except the crows. There had been a massacre here—of zombies, not men. The men who did it were also gone, but Danny couldn't guess where. She was definitely looking at a pitched battle, though. There were bullet scars all over the place, evidence they'd been shooting wild.

A further clue to recent events presented itself on the platform side of the train. The tarpaulin over the flatcar was spattered with blood in irregular, looping lines. The blood was dark red, turned to varnish by the sun, but unmistakably human. That was arterial spray from someone stumbling around on the flatcar itself. Maybe the victim got shot or bitten. Either way, the injury told Danny there had been living casualties at the train. That meant they had been driven back to it, or driven away from it. Driven away was Danny's guess. Otherwise, why would the train still be in the station, laden with fighting machines?

She found a corpse wearing military boots and the same digital camouflage as the train. The young man's throat was torn out. Brass shell casings littered the ground around him. Whoever had mounted the defense had not been able to retrieve their dead from the field. There might not have been any left alive.

Danny realized there were flies crawling all over her exposed skin. She waved them off, and they immediately settled back down on her. The overpowering reek of corpses was making her throat burn. She needed to get away from here. She moved toward the embankment and paused. No signs of zombies, no moaning or stirring among the corpses. So far, so good. Danny scrambled up the embankment, using the white rocks that spelled out the letter R in POTTER as stepping stones. Then she was up against a wooden fence at the top of the slope that ran along behind the hotel. There was a gate with concrete steps down at the far end of the fence, but Danny went the other way, where the fence ended at an empty lot and some dumpsters.

Still no zombie activity. It felt like every deserted battlefield she'd seen. The parking lot was at the other end of the hotel near the steps, but

Danny didn't want to approach it from the desert side. She wanted to come around the front of the hotel, so she could have a look at the street and find out what the hell happened here. It seemed like it might be important. If refugees had fled Potter, or some kind of military action had killed them (*killed Kelley, for example,* the voice in her head remarked), she needed to know. It was vital to the bigger-picture effort of finding her sister.

The street was thick with dust. The buildings created a natural funnel for the desert wind that blew up from the saline flats, and thick clouds of pale, sandy powder had settled over everything. There was no color. The dust obscured it. There were heaped shapes of bodies all along the sidewalks and against the many cars skewed in the street, some with open doors, some with bullet holes in the windshields. Danny could see hundreds of bodies from her position halfway down the block by the hotel, and there would be more on every street. Crows were picking at some of them, but not all. Danny suspected she was not alone here, although she was probably the only living human.

She knelt, keeping her head up, and picked up an empty shoe that lay on the pavement. Never break eye contact with your surroundings. She saw four corpses at which crows were picking a few yards away, and three they left alone. She took aim at one of the bodies the crows were avoiding. The shoe whirled through the air and came down with a *clump* against the leg of a body lying at the curb opposite the hotel.

Nothing happened. At first. Then, as Danny was about to move forward, the thing shifted its weight.

She saw the head turn, as if on rusty bearings. It was one of them, and it sought the source of the disturbance. When it saw nothing, it settled back down and became part of the gruesome scenery again.

Danny realized the street was a mistake. She would be better off taking a route through the hotel. If the zombies were in some kind of suspended animation right now, it wouldn't last. However they did it, they would sense her, as the ones in Agua Rojo had done.

She went in through the kitchen door by the hotel's dumpsters, and almost immediately found another zombie. It had been slumped against the walk-in freezer, at the end of the central aisle lined with cooktops and fryers. A Hispanic male, dressed in cook whites and black check pants. The fabric was stained and slimy at armpits and crotch. The zombie began to move a few seconds after Danny entered the room. There was a two-foot rolling pin made of marble in a rack only a yard from her hand. Long before the zombie had gained its feet, Danny snatched up the rolling pin, then crushed the monster's skull with a single overhand stroke, caving in the tall white chef's hat. Black fluid poured out of the hat and spattered the white uniform.

Aiming a second blow with the rolling pin, Danny dropped the coiled hose and the plastic jugs. She gathered them back up in a messy bundle and moved deeper into the hotel, gripping the rolling pin. She might keep it. It was better than a baseball bat.

The hotel was silent. There were too many doors for safety. Sidling past each doorway, ready to strike, she found an elderly female sitting in an office down the hall beyond the kitchen. Her hair was white, knotted atop her head, and she wore an old-fashioned black dress with a high collar. When Danny moved into the doorway, the old woman looked up. The eyes were dead.

The undead thing rose to its feet, taking halting steps toward Danny. She considered smashing its head the way she'd done to the cook—but instead, Danny simply closed the office door. The old zombie scratched at the other side of the wood, but it didn't have the wit to operate the doorknob.

There was a dining room beyond the office, in which Danny found a plump female zombie that had once been dark-skinned, but was now an eerie gunmetal color. It was dressed in some kind of aproned pink outfit, maybe a chambermaid. There was no door to close, here. Danny would have to kill this one. She put down the jugs and the hose and broke eye contact with the walking corpse. When she looked up again, it was shockingly close to her. It came at Danny with a speed she hadn't reckoned on.

She struck it haphazardly across the face with the rolling pin, knocking the nose and jaw profoundly out of alignment. The creature stopped, but only to reorient itself to Danny's position. Its fat hands whipped out at her. Danny swung the rolling pin again, and this time one of the zombie's slack, jowled arms came up in a distinct gesture of self-defense. The bones cracked, and the hand flopped loosely around at the end of the arm. Unfazed, it renewed the attack. Panic surged up inside Danny's chest.

The thing's broken jaw worked up and down, the lower teeth so dislocated they waved out of the side of the face. Danny whacked it again, this time straight down on top of the head. The chambermaid collapsed, vomiting one long spurt of black liquid at her boots, then was still.

Danny's heart was pounding. This zombie was fast—faster than any of the ones she had seen so far.

The adrenaline kicked her thinking into gear. There were more capable zombies out there. Maybe it was because this one had been indoors, not rotting in the sun. It was still slower than even the dullest human being, but this one could *move*. Maybe some of the undead were faster than usual, the infection or chemical or whatever it was working differently on their nervous systems. Danny would have to factor that into her plans. Even here in Potter, she would have to amend her approach: She didn't want to find herself surrounded if they could react with the speed of this one.

Danny was still formulating a fresh plan when a hand fell stiffly on her shoulder.

Raw fear jetted into her system and she spun free, the rolling pin already coming up—it was the old woman from the office. Behind it the office door stood open. She wasn't any faster than the others. *But she had opened that door.*

Danny clipped the old thing in the mouth with the rolling pin on the upswing, then clubbed the white-haired head to the floor on the return stroke. The thin arms reached for her, even as the creature fell. The scars on Danny's back prickled and itched with the sudden injection of fear. Danny stomped once, hard, on the wrinkled, sunken face. The skull broke beneath her foot like a china teapot wrapped in rags. The thing shuddered and went still. Danny felt growing terror, and she forced it to subside. Terror led to panic, and panic killed.

There were French doors at the rear of the dining room. They opened on to a patio at the back of the hotel. The patio ended in a low, gated iron fence, and beyond that was the parking lot. Danny moved swiftly. Beyond the fence was space for thirty or forty cars. The lot was full. The entire scene, from the hedges around the parking area, to the buildings, the paving, and the cars, was entirely floured in pale dust. There were bodies here, as well. Danny could see the head and shoulders of a corpse or zombie propped up inside a Jeep with a rag top and no doors. Was that only rotting tissue, or was it a threat? There were more of them on the ground, all around. One was an infant. They were motionless, but no crows had ventured into the enclosed yard. Several birds were perched on wires overhead, but none had settled in the parking area.

Danny was at the French doors now, crouching. She pulled the hose off her shoulder and uncoiled it. It was much too long. She had intended to siphon two gas tanks at once, but she would never have time. She cut the hose five feet from one end. That would be enough. She checked the action of the shotgun. There were too many things to carry. The rolling pin would have to stay behind.

There was a minivan near the patio gate. It might offer some cover for Danny while she sucked the gas through the pipe. After that, the siphoning action would work on its own, and she could keep moving around the lot if she had to. Gravity would take care of the rest. Even if a dozen zombies were coming for her, as long as she could eventually make it back around to the jug and run away with it, her mission was accomplished. A gallon of gas was enough to get her somewhere safer. But the minivan would also obscure her view.

She saw one of the 1980s Mustangs like her first, a few cars back from her position. An ugly piece of shit. But it offered a nice view all around, being a low vehicle. She could try taking the gas from that one. But would anybody that drove one of those mullet-mobiles keep the tank topped up? A better car might have more gas in it, simply because the owner could afford it.

Something was moving around inside the hotel. Somewhere behind her. Maybe there had been a zombie upstairs that was coming down to investigate. She had to make a choice, now.

Danny pushed the French doors open and moved outside. The heat inside and out was equally oppressive, but the air outside was tainted with the stink of rotting bodies. Nothing on the patio to be worried about: She saw a corpse, but it was a proper one, with the head bashed in. An iron umbrella stand lay next to it. There were useful skull-smashing weapons everywhere, if you were willing to improvise.

Danny kept her body parallel to the ground and scooted to the hedge, then looked over the top of it. The longer she could delay her discovery, the better her chances of getting the vital gasoline. She scanned the cars and saw, from her fresh angle, an ideal candidate: a vintage two-door Jaguar in good condition. It wouldn't have a locking gas cap, it would have a short filler tube, and it wasn't too far into the parking lot.

Danny checked the ground for zombies. None between her and the minivan, at least. She hustled across that distance, then checked again, keeping her motions sure and swift. Momentum was key. She made it to the ugly Mustang, then scuttled crabwise to the Jaguar, keeping an eye on two bodies she could now see lying on the far side of the minivan. They might get active. She pried the filler door on the Jag's gas tank open and fed the hose in. The tang of gasoline fumes joined the thick, dull smell of decaying meat.

A cloud of crows rose into the air. Danny followed them with her eyes, sucking the air out of the free end of the hose. She could taste the gasoline vapors, and wished she had found a narrower tube. The hose took almost more vacuum pressure than she could create with her lungs. She could feel the resistance inside it, the counterweight from the rising column of gasoline.

And then she heard the moaning.

The undead beside the minivan stirred in the dirt. They weren't up yet. They were emerging from the trance or coma they had been in. Prey was here at last.

One of the zombies was looking around now, its trunk supported on its arms. It hadn't yet stood up. Danny saw another one on the edge of her vision, and turned to see a male zombie around her age. It was lurching toward her on naked feet.

She sucked again at the hose, the negative pressure making her ears hurt deep inside at the corners of her jaw. This wasn't going to work.

The minivan zombies had seen her now. She checked on the position of the male coming at her across the parking lot, and beyond it, she saw an old Mustang Fastback.

It looked a lot like hers. It was the right year, or appeared to be. It had the side markers in back so it was at least a '68. But she couldn't tell what color it was. The discovery threw her concentration off, and she gasped, and the column of fuel fell back down the inside of the hose and she had lost her chance to get the siphon working.

Now she had another problem, as well: She couldn't leave this parking lot without checking that car. She had to know.

Danny didn't have a plan anymore. She threw herself across the hood of the Jaguar, raising a cloud of dust, and landed almost on top of a corpse on the other side. It didn't react. It was dead matter. But a foul, choking stench hissed out of it, obliterating the stink of gasoline.

Danny saw the zombies around her—there were six of them—become confused. She didn't know how else to identify their behavior. They looked around as if blinded, and they moaned out of sync with each other. They lost the forward impetus that had carried them toward her.

Danny felt an urgent need to vomit. The stink of the corpse she had stamped on was so intense it was like a smoke her lungs couldn't pull down. She retched once, then ran at the male zombie. It sensed her at last, and raised its arms. Danny rammed the butt of the shotgun into its face, but didn't pause to deliver the killing blow. She kept moving, and a dozen strides later the Mustang was right in front of her.

Its color was impossible to guess under the dust—dark, was all she could tell. Danny rushed forward and reached out, ignoring the zombies that now surged stiff-legged after her, and the half-dozen others that were spilling through the entrance of the parking lot. She ran her fingers across the dust, and crimson streaks were left behind, so red and wet she checked her fingers to see if she was bleeding.

It was not blood. It was Candyapple Red paint.

Danny turned around and fired the shotgun into the nearest mass of zombies. She didn't aim. It tore a glistening black swath through the dusty bodies. They swayed backward and kept coming. Danny reached out again and grasped the door handle. Depressed the button. It wasn't locked. There was a good, solid Detroit *click* and the door was open.

Danny flung herself inside the car. It was a furnace-hot twilight in there, the dust on the windows cutting half the sunlight. There was no view out, except through the driver's side window where the dust had fallen away when Danny slammed the door. The zombies were five yards from the car. She slapped down the door lock buttons and gasped for breath, supernovas bursting behind her eyes. She had scarcely drawn breath since her boot sank into the corpse. Then she looked around to ascertain the thing of which she was already sure.

This particular '68 interior was black on black. Totally stock. There was the thin-rimmed, two-spoke steering wheel with its seven decorative medallions. The crooked chrome shifter on the carpeted transmission hump. The five round instruments in the sleek wood-grain dashboard. *Breathe, Danny.*

Tucked under the chrome strip along the lower face of the dash, a receipt for gas from Riverton Junction Texico.

On the passenger seat was the leather jacket Danny had left in the car the last time she drove it.

As impossible as she'd begun to think it was, she was sitting inside her own beloved Mustang.

With the paroxysm of relief came the stark realization that the trail had run cold. She'd found the car, but she hadn't found Kelley.

She turned her eyes on the zombies. They were anonymous in death, slack-skinned and characterless and cement-white with dust except for the wet punctures of their eyes. Danny saw that these had been secreting snot from their tear ducts; there were dark, gelatinous strings running down their cheeks from the eyes, like beached sea turtles.

None of these zombies looked like Kelley. But there were thousands lying in the streets of this town. Danny saw into a future like a madman's vision of hell, in which she had to search every decaying face—and even then, she would not know. How many more of these things had wandered cross-country? How many dead were lying in the brush, the ravines, the sewers? How many turned to ash in the fires? There was so little chance of finding her sister.

But you found the Mustang.

For once, Danny agreed with the voice. But with the knowledge that she had reached her first impossible goal came terrible responsibility. There was so much more to do, and now she was trapped inside a car, surrounded by hundreds of ravenous walking dead.

She didn't have the ignition key.

Again Danny felt that sensation of tipping over the edge, of the great wheel of life turning beneath her feet, of staring into the void. Kelley had put the gas receipt right where Danny always put them. The car was in perfect order. It was ready to go, requiring only the key to bring it to life.

Danny realized, with a dismal feeling, that she would have to jump-start the vehicle. As a cop, she could jump-start a bicycle, but she wasn't fast at it. The process might take longer than she had to live. The undead were right outside, separated only by a sheet of glass.

Then again, Kelley might have been observing Danny's strict discipline regarding the vehicle, even after she stole it from the driveway. She'd even tucked the gas receipt right where Danny put them herself.

If Kelley observed Danny's habits with the Mustang to the letter, it was possible she would yet save Danny's life. The zombies were on the car now, their hands and faces making smears in the dust on the windshield, clearing patches that looked onto the nightmare outside. Thumping on the roof, clawing at the windows. Danny could smell them in the fetid air. One of the things dragged peeling lips across the windshield, its graphite-colored tongue thrusting against the glass, teeth scraping. It was like the view from a coffin being dug up by cannibals. Right now would be an excellent time for a drink, an excellent time for a long, burning swallow of something strong, but there wasn't one to be had. Danny was either sitting in her own tomb, or—

Sweating profusely, Danny reached up and flipped down the driver's side sun visor.

The keys dropped into her lap.

PART THREE

BEST-LAID PLANS

1

Some part of Danny had curled up and gone to sleep, but the rest of her remained in constant motion, methodical and focused on the one and only task besides brute survival. For this she didn't need a working hypothesis, she only needed a pen.

She was drawing lines over every route she covered on the map, with scribbled notes wherever there was a town: *Culper, 350, NL, NK, food, drugs, hdwr, Z.* This was the name of the town, the population, NL for "no life," NK for no sign of Kelley. Then what stores in town might be useful. And finally, Z for zombies.

Danny had left the police interceptor by the side of the road outside Potter, taking the time to push it onto the scenic overlook and cover it with a blue plastic tarp she'd found outside town. She weighted the tarp down with rocks and guessed that inside a few days it would be so dusty as to become invisible. If somebody got into the vehicle and vandalized it, no worries. She had her pick of thousands, out there in the world.

She kept the Mustang's police-band radio on at all times now, the glove box door hanging open to expose the faceplate and microphone of the miniature detective-style unit that was Danny's only concession to modifying the otherwise factory stock car. Things were happening in the world outside her remote desert beat. There were a lot of survivors out there.

Danny heard someone on the radio speculate that half of the population was still alive. So 150 million Americans, more or less. But according to the voices in the ether, they were engaged in costly battles with the zombies for possession of the cities, trying to clear out densely concentrated areas such as Chicago, Manhattan, and Miami. Denver was an inferno, as were San Diego, Los Angeles, and Seattle. Part of San Francisco was on fire. Hundreds of smaller towns were burning.

Much of humanity, it seemed, had banded back together in large groups. That was an ancient survival strategy, of course, and mankind was returning to basics. It made no sense to Danny. For most people, having someone on your flank, even if that person didn't know shit about survival, was a comfort. For herself, and probably a lot of ex-warriors, it was better to be alone. Better to trust your own reflexes than to put your hope in some civilian with an undeveloped sixth sense that thought you could ever relax, even for one minute, and didn't know how to properly clear a building. And sometimes, even a seasoned partner could be dangerous—you never want to be the slowest contestant in a foot race against the Devil. Danny was glad to be solo.

It had been two days since she had seen another living human being. She listened to voices on the radio, some of which she was starting to recognize, but it wasn't the same as company. She never spoke back to them. She didn't want to get into arguments about joining a bunch of idiots calling themselves "Wolverines," "Rebel Alliance," or "Ghostbusters." Most of all, these bands of survivors were sloppy. Every few hours, somebody somewhere would radio in for help because somebody else was bitten, or missing, or they were surrounded. And then the other groups would fall silent for a while, because in the end, even if they were playing at being soldiers, they were merely informal bands of people trying to survive.

A variety of survival tactics had been adopted, with mixed success. Those that adopted a fortress approach did well at first; they were usually near the big population centers where the zombies were thickest. But supplies were running out.

There were others that kept moving, the way Danny had wanted to do with her own convoy out of Forest Peak. But everybody was reliving *The Road Warrior* now that they knew the infrastructure was gone. Gangs were forming, casual alliances of hard-asses looking not only to survive, but to prosper. They were looting, they were raiding encampments, they were raping and killing. Danny knew her tribe back at Boscombe Field wouldn't last half an hour against these marauders.

There was something else, but Danny assumed it wasn't significant: A couple of groups had said they found help. Both of them dropped out of radio contact immediately afterward. Danny wondered what kind of help they had found. She didn't intend to find out. For once, Danny was placing a high price on her own life: Without it, she could never find Kelley. Still, there was a foul twist in her gut when she heard those Mayday calls on the radio and maintained her own silence. She was the Sheriff of Nowhere.

The last of the supplies Danny laid in was a case of bourbon.

Danny drank her way northward, drawing lines on her map.

2

Long before she could see the city, Danny could smell the smoke, and then Danny saw the thick sooty band along the horizon, and then she was chugging along the built-up waterfront toward San Francisco. The air stank of smoke and decomposition. The city was on fire. But it was not burning where she was going.

Danny had stopped at a deserted little beachfront hamlet, hardly a town, about ten miles south of San Francisco. All the seaworthy boats in the place were gone, but she had found an unwieldy, twelve-foot Jon boat, too big to row, with the engine removed for servicing. Danny found a clamp-on outboard in a crate at the marina's machine shop. She was fairly sure she had attached it wrong, but the propeller reached into the water and the gas line flowed okay, so she fired the motor up and aimed the craft north.

She brought the fishing boat into a notch at the throat of Pier 45, which a large Victorian-style signboard proclaimed to be Fisherman's Wharf. The pier was defended by a bow-shaped breakwater of concrete. In modern times it had become a parking spot for privately owned pleasure craft and charter boats. As Danny had discovered elsewhere during her two-day journey along the coast, everything on the water with sails or an engine had long since been piloted away; the water was the only safe route out of the city. God only knew what had happened to all the boat people. Maybe they starved. Maybe they were all in a fleet, headed for Hawaii to start a new society based on peace and understanding.

Danny was surprised at the small scale of the pier's marina. Fewer than a hundred slips. In San Pedro, south of Los Angeles, there were tens of thousands of places to keep a boat. Here in San Francisco these few precious slips were open for the taking for probably the first time in memory—not a rowing dinghy remained. The water was deep and mysterious and thick with effluent from the city. Not just ordinary urban flotsam, but oily sludge, ashes, and charred refuse, the drainage of a vast wound. Bags and backpacks bobbed in the tide. Shoes and shirts. Toys. A human head drifted past, mouth sagging into the water as if to drink the sea. The water stank so badly she could taste the smell.

Danny nosed the boat toward a makeshift barbed-wire fence that lined Jefferson Street at the water's edge, where several men in improvised commando costumes stood with weapons raised. They were armed with shotguns and rifles and looked as if killing was little more than expediency now, stripped of meaning. Danny knew the look well. She was wearing it herself.

"Don't shoot yet," the one man without a long gun said. He carried a pistol, and he appeared to be in charge, based upon his irritated expression.

"It's a zero," one of the others said, a young man in a black beret. "Look at it."

"Zeros can't drive a boat," the man in charge said.

"It's a zero," a black man said. He had white in his hair, or ashes. Danny could not tell at this distance. All of the men had some kind of white cream smeared beneath their noses.

"What's a zero?" she called, killing the engine. Her voice relaxed their trigger fingers a little. They did not respond. The boat ground up against the concrete a few moments later. At a gesture from the man in charge, the others stepped through a gap in the fence and Danny was hauled up by her arms onto the pier.

The silence was filled with questions. Back here among the living, Danny realized, she knew nothing. Half a dozen pairs of eyes with complex, working brains behind them, not just dead nerves and teeth. She would have to relearn how to interact, and what was going on, and who was in charge. It wouldn't be her for a while. She would have to play along. She would have to remember to fear a gun in the hands of an amateur.

Right now she was too tired to care. They were pathetic, these men. Like the hunters that came from the city to shoot deer up in Forest Peak, barely capable of not shooting themselves, let alone bagging game. That these people were salty after a few days of mass murder didn't make them soldiers.

"You bit?" the man in charge said to Danny.

"No."

"You look bit."

"Fuck you, cocksucker," Danny exclaimed, forgetting her nonconfrontational strategy.

"I'm Mitchell Gold," the man in charge said. "This is my part of the perimeter." He drew a compact satellite transmitter from his back belt and spoke into it. Danny thought she would very much like one of those radios. She would like some technological edge. A clue. Anything.

"Danny Adelman," Danny said. "I'm a sheriff from down near Los Angeles."

"Long way," Mitchell said.

"Yeah, there's a lot of dead walking around," Danny said. She spat on the ground but the taste of smoke remained in her mouth. "It's zeros, huh?" she continued. "The zombies."

"That's the official designation," the black man said. "Zeros. Stupid fucking name because you can't say a number with a zero in it without everybody flips out. You gotta say 'naught,' which I for one never fucking remember."

The conversation was interrupted by the gurgle of the Chinese engine turning over. It was Beret Boy: He'd climbed down into the boat and fired her up. He was holding his shotgun on his companions. The men who had been silent so far raised their guns in his direction but looked at Mitchell.

"Don't try to stop me. I'm going," Beret Boy said.

"Needledick," the black man muttered.

"Fuck it, let him go," said Mitchell. "He can't shoot worth a damn anyway."

They watched the boat lurch backward out of the mooring into which Danny had eased it. The kid knew nothing about handling watercraft. He crashed the hull of the boat against a bollard in the pier, knocking himself into the scuppers. The shotgun flew overboard. The engine quit. The boy got back to his feet, restarted the engine after several gargling attempts, then spun the wheel and got the boat pointed out to sea. A couple of civilians who had been working their way among the buildings on the pier charged at the boat; the male hurled himself into the water and began to swim after it with flailing strokes, but the boat was already well out of reach. Danny lost interest.

"Take me to your leader," she said, without any ironic intent.

"Somebody go take them into custody," Mitchell said, waving his pistol down the pier at the civilians. He drew a tube of Vicks Vapo Rub from his shirt pocket. "Put this under your nose, it cuts the smell." Danny took this for a goodwill gesture. But Mitchell had an eager look on his face. It wasn't simply a friendly gesture. He wanted something. "So," he said, aiming at nonchalance, "you got any news from down south?"

This was obviously the magic question, based on the nearly comical expression of expectation Mitchell wore. The answer was worth more than a squeeze of nose ointment.

So Danny said "yes," and within minutes she was in a dusty Cadillac sport utility vehicle with dried blood splashed all over the headliner, cruising into the city.

The smoke rose up among the hills beyond downtown, a boiling black curtain behind the sunlit buildings with their optimistic geometrical shapes in the financial center. Daly City was engulfed in fire, Danny assumed, and the entire South City area. They were thoroughly cut off from the mainland. If you could swim a couple of miles over to Sausalito, you could get away. If Sausalito wasn't infested. Otherwise, the population of downtown San Francisco, diminished as it might be, was trapped.

The light was amber-colored and dim from the smoke, the illusion of a sunset lasting all day. The air stank. Streets were mostly clear of debris, but the sidewalks were crowded with wrecked vehicles and twisted bicycle frames. Bulldozers stood idle at some intersections. Traffic lights were dark. There were burnt areas on the pavement and dark stains of blood or oil. Broken plate glass. A Starbucks with a Ford Taurus hanging out of the window. A fire hydrant, broken off pavement-high like a tooth at the gum line, spurted water into the air; nobody paid it any attention. It might have been like that for days. A river ran from the stump of the hydrant downhill toward the bay. Here there were none of the tumbled corpses Danny had come to see as part of the landscape, the ones that were not coming back. The place had been swept of the worst.

They drove past Telegraph Hill, and Danny heard sporadic gunfire from up there. Sharpshooters on Coit Tower, maybe. Or executions. There was a distinct feeling of martial law in the absence of people on the street; she saw pallid, grimy faces at windows, and knots of armed men and women patrolling around their little fiefdoms of a single city block. Lots of those good military satellite radios. A couple of pickup trucks loaded with canned goods cruised past with rifle-toting escorts atop the loads.

Mitchell drove Danny along Columbus Avenue to a roadblock where it turned into Montgomery, in the shadow of the Transamerica Pyramid. The Cadillac crept along in a queue of a dozen other vehicles. One was turned back; it appeared to contain a wounded woman in the backseat. A couple of pickups containing food were waved in past the barricades without delay. Danny found herself examining every female face, as if in all the world there were so few women left she would be certain to find her sister. Just like that.

She didn't, of course.

The barricade was manned—and it was only men—by some kind of mercenaries, very much like those she spent a lot of time disliking in Iraq. As they got close, she recognized the digital camouflage pattern she had seen back in Potter, adorning the equipment and corpses strewn around the railway station there. These privateers had the best gear. They had the body armor, the one-piece wrap-around shades, and the massive tactical wristwatches that got in your way in a genuine crisis. Their sleeve patches bore a screaming eagle—or, presumably, a hawk— rendered in gold thread over an American flag, the legend *Hawkstone Security* across the bottom.

When Mitchell identified himself and Danny, the mercenaries inspected her like a soiled diaper, then waved them both through. Whatever security they were providing it wasn't antizero. It was antipersonnel. They were keeping a tight lid on the civilians. Whose authority, Danny wondered, were they working under? The Fed? The state of California? The city? Was this a full-scale coup she'd walked into?

Mitchell pulled the Cadillac up onto the sidewalk in front of the pyramid. There were a lot of big, heavy vehicles parked there, right up to the patio wall. Nobody was worrying about fuel economy lately.

They climbed out of the SUV and crossed below the thick X-bracing that formed the base of the structure, above which the building looked like the point of some impossibly large spear. *Or a missile,* Danny thought. She'd never been in downtown San Francisco before; the closest she got was a one-night stopover a few days before her deployment at a friend's place up near Golden Gate Park. They'd spent the time screwing, not sightseeing. Old memories flitted past in her mind but were of no more significance to her now than dead leaves.

"There's a plaque in the park around back dedicated to these two dogs," Mitchell said, but lost interest in his own story. They entered the angular lobby past five more of the Hawkstone mercenaries, their automatic weapons laden with night sights and grenade launchers and assorted useless after-market crap.

Mitchell stopped at the elevator and leaned in close, speaking with a low and rapid voice. "You're going to be meeting Senator Vivian Anka. She happened to be in town when this thing happened, and she's pretty pissed off about it. She's kind of—she's a little paranoid. Just play it cool, okay? These Hawkstone guys—"

The elevator bell rang, the doors slid open. Inside the car was another of the hired mercenaries. He wrinkled his nose. They rode up the tower in silence.

The thing that shocked Danny most was the suits. These people were clean, well-dressed, and wore suits with neckties. Their faces were haggard; at least they had the decency to lose sleep. But up here above the city, with spectacular views of Nob Hill and the bay, it still seemed as if life could return to normal at any moment. The power worked, the phones worked, at least within the building; there were secretaries and assistants scuttling around, and the air smelled clean and conditioned. While they stood in a waiting area and looked out of the thirty-third story windows onto the city, Mitchell explained briefly that the government had moved from the Civic Center because the huge number of homeless people in the neighborhood meant a high concentration of zeros hidden away in every corner.

"At first the CDC was running the operation, but they got eaten. You can't run in a pressurized cleansuit. We cleared most of Chinatown but the area around St. Francis Memorial Hospital was still infested," he said, staring into the distance. "The Presidio was gone, and Golden Gate Bridge was blocked off in both directions. The Haight was like a slaughterhouse."

At first Danny wasn't listening, but she began to take interest as Mitchell waved vaguely in the direction of the landmarks he described. She wanted a map of the city. She had a feeling things were even worse than they appeared: If Mitchell's account was accurate, the entire area to the north was swarming with the undead, and they were advancing from the west. Danny didn't know how many people remained alive in town, but if it was a quarter million, there soon wouldn't be anywhere to keep them indoors. They were about to be driven into the bay.

There was one good thing about the situation, although only for her. Survivors would be compressed into the minimum amount of space. Easier to find a runaway girl from Forest Peak, if there was one. The voice in her head started to tell her she was crazy, her whole mission was crazy. It had been telling Danny this since she left Boscombe Field.

An aide to Senator Anka approached them, cutting off Danny's internal monologue. The aide walked as if his shoes were fragile. He bore with him two cups of coffee in cardboard sleeves. The smell of it made Danny salivate. She hadn't had coffee since the day before the world ended. This was fresh and black.

"I'm Eric Deforza," he said. "Welcome to San Francisco. I hear you came all the way from Los Angeles?"

"Long way," Danny said, burning her mouth on the delicious, bitter drink. It cut through the stale alcohol sugar on her tongue and the heat brought her belly back to life. She was suddenly ravenous.

"You drove in a car?" Eric said.

"Police cruiser. Had a convoy of civilians with me. They're in a safe place now. I don't know how long that situation will last."

"Ought to get some kind of medal for that."

"Right," Danny said, thinking of the Purple Heart ribbon she'd buried in a bureau drawer back home. Eric wasn't getting much conversational purchase with Danny, so he turned to Mitchell.

"Anybody else come along today?"

"Nobody," Mitchell said. "Fires kind of warn people off."

"What brings her here?"

"Ask her," Mitchell said. Eric turned back to Danny.

"Looking for somebody in charge," Danny said. It wasn't her final goal, only her immediate goal, but true enough for now. "First place I found so far where anybody's fighting back."

Eric's face went pale. "In the entire state?"

"As far as I saw it, yeah," Danny said. She knew she ought to be embroidering, adding in details to make her story sound more interesting, but she lacked the impetus. She hadn't actually seen much of the state, despite the distance she'd traveled; she had avoided anyplace with a population over a couple of thousand, sticking to back roads and old highways from before the freeway system.

She studied Eric's face. He was scared to death. Something was bothering her about this whole setup. Here she was in possibly the only major seat of government left in California, showing up without credentials, filthy as a hyena, and she had been whisked straight to the most powerful person in town. Where were the layers of bureaucrats, the paper-pushers and petty tyrants in charge of filtering out people like her? Did they really imagine she'd showed up without an agenda of her own?

This suggested to Danny that despite the appearance of official coordination here atop the pyramid, they were only barely in control of the situation, and altogether in the dark as far as information went. This was disheartening, but it made Danny's task simpler. They had nothing to offer her besides data. She had to find out what she wanted to know, and then she could go. Nothing to hold her. No brave band of survivors to join. This was merely the last vestige of the old system, on its way out.

Eric had been saying something. Danny didn't hear it. Mitchell was on his feet, so Danny stood up. Eric repeated his statement: "Follow me, please?" Danny walked behind him across the veined marble floor.

"Ma'am," Danny said to the senator. She felt self-conscious for the first time since the crisis began. Danny was hardwired to respond to authority figures, even civilian ones, and she was not shipshape for this interview. There was some kind of expensive scent in the air. Senator Anka wore a silk scarf knotted loosely at her throat. It was printed with golden anchors and horseshoes on a navy blue background. Her charcoal wool skirt suit was immaculate, tailored to lengthen her short figure, and somehow managed to carry the precision of a uniform while remaining feminine and delicate. Anka's skin looked as soft as chamois and hung at her jaw but was tight around the eyes. Almost time for a new facelift. Danny didn't use words like "feminine" or "delicate" in her mind when contemplating the congresswoman; it was shorthand as always. "Money," was the summary of Anka's appearance. The rest was implied. Danny took all of this in at a glance as she was led into the inner sanctum, a beige-carpeted corner office with thick, flame-mahogany veneered furniture and golfing prints on the walls. Some male executive's office, before the crisis.

Danny wasn't offered a chair, obviously because they'd never get the stink out of it once she was gone. Danny stood at ease in the center of the floor, with Anka behind the desk and a couple of junior aides seated on a bench against the wall farthest from the windows, the female one taking notes. Kids younger than Eric. There was a vase of flowers on the desk, but the flowers were dying, dropping petals. *Like the entire city,* Danny thought.

"So you're from Los Angeles," Anka said. "Long drive."

"Yeah," Danny said, and felt stupid. You needed a patter for these occasions.

"Did you come here alone?"

"I brought a group out from the San Bernardino mountains. They're in a safe place while I scout around up here."

"Part of the Eisenmann Plan, presumably. What brings you to San Francisco?"

"I have people up here," Danny said, and wished she'd said something more clever. Again, there were obviously right answers, things they wanted to hear, and Danny could tell she'd given the wrong answer. So she continued, "Los Angeles is on fire. You must have heard. It's swarming with zom—with zeros. Police and Rescue was down within five hours of the outbreak. I was in an isolated community. We got out on a wave of dead."

"We heard all about that," Anka said. "Los Angeles went a little sooner than elsewhere. It was on the news, while there was still news. Now we don't even have the internet." Danny could see her audience losing interest. These people were hungry for real facts, something useful. They were more isolated than Danny had at first imagined. Maybe it was her who needed to be asking questions, not the senator.

"I can be more useful if I have some idea of the situation," Danny said. "Don't want to repeat what you already know. I saw a lot of action between here and the Southland and I can maybe fill in the blanks. Roads, railways, towns, some are open. Some are not."

Senator Anka leaned forward, revealing a string of irregular pearls like baby's teeth that dangled in her ruffled cleavage. It seemed Danny had passed some kind of initial inspection. Now, apparently, they could talk. "Find her a chair, Kyle," Anka said, and the male aide hustled out of the room. He returned moments later with a steel folding model. Danny was grateful. She sat, and her bones ached in concert. Anka opened her sparkling red mouth and let it hang, waiting for the words to enter it, certain they would come. Her job in better times was to speak. She began:

"Some days ago, as I assume you know, terrorists attacked sixty-three world cities with a biological weapon. It may have been more cities. We don't have complete data. The attacks were coordinated and occurred within a half-hour period, worldwide. The biological agent is unknown but believed to be engineered, because there's no disease like it. We have laboratory people working on that in Denver, here, and in Virginia. Or we think so. D.C. has broken contact, but that's part of the program for these kinds of situations. Don't want to let them know who they've gotten or not gotten at the federal level. Whoever they might be."

The senator sounded bitter at this. Danny imagined a prominent member of the party in power would not be amused to find herself out of the loop. Maybe she was missing the caviar down in the luxury fallout shelters Washington was rumored to have.

The famous voice smoothed out again: "All of which information is not at your pay grade. But we're in this together."

"And then?" Danny said. She realized she was biting rags of skin from around her fingernails, making them bleed through the dirt. She folded her hands. The senator's hands, Danny observed, looked much older than the rest of her, the skin papery and spotted, knuckles prominent. Anka selected her facts and went on.

"There is a set of contingency plans for biological attack, but not on this scale. The disease moved swiftly."

"I saw it," Danny said. "People went crazy and ran and when they ran they spread it to the next people. It spread as fast as we can run."

"Or drive," Anka added. "Most people had only ten minutes from exposure before they collapsed, but it could incubate for hours in the right person. You may have seen this. We even have some immune carriers isolated at the medical center near here. Infected, capable of transmission, but themselves unaffected by symptoms. The virus seems capable of changing its methods."

"I want to talk to you about that," Danny said. "They're getting smarter. The—the zeros."

Anka's eyes cut to the aides, who were listening politely. She gave her head a single, slight shake. Danny didn't pursue the subject.

"Merely a side effect," Anka said, a bit of nonsense to keep the silence from becoming punctuation. She hurried on: "The main thing is the disease no longer communicates by air. Only through bites or introduction into the bloodstream. Which is a good thing. A positive development. It's much safer now."

"I hadn't thought of it quite that way," Danny said.

"We must be positive even as we are realistic, yes? Our scientists call this *tropism,* I believe. The virus is adapting itself to the host. It was difficult enough when the afflicted collapsed and died of the airborne form of the disease. That alone was catastrophic. But then they rose up again, apparently helpless, and survivors in the tens of thousands everywhere began taking them to first responders. Hospitals, police, fire stations, even public offices, everywhere was crammed with these so-called zeros. It was an impossible situation. Then when they began to attack, to feed, if you will, the first of the living to succumb were of course the professionals trained to deal with a crisis."

"Those paramilitary contractors guarding the building seem to be in pretty good shape."

"They have saved our bacon, so to speak. Without them we'd be in chaos. Private enterprise is always the best way to go, and I say that despite my status as a career public servant. Nothing like profits to motivate a person. Of course presently we're measuring profits in IOUs, but still. In any case they weren't on the front lines initially, so they enjoyed the opportunity to respond from positions outside the epicenters of the disease. Which they did, securing strongholds such as this one, and guiding the sweeps to clear the streets and buildings. We owe them the admirable calm that pertains outside today, which I'm sure you observed."

"Yes," Danny said. She didn't have much of an opinion of the calm outside yet, but she thought she probably didn't like it. It was shoot-on-sight calm. Senator Anka nodded and continued.

"Of course we suffered a massive influx of panicked citizens from all directions, and they brought the sickness with them. That's why we're allowing the fires to burn, to help cleanse some of the worst areas." *And because you have nobody to fight the fires,* Danny thought, remembering the hydrant spurting down the street outside. "The private security people have done wonders to sort that out, and we've started organizing everyone into local and nonlocal populations so we can determine how best to house them and possibly move them if the safe area requires adjustment. It also represents a database of survivors, which we will need eventually. It's all on computers right here in this building."

Danny's heart was racing: They were taking names of outsiders. Lists of refugees. Kelley.

She missed some of what the senator was saying, tuning back in halfway through: ". . . Despite which, on a larger scale, we lost the state capital; if you came up the coast, you know that. So this is essentially our game to play at the present time. You lost San Diego in the south. Silicon Valley is remarkable well-preserved thus far, thanks to the many gated communities and the high vacancy rates in the areas hardest hit by the economy. But a number of the zeros are coming up, migrating, so to speak, from Mexico and San Diego and there may be a contagion problem within a few days. It's a disease, you understand. A public health crisis, and it has to be addressed as such. It's *not* a military situation."

Danny involuntarily shook her head. "Does Washington agree with that? The Pentagon?"

Anka crimped her mouth into a small, patronizing smile.

"I'm not dealing with Washington, Sheriff. Our communications systems are working well on the West Coast but we have temporarily lost contact with the Eastern Seaboard, I regret to say. I thought I made that clear. The reasons for this will come out in the congressional hearings I will most certainly introduce once this situation has blown over. But don't imagine I'm without allies. We have contact with installations in Colorado and North Dakota, Texas, and Alaska. More will go online as things stabilize. Am I telling you anything you don't know?"

Danny shrugged. It was all news to her; it just wasn't important. She owed these people something, however. They needed to know what she'd seen in Potter.

"Thanks for the briefing. Lemme tell you a couple things," Danny said. "About those things. You want to deal with this like it was the flu or something, you will lose a lot of people. This is a military situation, no question. I gotta disagree with you on that. They *eat* people. They die if you smash their brains. The disease angle I'll buy, sure, if that's where it comes from, but it's not what's killing people now. Those zeros are what's killing people."

Anka's face was puckered with distaste. She wasn't looking for advice. "You fancy yourself quite an expert, I take it. You might be interested to know I get twice-daily briefings from our top people on the ground, here."

"No offense meant, ma'am," Danny said. She could see Senator Anka was becoming angry, but what mattered right now was speaking the truth. "If you get briefings, you probably heard they can hibernate while waiting for people to show up. Don't shake your head at me," she added.

Anka was all but sticking her fingers in her ears, but the aides were sitting bolt upright, staring at Danny. Good. At least somebody was listening. Danny kept on talking, her ears hot with anger, looking at Anka but aiming her words at the aides.

"Did your briefings tell you how they find living people? The zeros, ma'am, they hunt by sense of smell. I'm sure of it. They can see and hear, but that doesn't tell them who's who. They smell the living. I've watched them in action. You can be perfectly still and quiet and they home right in on you anyway. But if there's a real bad smell in the air, they can't lock on. I seen it. They hunt by smell. I think maybe they can smell our breath."

Senator Anka rose to her feet. She was trembling. She turned to the window. Her hands were knotted into small, triangular fists.

"You think you know more than we do?" she said, in her best speech-making voice. "We have scientists, *real* scientists, at work in locations around this area. Promising them a fortune because they won't work voluntarily. When I get back to D.C., of course, my surviving colleagues will refuse to reimburse the expense, but you know what I said? I said, 'This isn't about money.' I certainly hope the voters appreciate that fact."

She turned to face Danny, but her eyes took in the aides, as well, daring them not to listen: "Oh, yes, I too have sacrificed. I worked so hard for a transformation of the way they do business in Washington, and what is my reward? I am accused of being an insider, of being nothing more than a career player. Don't talk to me about partisan politics. I've spent years reaching across the damn aisle and my reward has been opprobrium at every turn! Obloquy! Have you ever heard of anybody in the entire Congress that worked harder to push the president to the center, to get him right there in that sweet spot where Middle America is comfortable? Of course not. I'm the one. He might still be alive if he listened to me sooner. And now—this. Don't lecture *me*, you ragamuffin!"

Danny realized her mouth was hanging open. She closed it with a *click.* The good senator was out of her well-groomed mind.

Danny thought it was probably best to try one more time, then get the hell out of Madame Ahab's presence. The aides were listening; they might pass word to people who still had a toe dipped in the reality pool.

"That's a heck of a burden you're carrying, Senator. Listen, I got one more important thing to tell you about those things. The zeros, not the voters, I mean. It's important. They're getting smarter and faster. The ones nearest the epicenters, like here? They're dumbasses, if you'll excuse me. The farther out you get, the better they get. You know? I don't think it's how *far,* though. I think it's *when* they got infected and died. The ones that came up real recently are a lot different from the first ones. They're . . . you know. Getting smarter."

Danny remembered the word she wanted: *evolving.* But it was too late. The senator wasn't listening, anyway. She had bent over the edge of her desk, scribbling notes with a silver fountain pen. Not, Danny suspected, notes about the lifestyle of zeros as reported by a sheriff from San Bernardino. The senator threw down the pen, folded the sheet of paper, and held it over her head as if signaling a waiter. She kept her arm straight; the sheet rattled in her grip. She would not look up. She wasn't going to look at anyone, now. She snapped the paper in the air, once, signaling her impatience. She was sulking, Danny considered. Who knew. The aides glanced at each other, Danny saw, with a distinct roll of the eyes; then the female took the sheet of paper and left the room.

"You think you know so much," Anka muttered. "Everybody knows more than I do, stuck here incommunicado with all my potential for leadership bottled up in this ridiculous architectural folly. They have their orders, naturally. Hawkstone, excellent people, but they don't get their paychecks from me. That's the problem: We have privatized too much. Money talks. Since the downturn, *only* money talks, preferably gold. What happened to loyalty and love of country? *Patrie,* if you will? I've been overridden, probably by the minority leadership. They've been waiting for this. This is their chance to humiliate me for their defeats."

"I appreciate you giving me the big-picture stuff," Danny said, to break the expanding silence. She got to her feet, ready to be ushered out. But Anka seemed to gather herself back together, to become present. She met Danny's eyes with her own. The dark mood appeared to have evaporated. She even smiled back with her gleaming political teeth.

Danny tried one more time: "I can offer your people some tactical information on dealing with those things. And I can give you some routes downstate, plus some idea where the major concentrations are, if you need to evacuate." Danny was putting her cards on the table. They weren't very good cards, now that she named them. But it sounded as if the unhinged senator was as isolated as Danny was. Even the illusion of information might now be useful. "I also have an idea of where the survivors are coming from. If you can give me lists of people you've taken in, and where they came from, maybe I can cross-check those with what I know and fill in some of the picture."

"That would be excellent," Senator Anka said. Danny could feel the older woman's interest draining away. Anka had been so desperate for information she'd allowed this disgusting creature into her inner sanctum, and now she wanted to get her out as quickly as she could. It was written on her face for Danny to see. "I'll have my people liaise with you downstairs," she continued. "Sometime soon. They'll report back to me. Is there anything else you want to know?"

Danny thought of coming right out and asking for help searching for her sister, but she'd already started to play that angle by asking for access to personnel lists. She had a strong hunch that the direct approach would not work. These people didn't have the time or resources for personal concerns. They'd probably lost everyone themselves. Danny would become just another frantic relative instead of a useful professional resource. She didn't think she would be granted another audience with the Great Lady, so this was it, her only chance at a bird's-eye view of the crisis nationwide. There had to be something else worth knowing. It was so little she'd been told.

But there might not be any more information. Danny thought of the wildfires that sometimes swept her home region, scorching the mountainsides. How, in those crises, they were always looking for eyewitness accounts to make sense of the bigger situation, and how the eyewitnesses always wanted the big picture back: how much of the fire was contained, how many people had been evacuated.

"One thing," Danny said. "About how much has this situation been contained?"

"Contained?" Anka repeated. Her face was blank.

"I mean is it spreading, is the problem under control, are we at 20 percent, 50 percent?"

"We don't think of it in those terms," the senator said, and Danny had her answer.

A thin streak of anger passed through Danny's mind. She wanted to snap at this slick woman with her illusions of power and control, knock her out of the trance she was in. At a gesture, the male aide stood up and crossed to Danny, as if to take her chair. Interview over. Danny wasn't quite finished. She wanted to get the last word.

"Why did you choose this building for your HQ?" Danny asked.

Anka was surprised by the question. "Why do you ask?"

"You planning to use a chopper to get out of town when the zeros break through?"

Danny stood up and leaned over the desk. The senator's face became cold and haughty, like photographs Danny had seen.

"I *do* have a helicopter at my disposal," Anka said, her voice high and self-righteous. "But we won't be fleeing the city, thank you."

Danny shrugged and turned to the door. "Good," she said, pausing in the doorway, "because this here is the only building in town that hasn't got a roof to land it on."

With that, Danny walked out of the room. The male aide closed the door on her back and Danny could hear Senator Anka's voice raised in anger behind the inch-thick wooden panel.

Mitchell met her in the waiting area, and Eric silently escorted them to the elevator and the grim private security man inside. The senator hadn't shaken her hand, Danny realized, coming in or going out. Probably scared to death of the contagion. She didn't understand it wasn't the disease they had to worry about; it was the undead. She had said this wasn't a military situation. She was dead wrong. And the way Anka's eyes went cold at Danny's use of the word "containment" was significant. The most important thing of all. How much was the problem contained? The number, appropriately enough, that Vivian Anka hadn't said—was zero.

The barracks had been an internet service company's worker-bee offices until the rise of the dead. Now the chest-high purple-gray cubicle walls partitioned off sleeping spaces: two per cubicle on the floor, sometimes a third crashed out on the desk surface above. There were little vinyl action figures and framed photos and Dilbert cartoons cluttering the margins of the cubicles, along with half-deflated Mylar birthday balloons, novelty calendars, dying plants in plastic pots, and junk-food wrappers.

Mitchell led Danny to a cubicle halfway along the second floor. It was occupied by a young Native-American-looking woman lying in a sleeping bag. She had two black eyes and her nose in a splint. Her copper-colored skin was yellow at the high points; she looked as if she hadn't slept in days. She recoiled involuntarily when she saw Danny, and stood up, the sleeping bag pooling at her feet.

"Yanaba, this is Danielle. She'll be your roomie for a while. Don't worry, we'll get her cleaned up."

Mitchell walked away with that, leaving Yanaba and Danny standing in awkward silence.

"You want a shower?" Yanaba finally said. There were no pleasantries to exchange, after all. They were not pleased to meet each other and Danny was not welcome. They were merely *there,* and that was that. "There's a sign-up sheet by the stairwell," Yanaba continued. "It's probably wide open right now." She spoke in a slow, deliberate cadence, as if reading her words from an invisible page.

Danny grunted and walked down the hall. An hour later she was clean, the remains of her uniform were in an industrial laundry in the commandeered hotel basement next door (the hotel rooms were obviously reserved for the Hawkstone paramilitary elite, with lesser folks crashing wherever there was cover), and Danny was wearing jeans and a faded T-shirt that had *Datacon 2006* written across the chest.

Mitchell was gone, presumably back to his post. Danny didn't know if Yanaba was still in the designated cubicle, because she didn't bother going back to it. She'd brought nothing with her but the uniform. The Mustang with her accumulated gear inside was hidden a mile from the marina from which she had embarked on her coastal voyage.

Danny found herself patrolling the building, looking at it from a security standpoint: it was a piss-poor place to be when the zeros broke through the front lines, as Danny had no doubt they would. Huge walls of glass, fire doors and blind alleys, little stairways leading up the outside of the structure onto the roof, where there was an employee patio and some highly insecure plate-glass doors. It was fine security against intelligent human beings, but Danny had seen the flesh-eaters push their way through a wall of glass back in Forest Peak. She knew the only deterrent for them was sheer structural resistance.

Still, this was a temporary arrangement. She didn't have to put up with it for long.

A man in a window cleaner's coveralls approached Danny as the sun was going down behind the smoke, casting the city in bronze. He was lean and tough and his eyes never stopped checking the environment around him. Either ex-military or a street person, Danny thought. *Or both, like you and Wulf,* the head-voice added. His cheeks were caved in and strapped with creases. He looked old. He was not as old as he looked.

"You're Sheriff Adelman, right?" he said. Danny nodded. "You match the description. I'm Kaufman. Welcome to Oz."

Danny followed him down to the lobby. Across the plaza outside, a convoy of minivans and a Jeep was idling at the curb. "All able-bodied personnel take a shift on security," Kaufman said. "And they put you top of the list. You look like you know what you're doing," he added, with an appraising glance at Danny. They exited the lobby.

Men and women were hunched inside the vehicles, a capacity crowd. Rifles and shotguns bristled between their knees. Kaufman kept up a steady patter on the way to the street: It wasn't idle chat. He had information to convey as they crossed the plaza.

"We go out in teams of five, one per vehicle. We have maps. Designated blocks. Each team takes its block and we put a man on every side of the block, with one man patrolling clockwise around it. We radio in after every rotation, and we switch off who's doing the walking. Everybody gets some exercise. There are supposed to be shooters on the roofs all around, so if you call in a problem, the shooter goes to the nearest vantage point and covers your ass until backup shows up. If there's no shooter in your position you deal with it. Tell you the truth there won't be a shooter. Anybody that can shoot gets recruited by those Hawkstone vigilantes."

"Why don't they patrol, too?" Danny asked, as they approached the vehicles. "They have the best gear. They have those Bradleys. They have the training."

Kaufman made a noise of contempt in his throat.

"Those pricks don't do shit. They're in charge, and nobody else. They have some kind of agenda, and we're trying to figure out what the fuck it is. So-called leadership is shitting a brick up there in the Pyramid."

"I met the senator today," Danny said.

"She say anything useful?"

"She doesn't know shit," Danny said.

"So to put things in perspective, you went up to the thirty-third floor, am I right?" Kaufman said. "To meet the highest-ranking civilian in town. And yet—the Pyramid is forty-eight floors, you know. Those Hawkstone *Shutzstaffel* have the top."

They climbed into a liver-colored Astrovan and Kaufman slid the door shut behind them. Somebody in the backseat passed Danny a deer rifle and a utility knife. The man in the passenger seat handed her one of those solid-state flashlights that are supposed to last a lifetime but get lost in a couple of months.

"Welcome to the zone," the man said, and turned around to look out the windshield as they rolled toward the perimeter.

Danny marched with the rest, shining the weak flashlight into every shadow, every angle in the architecture. Kaufman said the entire area had been cleared of zeros. When was the last time they checked? Although the street was empty, there were hundreds of people huddled indoors. Apparently minimum occupancy was ten to a room, at this point. The office building with its three-to-a-cubicle population represented elite status. There were no lights inside the windows, no voices, no music drifting out. There was a whiff of human excrement in the air, even outside, even with the stench of the fires. Indoors must have been unbearable.

The curfew under which these people were living was even harsher than the lockdowns in Iraq that Danny had participated in. Because of the zombies. Absolute silence, absolute darkness was required. Hide like rabbits, day and night. It was a stupid arrangement, Danny thought. All this manpower locked up and doing nothing. They needed to make downtown into a fortress, not a prison. They needed something to do. They needed to participate in their own defense. It could only be a matter of time, and not much of that, before the zeros got through. Then all these buildings crammed with people would become enormous meat lockers.

It was three in the morning and Danny had made two circuits around the block, besides standing guard on east and south sides while others in her team did the patrolling. Now and then she would see the flicker of a candle or flashlight in one of the windows of the apartment buildings of which her territory was comprised. There was no power for the street lights, but the fires half a mile away cast a red glow over everything, reflected in the clouds of smoke. No stars, no moon. The smoke obscured everything. Shadows seemed deeper and darker, tinged a velvety purple. The street-level frontages were shops, mostly; Danny could see vague shapes of people inside, sleeping in rows on the floor between the display racks and merchandise. Danny could not imagine sleeping in such an exposed situation. Then again, she didn't sleep much anyway.

With nothing to do but stand guard or walk the block, her thoughts circled around in the same way, always returning to the same points, searching for an analysis that would suggest her next line of action. She wasn't drinking, so her mind was clear. This was not an advantage. It meant she couldn't stifle the thoughts that swarmed like bats and distracted her from her reasoning. She considered the strange interview with the senator. Paranoid? Sheltered? What the hell had it all meant? Danny felt as if she'd been brought in mainly to give Senator Anka a distraction, not to offer information.

The politician might have been famous, and she might once have been powerful, but right now she was more like some kind of sideshow. At least that's how it seemed to Danny. She remembered how the woman had reacted when Danny observed that the helicopter didn't have a roof to land on in her building. It must have been what the mercenaries promised her: Keep up the good work, act like a leader, and when the city falls beneath the teeth of the undead, we'll give you a lift in our helicopter. Only you'll have to brave the zeros swarming the streets if you want to *get* to the helicopter, because we put you in a pointed building with no landing place on top.

The weird thing was, anybody could have figured it out. Danny was pretty sure everyone but Anka already knew it. The Great Woman was so sheltered she had stopped thinking for herself. Or she actually believed she was going to be safe in her tower indefinitely.

How did this affect Danny's plans? It meant there was no working government, not in California, not (if the senator was right) in America. There was no organized resistance. So moving forward, Danny was going to have to work with the next-biggest bully. That probably meant Hawkstone right now, and after that, whatever military units coordinated a defense and started taking command. The only problem was, she hated the mercenary system and all the assholes in it. She had dealt with men like that during her tours of duty. They were sociopath cowboys, overpaid and undertrained. Ex-military men or ex-cops, mostly. Addicted to fast money, adrenaline, testosterone, gunpowder, and usually crank. Now they were doubly amped up because they were in danger at home, not in some desert on the ass-end of the world.

So the first line of reckoning was what to do about staying out of human-generated trouble until she found Kelley. The second issue to think about was how to accomplish the task itself.

Kelley was either somewhere, or she was dead. America was a big place, zombies or no zombies. In the days since Kelley left her note and fled the Adelman household, she could have gotten to the East Coast, Alaska, Panama, or for that matter anywhere in the world, if she bought a plane ticket. And if the world hadn't chosen that particular moment to end.

As it was, Danny knew that Kelley had not taken the Mustang any farther than Potter. For some reason, she'd put the keys up under the sun visor and walked away. That suggested (if she hadn't just walked away to take a bathroom break, and never returned) that Kelley either met her boyfriend, presumably Barry Davis, with the plan of taking his ride the rest of the way to their destination, or they were meeting up with the intention of taking a train in Potter. But Danny didn't have the crucial timeline of events. It was also possible the two of them got that far when the crisis broke out, the mercenaries gunned them down, and Danny had missed seeing Kelley's rotting corpse in the mountain of them dumped by the railroad tracks. Maybe she had walked away from the car at gunpoint.

Danny worked the problem from every angle, fitting her meager store of facts together on all sides, at every angle, trying to find a match. Nothing so far. Did her jacket on the passenger seat of the Mustang mean Kelley had traveled alone? Did Kelley wear it out of the house and leave it behind? Did it matter? Danny didn't even know what was relevant. Maybe Kelley drove the car to Potter, set off on foot, and was halfway to Nevada with a backpack full of trail mix, completely unaware of the disaster. Maybe Kelley died back in Riverton, where Danny met Topper and Ernie. Somebody killed her and jumped into the gassed-up Mustang and drove to Potter because it was the next big place to go. There were too many possible outcomes. All of them included the random chance of being savaged by an undead cannibal.

It was all too much. Danny walked the beat and thought and argued with herself and came up with nothing.

There was another issue that claimed her attention, the concern that hung over all the rest: Kelley or no Kelley, what next?

It was *not* too much to say that the end of the world had arrived. Not the comic-book End Times as described by the evangelicals, a great big biblical special-effects extravaganza with asteroids and hellfire and Death on a Pale Horse: There was no righteous Creator overseeing this crisis. No mercy, no meaning, and there were no chosen people. People of every faith, atheists, sinners, and saints, they were all among the reanimated dead walking the earth, in search of flesh to tear from the limbs of the living. The end of the world was here, and as always—like all the rest of the end-of-the-world calamities mankind had survived—it was up to the unimaginative, fighting, enduring types, like Danny (for so she considered herself), to pick up the pieces and carry on. The ones that got wiped out were the interesting people.

So what next? Was it going to be six months of waiting for the zeros to rot off their own bones, to decay until they could no longer attack? Or did the living flesh they consumed keep them going, arrest the processes of death? For all Danny knew, they were now immortal unless destroyed. The chef in the hotel kitchen back in Potter had huge, stinking stains under his arms and at his crotch. Was that rotten sweat and shit, or was he starting to decompose? *Jesus,* Danny thought. *Even to think this stuff is insane. Now I'm making plans around it.*

But there had to be something beyond the current mission. A bigger game plan. Danny could only think of two ideas. The first was obvious. Find a cure, an antidote. Something to wipe the zombies out. Something to stop the virus, to immunize the living against infection. That wasn't something she could do, of course. But she could help others to do it. Senator Anka had said there were scientists working on it, right here in the city.

Danny didn't think they would be doing it there much longer: Even with the distant boom of the fires, she could hear moaning out there in the night. It was only a matter of time before the defenses fell; she herself was going to be as far from the city as possible when that moment arrived, regardless of what anybody else had in mind.

Another option wasn't obvious to Danny at all, because it went against the way she thought and acted. But there wasn't anything else viable to do. Get back to her little tribe of people at Boscombe Field, maybe pick up some others along the way, and find a safe place to wait out the storm. Live off the land. Hunt and grow seeds into crops. Hell, Amy could raise rabbits and pigs and horses and maybe Danny could eventually convince her to let them eat a few. Danny had a good cross-section of talents among them: Topper and Ernie knew machines. They could work metal. They could handle tools as well as weapons.

Troy knew what to do in an emergency. In his way he was as capable as Danny herself, if not as seasoned by adverse experience. Wulf was a hunter, a tracker. A survivor. Amy was also a doctor, if they needed one. The Mexican woman, Maria, was a born accomplisher, somebody who did things without being asked and didn't stop until a thing was done. Patrick could remind them not to descend into barbarism. There was the quiet baby and blue-haired Michelle and her brother Jimmy James, who represented the future.

Others had value, too. Danny didn't really know them. Some of the faces she could only barely conjure in her mind. She'd been away from them as long as she'd been with them, now. They were all a resource to be used for survival. Not only a resource, though—it didn't sit right in Danny's mind to think of them that way, although that was her first instinct. More than that, they were her people. They were in this thing with her. And once she admitted that, she knew she had let them down. She had put her personal crusade first, when none of them had done the same. They all had families, loved ones, friends. Were they any less sisters or brothers than Danny?

The answer to that question hurt. They were *more* so than Danny.

That's why she had left them behind to search for her sister: To Kelley, she was less family, less loved one, less friend. The farewell note was engraved in her memory, verbatim. It ached unbearably, cut into her soul one word at a time. Now, just a few days too late, she was trying to make amends to the sister she'd let down for most of her life. But in doing so, she had let the others down, abandoned them.

Danny was grappling with ideas of a kind she'd never had to deal with before. It scared her. This was the stuff she'd been running from all her life, and if she stopped running now, it would mean she'd been wrong all those years. Her motto had always been *I can handle this.* If she fell back on a bunch of incompetent civilians, she wasn't stronger. She was weaker.

What she'd never considered was the idea that "stronger" wasn't the only virtue. There were other things. Being a good friend, maybe. Not only being close to people, but *needing* them. She'd always thought of that as a weakness, but it was also a strength.

And Kelley—what did Danny even need her for? Maybe hope. Maybe atonement. Maybe she simply loved her, and that was all there was to it.

Soon she would have to go back. This whole junket to San Francisco was a terrible sidetrack, and now she was hooked into some kind of poorly run, counterproductive system even less effective than the theaters of war she'd been in overseas. *This is getting to be a habit with me,* she thought. *Seeking out disasters to be part of.* Like she had to find situations where her somewhat brutal talents would be needed. Danny knew, down inside herself where she seldom ventured to explore, that something had now changed. Even if Amy and all the others didn't need her, and were prospering at the airfield, the fact remained: She needed them.

3

The dawn after Danny slipped away in the night, it was Maria who discovered her absence.

Maria was up early, as was her habit. The sun was below the horizon, washing the sky behind the mountains with pale pastel colors. Maria had been sleeping on a folding cot by the radio. Now she said a brief prayer to the God she wasn't so sure she understood anymore. Then she went downstairs and looked into the office, where she saw the empty couch with a blanket rumpled up on it. The red-haired *renegada* sheriff lady wasn't in there. Not surprising: She hardly ever slept. Probably patrolling the fence.

Maria went outside into the cool, dewy air and breathed in the freshness of it before the sun could rise and bake it dry. On her way back into the tower, she saw a piece of paper, folded double and taped to the glass door. She hadn't noticed it on the way out. The paper had "FOR AMY" written on it in big block letters. Maria opened it, and read:

> *Amy: Keep them here. Back with Kelley.*
>> *Danny*

Maria knew who Kelley was, because Amy had told her about Danny's personal troubles, and the long, bitter note Kelley had written. But at first Maria didn't understand. Keep who here? Herself and the others? Did Danny know where Kelley *was*? How long would it take to get her, a day? A week?

Before she even knew she was on the move, Maria found herself shaking Amy awake in the dormitory of the terminal. Amy drifted up from an exhausted sleep, eyes rolling, mumbling. Some of the others woke up; the boy Jimmy James sat up in his top bunk and watched them with wary eyes that looked too old for his face. Maria thrust the note into Amy's hands.

"Scrambled, with rye toast, dry," Amy said, and blinked, and looked at Maria's tense face. Then the note. She woke up in a hurry.

"God *darnit*, Danny," she said. "You big *dumbhead*."

It was time to prepare for a long stay at the airfield. Amy didn't know how long they would need to remain there, and she didn't know how long Danny would be gone—if she even planned to return. Amy swore Maria to silence regarding the contents of the note; it wasn't that the note itself contained anything incriminating, but rather that it contained so little.

She called a general meeting and told the others that Danny was on a mission, and there was nothing to worry about. "I think you all know by now she's a lone wolf type," Amy said, "and she always comes back. She'll probably bring the cavalry with her."

Nobody seemed to be worried. Except Patrick, but he didn't say anything. He could read Amy. That made her nervous. She knew herself to be highly legible, to the right person. The boy Jimmy James was another one. He knew something was up. But he also kept his silence, although that was more due to his nature than to an awareness of a need for discretion. So Amy bluffed her way through it, some twenty or twenty-five faces turned in her direction looking as if they believed her and were interested in what she had to say, to varying degrees.

"These jobs are things Danny suggested to me," Amy lied, "things we can do while she's gone. She says they're, um, vital efforts to ensure our, um, long-term viability. In those words pretty much."

"Sheriff don't want to do the manual labor," Topper complained.

Think anything you want, was Amy's fervent wish. *Just don't think too hard.*

The first project she'd come up with was a simple matter of efficiency. The airfield had a finite supply of water, and so far they had used it with abandon. Now it was time to start conserving the stuff. That meant arranging some long-drop toilet facilities. At seven gallons a flush, they needed to start crapping in a hole. There was a general groan of dismay at this, but these people were all from the Southland. They knew about water shortages. Simon the accountant raised his hand: "I guess we can't wash the driveway with a hose, either," he said. That got a laugh. Mostly from Amy, who was on the verge of hysteria.

Amy gave Topper and Ernie the task of figuring out where the drainpipes went, and diverting the bathing and washing water so it could be collected. She wasn't sure what they were collecting it for, but that's what they seemed to do in the magazine articles on resource conservation she never quite got around to properly reading. Maybe they could grow their own corn with it, someday. Primarily it was an unpleasant, demanding job that would keep the restless bikers occupied for a couple of days. That was something Danny had explained to Amy a while back: Leadership is the act of causing other people to invest themselves in difficult work. You can't go easy on people and lead them at the same time. If you go easy on them, they will either self-destruct or find a different leader. *Human nature,* Danny would say. *Fucking ridiculous.* And then she'd pour herself another shot.

Leadership didn't come naturally to Amy. *People* didn't come naturally to her. She was going to have to figure it out until Danny got back, assuming she did, assuming she didn't get all dead and start chomping around. Amy's plan was simple: Do what Danny would do. Except, of course, the part where she took off and left everybody behind.

The second project was simpler, and Troy Huppert was happy to lead the effort. He took a team of ten people around the entire perimeter fence, looking for places that required reinforcement. Then they set to work building up those weak spots. There weren't many, but, as Troy said, it only took one.

Those two zombies moved slowly along the fence, hooking their gray fingers through the wire, always trying to get close to the living that were at work on the other side of the mesh. The small girl's empty sleeve of torn skin swayed as she moved. It was sickening to look at, but nobody went for long without glancing at the undead that yearned to get among them. The consensus was that these two zombies should be dispatched very soon. It was too much to handle, having them watching.

For the remaining people in the assembly, Amy concocted minor jobs: cleaning, stock taking of food and supplies, simple maintenance. Patrick was in charge of this cluster of tasks, and obviously grateful for something to do. They might be here another couple of days, or it might be six months. Amy wanted to proceed under the latter assumption. That meant knowing exactly what they had to work with, and taking care of it. This didn't require visualizing what Danny would do: As a country veterinarian, Amy knew all about conservation and maintenance of supplies. Her business lived by the careful shepherding of expensive materials for as long as they would last, juggling availability with expiration dates.

Maria stayed up in the tower with the radio. Ernie posted watch. Amy realized there was only one person who didn't know what to do that day: herself.

After a brief inspection of Topper and Ernie's trench-digging efforts, which had yielded several lengths of old rust-furred iron pipe, Amy decided she might be well employed watching the road for any sign of Danny's return. So she sat herself on the bumper of one of the minnows, a pickup truck with a fiberglass cap, and kept her eye on the ribbon of asphalt that wiggled away through the scrub desert.

She sat there for half an hour before she realized she could see something approaching. It was a cloud of dust. At first she thought it was a dust devil, one of those tiny cyclones that whirled up off the sand and threw litter around before blowing itself out.

But this one didn't blow out. It grew.

Eventually Amy could see the dark ciphers of vehicles emerging from the horizon, growing as they approached. Three or four of them. Then Amy found Wulf at her elbow. He was also watching, his rumpled eyes squinting into the hard light.

"I guess we shouldn't have counted on staying alone out here," Amy said.

"Military," Wulf said.

"You can't tell that from here."

"They're spaced out perfect. Hundred meters each. It's a convoy. *Xin chao*, Doc. I'm outta here," he said, and slung his rifle over his shoulder. He shambled over to the nearest hangar and emerged a few moments later with a child's nylon backpack. It had a unicorn embroidered on it.

"You've been waiting for this," Amy protested. "You're just like Danny. You can't wait to let everybody down."

"Didn't make no fuckin' promises to nobody," Wulf muttered. "Keys."

Amy had the key to the new padlock that held the gates shut. She let Wulf out without further discussion, knowing there was none to be had. He really was a lot like Danny, obstinate and alone. Wulf didn't walk down the road, but disappeared with surprising speed into the rutted landscape uphill of the airfield. Amy felt a little tickle of fear in the back of her belly. Those vehicles approaching represented change. A new situation. Amy was sick of new situations. At the time she wouldn't have thought of this as a premonition. Later, she would describe it exactly that way.

There were three vehicles, a pair of military Humvees with the deep, buttressed suspensions that gave them impossible ground clearance; both had .50 caliber machine guns mounted on the roofs. Behind them was a hulking machine that Amy thought looked like a tank on wheels instead of treads, its turret bristling with weapons. All three vehicles were painted in an angular black-and-gray camouflage pattern Amy didn't remember seeing before. Danny would have recognized it.

The word HAWKSTONE was lettered discreetly on the cab doors of the vehicles, accented with a logo: a simplified eagle's head over an American flag. Amy guessed this meant they were some kind of private outfit, but for all she knew there was a Hawkstone branch of the Marines or something. Big Red One, Screaming Eagles, and all that fierce-sounding stuff Danny was into. A stocky man wearing the same camouflage as the vehicles sprang out of the lead Humvee almost before it stopped moving. He came right up to the gates and banged on the metal frame with a fancy assault weapon, as if Amy and the half-dozen others now gathered behind the gates couldn't see him.

"Hi," Amy said, aware it might sound somewhat lame.

"Open up on the double," the man said, and waved at his companions in the second Humvee. Two men climbed down from the cargo area in back, carrying a third man between them in a fireman's lift. The third man's leg was saturated with blood streaming from the thigh, and he looked pale and ill.

Topper came right up to the gate and squared off in front of the man with the gun. "What's your business?" he said.

"We got wounded," the stocky man replied.

"I see that. And you're waving a gun around."

"Open the fucking gates," the man said, and Amy stepped between them and released the padlock.

There was a great bustle of activity as the wounded man was carried into the terminal building and laid out on the Ping-Pong table in the rec room, his head propped up on a greasy old sofa cushion, a hastily stripped bedsheet beneath him. Everyone who wasn't helping was watching, so it seemed almost incidental that the two Humvees and the big, tanklike vehicle, an M1117 ASV, rolled through the gates and took up prominent positions in the center of the airfield parking lot. Their noses were pointed in an arc outward, tail-to-tail, creating a defensible center and a comprehensive field of fire—but not out at the desert. Inward, toward the airfield.

The new arrivals moved with such purpose that it wasn't questioned. Patrick returned from the motor home with the big duffel bag of medical supplies they'd accumulated, only to find himself having to ask permission to enter the terminal building from a pair of muscular, uniformed men holding machine guns across their chests.

He knew instantly that everything had changed. The problem wasn't just zombies anymore.

Amy tried to remember how many of these people knew she wasn't a doctor. The short, stocky guy in uniform was addressed as "Murdo"; he was clearly in charge. Head like a fist, fringed with dense, black hair, balding in back to reveal an almost perfectly round cap of gleaming scalp.

These must be guys like the mercenaries Danny complained about dealing with in Iraq—hotshots with fancy guns and no particular allegiance to the Geneva Conventions.

Murdo called the huge men that flanked him Reese and Boudreau. Boudreau had to be six-five, his nose broken more than once so it tapered the wrong way—getting broader and more prominent between his eyes, almost flat above his mouth. Reese had no fat on him, not a spare scrap of flesh: His anatomy showed through the skin like steel cables on an iron frame.

The wounded man's name was Jones, because Murdo kept repeating that "Jones fucked us," when he wasn't shouting at people to get back or telling his men to secure their position.

Amy hadn't intended to volunteer her medical services, but several of the civilians she'd been traveling with pointed her out to Murdo and said she was a doctor. Amy regretted that particular subterfuge. Troy wasn't there to disagree, because he had been marched away along with Topper, Ernie, and a couple of other men who looked physically capable. Where they were now, Amy did not know. Their guard was Parker, a black man with a massive neck wider than his head.

She had never explained to these others that she was only a veterinarian. It wouldn't be good for morale: hers or theirs. She still had an inferiority complex when it came to human doctors. Now she wished very much that she hadn't let the matter slide.

Murdo pounded on the table. "You!" he barked at Amy. "Jones here needs some repairs. So let's get going with it."

Now was the time to come clean, Amy knew, before this went any further. If she messed up and lost this poor kid with the bullet in his leg, there would be heck to pay. If she told them all what she really was, they couldn't possibly make her operate. Patrick knew her secret, as well; surely *he* would say something. Everyone was crowding in, the men with guns and the civilians both, pressing close, caught up in the panic. Jones was wailing with pain.

"Listen to me," Amy said. "I'm not—"

A deafening noise threw everybody down on the floor except the men in uniform. The air went rank with cordite stink. Bent-nosed Boudreau had fired a bullet into the ceiling. The shell casing jingled on the linoleum.

"There's no time for this shit," Murdo said. "You all keep the fuck back and let the little lady do her thing."

The others did what he said, wet-eyed and afraid.

Amy looked at Jones. His skin was pale, like beeswax. He was sweating.

His mouth was contorted with pain. Amy visualized a horse in the same situation. That didn't work. A dog? More like it. This was not a man—it was a dog with very straight back legs. It had an injured limb, and Amy had to repair it. Same basic hydraulics, same structures. Different response to anesthetics, but she didn't have any animal tranquilizers, so it was hard to go wrong there.

"Patrick, you're my assistant. We need to wash up, and then let's get to work."

A minute later they were scrubbing their hands in the men's room, hissing at each other in urgent whispers.

"I can't do this—the sight of blood makes me faint," Patrick said.

"Faint later," Amy said. "We have to get this guy patched up and get them all out of here as fast as we can, because they're psycho-birdies, in case you didn't notice."

"You think they'll just shake our hands and leave?" Patrick snorted. "Duh. They're gonna look around here and figure out they have it made, and they'll sit out the situation with us as their servants. Trust me on this. I used to be a waiter. Them, you don't want to wait on."

"Either way, we have to do this. We don't have a choice. It's going to look really gross, so do what I say and don't think about it."

"Oh, yeah, *right.* Great advice."

"You want great advice?" Amy whispered, trying not to shout. She was pulling on a pair of latex gloves.

"Yes, I want great advice."

"Don't puke in the wound."

Even with all the horror Patrick had seen in the last fortnight or so, the sight of serious injuries still made him feel light-headed and ill. Amy lifted the sticky cloth away, strings of coagulated blood stretching and breaking. Pale flesh stained with red, the hairs glued down. Around the entry wound a puffed-up doughnut of skin. The crater itself, a purple-black orifice, didn't look as bad as Patrick expected. Amy had him pass along fistfuls of gauze, the sterile water, and any kind of antiseptic wipes he could find in their medical kit duffel bag; Patrick was hopeful she was just going to clean the skin and wrap the thing up, job done.

"Look for liquid iodine or something," Amy said. "There might be some peroxide in a brown bottle, that'll work." Patrick knew exactly what peroxide looked like. There was a full bottle in the duffel. He handed it over. Amy sloshed the liquid liberally all over the leg injury. It foamed up, brown and fragrant, hissing. Jones screamed.

"Just what the *fuck* do you think you're doing?" Murdo shouted.

"Just the fuck doing my *job,* Mr. Fucker Man," Amy replied. As if to punctuate her response, she swabbed raw iodine on the wound, and Jones screamed again; Reese and Boudreau had to hold him down, Reese on the arms and Boudreau on the knees. By way of comfort they kept telling the writhing Jones not to be a fucking pussy.

In a level voice, Amy said, "Jones, how much do you weigh? One-eighty?"

The wounded man nodded, his teeth clenched so tight he couldn't speak. Amy gestured with her chin: "Patrick, look for a box of little glass bottles labeled 'Procaine Penicillin.'" He located the box and removed a couple of the bottles. "Now," Amy continued, "look for a syringe. It will be in a paper packet." Patrick handed bottles and syringe to Amy.

Patrick was absolutely going to pass out. No question.

Amy unwrapped the syringe and removed the plastic cap from the needle. She inserted the needle through the cap of a procaine bottle and drew the contents up into the syringe. She was about to press the needle into the ragged flesh at the edge of the wound when Patrick interrupted. He couldn't help himself. Mostly, he was trying to postpone the moment when the needle entered the wound.

"Um—aren't you supposed to squirt the bubbles out of the needle first?"

"You think there's no air in there now?" Amy said, and sank the needle to the hilt right down inside the bullet hole.

Patrick made a croaking sound. Even Murdo took half a step back. But Jones didn't seem to feel this additional outrage to his system. Amy picked up the second vial of procaine and injected that one, as well. Into the skin, rather than deep in the meat of the leg. Then she set the syringe aside.

"Don't anybody touch that," she said. "I'll probably need it again. Tweezers, hemostat, scalpel, please."

Before Patrick had a chance to overthink the situation, Amy was deep in the wound. She cut it open wider with the scalpel, had Patrick shine the flashlight down in the throat of the injury, and found what was looking for. Clamped it off with the hemostats. Then, with the long-nosed tweezers, she fished down to the depths, burrowing around for the bullet itself. The hemostats seemed to move of their own volition, like silvery wading birds with sharp beaks. While Amy worked, she began to talk.

"So how did he come by this?" Amy said. "Zombies can't shoot."

"Zeros," Murdo said.

"Zeros who?"

"Zeros is what we call 'em. Not zombies."

"Okay, a zero didn't shoot him. Am I right?"

"Yeah," said Reese. "He shot himself."

"What caliber?"

"Nine millimeter," Jones himself replied. His voice was tight. He was scared. "Pistol. I fucked up."

"Got stuck with a tyro," Murdo said. "Jones, lie still. If you bleed out, we're gonna have to shoot you in the head. You want your momma should see you like that?"

"Nossir." Jones was struggling, obviously feeling Amy's exploration of the wound. He forced himself to lie still, but his face was rigid with the effort.

"We called for a chopper," Murdo said. "No chopper. Lost contact with our main unit four days back. Supposed to rendezvous."

"So, Jones, you shot yourself?" Amy said. "How long ago? A day?"

"Yesterday night," he gasped.

"And since then you've been dealing with it?"

"Like a little baby girl," Boudreau offered, renewing his grip on Jones's knees. Patrick was acutely aware of how close he was to this huge, ugly man: all sour sweat, arm hair, and the whistle of breath through distorted nostrils. Not an appealing encounter. Patrick found he was staring at Boudreau to avoid seeing what Amy was doing. But he had to look, because she'd found something.

"No jacket," Amy said. "Lead slug. You're lucky this didn't fragment too bad, but I think it hit the bone."

Amy retrieved a piece of dark metal the size of a pencil eraser from Jones's leg. Patrick felt an oily tide in the back of his throat, choked it down, and tried to breathe past the acid that surged behind his teeth. This squashed, bloody bit of metal had torn into this man's leg at some huge speed and now Amy was pulling it out the way it came in. Almost too much to bear. He handed her wads of gauze and more of the iodine towelettes and tried to keep himself coherent.

Amy fished out another three or four bits of metal, then a pale sliver of bone that looked like a chewed-up toothpick.

"I don't see anything else, but no warranty is express or implied," Amy said, and then: "Needle and gut, please."

A few minutes later, stitching complete, there was a sterile bandage over the whole thing. Amy released the tourniquet from around Jones's leg, and nothing seemed to happen. The bandage did not turn red. It might have actually worked.

"Can you feel your toes?" Amy asked. But Jones was unconscious.

The Ping-Pong table was a mess of bloody gauze and orange iodine stain, the sheet was ruined, her shirt (and Patrick's, he now observed) spattered with blood and disinfectant. The air had a hospital stink, but also reeked of armpits and fear. Empty first-aid wrappers and packets littered the floor. Jones was breathing fast but his body was limp. His companions let go of him and stepped back. Amy passed her arm across her forehead.

"No charge," she said. "Don't put any weight on that for a few days. Now put those guns away."

Murdo looked at Jones's face, and it was hard to say whether his expression was one of concern or irritation. He looked unsatisfied. Then he brought his eyes up, taking everybody in.

"This entire installation is under our control until further notice," he announced. "Martial law, shoot to kill, you know the drill. Follow my orders, we'll all get along. Fuck with us whatsoever and things will get ugly."

"Under whose authority?" Amy asked. Patrick had his head between his knees. He was recovering from an intense desire to be sick.

"Smith and Wesson," Murdo replied, and walked outside. Boudreau and Reese walked out behind him, and Parker and another man with a shaved head stepped inside the door and stood there with their guns across their chests, eyes as blank as buttons.

"No need to thank me," Amy said.

4

Nobody slept well that night. They'd had so little time without danger staring them in the face, and now instead of the living dead it was assholes with guns.

By morning, Topper had gotten himself beaten to the ground in an altercation with the bald mercenary, whose name was Estevez. Estevez had an illegible tattoo up under his right ear, and another of a teardrop under his left eye. Topper couldn't properly fight back, because he was the one without a gun—and if he *won* the fight, he might still get shot. So he ended up humiliated and bleeding, curled in a ball on the floor of Hangar 2.

The two zombies that had been hanging around outside the fence had started lying on the ground for hours at a time, as if sleeping, until one of the living came close. The next time the zombies stood up, there was a Hawkstone man with a machine gun on the other side of the mesh. All the survivors rushed outside at the sound of gunfire. There wasn't much to see. Just another couple of corpses now. Murdo selected a work party and sent them out to bury the bodies. He didn't allow them a firearm in case there were more of the undead around. "Plenty of rocks out there," he said. "Brain 'em."

Maria was relieved of radio duty. That job fell to one of the paramilitary men, called Flamingo by the others; his face was pink, prematurely creased, and spattered with cancerous-looking freckles. The mercenaries weren't inaccurate with nicknames: in addition to his complexion, Flamingo had enormous arms and skinny legs. There were two other members of the Hawkstone team, for a total of nine: black-haired, blue-eyed Ace, whose face was so immobile it appeared he suffered some kind of paralysis, and Molini. Molini had a single eyebrow identical to his mustache; these features bracketed a nose like an axe blade.

Murdo mostly ignored his civilian charges, preferring to order his men around. Amy thought that was a bad way to do things. It wasn't Danny's approach, that was for sure. But now that the zombies were buried, everybody was idle, sitting around in the rec room or the dormitories, talking in quiet voices. This irritated Molini and Boudreau, the guards at the door—they were sure the conversation was about them. In fact, people were primarily talking about what they would do after things settled down. Outside, the torn-up dirt where Topper and Ernie had undertaken the plumbing project remained as it was. There would be no further improvements. Topper's right eye had puffed shut and his lower lip had split open like a grape; as a result of the fight, he and Ernie were currently confined to the rec room, where they glowered in the corner.

Amy did what she could to defuse the situation through Murdo, catching him as he passed through the terminal.

"Hi," she began, wishing she had a better arsenal of conversation starters. "We should talk."

"Yeah?" Murdo said. He had a way of getting about five inches too close when he spoke to people. It made him look even shorter.

"See, we haven't been here all that long ourselves. And we've been through a lot the last few days. I'm sure you guys have, too. The thing is, we need to all remember we're in this together, you know?"

"So true," Murdo said. Amy was encouraged.

"Because right now there aren't any police or the normal army . . . the regular army, you know what I mean, the official one . . . and there's a lot of looting and stuff. But we're not the ones doing it. We're actually a pretty low-key bunch of people. Right? I mean we are, right?"

"Like newborn lambs. Are we having a chat, or are you going somewhere with this?"

Amy took a long breath. *Here goes.* "I'm saying what I think we'd all prefer is if you could quit guarding us like we were some kind of prisoners, okay? Let us do what we were doing before. There's no point to all this Stalag 13 bull-pucky. I fixed up your buddy's leg, I helped you out, and you are *way* not helping us back."

Murdo nodded, an expression of great thoughtfulness on his squat face.

"You've got a good point there. We come barging in like we own the place, we post guards, and we take immediate, violent action against anybody that resists. That's what you're talking about, am I right?"

"I'm so glad you understand," Amy said, letting the breath go.

Murdo reached up and placed one of his thick hands against the base of Amy's neck. Her "space violated" alarms went off, but she tried not to cringe. He was cooperating, after all. She didn't want to offend him.

"You're a reasonable woman, so I'll explain the situation and I'm sure you'll be with me all the way," Murdo began. "This entire nation was placed under martial law during the first ten hours of this crisis, you know that? No? It was. Coast to coast. You know what that means?" Murdo didn't wait for an answer. Veins were rising in his neck and his face was turning red. "*We're* the law. We're the Army, the Navy, and the FBI."

Amy tried to speak, but Murdo's hand tightened on her neck and he winched his face to within inches of hers, his voice rising: "Our job is to maintain order, you understand? Not, I repeat *not* to babysit a bunch of fucking helpless *fucks* like you people. You got some kind of idea we're not hardcore, is that what you're saying? You think we're not killers?" He threw Amy away from him.

She stumbled backward into a table and gripped the edge of it with both hands and he closed in on her, raging: "You don't know shit. We're the bad-dest of the bad. Stone cold. So you back the fuck off, you keep the rest of these fucking shitstains organized, and once we regain contact with com-mand, you're free to go wherever the fuck you want to go. You can have cake and ice cream, I don't give a shit. Meanwhile the best thing you can do is keep your fucking *people* under control. I don't want my boys to mistake anybody for a zero."

Without waiting for a response, Murdo turned and strode away. The in-terview hadn't gone as well as Amy hoped it would.

By late afternoon the Hawkstone men were sick of patrolling the fence. Some of them argued with Murdo, out on the runway at a good distance from the terminal. But their voices bounced off the sheet-metal hangar walls and straight into the rec room, where the survivors listened in miser-able silence through the open windows.

Murdo was barely in control of his men. That much was obvious. He didn't keep them occupied enough, except standing around guarding things that didn't need guards. And they had been on the move for days, so sitting still felt weird to them. Reese and Ace seemed especially antagonistic. Amy caught one of their convocations, a hissed argument just outside the termi-nal's front doorway. She could see them through the open rec room window nearest the door, if she pressed up close to the frame. It sounded to Amy like the subject was a recurring theme between them.

"Murdo, gimme a fucking break," Reese hissed. "They said find a secure location and *wait for orders*? How could they say that if they didn't know they were gonna drop out of contact?"

"Maybe they *did* know," Murdo replied, almost whining. "I don't ques-tion my orders. Neither should you, Reese."

"So either they *knew* they were gonna have a communications blackout, and didn't tell us, or they didn't see it coming. Either way, we should get the fuck up there and see what's happening, not sit here blowing farts with the fucking Partridge Family."

Reese and Murdo were less than a foot apart, now. Ace stepped back from them and spat on the tarmac by Murdo's boot.

"Murdo ain't got the guts to go up there," Ace said, his voice as expres-sionless as his features.

Murdo rounded on him and shoved his lumpy face right up under Ace's nose. "Stand down, boy."

"Ain't your boy."

"We stay right here until word comes down. We don't know what's happening with HQ. We weren't authorized to speculate. Our job is to hurry the fuck up and fucking wait."

They moved away from the building, and the rest of the conversation wasn't audible to Amy.

The gunmen had only arrived twenty-four hours earlier, and already things were badly off-track. She didn't know how to make it better. If Danny had been here, she might have figured out what to do—or they might have shot her by now. But Danny wasn't here. Amy was responsible. She had to keep the situation under some kind of control. But control had been taken from her, if she ever had it, and Murdo didn't seem to be able to handle it himself.

Half an hour later, Murdo strode into the terminal and zeroed in on Amy.

"I want another little meeting with you," he said.

"I'm right here," Amy said.

"Alone."

Amy was intimidated by physical men. She liked Patrick because he was not physical—he lived in his emotions, his thinking. A guy like Topper was different. He frightened Amy. He was big and fierce and expressed himself through his arms—steering, building, dismantling, dominating his environment with massive strength, the brachioradialis muscles thick as rattlesnakes coiled around his forearms. And Murdo's men had dominated him.

So now Amy was walking behind the hangar with Murdo, a short, solid physical man with cords of anger in his neck. She remembered walking behind the Skyline High football bleachers with Sean Mackey, a brawny kid who looked twenty-five at age sixteen. He was an athlete, a consummate jock. He lured Amy back there, where nobody could see but the trees, and made her do things. His pretext was her superior knowledge of the assigned book in English class; he said he needed help, but he was embarrassed to be seen discussing it in front of anybody. *Discussing it with me, anyway,* Amy had thought at the time.

It was an inspired strategy on Mackey's part: Amy's miserable self-image was certain he had no physical interest in her. She genuinely believed he wanted to pick her brains. So she was flattered, too. What made it even worse was Amy's realization, in hindsight, that he probably didn't have any physical interest in her. He was simply taking away power from a brainy chick who threatened his sense of absolute mastery. Once she'd been talked into letting him come in her mouth while he tugged at her small nipples, her power went away. She was no better than the cheerleaders and debutantes who willingly gave themselves to him. *Not so smart after all,* Amy had chided herself. It still made her face burn to remember the flattering things he'd said back there at the tree line behind the stadium, how he sounded surprised to find her so pretty, how smart was beautiful, can I touch your skin? She never told anybody at the time, not even Danny, although Danny sensed something serious was amiss. Nobody would have asked to touch Danny, back then—she had the worst case of pimples.

Amy never called it rape, what Sean Mackey did, because she'd gone willingly to the slaughter. Not that she found him attractive or interesting or anything, except intimidating. He didn't force himself upon her. He merely stepped behind her defenses.

This old, sore history was bubbling hot in Amy's mind as she followed the squat, intent Murdo behind the hangar. *He had better not try anything,* she thought. *He'd better only have something private to say.* But this was not a man with private thoughts. Amy wondered if she would scream or fight back until he knifed her or shot her or used his pepper spray on her. Even as she planned her defense, she knew deep inside it was all bullshit. She would do what he wanted, take the abuse rather than risk her life, and tell nobody. No . . . someday, she would tell Danny.

They were standing in the shadow of the hangar, which reached up onto the flank of the nearest hill past the fence. Copper-colored light glazed the desert and made it look like the work of a metalsmith's hammer. It was hot and dry but a light breeze signified that the night would be cool. Amy's arms were knotted across her chest. Murdo leaned against the fence looking out, his weight on one arm. His breathing was thick. Amy felt a chill inside her. If this blustering, dangerous little man decided to do something to her, he would kill her when he was finished. The act itself wouldn't satisfy. He'd want to erase the evidence, too.

Amy waited. He could do the talking, make the demands. But Amy did not intend to meet him halfway, or most of the way, as she had done long ago. Murdo scrubbed his bristling scalp with his free hand, then spoke without turning to look at Amy.

"Don't freak out. I ain't gonna fuck you."

"What?"

"Said I ain't gonna fuck you. So quit standing there like I had my cock out."

"I didn't think you were. I mean I don't think you have your thing out, and I don't think you're going to do what you just said. No. I mean why would you, right? Actually." Amy was babbling with relief. She literally stopped her voice by putting her hand over her mouth. Murdo didn't remark on it. Now Amy recognized what emotion he was radiating. It wasn't aggression, it was defensiveness. He looked almost beaten.

And in that instant, she discovered this frightened her more than anything.

He locked his fist through the wire of the fence. "What you ain't got is the big picture of the situation at hand. See, I got that. I'm the type can see a long ways. That's why I'm in charge. And what I seen is some bullshit of the first water. Me, my boys. Then you and your bunch. That's the hierarchy. Now you're in charge of these other people. I want you right where you're at, so I don't have to babysit nobody. *You* babysit, because that's the hierarchy like I said. But the thing is this.

"My boys are concerned. They seen some action, and they ain't afraid. So I got 'em this far, and we're on our way to Potter. But we're supposed to wait till we got word from the top before we move in on Potter, because that's where we meet up with a shitload more of our boys and then we form a big ass-kicking unit and we sweep this whole fucking sector of the map so clean you could eat off it."

Murdo started to pace, slowly, along the fence. Amy couldn't believe it. He really did want to meet behind the hangar to make a confession. Or he was insane. She didn't know anything about men, apparently. He was still talking.

"Like I said before, we haven't heard from nobody top or bottom, because we ain't got the new radio codes for our digital squawk-boxes. Conventional-band is down. So the boys are thinking. I can't stop 'em thinking. I gotta keep their minds occupied until time comes we roll out of here, and I gotta defuse the situation."

"There's no fuse," Amy broke in.

"Big boys like these, you got a few big boys yourself, you think they're not gonna mix it up? Already did, last night. Your boy got his ass whupped, but that ain't good for nobody's morale. He'll want a rematch. Maybe you don't get it cause you're not real desirable, but all them boys are fixing to fight. How come? On account of the women."

"What women?" Amy was incredulous. What the hell was he talking about?

"All them ones in there. You got eighteen twats on you, all told, and near twice that many tits. That little one with the blue hair, Jesus *Christ* she's all right. You think those men of yours ain't done the math? They want to defend their supply. If we're stuck out here for six months, hell, six weeks, six days, you think there ain't a problem on the way?"

Amy was speechless. With all this awful stuff going on, this little man thought everybody was going sex-crazy? He was the crazy one. As far as she knew, nobody had even thought about sex since the dead fell down and got back up. It wasn't what you thought about in situations like this. Maybe it was different when you were shooting a hundred milligrams of epiandrosterone into your ass every day.

"You're kidding," she said, when she could find her voice.

"Here's the deal," Murdo continued. "I gotta keep my boys happy. They're not happy now. I can't keep 'em happy with your boys getting all up in their grilles. Somebody's got to get out of the way."

He's going to kill them, Amy realized. *He plans to shoot Troy and Topper and Simon and all the men.*

"Now I ain't gonna shoot them," Murdo said, and Amy jumped. "I ain't a mind reader. You're staring at my gun." He croaked. It was supposed to be a laugh. "So we agree on all that. Good. Now what to do, right? What to do." He pretended to think about it. "I know," he continued, two seconds later. "Here's what we do. Your guys *leave.*"

"Our guys leave?"

"Great idea. We won't stop them. Good luck, godspeed, and we'll all have a laugh and a few beers after all this shit is over with."

"Leave where?"

"Anywhere they want, as long as it's outside the range of our twenty-millimeter."

Amy could think of some things to say about Murdo's twenty-millimeter herself, but her head got crowded. He didn't just want to get rid of the civilian men because they were a threat. He wanted all the women. Amy's guts coiled up tight. He was telling her what was going to happen, and he expected *her* to handle the transition.

To make it easy for him.

Amy thought of the men she'd arrived with. Their party was more women than men, for whatever reason. Troy, Topper, Ernie, and Simon the accountant were the strongest ones. Then there was Patrick, and the college kid named Martin, very skinny; an older bald man whose name Amy didn't know; a thick, jowly man named Juan who always held his head tilted back as if he were looking for something up in the sky, although his eyes were pointed forward; and another two or three men of modest build. She figured if she couldn't remember their names, they probably weren't threatening.

Amy realized Murdo was looking at her, waiting.

"What?" Amy said.

"I'm waiting for you to get on board with this thing."

"Mister," Amy said, her voice high and tense, "your idea *sucks.* You think I'm going to tell my guys to leave so your guys can have your way—"

"Whoa, there," Murdo said, his palms held upright in front of him. "Nobody's saying we're gonna turn this place into our own private whorehouse. We're saying we gotta separate the competing males before somebody gets hurt."

"Somebody already did get hurt."

"I rest my motherfucking case."

Murdo called everyone to stand out in the parking area, with his men ranged around the perimeter holding their guns like so many jointed plastic action figures. It wasn't much of a crowd. Amy found herself appraising the women: Who would be the first? She was most worried about Michelle, and after that the college girl, Pfeiffer, Martin's girlfriend; there was Cammy, the freckled, redheaded African-American woman, too, with the tiny baby that never seemed to cry. She was very pretty and had a kind of innocent surprise on her face that would interest the men. The baby wouldn't pose much of an obstacle.

Amy herself might not be in much danger. She wasn't unattractive, but she had asexuality about perfected. Her head was swarming with scenarios for how this situation could devolve into mayhem. A couple of women who were older than her, MILPs or MILFs or whatever the term was—especially the one with the big, unlikely boobs—would definitely end up on the roster. The boob one was flirty, the kind of person who got attacked and then told she was "asking for it." Heck, they were all going to end up in trouble if these guys turned out to be into the gender power trip. As long as a woman cried, she could be eighty years old and they'd get the jollies they were after.

Adrenaline had been steaming through Amy's bloodstream since she walked back behind the hangar, and now she felt ill and wired and crazy. But there was no plan. She couldn't think what to do. They had the guns. It was their show. Murdo said: "We need some volunteers. Scouting party. You go out there, find an alternate safe location, and stay put. We'll find you later on. Here's who's on the list."

Murdo pointed at the men he wanted, and Ace and Parker separated them from the herd at gunpoint. Everybody was worried, now. They'd all seen the movies about World War II and they knew where this was going—the only thing missing was the boxcar. Topper started to protest, and Amy didn't think. She shouted, sudden and loud: "Topper, *no!* Just do what he says."

The anger and fear in her voice sliced through Topper's bravado and left him silent. He stood with the others. Patrick was crying, though silently.

Fifteen minutes later, the chosen ones were walking down the road through the desert, each carrying a couple days' worth of food on his back and a change of clothes if he had one. There was a touch of the epic about it, with the others who stayed behind clinging to the fence, some weeping, some daring to complain, but not loudly. Pfeiffer cried out Martin's name, once, and he looked back. One of the Humvees was turned to the fence, with Molino manning the rooftop machine gun. They were unarmed, these men going out on foot into the deadly landscape. Troy was carrying two gallons of water in a polyethylene container.

That was it. They had nothing else.

The sun went down, the tips of the mountains cooled from fiery red to pitch black against the glowing azure horizon, and then it was too dark to see as the little band of figures receded into the distance. The remaining survivors were herded into the rec room after the cull, where they sat quietly. A couple of the women were cooking spaghetti in the kitchen; Boudreau was detailed to keep an eye on them. Amy kept to herself, sitting on the floor in a corner with her hands twisting between her knees. She didn't respond to questions from any of her people. She only scowled at Murdo, who stood in the foyer, studying the group.

For Murdo's part, he didn't have much to say to the doctor. She'd been useful to him, patching up the incompetent Jones and keeping her men under control until the gates were locked behind them. Now she could go fuck herself. Murdo sure as hell wouldn't.

Murdo's primary focus was on watching the other civilians. See who showed signs of defiance. Anybody decided to act out, they were going to get made an example of. It was Management 101: Somebody has to get fucked up good, real early on, and then everybody else toes the line. He thought beating up that fat hairy biker asshole would take care of it, but these people *expected* men like him to get into fights and lose. Somebody else was going to have to get a hurt on. He thought he knew who.

His eyes kept returning to the little blond they called Patrick.

Amy fell asleep sitting in a chair in front of the women's dormitory at the top of the stairs. She was going to postpone the inevitable as long as she could: Maybe it wouldn't be inevitable, if help came, or Murdo's headquarters radioed him to go to Potter, or who knew what else. Zombies or zeros might come down out of the hills and eat everybody. Amy didn't know what she was hoping for. Anything would do. Even bad news was better than the worst-case scenario in front of her.

She woke up every few minutes, never sleeping more than half an hour at a stretch. Occasionally she would yield to the alarm that was going off inside her, get up, and tour the beds, looking for knife-wielding steroidal rapists. She wasn't the only one awake. The dishwatery woman, Linda Maas, was crying on a lower bunk, shiny trails of tears running from eye to ear as she lay there on her back in the dark.

Once, sometime after three in the morning, Amy went to where the mercenaries were sleeping: only four at a time, the rest on guard duty, except Murdo, who had privilege of rank, and claimed one of the private bedrooms. He slept with the door ajar. Amy slipped past, trying not to look at Murdo, obscene even in sleep, his mouth hanging open as if to shout. The rest were in the men's dormitory, although most of the mercenaries had dragged mattresses onto the floor and slept there. Beds weren't macho enough, apparently, or they didn't feel comfortable in beds they'd emptied by force.

She explained to Parker, who stood watch at the dormitory door, that she wanted to check on Jones.

Jones was awake, too.

"It hurts," he whispered, as if confessing his sins. "I mean it really hurts. And it's itchy."

"Don't scratch it," Amy said. "Or chew on it. Otherwise we have to put a cone around your neck."

Jones didn't understand the joke, and Amy thought better of explaining it. The poor man had enough worries. "Pain is good. Means the leg is still alive. That tourniquet could have killed it. And the itching is good, too. It means you're healing."

Jones was young and scared. He had little more in common with these others than the uniform. *But he was still a good German,* Amy thought. It wasn't enough to be better than the bad guys. You had to resist.

Amy undressed the wound and examined it.

"Looks pretty good," she said. "Did you really shoot yourself?"

"No way," Jones said. "I'm not that stupid. Ace did it. He was shooting a zero that came up on me. Missed it."

"Murdo said you did it to yourself."

"He's got his reasons."

"I guess he must. So, Jones, has he said what the next step is?"

"Next step? To what?" Jones was a little groggy—and none too sharp on a good day, Amy suspected.

"You know. I mean you're not going to stay here very long, right?"

"I'd like to."

"Sure, but we'll run out of water and stuff, right? And food. I guess he told you when you'd be going up to Potter probably."

"He doesn't tell me anything. Did he say something about going to Potter?"

"That's where you were going, I thought," Amy said.

"Yeah, but we didn't hear from Control so we went to plan B or C or whatever plan it is by now. Find a secure location and stay there until further orders."

Amy nodded as if only half-listening, examining the wound closely although there wasn't anything to see—or smell. She had brought fresh dressings for it, and took her time wrapping the leg up again. She didn't want to appear interested in anything other than medical matters. She thought Danny would find this clever. Danny would have slapped him until he talked.

"Right, that's normal procedure, sure," she muttered distractedly.

"Yeah." Jones winced. There was a lot of damaged muscle knitting itself back together inside his leg. Amy had known the shot came from a distance the moment she saw it: no contact burns, the slug didn't make it all the way through the leg, and the wound path went at a very strange angle for a self-inflicted injury. It made a lot more sense to imagine a man standing a hundred feet away fired that shot.

"So," Amy continued, just making idle conversation, "what happens if you never get further orders?"

"I guess Murdo would . . . shit, I don't know."

It had obviously never occurred to Jones that there might someday not be somebody up higher to answer to. He was struggling with the idea.

Amy pressed on, sensing she had an advantage: "What I don't get is why he sent most of our men away."

"When was this?" Jones looked bewildered.

"Two nights ago. Murdo's pretty ruthless. I'm surprised he let you live."

"We had to shoot one of our dudes that got bit on the arm," Jones said. "We called him the Sledge, right? Sledge was all like sick and infected and Murdo told Ace . . . Damn, you know? And Ace was like—*pam*." Jones made a gun out of his hand and mimicked the recoil of a pistol shot.

Amy wasn't ready for that. *They'd shot one of their own.* It explained their lack of remorse: Shoot your buddies, it gets a hell of a lot easier to shoot a stranger.

5

Danny understood the martial law thing. She'd been an enforcer of lockdowns, not long before.

People would go crazy. Holed up in some stranger's house with twenty other people, unwelcome, not wanting to be there in the first place, stuck until the curfew was lifted for a few hours. Which sometimes would be days on end. Surviving on canned goods and whatever you could make with flour and water, assuming there was any gas to cook with. Or any water. No power, so these squeezed populations were sweltering in temperatures that would eventually prove deadly.

There would be inconsolable infants, some little kids suffering loudly, crazy just to be allowed to run around, to be alive. They hadn't mastered suffering and stillness the way the adults had. So they were wild, screaming. The mind doesn't stop thinking in these circumstances. Rage breeds, fed upon the stench of urine and shit and unwashed skin, the fetid, motionless air, the rumble of armored vehicles down the pavement outside.

Hunger makes it stronger. Thirst gives it urgency. Something happens, a house-to-house search or a death in the street, and the rage explodes into action.

Danny went back to the office building after her shift on patrol was over, to rest on the floor beside Yanaba. The woman slept on her side with her fists up by her face, beads of sweat on her skin, a posture Danny thought looked very much like a sleeping infant.

Danny slept on her back, the reptilian scars compressed by her weight in such a way that the itching was lessened. She had her hands laced behind her head, elbows out, staring at the underside of the desk atop which some anonymous information workers had done their day's work. Wad of old gum up there. A sheet of particle board above her, a thin carpet beneath; nonetheless it beat the hell out of sleeping in the driver's seat of the Mustang with the seat back tilted down as far as it would go. She wondered how she was going to find Kelley, and she wondered how long it would be before she could get out of the city. This place wasn't going to survive. Danny dozed off without being aware of it, and knew nothing until she awoke to the sound of shouting.

It was midmorning. They let the night shift sleep in, of course. Yanaba was gone. Danny felt a moment of irritation that she'd slept through people moving around in her space, but then, she hadn't had a proper sleep in living memory. She was secure enough here, she was a part of the machine, invisible and functioning according to plan.

She rose, pulled on her cold, sweat-damp boots, and went to the window-wall. Outside there was a plaza bounded on two sides by streets and the other two sides by office buildings, with rows of buildings opposite. Danny overlooked it from the second floor. The plaza was paved with brick, and there was some kind of modern fountain in the center of it, rising up out of a series of low, curving brick walls. Fair cover in a gunfight, Danny noted, although you'd be stranded when the ammunition ran out. Everything was covered in a shroud of cinerary dust that whirled and billowed when the air shifted.

The far side of the plaza was almost obscured by smoke from the fires. It was raining fluffy ash. A small shift in the wind and now the fires were threatening to choke those it could not burn.

Something was happening. People were running down the street. Some of them cut diagonally across the plaza. One of the Hawkstone Humvees came racing through the crowd and came to a halt across the street at a guillotine angle, bisecting the crowd. Probably two hundred people, Danny estimated, were running around out there. Men jumped out of the Humvee and started knocking civilians down. There was a gunshot, and the Hawkstone mercenaries took cover. Their weapons came up and they started shooting. Danny hit the floor, scooting back away from the window, but continued to watch the action.

At first it didn't look like anybody got hit. The civilians changed course and scattered like a school of minnows, disappearing down alleys and into doorways. Some crouched behind the fountain walls, their backs to Danny. Now she could see two people were lying in the street, one waving an arm, the other motionless. The Hawkstone men advanced, pointing their weapons around, until they were able to drag the two wounded people back down the street to the Humvee. Yanked them up inside it. Three grumbling Bradleys rolled up now, parking in the plaza. More men jumped down out of them and started to round up whoever they could find. They had machine gunners covering the plaza with the snouts of their heavy weapons.

There was a commotion downstairs in the building, shouting and pleading. Something heavy fell over, maybe a filing cabinet. After a couple of minutes, during which time Danny reasoned with herself that she should get involved, but didn't move, there was the sound of doors banging open below, and then three struggling people, a woman and two men, were led out of the building, dragged along by a dozen others. They must have been part of the riot, and they'd been found hiding inside. Everybody knew who belonged or didn't belong.

Ten minutes later, it was as if nothing had happened. The street was empty again, except for the occasional officially sanctioned vehicle crammed with supplies and gunmen.

Danny had a vague plan in mind. It required she stay put for another couple of days, watching for opportunities. Sitting tight was always the hardest part of action. With a great show of calm, Danny went downstairs in search of coffee. Little things had become incalculable luxuries again, the way it was in a theater of war; private toilet stalls, hot coffee, the occasional shower. Water that didn't taste like a swimming pool. She should enjoy these things while they were available.

Danny came down the grand staircase toward a group of people in the lobby, all of them speaking in low, urgent voices about the excitement outside. The consensus was that it had been a riot. Somebody said it wasn't a riot, but that people were only fleeing the fires. The wind had changed, and the flames were reaching inhabited areas. Danny drifted over to listen to the conversation. She might need the information.

"People are flipping out," said a white kid with dreadlocks and large metal grommets in his earlobes.

"Dude, they can't take the heat from the Man, man," an older woman retorted, imitating the kid.

"Knock it off, Carol," said a tall, thin man with enormous spectacles. "People got shot out there. We could be next. They're animals."

"Those man-eating *things* out there are the animals," Carol replied, turning on Spectacles. "I'd rather have to put up with a little extra security than get eaten by monsters."

"A little extra *security*?" the dreadlocked kid said. "You saw that. They just *shot* people. That's not security, it's Nazi bullshit."

It occurred to Danny that this very conversation had probably been had regarding her own squad of Marines—but in Mesopotamian Arabic or Farsi.

A shorter man in a torn mustard-yellow cardigan chimed in. Danny recognized him from one of the minivan teams that had been on patrol the previous night. "You have to be out there to see what's happening," he said. "The safe zone is getting tighter every day. We went into an apartment building last night that literally had people sleeping upright on the stairs. There wasn't a level square foot of floor space left. It stank."

"At least they have somewhere to stay," Carol snapped. "We should be grateful those brave men are keeping us safe—not only from those things, but from the mob—people that don't know when they've got it good."

"Carol," Spectacles said, cleaning his glasses on the tail of his shirt. "We've worked together for years, right? We go way back. So don't take it the wrong way when I say you're one of the least sympathetic human beings I've ever known."

"Okay, then what happens to everybody," the dreadlocked kid said, "when there's no more room? They end up in the streets. But it's martial law. You can't be in the streets. It's a pressure cooker, man. That resistance out there, that was only the beginning. The situation is going to de*volve*."

"Freedom," Carol said with staunch finality, "isn't free."

The man in the cardigan saw Danny and nudged Spectacles. Heads turned in her direction. The chatter died out. Her appearance lately tended to have a conversation-stopping effect; maybe once her hair grew out and the injuries faded she'd blend in a little better. It wouldn't hurt if she had eyelashes or eyebrows. Wait till they saw her in a bikini. She passed among them, not making eye contact, and was glad there were not more of them. She hated the staring.

Danny went down to the room where the laundry was kept for pick-up, then changed into the remains of her uniform, clean but ragged, in the nearest bathroom. Attired in a way that suggested she might have some pretense to authority, she inquired of some competent-looking people in the lobby if there were any convoys headed in the direction of the Pyramid Building. An hour later she was on her way, rifle in hand, riding guard duty on a load of canned soup and packets of dried ravioli.

When she got to the guards in front of the Pyramid, she was carrying a box of cans on her shoulder. The driver of the truck, also laden with boxes, asserted her legitimacy as a "critical member of personnel"; she hadn't been given any papers to flash around, but it didn't matter. Despite the lockdown, few people seemed to have any credentials.

"That's it? You're with him, you're cool?" Danny muttered to the driver as they entered the building.

"You're as legitimate as the guy vouching for you," he said. "I bring these guys smokes. They like me." In the lobby they didn't cross to the elevators but went around behind the elevator core to the stairs, which led down into the basement storage areas. Danny would have kept vital supplies on an upper floor, to make them easier to defend, but this wasn't her fight. The entire basement of the building was stuffed with dry goods, medical equipment, and canned food, besides caches of ammunition and weapons in accessible locations. There were loading doors down there, some kind of access possible by truck, but she could see why they made everything come through the lobby. One less access point, one less hole in the defenses. Keep the loading doors shut so nobody in a nearby building decided to make a raid—and keep an eye on what came and went. The place smelled strongly of vegetable soup and diesel fuel. Danny imagined there must be a couple of ruptured cans in there somewhere. The diesel was for the generators, rumbling away in a sub-basement below the supplies. She could feel the vibration through her boots.

Once the groceries were all carried into the basement, Danny excused herself and asked at the front desk where the personnel files were being kept. The woman at the desk raised her eyebrows.

"I'm a cop," Danny said. "I'm looking for some known criminals." What the hell, at this point anybody would take anything for an excuse, as long as it sounded urgent.

She'd thought her story out in advance. It was quite a melodrama. If anybody asked, Danny was going to say she'd come up from Los Angeles in pursuit of some fugitives from the prison system down there, the worst of the worst, who broke out when everything went nuts. She had a list of names. Kelley's name was on the list, of course.

As it transpired, nobody asked her what her story was. She was directed to a windowless, beige room on the first floor. There was a tired man with a white mustache at the desk she approached; he and a dozen others were transcribing names from handwritten sheets into a computer database. Danny asked to see the list of refugee names.

"The list we got isn't going to do you any good," the tired man said.

"I'd like to have a look anyway," Danny said.

"Come back in a week," the man said, shaking his head.

"Sir—it's important."

The man's eyes narrowed. He turned his screen squarely away from Danny's field of view. "Who are you with?"

"I'm from a small town outside Los Angeles—" Danny said, preparing to tell her story, and got no further than that. The tired man waved his hand at her.

"You're not with Hawkstone or the city, am I right?"

"No," Danny said. "Please let me look at the list, it's important."

"They didn't ask you to come down here?"

"I'm not supposed to be here," Danny admitted. "This is a personal thing. I traveled three hundred miles for this."

The man leaned back in his squeaky chair and chuckled. It was a dry, mirthless sound, the sort of noise that follows a cruel, not especially funny joke.

"The joke's on you. Those goons upstairs told us we each had to input five hundred names an hour, or we'd be out on the street. So they hand us these piles of names they gather at the checkpoints"—here he gestured at a carton filled with grubby scraps of paper—"and we type any goddamn name in on the computer, and at the end of every shift we dump all this crap in the incinerator. In other words, there is no list."

Danny's eyes stung. The air outside was dense and gritty; the wind had shifted again, carrying with it a burden of filthy smoke and ash. If Danny wept, she could tell herself it was only the smoke. There was no difference, in the end: Either way, all that was left was ashes. She looked back at the Pyramid Building and wondered how long it would be before the place was inhabited only by walking corpses. It was time to get out of San Francisco before the whole place went down, get back to Boscombe Field, and do what she did best: brood on her own failures.

Danny drove out to the perimeter with her patrol team, rifle propped up between her knees, a knife in the pocket of her uniform pants. Her mind was fixed on a single goal: to get out of the fortified city. She took her first patrol of the assigned block. Two buildings opposite had caught fire during the day, and they were excusing the former inhabitants for coming and going in the smoldering wreckage during curfew hours. The entire block was illuminated by the small fires that ate at whatever was left besides charcoal and masonry. As the night wore on, people found places to lie down and were not seen again.

Danny found herself alone, sometime in the hour between very late and very early. She stood below the smoke rising over the city, its sound like the sound of falling snow, a kind of pressure in the ear, almost a nonsound. Beyond, the fires rumbled and muttered. Turbulent, muscular smoke rolled up into the atmosphere, candescent at the skyline where the red flames leaped up inside it, dancing with bright izles that flared and winked out. The smoke bellied overhead, black and hot and dry, raining down ash and cinders. The stench was awful: Sulfur and poison and the destruction of ordinary things filled Danny's nose.

She was desperate to be out of the city before dawn, on her way back to Boscombe Field, but haste at this point would be fatal. She decided to patrol in the usual fashion, looking for some opportunity to slip away and get through the barrier between the living and the dead. It would almost be safer among the zeros. At least they were predictable.

Halfway through Danny's first shift standing watch, her shoulders heaped with ash, she heard an engine approaching. A Humvee rolled up the block and came to a halt directly in front of her position. A man in camouflage with a shaggy chin beard leaned out of the passenger side window.

"You Danny?" he asked.

Danny didn't say anything. She had her T-shirt pulled up through her collar, over the lower half of her face, to keep the soot out. She thought fast: What did he want? Why? Who sent him? He shone a flashlight in her eyes to verify she was the one he was looking for. Then he hooked his thumb at the back of the vehicle.

"I can't leave my post," Danny said. "This is the side the zeros will come from."

The man in the Humvee said something into his radio.

"It's covered," he told Danny. Danny slung her rifle down from her shoulder and climbed in the back, that familiar wide, flat space with benches along the sides she'd spent so much time bouncing around in during her tours of duty. There were two Hawkstone men in there with her, both wearing hardware store respirator masks. She sat close to the open tail of the vehicle and kept her rifle at a careless attitude—one that would make it quick to aim, if they decided to try something.

In her rapid analysis of the situation she couldn't come up with any good-news reason for the attention. She was in trouble. Probably her useless stint down in the records room of the Pyramid Building. The tired man with the mustache might have ratted her out.

They drove in silence for a few minutes, first westward, then what looked like due south. The west side of the road was bordered by a massive barricade, composed mostly of crushed vehicles and chunks of architecture, bulldozed into a rough wall and bound with accordion wire. It ran, as far as Danny could see, all the way along the street, crushed up against the façades of the buildings and piled across the intersections to form an unbroken boundary twice the height of a man. The smoky, fire-blown darkness outside was punctuated in this new area by battery-powered area lamps, so the world alternated between deep, bloody brown shadows and pools of sickening green light. It appeared to be snowing heavily, but the air was parching hot.

The windshield wipers scraped ash off the glass. The driver was hunched over, visibility poor. Choking grit swirled in through the back of the Humvee. One of the lights caught the blade of a street sign, and Danny saw they were traveling along Guerrero Street. This meant nothing to her in terms of navigation, but she knew what the word meant: *warrior.* Ramirez had taught it to her, in the desert on the other side of the world.

They came to a broad intersection where a Bradley fighting vehicle stood, a gunner in night vision goggles manning the .50 caliber weapon on the roof. The cross-street was barricaded with razor wire set up on pylons. Close behind the barricade were fresh, bright flames and the lumpen silhouettes of massed undead, clawing at the barrier, eyes flashing yellow when they reflected the lights. There were thousands of them. The air boomed with fire and moaning from voiceless mouths.

Danny had come to the literal border between life and death.

She climbed out of the Humvee, her rifle swinging casually within a few degrees of the men she was with. They stood around, waiting for someone. The man with the chin beard spoke into his radio again. Danny very much wanted one of those radios. She also wanted one of the machine guns. Most of all, however, she wanted to not be standing here where the roar of the fires and the moaning of the undead mingled on the hot gusting breeze. The air was pregnant with combustion, as if it might itself burst into sheets of flame, so full of gas and heat.

This, Danny thought, *is the apocalypse.*

These were the possibilities: First, they would shoot her on the spot. In that case she was going to try to take out a couple of them before she died. Not much of a plan.

Next option: They were going to send her out there to die. In that case she would simply follow her original plan: run like hell. This plan lacked detail.

The third possibility was that they wanted her to look at the situation they were in, and suggest some strategic ideas based on her experiences out there on the other side of the line. That was the most logical conclusion to come to, and the least likely scenario as far as Danny was concerned. Nobody, in her considerable experience, did anything for good, logical reasons; they did things based on their own narrow preconceived ideas of how the world ought to work.

It might only be that. But Danny could feel the presence of death.

After she and her escort had stood in the sickly glow of the battery lamps long enough to gather a fresh coat of ash, a new variable entered the intersection.

It was a motorcycle, some kind of fast Japanese thing covered in plastic fairings. The rider let the bike drop on its side and walked away from it; it was nothing but a tool. Danny noticed that Chin-beard and the rest of the men around her stiffened at the approach of this figure. They didn't come to attention; the slack simply pulled out of their postures. They were tense. Danny held her rifle carelessly, as before, but her muscles were taut. If this was the executioner, she was taking the first shot.

As the rider approached, emerging from firelit outline into dimensional figure, Danny thought Death himself would have approved. Maybe this was the presence she felt.

He was clad entirely in leather. Against human teeth, there were no vulnerable points on this man. He was sealed into a thick, scraped-up leather riding suit, stiff with crash pads. The boots were overkill, Danny decided. About fifty buckled straps from knee to toe, which meant they were heavy as hell, and inflexible. But Danny thought the elbow-length gauntlets were a great idea. The man looked like a lean, black alligator, seamed and stitched with zippers. On his head he wore a yellow plastic construction helmet over a leather aviator's cap, ski goggles, and a respirator. Around his waist was a belt bristling with ugly instruments for piercing and striking, and a holster containing what looked like a Luger automatic from the Second World War.

For a few seconds, Danny was intimidated by this bizarre, invulnerable creature that strode toward her. In the next moment, it was all she could do not to laugh. He looked like he was late for a Halloween party as much as anything else. Very *Beyond Thunderdome.* He was so heavily clad he couldn't move half as fast as Danny, he probably couldn't hear very well, and his peripheral vision was shit. She could fuck this guy up.

The apparition before her pulled the face-concealing respirator down, and Danny got her next surprise. It was a woman. The tool belt and leathers had hidden her shape. The woman snapped the ski goggles up over the brim of the safety helmet and stared around at the men in the party, then examined Danny like a conquest of battle. Danny didn't say anything or show any reaction, her expression bland.

"So you're the tough guy," she purred. "They call me the Zero Killer." Her voice was like honey and bourbon. Pitched low. Her face was clean and smooth where the soot couldn't reach, a tribal pattern of grit marking the narrow, exposed margins between goggles and mask. Chin-beard hawked and spat into the feathery ash at their feet. He thumbed in Danny's direction.

"She don't know shit about the mission. Figured you could tell her," he said. He was being evasive, Danny thought. So there was going to be a big lie in the next part of the conversation, or maybe something was going to happen. This was exactly how people died. Your executioner turns out to be a bondage chick, you let your guard down, and you're dead. Danny couldn't let it happen like that. The woman turned squarely to Danny, dismissing the men from her attention; they kept standing around, their roles subtly shifted to that of entourage.

"Heard you fought your way up here from L.A.," the woman said.

"Yeah," Danny said. "What's up?" She didn't want to fuck around. *If this is it, let's get to the fighting.* She was getting tired from the long period of keeping her body tensed for the defense.

"I have an assignment out there," the woman said, "but I can't do it alone. It takes four hands. So far, everybody's died before we reach the objective. Not that I blame them."

"Huh," Danny said. The absurdity of her position was making her careless, but she couldn't find the edge. She was sinking into a state of disbelief. She might as well be talking to Bozo the Clown about a trip to the moon. But if this assignment would get Danny out of the city—

"You're smiling. What's funny?" the leatherwoman said.

"I just remembered an old joke," Danny said, no longer interested in these people. They weren't going to kill her, at least not on the spot. They had some elaborate plan worked out. Get Danny's back turned and sic some zombies on her a mile out there in the wasteland, for whatever reason. Shoot her in the head on a long walk to some photo opportunity the senator thought she'd enjoy seeing. Danny now realized she was more interested in *why* all this was happening than *what* was supposed to happen next. Which, of course, could be fatal. She focused her attention again. *Stay on point. You against the world. Starting with these weirdos.*

The men who flanked Danny were shifting uneasily. This woman clearly scared the shit out of them. Danny decided to dial the amusement back. Play the seasoned professional angle. Make Ms. Thunderdome feel like she was with an equal. Danny spoke into the silence.

"Look, I was walking the beat, these boys drug me all the way to the back of beyond here, and I don't know a goddamn thing. So how about you tell me what's happening? Because we're wasting time. I hate wasting time. Not much of it around."

Half an hour later, Danny and the leather-bound Liz Magnussen, aka "Zero Killer," were on their way into zombie territory. They had made a brief stop at a generator-powered construction trailer, where Danny was kitted up with gear: Over her uniform she wore a police-style motorcycle jacket of horsehide, yellow buckskin gloves, and a knit watch cap to keep her ears tucked away—they had lost a lot of people to infected bites on the ears. Danny refused the heavy riding chaps, calf-length linesman's boots, and leather skullcap. She gladly accepted one of the loaded belts of equipment they had hanging on coat pegs in the trailer.

It was a standard police belt with the basket-weave pattern stamped into it. The little sleeves that normally held pepper spray, spare clips, knife, and chewing gum had been opened up at the bottom to allow the shafts of weapons to pass through them. Other implements were held on with Velcro bands.

Magnussen demonstrated the use of them, with several admiring onlookers keeping well back. "We got some welding equipment and we've been making things up as we go along. This one is brand new—it's a brain pick." It was a steel bar with a cruciform end, each of the three tips of the cross sharpened like nails. "Thrust with the middle point. Go for the mouth. Up and in. Or you can swing it side to side like a hammer. I find it's easier backhand than forehand. Female wrists," she added, and a couple of the onlookers laughed.

Danny was intrigued by the woman's face: She had a Scandinavian name, but she looked at least half Asian. Could have been a showgirl, except for the crooked nose and the old, white scar that ran along the top of her upper lip.

Magnussen went on: "These brain picks have changed the game. I carry four of them, you have three on you now. If they get stuck in a zero you definitely don't want to dick around trying to pull one out while the rest are coming at you. Just grab another, like Kleenex."

"Yeah, no shit," Danny said, thinking how handy these things would have been the last couple of weeks. She didn't notice that the attention in the trailer had shifted to her: In her element now, she sounded as tough and competent as the "Zero Killer." No nerves, only professionalism.

Magnussen continued: "There's a bunch of other pig-stickers on there as well. Jab 'em and leave 'em is my advice, but you can't have too many weapons. One thing I found—aim for the nose. That slows the zeros down."

Danny nodded. "They hunt by sense of smell. I think they can smell our breath. I noticed you stop breathing, their attention kind of wanders."

Magnussen herself seemed impressed by this. "Right, exactly. That's why I wear the respirator. Cuts down on my human signature."

She detached another Velcro-affixed device from her belt, a length of iron pipe with a small loop of wire at one end and a screw-on cap at the other. The onlookers shifted even further away. Danny figured that one for a homemade grenade. Magnussen had half a dozen of them along the back of her belt, which also made an effective kidney protector—assuming the wire loops didn't get caught on something.

"Yank the wire and throw. Even if the wire doesn't come all the way out, assume you have ten seconds. We make 'em long-fused because this isn't man-to-man combat. This enemy never get out of the way when they see one coming. Filled with ball bearings or dimes. Who says money isn't worth anything anymore?"

Everyone but Danny laughed at that.

"I want one of those radios, too," Danny said, indicating Magnussen's satellite unit. There was a rack of them charging on the wall.

"No can do," a man said from the end of the trailer.

"Why not?" Danny asked. "This is life and death."

"Because you are not authorized—" the man began. Magnussen interrupted him:

"Give her one, Sheldon. Set it to six-seven-seven."

The man shrugged and complied. Danny took the precious radio and inserted it in her belt. But now Danny found her pants were coming down. She'd lost a lot of weight in all the excitement of the past couple of weeks. So she lightened her belt: One of the brain picks would do. All those other pointed weapons hanging down around her legs could end up in a self-inflicted wound that would leave her at the mercy of the zombies. She'd rather improvise than crawl. She'd done all her crawling elsewhere in the world.

Besides the brain picks, she kept four grenades and a big hunting knife. There were some other, more common implements: a multitool, a butane pencil torch, and a stubby high-intensity flashlight. She kept those, too.

"You aren't equipped for the assignment," Magnussen said, when Danny was done cutting down on her armament.

"Then why don't you tell me just exactly what the fuck it is?" Danny said, and stepped outside.

They trudged through the rubble and charred remains of what had been the Glen Park neighborhood of San Francisco. The corner where they crossed through the barricades was, to Danny's grim amusement, the intersection of Guerrero and Army streets. César Chávez was in there somewhere but the street-naming scheme didn't make sense, major routes blending into each other at odd moments. They sprinted down Guerrero until it became San Jose Avenue and then walked for a long way through the predawn darkness.

Zeros were everywhere in the beginning. They were massed up behind the barricade and it took considerable diversion to get Magnussen and Danny over the wall without a horde of the moaning creatures descending on them in such numbers they couldn't have gotten through. There was no question of using the gates—the zeros seemed to have figured out that was the way to the meat buffet.

"Anybody want anything while we're out?" Magnussen quipped, and again the others laughed. "I'm going to be *famous* when this is over," she whispered to Danny. *She's an attention freak,* Danny realized. *She's doing this like it's a reality show.*

The situation was slipping into insanity. Reality was rapidly losing its hold on the world.

They had to go up and over the obstacle, cross a ladder laid horizontally to the upstairs window of an apartment building, and then emerge on a fire escape on the opposite side. By that time they were a block away from where their confederates were acting as decoys, shouting and throwing debris at the undead.

Danny wasn't sure the survivors should have been taunting such a huge crowd of the things: It seemed to energize the zeros, to make them throw themselves at the barrier. But diversion was the only way to get past them. What was most disturbing about the hellish scene—besides the hideous burns and injuries evident on so many of the undead—was the way the zombies were streaming toward the barricade from all quarters of the city.

Danny and Magnussen ran for the first quarter-mile once they hit the pavement below the fire escape, their flashlight beams whirling. There was no other way to avoid being overwhelmed by the sheer number of their enemy. It pleased Danny to observe she had better endurance than her counterpart, and it wasn't only the heavy Road Warrior boots. Danny was more fit.

They were headed for what Magnussen called "280." In Los Angeles it was *the* 405 or *the* 134. Here they only said the number, which was confusing. *The* 280 ran diagonally from the southwest to the northeast of the city, heading for Oakland. The mission was fairly simple, but it had so far claimed a number of qualified lives—Magnussen had made it by herself as far as their goal, but one person couldn't simultaneously take care of business and take care of herself. She'd heard from the people "back at command" that Danny's exploits had marked her as maybe the best potential scout to have entered the city since the fall of Chinatown.

They compared notes on the abilities of the zeros. Danny related her experiences with faster, more adept ones; Magnussen had seen some relatively bright examples but didn't entirely believe Danny's tale of problem-solving zombies. "The door must not have latched," she said, of the old female zombie that had attacked Danny in the Potter hotel, turning a doorknob to get at her. Then Magnussen added, "Because if they get smart, we're done."

So far, those in the San Francisco area were the slow, stupid variety. Magnussen certainly took the situation seriously enough despite her quips; she was at the top of the zombie-fighting heap in this town. But she had contempt for her foe. That would end in disaster someday. For that matter, Danny didn't trust her companion in the least; she was positive she'd been chosen to go on this mission with Magnussen because they needed someone expendable. Even if Danny made it back, she had a feeling the gates wouldn't open for both of them. Not if it meant Magnussen would have to share the limelight. Not if Vivian Anka wanted to "get her back." But maybe Danny was getting paranoid. Sure she was. That's why she was still alive. It didn't matter what they had planned for her in the city, anyway. She had no intention of returning.

Magnussen was leading her straight out of the hot zone. In return, Danny would get Magnussen to the objective, wish her well, then commandeer a vehicle and bug out back to Boscombe Field.

"What's your story?" Danny asked, as they marched along, double-time. There was a long tail of zeros coming up behind them, but Magnussen didn't seem concerned. The women were moving faster than the zombies, and the undead lost interest once the human scent faded, so the numbers that followed along never increased beyond thirty or forty, and they were well behind.

Since running the gauntlet outside the perimeter barricade, they hadn't come within twenty feet of a zero. No point in seeking a fight. Almost all of the undead in this area were burnt, some profoundly so, barely able to move; they had shambled in from the nearby fire-swept districts. Danny kept her eye on the freshest-looking specimens, because those could have traveled from outside the fire zone. They might be smarter.

Magnussen didn't answer her question. Danny didn't press the point.

They fast-walked, sometimes jogging, for three or four miles through the night. The best way to see ahead was to flick the flashlights rapidly back and forth across their path; it created a 3-D effect that made human shapes leap out of the background darkness.

Magnussen raised her hand and stopped. She drew a brain pick from her belt. "There's a hell of a lot of them up ahead, and then we're at 280. There's a fence, and they collect up against it. We're gonna take a shortcut down Cuvier Street, where it's not going to be populated as bad, but it's real narrow and there's cars all over the place. Two blocks and a U-turn at the end. There's a wall and an embankment down to the freeway there. You can't see over the wall. So we're gonna do a Hail Mary."

Their objective, as Magnussen had explained it, was to reach a convoy of Army vehicles that had gotten bogged down during the second day of the crisis, northbound on the freeway in what was known as the Sunnyside neighborhood. Helicopter flyovers by Hawkstone men had revealed the convoy included a flatbed truck with "a highly desirable military payload," the deployment of which could create an exit corridor from the downtown area to a safe zone outside the city. Danny didn't point out that there *was* no safe zone outside the city; anywhere had to be better than this. There must have been half a million zeros massed around the downtown with its chewy, delicious center.

Magnussen warned Danny that there would be numerous zeros in uniforms and body armor around the objective, which made them a hell of a lot harder to kill. None of them were living. She shouldn't hesitate to take them down. In addition to the Army unit that had originally been driving the armaments, they had subsequently lost a Hawkstone helicopter unit there, back when Hawkstone was still at the leading edge of the fight. Now the remains of the Army and Hawkstone men were shuffling around, hungry for prey, still inadvertently guarding their payload.

Danny and Magnussen had briefly discussed who would do what. Their task was to get the flatbed moving. The freeway was a mass of wreckage and destruction to the north, where it became the Embarcadero and formed one of the boundaries of the inhabited zone of the city. But it looked like they could drive a machine as heavy as the flatbed through the light scatter of abandoned vehicles up to that point. From there it would be possible for a good-sized squad of people to come through the defensive line, retrieve the payload, and make it back to safety.

The problem, however, was that the foremost vehicle in the convoy was one of the massive, dinosaurlike Cougar MRAPs, a cross between an armored car and a cement truck. It was squarely blocking the freeway. The monstrous vehicle would have to be moved; the flatbed couldn't shove its thirty-two-thousand-pound mass out of the way.

Magnussen could operate a nonsychronous gearbox, so she would drive the flatbed. The MRAP was an automatic.

Danny was entirely on board with the plan, except for one detail. There was no way she would be returning to the cab of the flatbed with Magnussen. She was on her own after Danny got the Cougar out of the way. In fact, Danny was going to commandeer the Cougar to get herself out of the urban area in high style. Somehow she didn't think Magnussen would mind very much seeing her rival for the "Queen of the Zombie Killers" crown leave town.

Although it wasn't entirely fair to abandon Magnussen before the return journey, Danny had a feeling she would be far better off ducking out early. She tried to tell herself she was thinking too much: Ms. Zero Killer seemed, if not friendly, at least professional. Danny had been observing her unusual companion in action—she obviously got off on the superhero stuff, dressing up like Batman and carrying a belt full of weapons. A showoff. Danny had also noticed Magnussen playing up the dangers for her colleagues, back behind the perimeter. She was making the most of the situation.

Danny didn't think she had any mischief in mind—the situation was dangerous enough as it was, without any cloak-and-dagger stuff. But she would have to be very alert for the moment when she was no longer indispensable, and maybe get out of there before that moment arrived. One never knew. After all, none of Magnussen's previous companions had come back alive.

They stood looking down the shortcut of Cuvier Street, with dawn beginning to creep up the sky out past where the fires burned, glimmering through the pall of smoke that hung over the entire horizon. The zeros that had been following them were getting closer, moaning with lust for flesh. Others emerged from the buildings around them. This neighborhood had so far escaped the fires. Danny assumed there must be living people in some of these structures, drinking toilet water and living on canned beans or handfuls of flour or whatever they had. Could be thousands, still alive, huddled in terror. Nothing could be done for them. This entire exercise was for the benefit of what was left of the urban core. She saw nothing beyond the common, stupid zombies that infested most places. None of the fast ones. Maybe it was a fluke, the clever ones found only in Potter. She didn't dare hope so.

The dark street was a tangle of automobiles and furniture. It looked like some people had attempted a crude barricade in the middle of the block. There were bodies in the street, several torn to pieces, several others intact; Danny knew those would come after them. They had only paused for a few seconds. Danny's mind was racing. There wasn't much to think about, now. She and her leather-clad companion simply had to sprint through that obstacle course and get over the wall and once they got to the freeway there was going to be an entirely new fight.

Danny drew her own brain pick and slipped one of the primitive grenades out of her belt. "I think we should blast ourselves a little room," she said. Magnussen nodded. She wasn't wearing her respirator now; it hung loosely around her neck. No point masking her breath signature if there was someone without a mask by her side. They took hold of the wires in their bombs.

"How accurate are the fuses on these things?" Danny asked.

"Don't wait around," Magnussen said, and they pulled and threw at the same moment.

Danny threw her grenade down Cuvier, arcing it high up into the darkness. It rattled to the pavement and rolled under a Plymouth skewed across the street. Magnussen threw hers back the way they came, lobbing it low so it came to rest against the feet of one of the zombies pursuing them, a male in the middle of the nearest pack, which had around twenty individuals in it. Both women threw themselves full-length on the ground. Danny had never used anything with such a long delay—after three or four seconds, she expected to hear an explosion. It took so long for these delayed-fuse grenades she thought they must be duds. She could hear the one behind them clinking along the pavement as the zombie shuffled over it. Finally she looked up. At that moment, both weapons exploded.

Hers produced a satisfying concussion, blasting apart the tires of the

Plymouth and shredding everything around it. The car rose in the air at least six feet, then crashed straight down on its axles and began to burn. Danny was momentarily blinded, her teeth rattling together. The explosion was several times greater than that of a military M-26 grenade. All the glass in the buildings on both sides of the blast disintegrated, and the siding and stucco of the walls belched fragments and dust. Shrapnel whickered over their heads. Magnussen's grenade was closer, and the ground shock bounced them off the pavement. Danny didn't see what damage it did, but she heard pattering in the rooftops and on the asphalt. Gobbets of reeking flesh rained down on them.

"Go," Magnussen said. Although Danny's vision was still swimming with amorphous green afterimages of the explosion, she went.

They ran like Olympic sprinters, hurdling over debris, dodging cars and pickups. The zeros were torn to bits at the near end of the first block; they made it to the end of the block without anything even getting to its feet.

Across the intersection on the second block, they were in some trouble. A lot of the undead had come out to see what made the noise. *Fuck it,* Danny thought, and ran as fast as she could, her boots slapping on the road, arms pumping. Simple plans worked best. She was going to run so damn fast they couldn't catch up with her. She got three houses down the block before it was time for a new plan. Magnussen wasn't with her. Danny looked back; her companion was out of sight. She had taken a different route when they reached the intersection. Or, for all Danny knew, she was heading back to base, mission accomplished, Danny dead.

As she looked over her shoulder, Danny lost track of the zeros nearest to her. One of them stumbled into her path and she slammed into it, knocking the breath out of herself. She tumbled and rolled and thumped heavily into the side of an old Volkswagen Beetle, the running board crashing into her ribs.

There was no air inside her. She got to her feet, winded to the point of panic, and as she tried to refill her lungs, the next two zombies arrived. They reached for her, and their fingers—now soft and decaying—slithered across the leather of her jacket. She ripped the brain pick from her belt and shoved it into the nearest face, yanked it out, and stuck it into the temple of the next one. It didn't work very well—the heads rocked back, decreasing penetration. The thing she had run into was at her feet, crawling. It grabbed her legs, and the tattered fabric of her uniform trousers was not going to stop its teeth from taking a chunk of meat. Danny kicked it in the head, shoved past the ones she had wounded—the brain was farther back in the skull than she had imagined—and made herself run again, breathless as she was. This was Forest Peak all over again, except this time, she wasn't going to get help.

It was shoulder work now. She shoved through the mass of stinking, wet bodies. They were forcing her to a standstill with their numbers. Yet she realized the fingers weren't holding her, the teeth couldn't crush into her flesh with force enough to break the skin. The dynamics of the attack had changed. These hadn't fed in a week or more. They were coming apart, slimy as spoiled chicken. Their limbs moved poorly, senses dull. They often fell. Danny understood why Magnussen didn't believe her story of advanced-skill zombies. She'd been coming out here where they got *less* capable, not more so.

Magnussen's reputation as a zero destroyer was probably founded on these trips out into the distant areas of town, where the fight actually got *easier*. It was Magnussen's best-kept secret.

Danny was still electric with fear, but she found herself plowing through the things like a quarterback. She could almost tear their arms off. She was soaked in stinking fluids and scraps of gooey, dead skin like the flesh of octopus. She was a destroyer of monsters. Now: There was a weapon she could work with, a prybar stuck through the windshield of a car. She dragged it out and swung it like King Arthur and heads burst, jaws tore off, arms cracked and spun wildly on rags of flesh.

She didn't have to destroy them. She could disable them, turn them into twitching meat. Without arms, without jaws, without teeth, they could only rot. She remembered the great numbers of fire-damaged zeros back at the barricades. Hideous, terrifying things, red and black, webbed with fissures of white where the fat and tendons showed. Ears and noses scorched away, eyeballs like skinned knuckles. They were almost harmless, she realized. Those roasted muscles would have little success holding, biting. And with every day that went by, they got weaker.

Danny hacked her way through the things, and now she had her breath back, the fear had solidified into strength in her limbs, and she was easily destroying her foes. She was still afraid, but it was the simple fear she'd felt when hunting boar or crawling across some high ridge on a rock face in the mountains. It was clean fear. All she had to do was perform, and she would succeed. She reached the end of the second block and waded through a bed of ivy and long-abandoned shopping carts to the wall that overlooked the freeway. Danny had made it this far because her enemies were weak and she was strong. That suited her fine. She smelled the stink of herself, retched, spat, and started to climb the wall.

One of these days, Danny thought, Magnussen would report back to headquarters and announce, "The zeros are dying," and she would be hailed as the greatest champion the city had ever known. Meanwhile, she would have accomplished what? She might be hoarding money, or jewelry—gold and stones. Government bonds. She might be collecting material for the finest good life possible, scavenging herself into a retirement of luxury and comfort. Or maybe she wanted to be a superstar.

Danny felt hands grip her leg as she swung it over the far side of the wall: strong, fast hands. She recoiled, preparing to kick where the face ought to be, when she heard Magnussen's low, simmering voice.

"Step down and let's find some cover," she said.

Danny was seething. She wanted to break the exotic face of her guide through the wasteland. Smash her with the prybar. Magnussen had left Danny among the zombies without a word of warning, and now everything was supposed to be hunky-dory again. Danny didn't think so.

"What the fuck was that?" Danny hissed through her teeth.

"There were too many," Magnussen said. "Why didn't you follow me?"

Danny realized there was no point demanding explanations.

"I was ahead of you, is why," she said, and dropped the subject. Their weird partnership was almost done, anyway. Their objective was straight ahead.

6

A couple hundred feet away, the Army convoy stood on the freeway, among all the vehicles of everyday life abandoned there as well. It looked almost like a freeze-frame of ordinary traffic on a busy day. But this traffic was going to stay right where it was for a long time. The light in the sky was gathering. Sunrise was less than an hour away. The light was sufficient to reveal at least two dozen huddled shapes lying on the pavement among the military vehicles. There were others, as well, scattered as far as they could see among the civilian vehicles. Both women had doused their lights. No point providing an early warning.

Behind the wall, the wailing of hunger could be heard, but it didn't seem to have any effect on the zeros littering the freeway. They could be too rotten to move, Danny thought. But they'd been able to feed, of course, so they would be in better shape than the ones on the other side of the wall. That seemed to be a factor. Danny hoped the fast variety wouldn't be found in this area. They were still close to the epicenter, less than six miles. The smarter ones appeared eighty miles or more from the source. That would explain Magnussen's cavalier attitude toward the undead, although not her hanging Danny out for bait.

Danny would get herself up into the Cougar and get it out of the way of the flatbed. Then she was going to leave San Francisco behind forever. She kept repeating this idea to herself. Another five minutes, and she was on her way back to Boscombe Field.

"Give me one of your brain picks," Danny whispered. Magnussen reached back and eased one of the weapons off her belt, careful not to let the Velcro make its unmistakable sound.

The women's attention was fixed on the flatbed, which was three vehicles from the front in the twenty-vehicle formation, its payload obscured beneath camouflage-printed canvas. It was flanked on both sides by Humvees and utility SUVs, painted in an assortment of green and desert Army camouflage patterns. Several of these had crashed into the passenger vehicles in front of them. Down the road was the massive Cougar MRAP, slewed across lanes just as Magnussen had described. Although Danny and Magnussen had done little to advertise their presence, the shapes of corpses on the roadway were beginning to stir.

Danny's equilibrium was briefly thrown by the sight of the flatbed truck. The low-slung configuration of the vehicle, which resembled a construction crane tractor with the cab down between the front wheels, indicated it was a purpose-built missile carrier. Danny had seen them many times before. Although the payload was not visible, the only missile system in Danny's experience that would require a truck so *large*—the trend was always to smaller and smaller tactical missile deployment systems—was a Patriot Transporter/Erector/Launcher unit. A Patriot launcher would hold sixteen missiles in four "cans," or boxed launch tubes, each missile with a payload sufficient to vaporize a large building. It was far too much firepower for their purposes. It would be a disaster. *Tough shit,* Danny thought, dismissing her qualms. *It's a disaster already.*

It was time to move fast.

Danny hustled down the embankment alongside Magnussen, then they separated, Danny running for the Cougar, the Zero Killer cutting straight across lanes to the cab of the flatbed truck. The zombies were struggling to their feet, moaning, some already lurching toward the living prey. They were wrapped in body armor and Kevlar helmets, as Magnussen had said they were. The jaws were free to work. Danny kept clear of them.

The predawn light was at that tricky stage, like moonlight, when it appears to reveal much—but what it conceals is far greater. Any of those shadows could have grasping claws and slicing teeth hidden inside it. So Danny also kept clear of anything she couldn't see under or around.

This meant her route through the vehicles was sinuous. It took far longer to reach the Cougar than she had anticipated. Some of the stumbling zeros were converging on her target, not because they anticipated her goal, but because they were traveling the shortest route to intersect with her path. Two of them got there first. Both wore the Hawkstone camouflage. Big, once-brawny males. One was bare-headed, with the face skinned off from the bridge of the nose down to the chin. The thing had upper eyelids but none below, eyeballs sagging in a matrix of congealed flesh down onto the exposed cheekbones. The teeth showed in the lipless jaws like a picket fence. The other's uniform was black with old blood. It was missing the meat off its upper arms; the forearms hung uselessly from the stripped humerus bones, ragged uniform sleeves swaying in shreds from its shoulders. This one wore a helmet.

Behind Danny, three more were lurching toward her position, about ten feet from the driver's side door of the Cougar. The mutilated pair stood between her and the vehicle. Danny hefted the brain pick in one hand and the prybar in the other.

She decided to do things the bold way. She swung the prybar at the one with no face, shattering its teeth. Her soul recoiled to see the damage done: It was one thing to smash the face in its bag of skin, and another thing to see the teeth shatter and the pieces spill to the ground, with some of them dangling on ropes of nerve tissue from the jaws. She swung again and the hooked cat's paw at the end of the bar caved in its temple. One of the eyes burst on impact, spurting thin gray liquid. The thing went down.

It was still in action, struggling to get to her, but she'd scrambled its brain enough for her purpose. The second was protected by the helmet. That made things difficult. Danny had been in the fight for less than ten seconds; the space between her and the zeros behind her was closing by the moment, and she had to get up into the cab of the MRAP, which was not at all like climbing into a Suburban. The tires alone were chest-high on Danny. She had to scale a ladder up the side of the vehicle, then swing the door out above her head. If she opened it wrong, she would fall off the ladder. She had to make this quick and get up there immediately or she was going to get pulled down by the others that were closing in.

The stench of them seemed to fill the air with invisible, rotten jelly, making it difficult to draw breath.

Danny saw she wouldn't have to pierce the helmet to stop the zombie in front of her. It didn't have arms. Danny struck it savagely on the knee, the thing fell over sideways, and with three bounding strides she reached the side of the gigantic vehicle. Up the ladder—the latch handle was inset at the bottom of the door. She pulled down on the handle and the pneumatics swung the door open. She grabbed the frame to pull herself up, already aware of how close the half-dozen undead behind her were, and how easy it would be for one of them to tear off a chunk of her calf right now—the smell was mind-blowing. With a thrust of her arms, she lunged up into the cab of the MRAP. The stench hit her first, the swarm of raisin-fat flies next. The reanimated, decaying soldier hit her an instant later.

The thing had been in the cab of the Cougar for a long time. The soldier must have climbed up in there, wounded, and bled to death. When it returned to animation, it was trapped inside, and went into its hibernation state, all the while liquefying in the intense heat of the enclosed vehicle, baking day after day in the sun. That it could still move in its advanced state of decay was testament to the durability of the human design. Ropes of festering meat slid from its limbs, fizzing with bacteria. Its uniform was a sack filled with the liquor of burst guts. The stink of it was beyond endurance.

Danny's mind shut down. She simply hurled herself away from the thing as it threw its weight against her, snapping its jaws so that the lips tore free and hung like storm-drowned nightcrawlers. Danny flew through the air, five feet down and six feet out, and hit the pavement on her back with such violence that only the pain told her she wasn't dead. The grenades at her belt slammed into her vital organs and threatened to burst them. Her skull bounced off the asphalt, the knit cap offering no protection, and Danny saw the universe contract to a pinpoint, but consciousness came back in a fraction of a second—in time for the waves of agony from her back.

A moment later, the rotten thing in the cab of the MRAP fell upon her. It exploded. What seemed to be ten gallons of sewage belched into her face, then bowlfuls of warm rice. Not rice, though. Maggots.

Danny might have screamed. She couldn't tell. She struggled with stunned senses to get away from the thing, her head whirling from the blow on the pavement. Her body hurt to move, but she had to do something to get away from the nightmare of rotten meat and bones that sprawled across her body.

Beneath her something else was moving. She had fallen on the zero with no arms. Somewhere it was questing with its mouth to find purchase on her body.

The rest of the monsters were reaching down to get their piece of her. Moaning. Snapping their jaws.

Danny got her legs under her. The left one was not holding weight; she fell. She pushed herself away, rolling beneath the Cougar's powerful, V-shaped undercarriage. She didn't have anything to lose, and she had very little bandwidth available to think. Mostly she was trying not to pass out. So she reached around for one of the time-delay grenades, pulled the wire with clumsy fingers, and skidded it back the way she had come. Then she crawled as she had in the desert. Her clothes stuck to the pavement, glutinous with corpse ichor, larvae spilling in fistfuls from her hair. Her mouth writhed with them.

Danny dragged her unresponsive leg all the way beneath the vehicle, then into the approaching dawn light on the other side. She curled herself into an aching ball behind the wheel. She wondered how long ten seconds could possibly last. She wondered if the vehicle was equipped with the run-flat tire inserts. If it was, she might live. Otherwise, she was about to get blown in half. She put her hands over her ears and closed her eyes. Her brains were working again.

The grenade went off.

The shockwave threw Danny away from the wheel of the Cougar. She hardly felt it. On both sides of her a haze of shrapnel, organic matter, and fire filled the air; she received none of it in the silhouette of the massive, blast-resistant tire. The vehicle itself hardly rocked on its suspension, although the paint caught fire.

Danny crawled on elbows and knees away from the site of the explosion. She had no idea if she was the center of interest for a swarm of undead or the only thing moving on that section of road.

She kept crawling, and found she was moving back behind the MRAP. The foremost Humvee was right in front of her. She dragged herself toward it, then took a rest against its side. She didn't have a whole lot of energy. She spat to clear her mouth, then spat again, and dry heaved. Then she wanted to go to sleep. She couldn't go on fighting. It was her time. Her fortune in seconds was spent.

But there was something happening around her. The cavalry must have come. She saw people passing among the vehicles. They weren't zeros. They moved with purpose, hunched over for cover, slipping silent and intent between the cars. Danny supposed she should be pleased. These must be civilians who were holed up in this area, outside the so-called safe zone, and they came out of hiding when they heard the grenade go off. Maybe they would have a working shower, and some whiskey. She didn't call to the people who were now encircling the blast site. They would find her. She didn't have the breath in her body.

Then she heard something else. It was cursing. She turned her head slowly, the vertebrae that carried it protesting at the strain. It was the Zero Killer, Magnussen. She was trotting toward the MRAP, enraged, cursing hysterically. And she hadn't seen Danny.

"Fucking idiot," Danny heard, and "amateur," and "asshole cop." Magnussen efficiently stabbed one of the nearest zeros in the skull, leaving the knife in its head, and reached a brain pick from her belt. The Luger was in her other hand. Danny was almost touched at her devotion to duty: Magnussen was going to move the MRAP herself. Danny wondered why the others who had come out to see what was going on didn't emerge from hiding to help Magnussen, at least. They were so quiet. They probably figured Danny was dead, or undead.

The sun was a few minutes from rising now. Color was seeping into the world. Birds would be singing, if birds sang anymore. Danny painstakingly rotated her head back around to see what the new folks were doing.

She felt a wave of ice water spill through her veins, the pain of her body overridden by fear.

These weren't survivors circling around among the vehicles on the freeway. They were undead. And Danny realized what it was they were doing.

They were hunting.

In a pack.

7

Patrick walked past Ace at the wrong time, or in the wrong way, or Ace just wanted something to do.

"Don't you fucking look at me, faggot," Ace said.

"Why, does it turn you on?" Patrick replied, and continued on his way into the rec room. He didn't hear Ace coming until it was too late. Suddenly Patrick was spun around and a fist crashed into his nose and blood spewed out of it and Patrick was stumbling backward, his hands at his face. Ace punched him again, in the belly, and when Patrick jackknifed, the wind knocked out of him, Ace grabbed the smaller man's hair and propelled his skull into the wall, caving in the plaster.

Patrick collapsed. After he didn't get up for fifteen minutes, Amy was called in. She didn't know how bad the damage was, but Patrick was practically comatose, so she went to Murdo.

"Boys will be boys," Murdo said, when he'd heard the story.

"You can't let this happen," Amy said. "You have to punish that Ace of yours. Otherwise something worse is going to happen. Patrick might be brain-damaged."

"His kind are all brain-damaged," Murdo said, but agreed to let Amy move Patrick out to the White Whale, just to make sure none of the men decided to take another crack at him.

It was civilians who carried Patrick out to the motor home. Michelle volunteered to stay and watch over him. Jimmy James went with her. Amy was relieved at this, at least: Michelle was definitely in danger around these men, and her brother might be next in line for a beating. They could play computer games and listen to Patrick try to breathe.

Amy got the wounded man arranged on his bed, and although she couldn't reset the shattered bones of his nose, she was able to pry open an airway through the damage on either side, using a tongue depressor and wads of gauze pushed up into his nostrils. His face was a terrible mess. Both eyes were swelling up. He was probably better off unconscious.

Back in the terminal, the day wore on forever.

The survivors were dividing into uneasy factions now: Some wanted to *do* something about the situation; others wanted to try to make nice with the Hawkstone men; and the rest didn't want to do anything. They wanted to sulk in silence, if only because it bothered the hell out of *Turdo*, as the women had taken to calling him.

Juan kept fawning over Boudreau and the rest; at one point Maria happened to walk past him and let loose a low, rapid stream of Spanish that sounded like a lot of dirty words to Amy. Juan cringed and scuttled away. Amy was sympathetic to Juan's plight: He was eligible for the next beating, if Jimmy James and Patrick weren't around. He was also the next one in line to get sent out into the wasteland, if the mercenaries decided to get rid of anybody else. Juan would do anything to avoid that fate. Maybe even join the cause of his captors.

As it happened, the next victim was a woman.

It began at dawn with the screaming of the usually silent baby. Amy bolted out of the chair she was sleeping in. The baby was at the far end of the dormitory. Amy dashed down the aisle between the bunks and found the child alone in bed, wiggling his little arms and legs, his face a red, puckered ring around the screaming toothless mouth. The bedclothes were rumpled and still warm, but his mother was not there.

By now most of the women had gathered to see what was going on. Amy shoved through them—they would handle the baby, somehow; she didn't know what to do except offer him a glass of water. She ran out of the room. There was no guard by the exterior door, only an empty chair. Amy tried to think what was happening. The washrooms. She turned on her heels and ran down the stairs toward the Aviatrix's room, taking the steps three at a time.

The door was jammed shut. Amy shoved hard, shoved again. She could hear chair legs shuddering over the slick floor tiles. She kicked the door, and it squeaked open another inch. Now she could get her hand through the gap. She felt the back of a plastic stacking chair wedged under the door handle. Shook it free and swung the door open, just as Murdo and Ace came racing down from the men's dormitory, guns in hand, wearing their cargo pants but no shirts or boots.

They could all see inside the bathroom. They all saw the same thing.

Murdo wasn't going to be able to play this one as a he-said-she-said. Because Cammy was jammed up in the corner by the paper towel dispensers, and he—the Flamingo—was crushed up against her, one hand twisted down at her groin, the other at her throat. The woman was terrified, the whites showing all the way around her eyes. She looked at Amy and there was pleading on her face, but silent pleading, because the Flamingo was choking her silent.

Amy didn't make a plan. She simply grabbed the plastic chair, raised it over her left shoulder, and charged. She swung it at the pink-skinned, pink-haired man, her eyes fixed on the back of his neck. *I hope I kill him,* Amy thought, and an instant later the chair wasn't in her hands.

She careened into the man, his hard muscles unyielding, and because the chair was gone she was off-balance and fell. She was back up on her knees within half a second. Flamingo hadn't even turned all the way around. Amy started punching, aiming for his legs, his crotch, anything to stop him. He kicked her away before she landed a single worthwhile blow, and then strong hands were dragging her backward. Ace towed Amy along the floor with one hand twisted into her hair and the other hand shoving his pistol in her face. She could smell the tang of the gun oil. She was spitting with fury; injustice like a cliff towered above her and she wanted to smash it down. Flamingo, she saw, had turned to Murdo. Murdo was holding the chair he'd pulled out of Amy's hands. There was a crazy daisy sticker on the chair.

Flamingo had his back to Cammy, his hands held out to Murdo, shaking his head in a now-let's-be-reasonable kind of way, a bashful little smile on his piebald face. It might have ended there, boys will be boys, everybody back to your own beds. Except Cammy's foot appeared from behind Flamingo, with the suddenness of a magic trick, in the fork between his legs. His trouser legs jumped halfway up his shins. The blow made a noise like a preacher whacking his Bible in midsermon.

"That's for Patrick, you *asshole*!" Cammy shouted. Flamingo went down in slow motion, his neck rigged with tendons like a schooner in a high wind, teeth bared, eyes bulging. Ace let go of Amy's hair. One moment Cammy was there, blazing with life, tall with defiance. The next moment there was a crisp, ear-splitting report that buzzed off the tiles, and the wall behind Cammy was blooming with red roses. Her head snapped back and she fell to the floor, dead. Flamingo lay on his side clutching his testicles while the blood flowed out of Cammy in the shape of a monstrous red hand, its fingers crawling along the grout lines, oozing toward the fallen man, as if to avenge its dead. Amy looked away.

Jones was leaning against the doorframe, his wounded leg held stiffly at an angle in front of him. His face was sheet-rumpled, his hair awry. He stared at the bloody scene, then spoke to Murdo: "Sir? What the *fuck* is going on?"

8

Danny tried to shout, but her voice was gone along with her strength. She didn't want herself or Liz Magnussen to die at the teeth of the undead wolf-pack that was encircling them. Her mind was still tumbling around from the crack on the head she'd received. Magnussen, oblivious to the approaching danger, continued to curse out loud. She put two shots from her Luger into one of the sluggish undead by the MRAP that Danny's grenade hadn't blown apart. The others were motionless, or struggling with shattered limbs, unable to attack. Danny croaked, then tried again; it sounded more like the zombie moan than anything else. She tried to wave her hands. One of them lifted up a few inches, then fell back. She turned her protesting neck to follow how far the hunter zeros had gotten in their careful stalking of their live prey.

There was one eight feet away from Danny.

It was so close, she could hear the rustle of its scabby tongue behind yellow teeth. The thing was looking directly at her with frost-dimmed eyes. When it saw her, it froze in position, knees bent, one leg forward, both arms held crookedly out before it with fingers extended. It stood like that, motionless, for several seconds.

Then it scented the air like an animal, hooking its shrunken nose into the dawn breeze. *It smells me,* Danny thought. She was helpless. It had her.

The zero moved, but not toward Danny. It hunched down low and slunk away to the next position of concealment, behind a dusty hatchback. Danny's heart flooded with emotion.

It saw her and didn't want to eat her.

It smelled her and moved on.

She could hardly move, and her throat would not speak. An evil thought came to her: If the thing didn't attack, she must *already be* one of them.

Yet she felt pain, not hunger.

She felt fear for the living woman who was now up the ladder of the MRAP, shouting her disgust at the stench inside the cab.

Get in and shut the door, you stupid bitch! Danny screamed inside herself. She tried to make the words come out but her vocal cords were unstrung and she could only gasp, sucking in a throatful of putrid gas.

Then Danny understood why she herself was still alive: She was soaked in the sludge of the far-rotten soldier's corpse. She stank so powerfully it would make a graveyard rat puke. On her, the zombie couldn't smell the living breath, the warmth of her blood. It could only smell its own, decaying kind.

Danny bent her eyes toward the Cougar MRAP.

Magnussen didn't get into the cab, having discovered the same unbearable filth that had knocked Danny back. Instead she waved her hands around to clear the flies from her face and started searching the pavement for something. Maybe a rag to wipe up the rotten guts on the front seat.

She kept an eye on the nearest of the shuffling, slow zeros that were making their way toward her, but Danny had cleared a considerable radius with the explosion. Magnussen thought she had plenty of time.

What Magnussen was not anticipating (*because you wouldn't fucking listen,* shouted the voice inside Danny's head) was the stealthy approach of undead with fast reflexes, hunting instincts, and the ability to use concealment to get close to their prey.

Several others of the stalking pack had moved within twenty feet of the Cougar.

Magnussen had something less than fifteen seconds to get inside that vehicle and slam the door. If she did, she was safe as houses. She was surrounded by inch-thick steel plate, triple bulletproof glass, and a variety of armaments and survival gear.

Who gives a shit what it smells like, in the name of God, Danny shouted, silently. *Get in.*

Danny tried again to wave her companion away, to get her attention, and this time she was able to lift both hands. Life was returning to her limbs. She wasn't dead; her body was only rebooting. She still couldn't speak.

Then she had an idea. Danny dragged her numb fingers around behind her belt, knuckles scraping on the pavement, and groped them across the tattered band of leather, looking for the satellite radio. It was gone. But there was a single pipe grenade left. She willed her fingers to close around it and they did, in the same slow, imprecise way as the artificial hands she'd seen at the veteran's rehab center when she was learning to use her legs again.

She got the grenade clear of the belt and pulled her arm around by force of will until she could grasp the pipe with both hands. She probably couldn't throw it far enough to avoid killing herself, but she didn't particularly relish surviving much longer, anyway. This was a better way to die. There were six or seven of the hunting zombies gathered behind vehicles all around Magnussen now, and Danny couldn't figure out why her companion hadn't seen them.

But she knew the answer already. *Because she doesn't believe in them, of course.*

Danny turned her eyes to the grenade. She gathered her will, sending conscious commands to her arms. She pulled the fuse wire with all the force she could muster, and it didn't move. She pulled again, and now that her arms were familiar with the orders they yanked apart and the wire came smartly out of the grenade. There was a little whiff of fuse smoke that nipped inside Danny's nostrils, breaking through the stench of corpses. This was it. If things went the way she thought they might, she was about to be blown apart, either by dimes or ball bearings. She preferred dimes, if given a choice. Classier.

She turned her body like a rusty spring and threw the grenade as hard as she could.

To Danny's surprise, the missile sailed briskly into the air and clanked down among the cars, not far from a pair of the crouching zeros. Magnussen heard the noise, and turned, pistol raised, searching with her eyes. Danny tried once more to shout.

At last, Magnussen saw the zombies. They broke cover at the same moment, oblivious to the importance of the grenade, but recognizing their quarry was alerted to them.

Silent as lions they came on, jaws open.

Magnussen fired three shots in rapid succession, pivoting her arm straight out in front of her to sweep the pack as it charged. One of the things went heavily down, then the rest were upon her.

She screamed, a low, angry cry, that honeyed singer's voice lending melody even to this. The zeros slammed her against the hull of the MRAP.

Danny couldn't see clearly—Magnussen was obscured between the fenders of the vehicle. Danny saw the monsters grabbing her arms, biting, trying to tear through the leather.

How long had it been since she threw the grenade? Five seconds? Six? It seemed as if ten minutes had passed since the fuse had flared to life.

Magnussen had one arm free of her tormentors and was shouting, swinging a brain pick side-to-side. She nailed one of the things, caught it in the head and it fell, its legs kicking as if electrified. But now Magnussen's hands were empty. Another of the undead lunged in, teeth flashing, and she was shoved back completely out of sight and her hoarse shouts turned to a high, gurgling whistle. Danny was too far away to tell if it was human blood or zombie ink, but something squirted through the air.

Seven, eight.

The grenade exploded. A blazing automobile door sailed high overhead and crashed down out of sight beyond Danny's position. She blinked as the explosion drove a wave of hot, gritty air into her face. The MRAP rocked back on its wheels, then lurched down again. Cars burst into flame; gasoline tanks ruptured and blew. Black, greasy smoke coiled into the light of the newly risen sun, which was burning a bright crescent into the eastern horizon of rooftops.

One of the undead hunters stumbled out of the smoke, flames clambering over its ragged flesh. It stumbled, sought balance against a car, then continued. Eventually the thing fell down, and struggled, and lay still.

Danny drove the Humvee along the obstacle course of the freeway, away from San Francisco. She bulled the heavy truck through the smaller vehicles. This wasn't detail work. She simply had to make some distance. The military Hummers were equipped with an on-off switch, not keys, so it had been the work of a few seconds to get the machine running and maneuver her way into the maze of motionless vehicles.

All along her route she saw the hunting undead: dozens of them at first, then hundreds, then thousands of these alert, swift-moving zeros, all swarming in the direction of the city and its stench of living things.

The sun was not long up in the sky when she saw another phenomenon that made her pull up onto an overpass raised on concrete pillars high in the air. *Half Moon Bay Road,* the sign said. She stopped the Humvee. She was fairly safe inside the vehicle, which had a fully enclosed cab, but it was extremely dangerous to be out in the open. There was a backpack on the floor of the passenger side. Danny found a couple of vacuum-packed meals in there, a copy of *Car and Driver*, two clips of 9mm ammunition, and a pair of compact binoculars.

Danny checked her position carefully before she emerged, the overpass giving her a commanding view of several miles of road in both directions. She climbed up on the roof, carefully because her legs were weak as a newborn foal's, and sighted through the binoculars.

Danny didn't know exactly where she was. The road was on high ground. Downhill from the freeway were master-planned subdivisions, identical houses on streets that branched into ever-smaller streets, like limbs on a tree. Beyond that was the bay. On the other side was a long, narrow reservoir fringed with trees. It butted up against forested hills. Danny had seen something happening out among the houses that made her wonder. She saw it for mile after mile, and still couldn't comprehend it. So now she searched the distant streets with the binoculars.

They were there.

The figures she discerned were tiny, this far away, but she could see they were upright, human—the undead. In some places there were one or two of them; in other places, hundreds had gathered.

They were all facing north. *All* of them. Danny sought out the nearest streets, not far from her elevated position, and there were more of them there. She feathered the focus ring and now she could see the faces of the nearest ones. They were chomping. Or rather, they were clacking their jaws. They looked like wooden puppets, nutcrackers, mouths snapping open and shut. Now she thought she could even hear the sound, which she had originally believed to be the rustling of grass. It was the snapping of hundreds of thousands of hungry teeth. All biting at the air, all facing north, all aimed toward the city.

9

Since the incident that morning, Murdo was never without a pistol in his hand. Discipline with his men had broken down completely by midday. They were arguing among themselves. There was a fistfight between Ace and Parker, Ace accusing Parker of siding with the slain woman because she was "half coon."

Murdo brooded alone in the control tower for several hours. The civilians were rounded up and locked down in the dining room, with guards on every exit. It was Reese and Boudreau who carried Cammy out of the ladies' room, wrapped in a plastic dropcloth, her bloodless, yellow-gray feet protruding from the polyethylene. Maria demanded to know what they were going to do with her.

"She's dead," Boudreau replied, as if Maria was suggesting necrophilia. They wrestled the bound corpse across the parking lot, threading between their hulking vehicles. Estevez unlocked the gates and they carried Cammy's body away out into the scrubland. Both men came running back into the compound within a minute and a half, reporting to their compatriots before Reese trotted up into the conning tower to inform Murdo.

None of the civilians could see what the fuss was about, but the normally macho men were clearly shaken. The dining room was on the runway side of the building; none of the windows looked out on the front gates. As it was, the civilians didn't have long to wait before the news reached them. Estevez climbed into the M1117 ASV and manned the gun turret and when Murdo came down out of the tower, he shouted, "Zeros!" and pointed out into the desert.

There were gunshots. Several of the survivors got down on the floor. Pfeiffer posted a lookout by the window.

"They're shooting outside the fence," she said.

Minutes later, the mercenaries came back in, this time with Murdo among them, chest out, head thrown back. They had their old swagger back, as if they'd been out hunting bear.

"You'll be glad to know," Murdo said, in a too-loud, expansive voice, "We took care of about ten zeros that were on their way here for the free buffet." He looked around at the civilians as if he expected them to thank him. He met the hostile eyes and took a step backward, then drew himself up to his modest full height.

"Let's all try to remember that we had an accident here. An unfortunate accident. But now we saved all your lives. We did it without hesitation, we did it without making any demands out of you people. We did our duty as sworn contractors to the United States government, if any. I didn't come back in here expecting to be hailed as a conquering hero. But I do expect you people to show some fucking *respect* for the men who just saved your *asses*."

By the end of his speech his face was red and he had his head thrust forward again in that characteristic, belligerent posture that was his natural stance. Nobody spoke for a few seconds. Then Linda Maas, who seemed to have found some inner fire, stood up and raised her hand. Without waiting to be acknowledged by Murdo, she said, "Were they attracted by the smell of fresh meat? Was it the body out there? You creeps didn't even bury her, did you."

"We didn't have *time,*" Reese shouted, at the top of his lungs. His hand rose up to rest on the pommel of his automatic. Murdo stepped in front of Reese with his back to the civilians.

"You listen here," Murdo said to Reese, but for the general audience. "These people are spoiled, soft, and ungrateful: Civilians are like that everywhere in the world. They don't know the cost in blood, sweat, and tears it takes to bring peace to a troubled land, you hear me?" By now Murdo was inches from Reese, looking up into the taller man's face with glittering, bloodshot eyes. "Now you and me, we get no respect. We're not Army. We're not Marines or Air Force or Navy."

Murdo stepped back so he could take in all his men with an encompassing look, warming to his speech. He placed his hand on Reese's arm and squeezed.

"Hell, we're not even National Guard." This got a laugh out of the mercenaries. Murdo continued, on a roll now.

"We're plain old Americans, except we have a *code*. A code of discipline and loyalty and duty. In all this excitement, hell, we made mistakes. Freedom isn't free. But"—here he thrust a blunt finger heavenward—"the highest authority will forgive us what happens on the bloody fields of war, because it's not the dead that mourn, it's the living. Let's remember that. We mourn the dead. Fuck if I'm not mourning the dead right now, right here in my heart. And I will kill the first cocksucker says otherwise."

"So, what happens now?" Amy asked. This speech of his was leading somewhere.

Murdo ground a fist into his other hand. "I'll tell you what happens now. We're pulling out," he announced. "Too many zeros. This is no longer a secure location."

The sun was setting behind a mass of thick, shapeless cloud low on the horizon. The sky was shot through with faded purple and scratches of bright orange as the light drowned and the world fell into darkness. Supplies had been hurried into the vehicles over the course of the afternoon, with most of the edible stuff going into the ASV and the back of a Humvee controlled by the Hawkstone men; as a concession, some food was left in the RV so the civilians could eat on the road. Toilet paper, batteries, and the first-aid materials—whatever occurred to people—were piled up around Patrick's bed in the motor home.

The urgency of the situation wasn't clear to anybody but Murdo. Amy thought he must be going stir-crazy, and this was his way of dealing with it. There were undead out there in growing numbers, but she thought the living were safer at the airfield, at least until morning; who knew what would happen out there in the dark? But she kept her own counsel and did what she was told to do, like everyone else.

Once the vehicles were loaded to Murdo's satisfaction, the survivors were marched double-time to the White Whale. Murdo ordered them to halt at the door. "You and you," he said, indicating Reese and Estevez, "throw the fag out. Put him over there."

Amy surprised herself by shouting, as loudly as she could, "No! He's not even conscious!"

Murdo turned to her with his eyes strangely blank. "I don't give a side-ways fuck what he is, I'm not having another wounded on this bus. Jones is all we can handle. Reese, Estevez, do it."

"At least," Amy said, her voice quaking, "bring him inside the building."

Reese and Estevez muscled the unconscious body into the terminal. They were going to dump Patrick on the floor a foot inside the front door, but Amy barked, "Upstairs," and rather than argue, they carried him up the steps and tossed him on a bed in the men's dormitory. Amy tried to arrange Patrick's limbs in a restful pose, then threw a blanket over him.

"Okay," Reese said, when Amy didn't move from Patrick's bedside. "Let's go."

"What the fuck, man," Estevez said, looking to Reese. "Let's get the fuck out of here."

"Let's go," Reese repeated, to Amy.

"Come on, man. We ain't got a whole shitload of time." Estevez slapped Reese on the arm.

Reese turned on Estevez. "She's the fuckin' doctor, man. We gotta take the doctor with us. She don't need to stay here nursing Boy George."

Amy had an inspiration, beautiful in its simplicity.

"I'm not a doctor," she said. "I'm a veterinarian."

That got them.

"Bullshit," Estevez said. "You sewed up Jones."

"Same as a dog, except taller," Amy said.

"Serious?" Reese asked.

"I'm a horse doctor," Amy said. The men looked confused. Reese pointed in the direction of the parking lot.

"Go tell Murdo," he said to Estevez. "Maybe she ain't shit."

She was an *animal* doctor, nothing more.

Murdo was embarrassed, and that made him angry. The refugees in the motor home had gotten a huge laugh out of it. Murdo couldn't believe they were laughing at *him,* of all people, who held their lives in his hand. Like that cocksucker who threw the shoes at the president a while back and everybody thought he was a hero. So what if Jones got doctored by an animal expert? It was all meat, right? But Murdo still felt the blush flaring away in his face. Maybe he should shoot the bitch, teach them a lesson. But he had a feeling if there was one more act of violence like that, these people would no longer come along easily.

"Tell you what," Murdo said to Estevez. "We're gonna leave her here like she wants. But on our way out, we're gonna chain the gates to the ASV, rip 'em off the hinges, and drag 'em a mile down the road. Then let's see if the lady veterinarian thinks it's so funny when all the zeros come pouring in looking for chow. What do you say?"

"I say hells to the yeah," Estevez replied.

So the engines were fired up on the M1117 Armored Security Vehicle and the two Humvees. Ace piloted one of the Humvees around in a broad circle until it was up behind the White Whale, which was the only civilian vehicle they were taking. Reese got back in beside Molini in the cab of the motor home. Murdo was in the ASV, because he was the boss. Parker was at the controls. Jones was laid out in the back of the second Humvee. It took Flamingo five minutes to get down the terminal stairs, his testicles were so sore.

Boudreau shot a couple of nearby zeros, unlocked the big gates, and swung them open. He had thirty feet of chain ready to attach the gates to the ASV, when the time came. The next nearest undead were probably five minutes out in the desert, maybe less. The convoy was ready to go, as soon as Flamingo quit fucking around: He was trying to urinate against the side of Hangar 1.

"What the fuck, asshole," Murdo said, climbing down out of the ASV.

"I can't piss," Flamingo said. "It feels like I got to go but I can't. She busted my dick."

"You got ten seconds to stow your junk, Flamingo. Then we roll."

The night was swallowing up the world, cold and dark. There was a wind rising. Murdo thought he could hear the moaning of the zeros out there in the dark, barren country. Then he thought he could hear an engine. Murdo turned to face the road, and Boudreau was watching, as well. There were headlights bouncing along out there in the distance. Coming down the road for the airfield. The vehicle couldn't have been headed anywhere else because there was nowhere else.

Moments later, they watched a grime-coated Candyapple Red 1968 Mustang roll to a stop a hundred feet from the gates.

10

Danny's ass was sore. So was everything else. But she was relieved to be back on the road to Boscombe Field. The return trip to the Mustang had been problem-free, but she was troubled by the thought of what was happening back in San Francisco. They might not have attacked yet, but those zeros with their canine intelligence and their silent, crouching stealth were going to overrun the defenses. There was no question. The urban core was surrounded by a perimeter of wire and rubble and cars. This barricade was designed to keep out rotting, two-legged things as stupid and single-minded as sharks. These new ones were cunning.

They could work together in packs. They were exponentially faster and smarter than the ones Danny had encountered in the hotel in Potter, and there were hundreds of thousands of them. She was afraid to speculate on how much further the living dead would evolve before the virus that animated them decided it was finished improving its kill ratio. Would the zeros someday be able to communicate? Use weapons? If that happened, the living would be destroyed.

To confront an opponent that could think, but felt no pain, no fear, and was incapable of mercy—that meant extinction.

Danny decided to ditch the Humvee in favor of the Mustang. She had all kinds of reasons for this, but the truth was she couldn't leave the Mustang behind. It represented everything: the last vestige of Kelley's trail, the last vestige of Danny's attempts at a real life. And it was such a sweet ride. Danny didn't have a lot of pleasures left. The 302 V-8 might be the last of them. That, and the bourbon.

Danny allowed herself a few pulls on a fresh fifth, but didn't drink herself stupid the way she had on the road north. She was on her way back to known things, now, and there was refuge in it. She wouldn't need the bottle for company. Merely the occasional sip, enough to take the edge off the pain that a handful of Vicodin couldn't get to.

Danny took a few more chances before she lit out again.

She was there at the seaside where she'd left the Mustang. It was exactly as she had left it, some days before. The coast was deserted.

Climbing into her beloved vehicle wearing such stinking, filth-saturated clothing seemed blasphemous. She wondered if zeros could swim. The beach was empty, and the nearby marina, and the motel, the boatyard, and all the little houses. She had swept the area for zeros previously, and none seemed to have wandered in since.

She had never been so alone.

The water would be cruelly cold. But you only live once, she thought. *If you're lucky,* the voice said. Danny stripped off her clothes and raced her battered body into the creaming surf. Despite the frigid water and a persistent worry that the severed head she'd seen at Fisherman's Wharf would rise up from the bottom and bite her on the ass, she floundered around in the surf for almost half an hour. She scampered back out of the water only once, to retrieve her long-suffering boots and swish them through the water, over and over, scooping up the sea and pouring it out again until the leather lost its slimy feel and they smelled like nothing except ocean. Then she swam, for the sheer joy of swimming.

When she emerged from the sea, she felt thoroughly alive. Her limbs were numb, so they didn't ache. The thick mat of scars that covered her back seemed to enjoy salt water, its astringency softening the rawhide until it almost felt like skin again. The air was a lot colder than she remembered it, and she didn't have a towel—or any clothes at all, unless she wanted to put on the reeking garbage she'd been wearing before.

She scanned the area around her. It was truly deserted, this little seasonal village tucked between the sea and the headlands. Fuck it. Danny arranged her boots to drain onto the sand, then walked up the beach, stark naked. Between the scars and the bruises she figured anybody who saw her from a distance would think she was wearing a tie-dyed wetsuit. Besides, wasn't the world getting beyond modesty now? It didn't matter if you were clothed or naked, only if you were alive or dead. It didn't matter if your thighs were laced with surgical scars and your back looked like the surface of Neptune. Just so long as you were a human being.

Still, she hoped nobody would see her.

Danny walked along the strand until she came to a surf shop. For protection she was carrying the tiller off a derelict sailboat. It would make a handy club. Although there was light overcast, she thought she was getting sunburned, and then she thought, *Not on your back, you aren't,* and she laughed to herself. She laughed out loud. It sounded like gunshots. She was quiet again.

The surf shop was unlocked. She went in, stilling the bell at the top with her fingers so it wouldn't jingle. She found some cargo shorts and a long-sleeve Tee with a cartoon shark holding a surfboard on it. She scuffed on a pair of flip-flops. They were no good for running, though. She found a sleek pair of surf shoes in her size and tried those on. She'd always thought they looked stupid, like ballet slippers. But now that she had them on, they were quite nice. Snug and light, with a sole as thin as an extra layer of skin on her foot.

Danny didn't look much like a cop, now. If, on her journey, she met people, she would prefer to have whatever authority a uniform could convey. It was shorthand for *Take me seriously.* Then she thought, *There might be a police station here.* Summer cops for when the crowds showed up to go boating and lie in the sun. Anyway, she didn't fancy running into any of the agile zombies in her current costume; she hadn't had to fight in slippers before. Danny made her way down the lone street in town, past the shuttered-up beachwear shops, the art gallery with its driftwood sculptures and whale paintings, never to be admired again; there was a real estate agency with the usual *For Sale* sign on the door.

She found what she was looking for without encountering anything that moved, except a seagull that watched her from atop a telephone pole. Her objective was a tiny building of concrete blocks. One door, one window, garage on the side. She said a silent prayer for forgiveness and lobbed a rock through the window of the Madras Bay Police & Beach Safety Department.

Half an hour later she was gunning the Mustang up the hill out of town, attired in a fresh tan uniform. The arm patches said only *Police,* it was cut to fit a man, and the pants were three inches too long, but Danny tucked the cuffs into her soggy boots and looked enough like a cop so she could almost imagine she had her dignity back. She buckled on her heavy police belt and pistol. Better yet. All that remained was to tuck Kelley's letter, secure in a plastic sandwich bag, into her breast pocket. Danny buttoned it up.

As she drove back to the highway, Danny thought of the scene she'd observed from the overpass outside the city.

Thousands of zeros, jaws working in concert with each other, like the realization of some shared instinct. Something locked up since before mankind stood on its hind legs, possibly so ancient it came from a time before animals walked at all. Why did the undead chomp the air like that? The sight of so many monsters clacking their sinewy jaws together reminded Danny of armies on a medieval battlefield, beating their shields with their spears as they marched to the slaughter. The zeros might have been anticipating the kill, tearing at warm throats in what was left of their imaginations.

But those things couldn't imagine, could they? Danny rejected the idea. They couldn't create, or build, or grow. They were only capable of destruction, however clever they became. So it must have been those things in their thousands were warming up for the kill. Nothing more. How many of them would taste fresh meat? How many would rot away of hunger because there were no more living things to destroy?

Danny was driving toward the sunset. She was worried now—she hadn't been able to contact Boscombe Field by the police radio in her glove box. It didn't necessarily mean anything; if things were quiet, they might have stopped monitoring the radio. But she would much have preferred to hear from them in advance of her arrival.

There was a massive bank of clouds on the horizon, stealing the sun away before its time. She turned off onto Ore Creek Highway and her pulse picked up a little. She was avoiding thoughts of Amy and Patrick and the rest. Topper and Ernie. Maria on the radio. Troy Huppert the city fireman. They might all be dead, overrun by the undead while she was gone, but she didn't think so. Behind that fence with supplies and soft beds, and so far from major human settlements, they should be fine. They'd be pissed off at her, of course, and she would have to act contrite, but they'd get over it. It hadn't been that long since Danny left. What could possibly have gone wrong?

A few miles of blacktop, the night coming down like an opera curtain. By the fading light she saw zeros, wandering in the desert. They were going the same way she was. The flat desert floor seemed to have become a kind of caravan route for the things. That couldn't be good.

There weren't as many as up there in San Francisco—there weren't enough *people* within two hundred miles of here—but there were a hell of a lot of them. They were the slow kind, she thought. They didn't have any coordination, and they didn't crouch-walk or attempt to keep out of sight. But then, she didn't know if the fast ones reserved their stalking technique for the kill. They might shamble along like all the others, until prey came along.

Danny had to force her foot up off the gas pedal. She was driving much too fast for such a poorly maintained road.

Then she saw lights in a hollow of the dark line of hills, and before long she could see the airfield. She slowed down. The yard of the airfield was brilliantly lit by pole-mounted fixtures. Lights meant life. That was good. Then, as she approached, she saw military vehicles in formation, lined up to drive out through the gates—including one of the thick, gun-turreted M1117 Guardian ASVs. Almost immune to attack, those were, except they had a distinct tendency to flip over on their backs because of a high center of gravity. Behind that was a Humvee, then the motor home, then another Humvee.

Regardless, Danny would have driven right through the open gates to meet them—except she was now close enough to see the camouflage with which the vehicles were painted. Her blood went cold and thin.

Hawkstone.

Murdo crammed in next to Estevez in the turret of the ASV, and watched as a cop stepped out of the vintage Mustang. A lady cop. She stood by the car. Left the door open. Cautious type. She must be the one the civilians talked about like she was the Queen of Sheba for getting them to the airfield alive. She was here precisely in time to fuck things up even further. The cop walked toward them, a dozen feet in front of the Mustang, but no closer.

"Estevez, you be ready to open up that big gun, you hear?" Murdo said, softly. "I don't need this shit."

Murdo clambered back through the hull of the ASV and lowered himself down to the ground from the side hatch. Pulled his uniform straight. Then he walked across toward Boudreau and stood in the middle of the gate, arms folded.

"You better come in," he called to the cop. "Shitload of zeros out there." His voice was pitched loud, to cover the distance between them.

"I saw them," the cop replied, in a big voice accustomed to authority. "I'd like to speak to someone there."

"I'm the one in charge," Murdo said.

What he didn't know was what to do next. The cop had no authority in this time of privatized martial law. He could kill her on the spot. He probably would. But he wanted to make sure she hadn't come from headquarters with fresh news. Could be the rest of the world was already on the rebound and they were sitting in the desert kicking each other in the nuts for no good reason.

"I'm looking for Amy Cutter. She's a doctor," Danny said. The short, thick man spat on the ground. The tall man with the prizefighter's face shook his head. She had definitely stepped in something. Danny was mortally afraid for Amy. She realized she had pinned the hopes she'd lost of ever seeing Kelley again on seeing Amy again, instead. Which was not very smart. Hope didn't get you through.

The short man spoke again after thinking awhile: "You mean the veterinarian? She left. She was here, but she left. We're relocating to command headquarters, so you need to get out of our way."

Danny couldn't see the motor home clearly, shielded as it was by the blaze of the brilliant headlamps of the ASV. But she didn't recognize whoever was sitting in the driver's seat. She thought she might be making a very serious mistake, standing out here in the open. There was a man on the 20mm cannon in the turret of the security vehicle, and these others were armed, as well. There was a big fifty on the roof of the foremost Humvee.

Also, Danny could hear the moaning. There were undead moving through the dark brush all around her. They would be changing course, heading in her direction. This was going to have to be a short conversation, one way or the other.

She tried again, guessing where "headquarters" would be for this man.

"I was just in San Francisco," she said. "It's gone."

"*Bullshit,*" he said, but Danny could tell he was rattled.

"The zombies—the zeros—are getting faster," she added.

"You're a world-class bullshitter," the man said.

Danny didn't feel like pursuing that line of discussion.

"Look, mister," she said. "If Amy Cutter left, where is everybody else? They in the Whale?"

"The Whale?" The man was looking at his comrade now. They were whispering.

"The motor home there," Danny amended. "You're taking it. I'd like to see who's inside."

"They all left," Murdo said.

"I'm Sheriff Adelman. Who are you?"

"Squad Leader Murdo. Hawkstone Security."

"So, *Murdo,*" Danny said, pronouncing his name like it was stuck to her boot, "what I want to know is this: Under what authority have you taken control of this location? What have you done with the civilians? We're on American soil. These are American citizens. They got some rights and you got some restrictions. *Posse comitatus* and shit."

Murdo shook his head. "The entire fucking nation is under martial law, Sheriff. Section ten-seventy-six. *Posse comitatus* is suspended."

"Don't blow smoke up my ass," Danny said, anger giving her voice wings. She wanted to go right up there and get eyeball-to-eyeball with this prick. Maybe even shoot him. "That crap was repealed in '08. I know the law. You don't know shit."

Murdo scuffed the ground with his toe, then laughed. It sounded like an effort. "I'm gonna give you count of ten to decide whether you're coming or going, okay? We're on a timetable." He pantomime-tapped his watch.

Then he whispered something to the gunner in the turret of the ASV. The gunner nodded and hunched over his weapon. Danny knew the posture well—he was braced to open fire.

At that moment, the terminal door banged open and Amy came hammering out of the building, shouting and waving her arms. Danny's heart squeezed halfway up her throat. Amy was alive. She was right there, and these bugfuckers were in the way.

"Danny, go! Go, go, *go!*" Amy shouted, and now one of the uniformed men was running at her from the Humvee and Amy was down on the ground.

Fury burst inside Danny's head: Her friend was being attacked, and she couldn't do anything about it. In fact, she needed to retreat *now.* That upgraded 20mm cannon would blow her apart like a dog-food balloon. She'd seen it in the war. A single round could pass through Danny, the Mustang's engine block, and the rest of the vehicle, yet still have enough power left to punch a two-foot pothole in the road.

She was already throwing herself into the Mustang when the big gun opened up and the world around her turned to hell.

She'd kept the Mustang idling and the door open. The first burst from the 20mm cannon went high. The supersonic crack of the rounds passing overhead at thirty-four hundred feet per second had Danny instinctively bent double as she leaped behind the wheel. Her left foot was still on the ground when she slammed the old Pony into reverse and slapped the accelerator to the floor. In a stinking cloud of tire smoke, she twisted the wheel around and the car reversed itself. The rear window and the windshield simultaneously exploded and the driver's side door, which was still swinging open, let out a deafening *bang* as one of the 20mm rounds whacked through it. The window glass turned to snow. Danny braced herself with her left hand on the windshield pillar to keep from being thrown out of the car as she bashed the shifter forward. The car got traction and jumped up the road. Danny was losing Amy *and* the Mustang to these sons of bitches.

She yanked the steering wheel left and right, fishtailing the car even as it accelerated, to break up the gunner's aim. The road ahead of her leaped into the glow of the headlights as if struck by a tornado, the heavy gun blowing the pavement apart. She pulled the wheel over and drove the Mustang off the road, into the brush. It was never going to be the same car again, but this was no time to worry about the paint job.

It had been eight seconds since the first burst of cannon fire and Danny was still alive.

She whipped the car through the rough desert brush, caught a zombie in the headlights, smashed it into the air over the hood, and now she had one headlamp, not two. She should douse the lights, she realized. But then they could see her taillights and she wouldn't be able to see shit. She kept on driving and wondered why the cannon wasn't turning the entire desert into a blizzard of steel.

There were zeros coming toward her through the bush. It had been fifteen seconds, and she was still alive.

Then she heard the bark of a grenade launcher. The first burst of fire came down in a tight formation close in front of the Mustang, and the desert floor was blasted into the air, rocks and dirt and bushes at once.

Danny drove, blinded by smoke and debris, into the explosions. The Mustang was choked by leaves and dust. The second salvo came down behind the car—except for the grenade that erupted beneath the rear axle.

Everything turned upside-down. The Mustang, the liquor, the first-aid gear, the hoard of ammunition and weapons and food and whatever crap Danny thought she might possibly need on a road trip through the zombie-infested American landscape. Gravity disappeared, then came back in the wrong direction.

Danny was caught by the force of the blast and thrown against the steering wheel, then whiplashed back into the seat, and then she was flung at the ceiling because down was up. The Mustang slammed on its side into the dirt, upside-down, and slid down an eight-foot drainage ditch, until Danny could almost rest her head on the ground below. Red flames lit the world up. It was all red and black and yellow. Nothing else.

Half-deaf, half-blind, and nearly senseless from the impact, Danny tucked her knees up under her and slid her feet through the empty frame of the driver's side door window. It couldn't have been more than three feet down to the bottom of the culvert she'd landed in. But she couldn't get free of the car. She needed to figure out why, because there were zombies and militiamen trying to kill her.

A high, clear note rang in her ears, and there was pressure in her head as if she was at the bottom of a swimming pool. Her thoughts were scrambled like old-fashioned television reception from the predigital days.

What was keeping her dangling under the car? Somehow her arm had gotten hooked around her chest. Her left arm, twisted around. Danny tried to reason the thing out. Something else exploded nearby, but she wasn't concerned about that. She attempted to get her arm free of the obstruction. No go. So she used her right hand to feel out what the problem might be, and now she understood. She had been holding the A pillar, the one that rose up from hood to roof and held the windshield in. The door had been open, then, banging on her knuckles.

Now the door was firmly closed, jammed tight against the stony wall of the culvert. But her fingers were still wrapped around the A pillar. That posed an insoluble problem to Danny's fuddled mind. The Mustang had become like a great big rat trap, and Danny was trapped in it. She smelled gasoline. She loved the smell of gasoline on a man. But not the smell of gasoline running out of the Mustang, especially as the car was on fire.

The threat of fire combined with the stink of gas cleared Danny's head enough so she could panic. Things couldn't get much worse. She needed to pry the door open and release her crushed fingers, which she expected was going to hurt like a motherfucker. Otherwise she was going to be burned alive, which was the Thing She Feared Most. So Danny groped around her for something to get the door open with. There were tools on her belt. Nothing that would fit in the gap of the door. Unless the barrel of her revolver. She pulled the weapon from the holster.

Pain was beginning to converge on her shoulder where her weight hung awkwardly on the trapped arm. She strained to get one knee on the window frame of the door and the other foot on the ground. Now she had a little leverage. She got the barrel of the gun into the rumpled gap between door and roof. She pried at it with all her weight. The gun was coming apart. She was bending the frame around the cylinder. The door shifted slightly. She could flex her fingers. Then the Mustang settled another half-inch, and Danny saw the gap tighten on her hand. The skin of her left index finger split open like a frying sausage.

She needed to make a plan come together fast, or she was definitely going to die.

Danny tried prying the door open again. Now the barrel of the gun wouldn't even fit in the gap. The space was half the width of her fingers. She heard herself whimpering, and made it stop. Now she could hear the moaning, out in the darkness.

Danny lowered her head down below the roof of the Mustang so she could see along the length of the culvert, lit by burning creosote bushes and fragrant mesquite. Two zeros were lurching in her direction, bent silhouettes in the leaping firelight.

She couldn't come up with a plan. By fire or teeth, she was going to die in the wreckage of her beloved 1968 Mustang unless she got herself clear of the vehicle, and her left hand was jammed into a sandwich of steel less than three-eighths of an inch wide.

Danny knew what she needed to do. All the bright hope inside her was still there, but she couldn't use it for anything. Someday, everybody had to die, and this was her day.

She raised the revolver to her temple, and didn't think any grand last thoughts, or send up a prayer to God, or even say good-bye to Kelley's memory. It was easier than that. She squeezed the trigger to send the fat bullet through her head, to blot out the stink of gasoline and the flames and the biting jaws that were coming for her.

The gun didn't fire.

She'd distorted the frame so much the hammer wouldn't fall.

Danny fumbled at her belt and found the knife she'd gotten in San Francisco. That was something. She could cut her throat. Or—Danny's pain-clouded mind saw a possibility. It was as bad an idea as she'd ever had, but it was better than cutting her throat.

Danny took the nickel-plated handcuffs from her belt, let the jaws fall open, and snapped them onto her left wrist, one bracelet at a time. The pain in her trapped fingers was unbelievable, filling the world. She cinched the cuffs tight. They ratcheted down until the bracelets sank into the skin of her arm. Still she squeezed them, until the flesh wouldn't compress anymore and she was working against the density of her own wrist bones. That would have to do. She could feel the pulse hammering in her arm against this obstacle, these constricting bands of steel. Good. Danny reached down with her good hand and drew out the knife.

The nearest zombie was twenty yards away, at most. There were several more behind it, lurching down the ditch toward the fire. The smoke from burning tires and gasoline was choking her. It didn't seem as if the gas tank was going to explode. It was going to burn itself out, which could take all night roasting her, but meanwhile flaming gasoline was streaming down the rear frame of the car, spattering in bright flaring droplets into the boiling pool of motor oil collected near Danny's foot. The heat was intense.

There was a rhythmic thumping in her ears, like a helicopter passing overhead. It was her own heartbeat. Danny raised the blade of the knife, a good sharp edge four inches long with a few serrations down by the hilt. It was a tight space, but she was able to get the blade in close to where her fingers were crushed against the frame of the Mustang. She held her breath. Thrust the knife into the gap. Blood spilled out despite the handcuffs, and a wire of white-hot agony snapped across Danny's brain.

She dropped the knife.

It bounced to the ground and skittered away under the roof of the car. Danny couldn't reach it. Her heart contracted to a pinpoint. She had nothing left to free herself from the coffin the Mustang had become.

Teeth.

Danny grasped her handcuffed wrist and stretched the flesh back as far as she could. She maneuvered her jaws until her teeth were jammed against the frame of the Mustang. Her knuckle, salty with blood, was between her lips. Danny thrust her head forward and bit down. The pain was so much bigger than her hand, crushed into its outline with punishing force.

She jammed her teeth into her flesh with strength renewed by fear, and the skin broke. Blood flowed. There was meat under there, rubbery cables, then the hard joint. She worked her teeth between the two bones that made up her knuckle. They fit together so closely. There was a *pop* when she forced them apart.

She chewed until she was choking in her own blood, the pain making her writhe. At last the finger snapped away from her hand. The zombies were so close, moaning with hunger, but they hadn't reached her yet.

Danny got through three of her fingers before she was released from the Mustang.

She fell to the dirt floor of the ditch and tucked her mutilated limb up against her chest. The sole of her boot was on fire. She crawled away from the blazing motor oil and hunched herself along. But the zeros were there. So after all that, she was going to get torn apart anyway.

She struggled to her feet. The boot, at least, wasn't burning anymore. There was a transcendental giddiness in her, now, all the pain and terror like vast electrified wings that could bear her away. The zero was there. It reached out to her, almost in welcome, its mouth open, teeth exposed—she could see the firelight reflecting off the back of its mottled throat—and then its head blew clean off its shoulders. A comical little spurt of black blood popped up from the ragged meat of its neck and the thing collapsed.

Then a great, dark shape leaped down from the upper world above the culvert—a shaggy, ugly thing with a wild, broken face. Danny did the only thing left. She blacked out.

PART FOUR
HEAVEN

1

Amy got her butt kicked. There was no question about that. It was almost worth it, the way Danny hightailed it like a jackrabbit back to that beautiful old stupid Mustang of hers. Danny did a fancy dive into the car and it was moving before she was even all the way in. Then the guy with the face tattoos was shooting at Danny with his huge tank gun, *buk-buk-buk-buk*. Danny got the car spun all the way around back to front and hit the gas. Amy could hear people shouting inside the motor home. Then Reese was pounding Amy silly and she couldn't really look anymore because she was taking a severe beating.

Reese stopped hitting her in order to watch the shooting. Murdo was screaming in a high-pitched voice and jumping up and down, waving his fists. The flame from the huge cannon leaped ten feet from the barrel. The lights of the Mustang turned from crisp outlines into dim glows as the landscape blew up around it.

Amy could hear metallic hammering noises, and assumed that was Danny getting blown to pieces. Amy was so used to Danny turning back up again—from that motorcycle accident when she was young, then from the war, and the war again, and another war, and now, coming back from her mission in the world of the undead—that she didn't experience shock or grief, but disbelief. This couldn't be it.

Danny couldn't finally be gone.

Then it looked as if Amy's faith was vindicated. Danny took the Mustang off-road, so much dust kicked up you couldn't even see where it was. It was like a smokescreen, and the gun was shooting up all over the place but they could still hear the Mustang's engine roaring away out there like a wounded bear. Danny was so smart, especially if everything was going wrong—she wasn't so good in a noncrisis but this was right up her alley.

The shooting stopped. Where they going to let Danny go? *Please let it stop,* Amy thought. *You have no idea what she's been through.* Then there was a *ching-thud, ching-thud* sound, two bursts of ten repetitions each, and a long moment later the desert blew up. They were shooting *bombs* at Danny. There was an explosion, and Amy saw the shape of the Mustang flip end-over-end, silhouetted against the halo of fire, and then it dropped into the flames and smoke and dirt and that was that.

Reese kicked Amy one more time, spat on her, and walked away, whooping with triumph. Murdo himself was hollering victory, clapping. Boudreau stood there watching the fires out in the desert, framed squarely in the gateway to the airfield. His posture was one of satisfaction, like a weary man admiring the snug house he had just finished building. Amy felt real hatred for these men. Hate and rage weren't things she understood, but they had roosted inside her and she was going to have to deal with them. They wanted her to hurt and kill, to get revenge. That's all the world had in it. Amy rejected these things, but the feeling, the black rage, burned on, like the fires in the desert that marked Danny's grave.

Murdo clapped Boudreau on the shoulder as he walked toward the ASV. Boudreau rocked his fist in the air. They were yelling many things to each other. Apparently, they were the winners.

Then Boudreau's ear blew off and he lurched backward and fell to the ground, dead, his skull emptied out by a high-velocity round. A second later they heard the gunshot. Murdo threw himself into the dirt, covered in blood and brains, and crawled under the ASV. Two more shots snapped through the night, but nobody else was hit. Reese sprinted inside the terminal building. The gates were still wide open, and now above the whoosh and crackle of the flames out in the desert they could hear the moaning. Undead were coming. Zeros.

Amy didn't feel as good as she usually did. She had never been physically beaten before, beyond the occasional parental spanking. It wasn't the pain so much as the fear it wouldn't stop.

Reese had clearly gone easy on her. He couldn't incapacitate the medic, veterinarian or not: He was only trying to slow her down. Which had the opposite effect, of course. If he couldn't afford to kill her, she could afford to give him the bird. Still, she was very sore. She felt a fresh wave of empathy for Patrick and didn't blame him for having a nice, quiet coma.

Amy got creaking to her feet and hobbled across the parking lot. She could hear Murdo down low, arguing with the men huddled inside the ASV as she limped past. She could hear agitated voices inside the White Whale. She skirted around Boudreau's corpse to the gates, and swung them shut, one at a time. She closed the padlock. One thing she wasn't concerned with was getting shot by whoever was out there in the night—she had a feeling it was somebody she knew.

She could see the zeros coming, now: some as rough outlines crossing in front of the firelight, some moving into the glow of the headlights on the vehicles. They were slow and shuffling and slack-jawed, that sound like the wind in winter trees coming out of their throats. The undead were finally here. And it seemed to Amy there were an awful lot of them.

Dawn took its time coming. The Hawkstone men were no longer in control. They used the civilians as a human shield to extricate themselves from their vehicles; that was Molini's idea. He suspected whoever shot Boudreau must be one of the men they'd ejected from the airfield, days before. Gun in hand, he formed up a weeping ring of survivors and sent them scuffling across the parking lot with himself in the middle. They pulled up next to each of the military vehicles, until all his comrades had been able to climb out and crouch behind the circle of human cover. They didn't know from what direction the gunshots came, although it seemed likely to be along the road. Not worth taking chances. They forced the huddle of civilians back into the terminal, and then made them close all the roller blinds on the windows, while the mercenaries remained firmly on the floor, shoving their guns around. Becky with the fake boobs had the baby in her arms again. She pulled down a roller blind in the men's dormitory. Flamingo was pressed against the wall with his gun aimed at her head. Patrick lay still between them.

"Goddamn coward," she said.

"Fuck you, whore," Flamingo said.

"This baby's mother had more balls than you." She strode past him, ignoring the gun.

2

The sky grew light that morning in a silvery overcast, the bank of clouds that had been on the horizon the previous day having moved in over the desert. It was hot and still. The overcast did nothing to cut the heat of the sun. All it did was dim the colors of the world, making the undead, with their leathery-gray skin and ragged, dingy clothes, look even more monochromatic. The trip through the desert had dried them out. Lips were pulled away from long teeth, eyes shrunken, bone structure telegraphing through the thin flesh. The fat ones in life had become as dry-skinned as all the rest, but the fat formed liquefying sacks around their waists, their thighs, and the upper parts of their arms. These dangled and swung like the infected udders of cows, leaking serum. The weight of this putrefying flesh dragged the loose skin in folds from their necks, their heads, giving them something of the look of droop-eyed hounds, their mouths pulled down in a caricature of a frown. The ones that had been slender in life were now angular stick insects, skeletons bound in hide, moving with difficulty as their tendons shrank and stiffened.

Around six-thirty, once the light was full, a bulky figure in the Hawkstone camouflage stepped out of the terminal. He looked around, his body poised for flight. Then he walked toward the corpse of Boudreau, unwilling, his steps as halting as if he were crossing a minefield. He made it to the body. The moaning of the undead went up loud and urgent. They could smell him. They wanted him. The chain link of the fence and gates bellied outward with the mass of the things. They wrung the wire with their fingers, clawing to get in.

The man took hold of the corpse's sleeve and started pulling it across the parking lot. The corpse was heavy, heavier than the man dragging it toward the terminal building. He stopped halfway across to wipe the sweat off his face with his sleeve, taking the opportunity to scan his surroundings. Then he turned back to the task. He got the body another yard toward the terminal before a spray of blood leaped out of his chest and he fell across the corpse, his boots clawing at the pavement until he bled to death and went limp. The report of the rifle followed the impact by almost a second.

•

Inside the terminal, Murdo cursed and punched the wall, leaving a row of dimples where his knuckles hit the plasterboard. For a while it looked like Juan, the fat Mexican, was going to make it. They had dressed him up in Jones's uniform, which didn't fit him very well but looked convincing enough from the kind of distance a sniper would be dealing with. Then they forced the blubbering, shiny-faced man out the door at gunpoint: He could go out there where it was a fifty-fifty chance he'd get shot, or he could stay in here where the chance was one hundred percent. All the way to Boudreau's body, Juan looked like he was still deciding which option suited him best. Then he seemed to gather courage. He was still alive, after all. Murdo thought the solid mass of zombies might be spoiling the shot for whoever was out there. It might have been true. But the sniper found a better angle, apparently, because he blew Juan's heart clean out of his body.

Now the zeros were going crazy, their hunger driving them against the fence, as if they could push themselves clear through it if they tried hard enough. Murdo's main concern was that they probably could. There were hundreds of them, with more on the way, and the fence rocked slightly as they thrust themselves upon it.

Meanwhile, inside the terminal, the civilian hostages wept and cursed.

3

Wulf got another one with a trick shot. He'd spent the morning of the third day after he rescued the sheriff getting himself into the high ground overlooking the airfield, and he was working his way along the ridge. These Hawkstone dipshits couldn't simultaneously search for his position and hide on the floor, so they had no idea where to find him, and they obviously didn't put on their thinking caps, either. Because right now there were very few safe places he could shoot from without getting eaten alive.

One of them was the stony ridge that ran parallel with the runway. He had a good six hundred feet of altitude at a fairly steep angle. From that height he could see down into the rooms of the terminal building, if the windows were clear. They had the place buttoned up pretty well now; all the blinds were drawn. But the blinds stood off the interior window frames a couple of inches. He noticed, in one of the upstairs sleeping rooms the men used, every now and then somebody would move the edge of the roller shade a little and have a quick look around. And when they did, Wulf could clearly see the silhouette of legs, a glimpse of them, between window frame and blind. Invisible from below. Obvious from above.

Now, Wulf didn't want to kill any noncombatants. He wasn't sure about the fat guy he'd shot, for example. He wasn't built like a fighter, and his uniform looked borrowed. So that might mean they were dressing up civilians and sending them out to die. Far from troubling Wulf, this merely added to the interest of the assignment. The possibility of an unforgivable error made the stakes higher. Sweetened the pot. Still, he had to make damn sure it wasn't a harmless woman, especially the one with the ten-gallon hats in her shirt. He thought he might have a chance with her, if he cleaned up a little.

He elevated the barrel of the rifle, adjusted for windage and gravity. The legs were there behind the window blind, and then the weight shifted and the curtain fell back into its usual position. They were about to move on.

Wulf fired, brought the target back into the scope, and waited.

There was no sign of whether he'd gotten a clean hit or not. There was a tiny black dot where the bullet had gone through the blind, half an inch from the window frame. A little haze around it. That would be the broken glass. Nothing else.

Wulf crawled backward on his belly until he was out of view. He didn't want to risk their locating him: That grenade launcher could turn the ridgeline into Mount Rushmore. He scrambled along a deep ledge until he found the notch that took him right over the other side of the ridge.

It was getting harder and harder to travel, what with all the zombies down there. Looked like a wildebeest herd, but it was all walking corpses. Some of them were struggling along trails that a mountain goat would have trouble with. Wulf had seen a couple fall, tumbling down the mountainside to land broken in the rocks. One of them even kept on crawling. They weren't afraid of anything, that was clear. Wulf was only afraid of them, nothing else (except maybe that Sheriff Adelman), so he figured that was about as good as it was going to get. All he had to do was stay up high and not fall off anything and break his back. The irony alone would kill him. And then he might get up dead and start looking for fresh meat.

Nothing else happened that day. Wulf was a man of infinite patience.

He waited.

Dawn came. Morning turned to day. Then the front door of the terminal building opened, and Wulf sighted on the figure below through the scope of his rifle. The man was wearing the Hawkstone camouflage.

The hunt was back on.

4

Danny opened her eyes.

The sun was shining. The sky was blue.

In the dream, she had been swimming. The water was warm and full of bright flashing fish. She dove down among the rocks and coral. There was no question of drowning. She could hold her breath forever. She swam down through a gap in the rocks, where the light was green and dim. Then she swam through a dark tunnel, ribbed and barreled like the inside of a cartoon whale. She swam upward toward the light, broke the surface, and found herself in a bathtub. It was in an all-white bathroom with a bedroom beyond. A fire burned in the fireplace.

Then she woke up.

"You look like Patrick," she murmured.

"I am Patrick," the man replied. This surprised Danny. The Patrick she remembered was on the pretty side of handsome. This man was not. His face was a symphony of yellows and browns, with notes of deep blue like the USDA ink stains on a side of beef. His nose was very different from Patrick's as well, all dented in, and one of his eyes was a raw, red slit between thick lids.

Only his hair looked the same.

"Hi," Danny said, and laughed a little. Laughing was physically painful, but it felt good anyway. It sounded like rocks grinding together. Of events at Boscombe Field, Danny had no recollection at all. She dimly remembered driving down the road, but nothing more.

"Take it easy," Patrick said. "We got you stuffed with all kinds of painkillers. Might make you kind of light-headed."

"Who's we?" Danny asked. She was floating in a haze, unable to connect even the most rudimentary pieces of information with each other.

The sun was behind Patrick's head, turning his blond hair into a golden halo. He was wearing a white T-shirt. It occurred to Danny that she might be dead, and this was heaven. Then she was disappointed to remember what she had been avoiding the memory of since she awoke: The world was overrun by walking dead that ate human flesh. So probably this wasn't heaven. She was glad she hadn't mentioned it to Patrick.

Patrick counted off on his fingers: "Topper and Ernie. Martin, Simon, Don. Troy's here. Even Wulf comes by every once in a while for food and water. He's not such a bad guy. He stayed right beside you the whole first night you were here. Went away before the sun came up."

As much as she enjoyed lying on her back being stoned, Danny felt like there was a great deal of data she was missing and her hypothesis was woefully out of date. She tried to push herself up into a sitting position but Patrick gently guided her back.

"Let me get you a pillow," he said, and hoisted himself up. Patrick was walking with the help of a stick, Danny observed. He was obviously in pain, but didn't make much of it. *That* was different. He used to complain about damn near everything; now he had something real to bitch about, he was bearing it with grace.

Danny drifted out of consciousness without knowing it.

When she awoke again, Topper was kneeling beside her. He had a fading black eye himself, though not quite as bad as Patrick's.

Patrick returned. He arranged a balled-up overcoat under Danny's head. She was lying on, or very close to, the ground, inside something like a big turtle shell. That much detective work she could handle. Topper knelt beside her and she smelled armpits and whiskey and motor oil. The motor oil smell disturbed her for a reason Danny could not summon before her mind. "How you feelin', Sheriff?"

"Feelin' no pain," Danny said, and smiled back.

"There's so much dope in your bloodstream we could probably sell your piss for fifty bucks a shot," Topper said.

Danny wanted to laugh again, but it seemed like a lot of effort, so she passed out instead.

They cleared the farmhouse room by room. Two men inside, both dead. They were not locals. Danny thought they were from the city, not the middle of nowhere where they had been patrolling flat sand to keep the date palms safe.

The woman in black was dead, someone said. Danny went outside again. She hadn't spared a thought for the woman since she'd run for the side of the farmhouse to get herself out of range of the windows.

Now Danny went out into the broiling hot yard and crossed the dirt to the place where the woman lay, dead, her eyes half-open and staring at a point somewhere beyond the center of the sky. Her lips were parted. Danny saw hard white teeth with dark patina between them.

The satchel mine the woman had been holding was kicked several meters away from the body. Danny would secure it in a few seconds. First, she leaned close to the dead woman, wanting to ask her: What were you doing? Why did he kill you? Who did you imagine I was? But the woman's eyes opened, and they were not eyes at all—they were mouths full of crooked teeth—

Danny returned to awareness at intervals throughout the remainder of the day and night. Unconsciousness, within which there was nothing, eventually gave way to sleep, where there were picture-plays of the waking world. At last Danny was able to remain awake for as much as an hour at a time.

Along with returning clarity of mind came the return of pain, to which she responded by demanding the others stop feeding her with tranquilizers. Her body needed a complete overhaul. And at some point the many things she had decided not to think about emerged, and demanded to be known. To distract herself, she studied her surroundings.

She was lying on an old mattress inside the stripped frame of an ancient automobile. There was no floor. It was only the hull. The roof formed a sunshade; there was no glass to keep in the heat of the day, and without the doors she could see a section of the scenery on either side. Piles of crushed and broken automobiles towered all around, flattened as if by their combined weight. There were heaps of chrome parts, old fenders and grilles. Iron racks bore windshields and door glass, arranged by make and model. Dumpsters full of alternators, engine blocks, motors, transmissions, and all the rest of the guts of cars stood in ranks below the walls of mashed vehicles. The place had been paved with concrete once, but the concrete had split and broken and now it was pavement, dirt, and lank brown grass in equal measures.

Topper explained to Danny during one of her brief lucid periods that they *were* in heaven. It was a wrecking yard, not three miles from Boscombe Field. He and Ernie had seen it on the day they arrived at the airfield. They made straight for the place when they were banished by the mercenaries. Danny asked about that, and Topper told her it was a long story for when she was fully awake.

They had a big old Chinese-made diesel generator, welding gear, a machine shop, and all the raw materials a man could ever ask for, if he was man enough to ask for raw materials. They even had a fridge full of beer. They were surrounded by a fortress of crushed cars and a tall sheet-metal fence. They had some projects going.

"We're going to put some gear together and retake that motherfucking airfield, for one thing," Topper said. "We're going to make ourselves some battle wagons!" He was excited now, his voice raised almost to a shout. Patrick came back and shooed him away.

Danny awoke in the night. There was a lump of moon in the sky, and bunches of stars. She could see a couple of the planets, although as always she had no idea which ones they were. Patrick was sleeping beside her inside the shell of the old car. They were lying under a heap of secondhand clothing. It was cool but not cold.

Danny's left hand itched like fury. It was driving her mad. Woke her up. It felt as if ants were inside the bones, making tunnels. She couldn't get her fingers to move.

So Danny extracted her hand from beneath the pile of clothes, and discovered it was bound inside a large wad of cotton gauze. She unhooked the butterfly clips that held the gauze in place, unwinding the long strips of bandage until her hand was exposed. It was too dark to see—even the pale gauze was little more than a blue-gray smudge in the shadows. Her hand was an astringent-smelling darkness in the greater darkness of the night.

So she felt her way up from the wrist with her other hand. The wrist was badly sprained, swollen and tender. Her palm was rough with abrasions. There was a crust, presumably blood, in all the creases of her hand. Then her fingers slipped up past her knuckles and there was nothing. She closed her good hand over the injured one.

Before she could understand what she was feeling, a massive fireball of pain leaped up her arm and blew her straight back into oblivion.

"You chewed off your fingers," Patrick explained. "That's what Wulf thinks. He found something in your mouth, apparently." Patrick shivered involuntarily.

Danny was trying to remember, squinting up into a pale gray sky, pink at the margins. Dawn was an hour away. She had bled a lot in the night; Patrick had awakened in the wee hours to find both of them sticky with blood. Despite his protestations, Danny had a close look at the damage by flashlight, before the fresh gauze went on. She had a thumb and a pinky finger, then three swollen knuckles with the skin sutured at the ends like sausage casing. The fingers were gone and there was blackening, ragged skin around the cinched-up wounds.

"Do you remember what happened?" he continued. "If one of those undead things did this, you could have some kind of infection . . ." he trailed off, leaving it unspoken. They could both guess what would happen.

"I don't remember anything after seeing the airfield down the road. There was somebody there. That's it. How long ago was that?"

"Two days," Patrick said, as if admitting something shameful.

"Two fuckin' days?" Danny wanted to sit up again. Patrick held her down with both hands. She lacked the strength to resist, and fell asleep again.

When Danny awoke, the sun was close to rising. She kept her eyes shut and started thinking about her new situation.

She felt she was at some kind of crossroads. She knew guys, people in rehab, soldiers and Marines dealing all the time with the Veterans' Administration, who were missing a hand, or both hands, or a foot or a couple of legs. Eyes, faces, what have you, missing. They spent so much of their time trying to increase the amount they were considered legally disabled. This was the "percentage." Twenty percent got you a certain stipend every month. Thirty, fifty, eighty percent disabled: They were all worth increasing sums. At a hundred percent you could practically live on the money the government allowed you, except of course you spent it all on the iron lung and diapers. Danny couldn't get a thin dime once she could walk again, because she had been deemed fully recovered. The VA didn't give a shit if you were ugly and deformed, as long as you could theoretically go out and get a job cleaning bedpans.

But now she was properly disabled. She was sporting half the stock number of hands. She had phantom limb syndrome, and everything—her nonexistent fingers continued to itch. She could probably get a handicap tag for the Mustang.

A tremor of doubt rattled through her mind. *The Mustang.* There was some question about the car, but she couldn't remember what it was.

The reverie fell apart. Danny wasn't fooling herself. She knew that even if there still was a Veterans' Administration (she thought of Harlan again, presumably rotting away in a bed, untended), even if parking was ever an issue again, she wasn't somebody who could call herself handicapped. She was going to have to put this thing behind her. She was going to have to figure out a system for living the same way she was before, only one-handed. *Which shouldn't be difficult,* the voice said. It never slept. *You weren't living very well before.* She had lost a part of herself, and come out alive. She was stronger than ever, because she had even less to lose.

She knew it was the painkillers, but Danny was exhilarated by this weird new situation. She had to share the moment with somebody. She didn't feel loss, as she expected to do. She didn't resent having to chew off her own fingers. Rather she felt impossibly alive. She felt irreducible. What she was had been reduced to its absolute essence, then reduced again, and then she was supposed to die. She didn't die. So everything ahead of her was extra time.

Danny rolled over on her good elbow and shook Patrick.

"Hey," she said, in an urgent whisper.

"What is it," Patrick whispered back.

"I'm invincible."

She passed out again. By midday, she had a raging fever.

Patrick kept asking for cool cloths to wipe Danny down, and the others kept bringing him filthy shop rags. Danny's face was getting progressively dirtier as the fever expanded, but if Patrick left her alone for ten minutes, her sweat flushed most of the grime off. He'd given her some oral antibiotics they'd found, but of course knowing nothing about antibiotics, Patrick might be treating her for malaria, for all he knew. Whatever the stuff was, it didn't seem to be helping.

Am I in love with this weather-beaten woman? Patrick wondered, as he tried again to rouse Danny enough to drink something. Stranger things had happened. Were happening, all over the world. No, he decided. He *loved* her, which wasn't the same. But it was still a big deal.

Danny was talking again. The fever brought up whatever was stewing in her subconscious, like dragging the bottom of a swamp with an oar. She murmured a great deal of gibberish, and sometimes spoke of her sister Kelley. Never *to* her. She spoke directly to Patrick when she recognized him, to the Amy in her mind's eye at other times; she spoke to someone named Zero Killer, and even once to Weaver, begging him to get down. But

Kelley was in the past now. Patrick kept her cool as he could, and frequently changed the looted thrift-store shirts tucked beneath her to serve as diapers. It remained a miracle to Patrick how often women could pee. Danny was starting to stink, Patrick realized. Not like body odor or the sickbed, but a rotten smell, like death.

Danny's stump of hand had swelled to three times its original diameter. There was no question: That was where the stink was coming from. The wounds, which Patrick had sewn shut himself as he'd seen Amy do, were weeping and purple where the stitches dug in, but turning gray at the edges. He was losing her. After all that Danny had been through, after all the enemies she had faced, it was the microscopic army that was going to beat her.

"Hey, Topper, heat me up a sharp piece of wire," Patrick said. "Like red-hot."

Topper took one look at Danny's hand, said, "Oh Jesus fuck," and walked away, shaking his head.

"It don't half fuckin' stink," Ernie said, handing the sterilized wire to Patrick at arm's length.

Patrick examined the bulb of Danny's hand, swollen now to the size of her folded knee, purple and hot to the touch. He was wasting time. Go for it. There was a moon-shaped hubcap in his lap, upturned like a salad bowl. He held Danny's limp arm over the basin formed by the hubcap, then— with a sharp inhalation—he thrust the sharpened wire into the palm of Danny's hand.

It popped.

An incredible quantity of stinking, bloody pus spurted out, marbled with whorls of amber and greenish cream. It spattered his secondhand jeans, then the stream lost pressure and steadied. The stench made him want very much to throw up. He swallowed and kept swallowing, but he couldn't help crying out. He said "oh, God, oh, my God," over and over. The liquid continued to run out, until it was dribbling. Much as he would rather have been stabbed to death with chopsticks, Patrick changed his grip on the purulent wound and started milking the puffy flesh. Gobs of congealed pus belched out of the puncture. Things that looked like chewed fat. Finally the wound ran blood. Patrick let it bleed for a minute, then doused the whole red mess in alcohol and wrapped it back up with fresh white bandage.

The hubcap in his lap was almost full. The hot liquid sloshed over his thumb as Patrick carried it away and poured it down a storm drain in the pavement. Then he vomited down the drain, and stayed like that with his head dangling and his hands on his knees for several minutes. Topper came by and slapped him on the back.

"You done a hell of a thing," Topper said. "Fuckin' Florence Fuckin' Nightingale, man."

"After all that she better not die," Patrick said, and heaved again.

Danny didn't die. It had been four days since she bit herself free of the Mustang. She was feeling much better. Damn good, even. The fever broke, the black clouds that raged and stormed inside her mind cleared away, and despite the gleaming pain she began to ask questions in earnest. That was the men's best proof that she was going to survive. She wanted to know what the plan was.

The men had come to this place only an hour or two after they were banished. The junkyard was located behind a butte of rock at the base of the mountains, separated from the airfield by a foothill upon which the airfield was backed. If you scaled the butte, which was not difficult because the stacked cars made an effective stairway up its flank, there was a flat place from which you could see the airfield with binoculars—or better yet, the Celestria eight-inch telescope they'd set up for that purpose. As Topper enthusiastically explained, because the bulk of the plan was his, they were currently beefing up a 9C1 Chevy Impala, the police car they'd found abandoned down the road. Danny remembered it: There had been an old, wizened zombie in the back.

"She looked like fuckin' King Tut, but she was still kicking," Topper chuckled. "I made Ernie do the braining on that one."

They had made some modifications to the basic police package that Topper thought Danny would like. In addition, they had an old Ford pickup running, not to mention Patrick's fire truck, and there were a couple of adequate Harleys that didn't need much work to be roadworthy. The plan was to creep up on the airfield at night, lights off, then all of a sudden ram the fence from the side behind the terminal building—not at the gates, where the grenade launcher and the 20mm cannon presented an obstacle, let alone about four hundred zombies. The rest of them would get in there through the gap and start killing anybody over six foot.

Along with her health, Danny's memory had returned. Not all of it, but she could now remember the early part of the confrontation she'd had with the Hawkstone men. And that the Mustang had gone to Pony Heaven.

"Their leader is five-nine at the most," Danny said, remembering Murdo.

She heard the plan out. It was suicidal, violent, and likely to result in civilian casualties, failure, and death, in that order. But it was a hell of a plan, nonetheless. Something bothered Danny, though.

"They were leaving when I got there. Where were they going? Did they say?" Danny asked.

"Their command was supposed to be in Potter," Patrick volunteered.

Danny tossed her good hand in the air. "It isn't. Do they know that?"

Patrick shrugged. "They don't know anything."

"Potter is a deathtrap," Danny barked. Something was bothering her, some fact that didn't fit the picture. "Wait a minute," she eventually said. "It's four days later. How come they're still at the airfield?"

Topper took off his greasy Kenworth gimme-cap and scratched the thin, scraggly hair underneath.

"That's where old Wulfie come in," Topper said. He looked uneasy. He clearly knew Danny might not approve of this part of the plan. But he bravely continued.

"See, Wolfman lit out right before those fuckwads showed up, right? He just disappeared the way he does. And he was like livin' on jackrabbits in the brush, because there weren't that many zombies around at the time. Watching the airfield. Never more than five hundred yards away and them twats didn't even know he was there. And he had his rifle, too. So when we got tossed out on our asses, he followed us here and we met up and told him the deal, and I already had this idea going, right? And he said he'd keep 'em there long as he could until we had ourselves set up."

"You guys," Danny said, shaking her head.

"So days are going by, right?" Topper was warming to his narrative. "Wulf is down there watching and he comes and briefs us on the intel from the field. He hears shouting sometimes. Then a few mornings back he hears a gunshot and that black chick with the little baby gets carried out dead. Those cocksuckers left her on the ground and ran. Once it was dark, Wulf buried her with rocks. By that time the zombies were showing up by the dozen, so he had to retreat to high ground, but that rifle of yours got a real good fuckin' scope on it. Wulf could see just fine. He sees they're pulling out. So he come back here and tells us about it and I says to him, shit, we're not ready. So he says he figures he can slow 'em down."

"Slow them down?" Danny said, and Topper heard the disapproval again. But he pressed on.

"Well, see that's where you come in. We were gonna put our plan in action—when all of a sudden the long-lost Sheriff Adelman pulls up to the airfield in a fine example of vintage American iron. Then those pricks blew you off the map. We're all real sorry about the 'Stang, incidentally. Wulf was right there. He saw it all happen not two hundred yards away."

"Three hundred," Ernie added.

"Three hundred," Topper amended. "You fucked up my story, Ernie."

"Sorry, Topper."

"Mind if I continue?"

"Please."

"So Wulf is right there under a quarter-mile away," Topper went on. Danny enjoyed simply hearing their voices, being among people she knew. They shared something. They survived together.

"He took a chance and crawled to your position," Topper said. "Fuckin' zombies were right there on you, practically. You're hung up under the car, then you're doing something, and before he gets to you you're free. He thought you were a zombie for a minute on account of what you done. Them cuffs was a good idea. He said your hand didn't bleed hardly at all. The Wolfman took out the zombies and carried you off a safe ways. Calls us to come quick, no lights."

"How are you communicating this whole time?" Danny asked.

Ernie produced a toy plastic walkie-talkie in a magenta case with stickers of a cartoon girl all over it.

"We got these at the store," Ernie said. "Toy department. You couldn't talk from one end of the trailer to the other with them goddamn toy radios we had when I was a kid, but these new ones got a good range on 'em. But the range ain't so good you can hear the whole way. So we done relays with 'em."

"That was Ernie's idea," Topper said. "He ain't as stupid as he smells. We set up a daisy chain with the radios: Wulf talks on the first one, we got a man halfway back gets Wulf's message, and he talks on the next one to send the message to our lookout, up top." Topper gestured to the butte, where Martin the skinny college kid was crouching above them.

"Go keep watch, for chrissakes," Topper shouted, catching sight of Martin. Martin walked away out of view across the top of the butte.

"Man, we're as bad as those pukes down at the airfield," Topper added, then went on, "Tell you the truth, Wulf was real mad about what happened to you. He shot one of those fuckers in the head right after he found you, just outta spite, and that give us all the idea to keep 'em where we want 'em. Any time one of them peckerwipes shows his self, we shoot him. Shit, they keep peeking out the windows, they might run out of men before we're even ready to move on the plan."

Having heard the whole story, what Danny meant to say was: *What an extraordinary series of actions. What an unprecedented situation. It is thought-provoking. I am impressed, and I am compelled.*

What she said was, "Fuck." And again, thoughtfully: "*Fuck.*"

They knew what she meant.

Danny ate for the first time in days, and ate well. Macaroni and cheese from a box, followed by cocktail franks from a jar. Then she felt sick, but it stayed down, and the next thing was thirst. She wanted beer, something cheap and American if they had it, but no light beer. Patrick brought her three large bottles of sparkling water. She complained, then drank all three bottles inside forty minutes. A while later she belched with such force that Ernie came to see what the noise was, a welding mask propped up on his forehead.

"Nice one, Sheriff," he said, and went back through the piles of wrecked cars to report the occasion to Topper.

Danny was back under the old car hull. It was a 1939 Buick, she had determined. Patrick was on radio relay duty at the listening post out in the desert, a spot relatively zombie-safe because it had an eight-foot cliff on one side and an old cow pen with heavy wire along the other. Still, an anxiety-producing place to be. Easily surrounded.

Topper came by to visit Danny; he was reeking of ozone from the arc welder in the shed. They were going to move her to the living quarters next, but they wanted her to be able to walk on her own. She thought she probably could. The men were shacked up inside a corrugated iron Quonset hut around the corner, where the interior parts and upholstery were kept by the previous owners; the men were sleeping on bench seats scavenged from old trucks. It was a bachelor's paradise, except for the absence of good-looking ladies. Pardon the implication, Topper added.

"I dunno how you survive all this," Topper mused.

"It's got me stumped, too," Danny said, and waited. When Topper didn't laugh, she prodded him with her good elbow.

"That's just wrong," Topper said.

Danny cawed with laughter. It wasn't a pretty laugh—it sounded like somebody sawing a sheet of tin, in fact—but then again, she wasn't accustomed to laughing.

Danny wanted very much to get into action. Her friends were down there. She couldn't remember what directly preceded her getting blown up and performing the self-amputation, but she knew Amy was in trouble. Danny remembered that she had seen her friend alive, but not what she saw. There were the stories of what had happened before, as well. The mercenaries from Hawkstone had beaten Patrick almost to death, and killed the young mother. For all Danny knew the baby was dead, too. According to the reports from Wulf, three Hawkstone men were dead or wounded, although one of them might have been somebody else dressed as a soldier, he had to admit. Danny admired the old man's candor. He might have shot a noncombatant; his bad, he accepted full responsibility.

He also knew there wasn't a working jail or courthouse on the West Coast.

Later, Danny tried to figure out how to eat with one hand. There was no physical rehabilitation anymore; she would have to invent new ways of doing a lot of things. Patrick knelt beside her and produced a rumpled plastic bag from his back pocket.

Inside was Kelley's note.

"You had it on you. Your uniform is cleaned up, too," Patrick said. Danny was touched. Only he would have bothered.

"I heard they beat you up pretty good and left you down at the airfield," Danny said. "How come *you're* here?"

Patrick drew invisible circles on the pavement with a piece of automotive trim.

"Those guys, those fake soldiers," Patrick said. "Murdo, the boss? He hated me. I think he was latent. He chose me for his special enemy. They all kept fucking with me. It was so obvious they wanted to make an example out of me, and I was so like, no way. Not happening. But even that upset them.

"I don't remember getting my ass kicked, thankfully," Patrick continued. "I don't even remember the next like three or four days."

They sat in silence for a while, then Patrick made a couple of false starts at speaking. He wanted to say something, but couldn't find the right way to put it.

"Why did you go?" he finally said.

Danny shook her head. "My sister. I was crazy to find her. I had to try. If it had been Weaver—you know what I mean?"

"You went out to look for her."

"All the way to San Francisco. She's gone. It's all gone. I realized out there, there's nothing left. Each other is all we got. It sounds gay, I know. I mean—"

"I know what you mean."

"Anyway, I shouldn't have left you guys."

"I guess you didn't have a choice." Patrick didn't sound convinced, but Danny knew she didn't have the right to insist on understanding. What had happened to him—and to all of the survivors—was as much her responsibility as it was the mercenaries'.

Out of her emotional depth, she changed the subject. "So what happened?"

"I woke up the next day. I was marinating in my own pee, but I was all bandaged up, so I know Amy was taking care of me. What happened was I was staring at this godawful spray-on acoustic ceiling material, and then one of them comes in, one of these Hawkstone gangsters. The Italian one. He takes one look at me like I'm worthless, and then he peeks out the window. Half an hour later he comes in and does it again. This time the boss is with him, this guy named Murdo. He's such an overcompensator."

"Was he the short one?"

"Total Porsche driver. He tells me I'm lucky I'm even alive, which is debatable based on the state my beautiful face is in. Then he tells me somebody is shooting at us, and he wants to know who. He thinks it was Topper. Of course I hadn't the foggiest, and I told him that. He comes over to smack me some more and just then Amy arrives and tells him if he hits me, I'll die. He says, so fucking what. I kid you not, his exact words. *So fucking what.* And right then, the window breaks. I thought the Italian Stallion broke it, but he's going like this—"

Here, Patrick pantomimed pressing his stomach with the heel of both hands.

"—And he falls down. And I had no idea that much blood could come out of somebody. It was unbelievable. He got shot, right then and there, just like Murdo said. Amy did whatever she was doing, tried to stop the bleeding, but she said it must have gone through his liver or something. He kept trying to fight her off. Then he died."

"So how many of them are left, as far as you know?" Danny was caught up in the narrative, but she was also building up her calculations, adding in factors, trying to come up with a way to spring the others out of captivity that didn't involve making a big hole in the fence for zeros to get through. Patrick shrugged.

"Murdo. Parker, this guy with a neck like this. Reese and Flamingo. Don't ask where he got his name. There's this psychopath called Ace, Amy told me he killed Cammy, the one with the baby? And there's Jones, this wounded one that Amy patched up. That's what started the whole thing."

Danny hadn't heard the story of Jones, yet. Patrick told her about it, and everything else that had happened. It took much of the afternoon. By that time, most of the other men were fairly drunk and shouting obscenities, roaring with laughter as they carried parts back and forth and clanged around with hammers and built whatever it was they were building.

Patrick was watching Danny's face. She didn't like the scrutiny. He seemed to be looking for something that ought to be there, but wasn't.

"I found the Mustang in Potter," Danny said, for the sake of breaking the silence. "End of the trail. After that, Kelley was gone. Dead or alive, I don't know." It all seemed so long ago.

"Then you went to San Francisco. And did what?"

"Nothing," Danny said, and meant it. The whole journey had been a waste of time. What happened wasn't worth recounting.

"I went for a swim in the ocean," Danny added, her voice freighted with guilt.

"You should have stayed," Patrick said, and contained within that small statement was the world of unintended consequences Danny had unleashed. He might forgive her someday, but she wouldn't.

She felt a flood of grief and could have cried, but cleared her throat instead: "So, how did you get out of Boscombe Field? Sounds like the place was locked down."

Patrick could see Danny wasn't going to tell him anything else about her adventures, so he closed his eyes to summon the history before him.

"Yeah. And now with the Italian dead the Hawkstone guys were really going cuckoo for their Cocoa Puffs, so to speak. Murdo went crazy. Not so much because he lost another man, I think, as because it could just as easily have been him that got hit. So next morning, I can walk a little, and Murdo dresses me up in the Flamingo's uniform, they all hide next to the windows with their guns, and Murdo tells me to go outside or they'll shoot me. I can totally see what the idea is, and everybody's yelling for me not to go out there because they did the same thing with Juan before, and he's dead. But what do I care, right? I *wanted* to die at that point.

"So I went outside. If Wulf shot me, they were going to shoot back in the direction the shot came from. I guess he recognized me, because nothing happened. Murdo was so mad *he* tried to shoot me from the front door, but Wulf shot the doorway up and all the big tough guys ended up on the floor. I went over to the hangar, got the fire truck out, and drove away."

"It's not that simple," Danny said. "The airfield must be swarming with zombies. Everybody's dead by now. Amy. The rest. You didn't open the gates full of zeros and shove through and then close the gates behind you. I mean you just didn't. You'd be dead."

"Oh, come on, Danielle, give other people a little credit. It's a truck full of fire-retardant foam. The gate has a big padlock with a key in it. All I had to do was drive over, unlock the padlock, and after a couple of minutes I figured out how to work the foam gun. I sprayed my way out!"

"Just like that?"

"Well, yes. That stuff is awful. The zombies went flying. They couldn't see or smell or hear or anything; they looked like Christmas decorations. They looked like the Stay Puft Marshmallow Man."

"No shit."

"I drove through the gates, and right away a bunch of the Ladies' Auxiliary came running from the terminal building and closed the gates behind me. I think like two zombies got through, and Wulf killed them both," he added, defensively.

Danny shook her head.

"If you don't believe me," Patrick protested, "the fire truck is right over there. Ask anybody."

"So how the hell do you know how to drive a fire truck?"

Patrick blushed. "Oh, so I'm not man enough for that? I can choose the curtains but I can't operate heavy machinery?"

Sarcasm was obviously lost on Danny. She waved her hand-stump dismissively at Patrick.

"Fire trucks are complex. They're not cars."

"It was only a small one. Like a moving truck."

Danny stared at him, her eyes slitted with suspicion.

"I used to date a fireman," Patrick confessed.

•

Danny found she could move around now without getting light-headed. She felt good, despite the pain; after years of prescriptions and drinking, she felt as if all the poison had left her body. Maybe it had, running out of the infected stump of her hand. With Patrick's assistance, Danny took a tour of the junkyard. It was probably originally a place for salvaging parts and selling the rest for scrap metal, but clearly someone had loved the bits and pieces, because there was now a comprehensive auto-building workshop there, full-scale, if hand-built. They had independent generator power, tools, a spray booth, pneumatics—it wasn't state-of-the-art, but it was everything a fellow needed. The front gates were a masterpiece of folk art. Coyote skulls and deer antlers sprouted from a deadly-looking metal sculpture surmounting a pair of huge iron doors on two-foot hinges. The gate belonged on a medieval castle. The doors were studded with hubcaps and wheels. Each door must have weighed five tons, but they were nicely balanced. Topper gave Danny the tour of the facilities and lamented the previous owner was not among them.

"He was my kind of motherfucker," Topper intoned, reverently. Then he helped Danny over to a rudely constructed garage, the door to which Ernie swung open on cue.

"Tadaaa," Ernie said.

"It's not beautiful," Patrick said. "But it has a certain something."

Danny said nothing. She limped past Topper and circled the machine, slowly. She could see the basic outline of the Chevy police special underneath. The paint was the same. But the vehicle had been built up from end to end. A frame of tubular steel, granular and blackened at the welds, mimicked the contours of the car, forming a cage around it. Panels of chain-link fence had been framed in iron and set into the tubular superstructure across all the windows. The doors had their own, independent frames welded straight onto the sheet metal. A row of mismatched off-road lamps were mounted on the roof above the police flashers. At each end of the car the factory bumpers had been pulled off and replaced with railroad ties, bolted on and bound with thick steel rope. Projecting out of the railroad ties was a pair of arms that extended two feet beyond the nose of the vehicle. Between the arms was stretched a length of slender cable.

"That what I think it is?" Danny said at last. She gestured at the cable with her injured hand.

"It's for cutting cheese," Topper said. When Danny said nothing else,

Topper added, "It's not done yet. We'd like to reduce the weight some, maybe get some gladiator action going."

"It's good," Danny said, realizing she needed to say something. "Damn good."

When the following dawn came, Danny had been awake for hours, contemplating the options before her. There was a quotation she remembered from Sun Tzu's *Art of War*, good advice even twenty-six hundred years later.

Do not interfere with an army that is returning home. When you surround an army, leave an outlet free. Do not press a desperate foe too hard.

It was time to create an outlet.

5

The shooting had stopped. Murdo sent several relays of civilians out. The women looked ridiculous in the oversized uniforms, but he even made Mrs. Tits go out holding a gun to Amy the veterinarian's head, and that didn't work, either. The sniper was either holding fire, or—more likely—he'd been chased away or eaten by the zeros. It was time to take a chance. Murdo had to decide which of his men was going to take it. But when he brought the subject up, the first thing that happened was Estevez worked the chambering mechanism on his submachine gun and said, "I think it's your turn, Mr. Man."

Murdo shouted at them. He raged. They all stood there, bigger and meaner than him. And then he saw it. In a single gesture, assuming he survived, he could make himself into the commander again, the respected leader. He could turn himself into a legend. All he had to do was get out that door and across to the ASV. Once he was inside, he was safe, he was armed to the teeth, and he was back on top.

He told them they were all pussies. Fuck it. Man to do a man's job. He went to the front door, splintered with bullet holes from Patrick's escape, and opened it a crack. Nothing. That wasn't how the sniper operated. He was sure the gunman was up on the ridgeline above the airfield—where else could he be, and not get bitten to death? But it was a mile of rough stone up there. A man could hide out for months in a place like that, picking off targets below; Murdo had spent time in Afghanistan with stone-cold killers who did exactly that for a living.

Murdo knew what to do. Get into the gun turret of the ASV and blast off with the grenade launcher, blow that whole ridgeline to shit. Even if the gunman wasn't up there, it would sure put the courage back in his boys.

He was hoping somebody would tell him not to go, don't risk it, let me take your place. Nobody said a thing. Hyperventilating freely, Murdo drew his pistol, then kicked the door open and threw himself outside. He hit the ground painfully and rolled, this way and that, thrusting himself from roll to roll with his legs. But he lost track of the ASV in all the rolling and worked his way too far out into the open. He wasn't dead yet, so he took a chance and scrambled to his feet and ran, body bent double, to the shelter of the massive vehicle's flank. He climbed up into the side hatch, gasping for breath, soaked with perspiration. No rifle shots. He made it. That would show those assholes who had what it took.

He reached down into the cockpit and switched on the power, then climbed up into the gunner's position. He would be exposed again, but he could keep his head down mostly because specific aim wasn't the issue here. Murdo powered up the weapons systems. There were still a few rounds left. Estevez talked like a big man, and yet he'd used up most of their explosives to blow up one little sports car.

Murdo swung the turret around until the ridgeline crossed his sights, elevated almost as high as the system would go. The rock face towered above. He opened fire, swinging across the side of the mountain. Then a second burst, swinging back, until the grenades ran out. The first salvo hit while the second was still on its way.

The entire mountainside sprouted blossoms of smoke and debris. Then the second salvo of grenades stitched along the rock face below the first impacts, and Murdo was extremely pleased to see the entire damn cliff come apart in long, smoking fissures, then collapse with the slow, rumbling majesty of an iceberg calving into the sea. The roar of so much rock coming down was deafening. The whole world trembled. A solid wall of dust and smoke billowed up and swept toward the airfield, and Murdo bellowed in triumph. He had won.

Then the airborne rain of broken stones came down.

Murdo dove for cover inside the ASV. For twenty seconds the rubble came whistling out of the sky. Glass broke, metal clanged and buckled, and the ground trembled with the hammering of rock. A boulder the size of a king mattress whirled down and cut the firefighting helicopter in half. Dozens of the undead outside the wire were struck down, some reduced to pulp. Then the cloud of dust from the hillside wafted across the rock-strewn asphalt, obscuring everything for twenty seconds.

When the pall lifted, Murdo looked out of the turret to see what he had wrought. The airfield was almost in ruins. There were holes in the roofs, and the tower windows were shattered. Part of the fence at the far end of the runway had collapsed. The front of one of the Humvees was crushed in by a man-sized chunk of rock and there were dents in all the rest of the vehicles, except the ASV, which had weathered the storm of rubble impassively, although it was thickly covered in debris. There were broken windows on the motor home, but it appeared to be intact otherwise. They might have a hard time driving across the parking area, though. There was that much rock thrown around.

Unintended consequences, but who the fuck cared? He was the man. Murdo waved at the terminal building. He saw faces at the broken windows, having a hesitant look outside, afraid.

"Come on, you pussies. Roll out!"

Wulf was happy to see Danny conscious again, but he would have preferred to keep on plugging away until he got all the Hawkstone men. He was pretty sure he could do it. But as usual, the sheriff insisted on moderation. On strategy. After all, the mercenaries might drive the women five miles up the road and leave them behind, not a shot fired or a life lost. So the men from the junkyard waited and watched. The spectacle of the mountain grenade bombing was worth the wait, certainly, although it looked for a while as if it had killed everyone below.

"You still wish you were up there?" Danny asked Wulf.

"If I was up there, he wouldn't a lived long enough to do it," Wulf muttered. The problem now was that the fence was compromised. The zeros were gathered primarily at the near end, where the gates were. But there were some at the far end, and they had already discovered the breach in the defenses. It would take them some time to make it down the length of the runway, but they were inside the perimeter. And there would be more. However, as they watched—through telescope, binoculars, and rifle scopes—they saw knots of people coming out of the terminal building. The mercenaries were forming rings of civilians in case the gunman was still out there.

"I could make headshots there, easy," Wulf said, to nobody in particular.

Danny was on the big telescope, but she couldn't discern who was who. She hoped Amy was down there among those hustling for the vehicles. Less than five minutes later, the convoy was rolling. They saw a bright flag of fire jump out of the 20mm cannon on the ASV, and the swarm of zombies at the gates seemed to glitter and burst into confetti. Something from a parade. They heard the distant rattle of the cannon a few moments later. The undead were falling, cut to pieces. The roadway turned black with guts and blood. Then the ASV jumped forward and rammed the gates open; the convoy rolled through the gap, slowly, the cannon still sweeping the swarm, then picking up speed. The ASV was plowing through the fringes of the crowd now, and then they were all driving away down the road, the motor home in the middle, the remaining Humvee at the back, and behind that stood what was left of Boscombe Field, the undead already stumbling in to claim it for themselves.

Wulf's toy radio spoke. It stuttered and spat fragments of words. Ernie thumbed his on, as well, and it echoed Wulf's.

"What band are those on?" Danny asked.

"Fuck if I know," Ernie said. "Any damn interference cuts 'em out."

Danny understood. Toy transmitters, like these radios, or remote-controlled cars, were designed to be easily overridden by stronger signals. It was a guarantee that some kid with a foot-long RC dune buggy wouldn't inadvertently cut out a fire department signal, or a police radio, rendering communications impossible during an emergency. Some devices that were supposed to be safe for use still did it: Certain cordless phones, for example, could break up a transmission as a squad car rolled past the house. As the convoy rolled up the road toward their position, the puny little toy radios were picking up transmissions from the transceivers aboard the vehicles.

The digital band signals would make no sense, of course. The military favored them for that reason, among many. Scrambled fragments of noise that had to be assembled into ones and naughts before a computer turned those into simulations of sounds. But the White Whale didn't have a satellite radio. It was good old-fashioned Citizen's Band. That meant Danny might possibly get to listen in. They all watched and waited as the convoy rumbled away from the airfield, a plume of dust rising up behind it. They all listened as the toy radios muttered and squawked. Then chunks of intelligible speech came through. Words and phrases. And finally Danny heard the word "Potter." Patrick was right.

"Is that thing gassed up?" Danny asked. "I'd like to take it for a spin."

Murdo led the convoy down the highway and was relieved to find far fewer zombies once they moved into the rougher hill country. They'd had to grease dozens of the things on the way to the main road, blowing them apart with the cannon or running them down. The massive swarm inching its way north through the lowlands worried him, because Potter was northward. It also worried him, or bothered him, that his men hadn't given him credit for his courageous actions of the morning. Hadn't he gotten them out of that place? Hadn't he been the one who went outside and braved the gunfire? They had no appreciation. When he hooked up with command he was going to request a new unit. These men were insubordinate. They would never stop laughing at him. Murdo understood that now. Never to his face, but the laughter would go on in private. It didn't matter.

He had a plan, and he was going to make it work. Even if something was wrong at Potter, that was where the supply train had stopped. There would be materiel there. The train was presumably long gone, but the supplies would be there. He knew it because the last transmission they'd gotten from command was ten minutes before the train pulled into Potter. Command had been on the train, along with some fine warmaking equipment and fifty seasoned men.

It was all going to work out.

Amy had seen the zombies surrounding the airfield, how dried-out they looked, and rotten. They couldn't last much longer. Their tissues would break down and they would collapse and die again, forever this time.

If Murdo and his bunch of meatheaded killers could have been persuaded to pitch in, instead of playing the heavies, they might have been able to hold out at the airfield even longer. They could have mounted some kind of defense. All of them together, the men, the women, the civilians and professional soldiers, might have been able to accomplish something. As it was, all they had achieved was to render the airfield uninhabitable for the next people who came along. Yet another refuge from the undead, lost to stupidity and fear and violent thinking. When Murdo got to Potter, what would he find? More of his idiot companions marching around with their guns and gung-ho? Would they be driving around shooting up crowds of zombies, as they had done on the way out of the airfield?

She remembered, when the gates swung open, how Reese, now in the driver's seat of the White Whale, had screamed with excitement. The claws of the zombies had torn at the outside of the motor home, blackened fingers with the bones jutting out of them. The wheels of the heavy machine had spun in the greasy slick of bowels, dirt, and blood on the road. The smoke from the spinning tires stank of grilled meat, a smell that left a taste in the mouth. The survivors were weeping, holding each other. The baby, uncharacteristically, wailed. Then that huge tank thing of Murdo's had plowed a path through the bodies, and the tires of the Whale had gripped, and they started to advance. They left the airfield behind but the stink remained with them.

Reese and Murdo were talking over the radio. Amy was listening. They all were. The question that hung over them was simple: Why had the mercenaries taken *anybody* with them? Before, it made some kind of sense. They had hostages, in case the menfolk tried something. But all the menfolk had done so far, and Amy was pretty sure this meant only Wulf, was shoot at them from a distance. Murdo made some cryptic remarks, couched in jargon, that sounded like they might refer to the civilians: Mention of "the cargo" and "tiger trap" caught Amy's attention. But there was nothing specific. All she knew for certain was this wasn't a humanitarian gesture. They weren't being saved for the sake of saving them. Danny would have known what they were up to.

Amy grieved for Danny, and on a bigger scale she grieved for the brief possibility that if they all worked together they could make some kind of future out of the disaster that had befallen the world. She didn't mourn for the murdered world, at least not in any direct sense. It had always been a strange, unforgiving place to her, all those people out there making each other miserable. They were still doing it, alive or dead. What she wanted was the chance to start over. That's what all this horror and destruction offered: a new start. Typical of human beings not to leap at the chance.

There was a series of curt commands from Murdo, and the convoy rolled to a stop at the intersection of the road to the airport and the Ore Creek Highway. Shoshone Springs, the place was called. Amy assumed this was because there were no Native Americans and no springs there. But there was something written on the blacktop.

They couldn't see what it said; the mass of the ASV blocked the view. Flamingo got out of the Humvee and checked the paint. Held his fingers up to show Murdo, leaning out of the ASV's side door. Wet paint, Amy guessed. A minute later the convoy was rolling again, heading in the direction of Potter. As they drove through the turn, Amy clambered over her miserable companions huddled in the living area, and made it across the bedroom just in time to look out the back window and catch the message written in sprawling, hot-pink spray paint across the intersection:

POTTER = DEATH

Amy thought it looked like Danny's handwriting. But Danny, of course, was dead. Amy supposed she would be seeing Danny's handwriting everywhere for a while, until the memories faded. That is, if she was alive long enough for memories to fade. She might be seeing Danny quite soon, in the most morbid sense of the phrase.

As the motor home hummed down the open road toward whatever unpleasant destiny Murdo had prepared, Amy wished she believed in heaven. It was one of her favorite wishes, although she kept it a secret, even from Danny. She had a very specific vision of the afterlife. It was not white clouds and angels in the sky plucking harps. Amy's heaven was green fields and forests full of all the animals she'd ever known, and a few people, too. Danny would be there, at age sixteen, before life started beating the joy out of her.

Amy thought of Danny again, probably half-eaten and rotten underneath the Mustang. Danny had a habit of mentioning things that would *be* heaven, but they were always excesses: If she could drink all night and not get hung over, that would be heaven. If she could fuck, eat, watch TV, and sleep at the same time, that would be heaven.

The sun was starting its descent in the sky, its light glancing in across the floor through the rubble-starred windows of the RV, but there were many hours of daylight left. Amy wondered how many of those hours she would see, and once more wished her heaven was real.

The convoy rolled over the last hill before Potter at four in the afternoon. They had made good time, but didn't rush it: Murdo knew there could be an ambush anywhere along the route. There had been three more graffiti warnings on the road, all of which he ignored. He knew that game. Get him to stop before he hooked up with reinforcements. Get him to doubt. Sow confusion among his men. Parker had threatened to stop the ASV, at one point. The message on the road was especially dire:

THE ZEROS
CAN HUNT
MEN

"What the fuck does that mean?" Parker said.

"It means they're using psychological warfare, dumbass," Murdo explained. Estevez, up in the turret, didn't seem upset by the messages scrawled on the road, but then, Murdo was pretty sure Estevez couldn't read. There was some backtalk on the radio. Reese was on the verge of mutiny again, and Flamingo was shitting himself.

"How do we know it's their people, not ours?" Flamingo asked. "They used code zero," he added.

"Everybody knows code zero," Murdo replied. "That fuckin' sheriff even knew it." It angered him to bring up the subject of that particular individual, so Murdo demanded five minutes of air silence.

At last they were close. Murdo saw a cloud of birds in the sky. A dusty blue tarpaulin flapped across the road as they motored past a scenic overlook. And then they were on the hill above Potter. The town looked sleepy and dull and calm. There was a final remark written there on the road at the crest of the hill, so fresh Murdo could smell the aerosol without descending from the M1117. It was straight to the point: The fuckers must have been running out of paint.

YOUR DEAD

"No, I'm not," Murdo said aloud.

The tarpaulin caught the breeze and tumbled away over the hill like a loose patch of sky. Murdo climbed up next to Estevez in the turret of the M1117, took the lens caps off his binoculars, and scanned the town of Potter, California, for signs of Hawkstone's presence. And he couldn't believe his luck. There was the train, three hundred feet of glorious Hawkstone camouflage with the screaming eagle on the side and some serious rock-and-roll hardware on the flatcars in the rear. Five passenger cars that would carry upward of ninety men each. They were back in business. But things might not be as they seemed. He remembered the warning from the dead sheriff: *The zeros are getting faster.* Murdo was no fool. He'd brought all those troublesome civilian assholes for a reason: They were going to walk into town. If they made it, Murdo was going to drive.

6

The visibility in the firefighting mask wasn't very good, and the oxygen cylinder on her back raised hell with the scars, but at least she wasn't leaving a plume of breath smell behind her. Danny was on foot. She knew something was wrong, even more wrong than the last time she was here. High overhead, a fleet of vultures was circling. The crows were watching from the tress and wires overhead. Days before, the streets of Potter had been strewn with ordinary corpses and comatose zeros, waiting for prey. Hundreds of them. Now there were only corpses. The zeros were gone. And it wasn't because the zeros had finally perished of hunger. There weren't enough bodies in the street.

Something had driven the undead out. Danny thought she knew what that was. She remembered the way the undead were massed along the barrier that divided San Francisco. Tens of thousands of them clawing at the wire and rubble, trying to get in. At the time, Danny had thought it odd that they were struggling at the barrier in such numbers; if they hunted by sense of smell, surely the smoke of the fires would have masked the breath of living things? They weren't supernatural. They operated according to simple rules. She couldn't believe they were smelling the humanity huddled downwind of them, with the fires upwind. But Danny had had other things on her mind at the time. She dismissed the question because it didn't influence her hypothesis of the moment.

But now, her boots gritting in the thick dust settled over Main Street, Danny thought the question had become pertinent in the extreme. She had a theory about what the zeros had been doing back there at the barrier.

They weren't trying to get at the humanity on the other side. They were trying to get away from the hunters on *their* side.

She thought of the hunters, how they moved so silently together, each working in concert with the rest of the pack. They had—was it discipline? Better instincts? They had the edge, Danny knew that much. And the more she thought about it, the more sure she became. The lesser ones, the moaning, stupid zombies, had been trying to escape the clever ones. Danny's mind was working fast, but her eyes kept watch on every angle of concealment, every possible approach. She needed to find a zombie. She didn't need them to find her.

She thought of the mission she had undertaken in San Francisco. The slow specimens Danny and Magnussen had encountered on the freeway at first—they must not have known the swift ones were nearby. The hunters hadn't gotten onto the freeway until then. The clever dead were scavenging through the neighborhoods where the living could still be found, huddled in attics and back rooms, thinking they might survive. That was why the surface streets were unexpectedly crowded with the undead on the far side of the freeway. They were migrating, just like the ones out in the desert. Migrating away from the approach of the hunters from outside the city. It was the arrival of Danny and Magnussen that attracted the hunters to come up onto the road.

Everything made sense when considered in this light. Danny felt sweat running down her sides and the prickling in her back was fierce. She carried a length of iron rod in her good hand, useful as a club, among other things.

Over her stump-hand she wore something Topper had assembled to her specifications. It was a kind of steel glove, spattered with bright pink paint from the spray cans, shaped like a cowbell where it fitted over her hand, and strapped to her wrist with a long belt of tire-tube rubber. Welded to the end where her fingers would have been was a six-inch spike shaped like the tip of a fireplace poker—a stabbing point with a curved hook at the base. Danny's injury was encased in metal, only her thumb protruding through an opening in the side. Her main concern was avoiding infection. Not the zombie disease, to which she was apparently immune, but a rematch with the ordinary infection that had nearly killed her. She didn't anticipate using the spike as a weapon. It would probably hurt so much she would black out.

It was a pity the zeros were incapable of fear, Danny considered: *They would fear this bad-ass hook.* Then it occurred to her the monsters *could* feel fear, but only of their own kind. And only of the superior ones. *Just like the living.* The problem Danny hadn't anticipated was the absence of zombies. Without them, she would soon be nothing but another dead cop. But somehow, with the ones she'd seen before missing from the street, she thought the problem wasn't that there were *no* zombies in town. They were here. They were just a hell of a lot better at not being seen.

She saw one at last. One of the stupid ones. It had a broken leg, the foot pointing around backward. It was dragging the limb along a side street that bordered the park at the edge of town opposite the hotel; its course would take it out into the open desert. The park was a small wilderness of trees, dead rosebushes, and low walls. A lot of places a capable hunter could hide. But Danny had very little time to waste. It was this specimen, or she would have to switch to plan B. And she didn't have a plan B.

She abandoned caution. Move. She came up swiftly behind the zombie. It was a female of middle size. Perfect. It lurched along beside a big, stone Spanish-style fountain that hadn't worked in years, the centerpiece of the park back when railroads still meant something.

"Din-dins," Danny said, her voice muffled by the firefighting mask. "Yummy." She wished she could come up with better quips. But it worked.

The zombie heard Danny and forgot its efforts to get away from town. It came for her, the broken leg bending at a nauseating angle as it reversed course. The thing was dried-out looking, shriveled. The lips wouldn't close and the eyelids were stretched tight, the once-brown hair now faded and dusty, missing in clumps. Its flesh looked too small for its skeleton.

It followed Danny through the park. She hadn't anticipated finding one with a bad leg. It was taking forever. She could keep away from it at a stroll. But this was going to have to do. She only hoped the Hawkstone men didn't show up before she was ready. More than that, she hoped the hunters hadn't caught her scent. The breathing apparatus ought to help, but their senses were heightened. She could feel the cloudy eyes upon her, watching, waiting. She hoped that was only nerves. She checked the trees around her. The crows were still there.

As long as the crows stayed in the trees, Danny was safe.

The M1117 Armored Security Vehicle idled near a small, square, stucco house outside of town. There was a concrete Virgin Mary in the front yard. Estevez had his hands on the firing grips of the 20mm cannon, but Murdo had given him strict instructions not to shoot unless the women made a run for it. The civilians walked toward town with their hands up, except the woman carrying the baby. Murdo figured her hands were as good as up. The veterinarian was out front, stomping along so she would get killed first. Or whatever her motivation was. Murdo guessed she was just trying to show them who was boss.

Knock yourself out, Doc. Hope there ain't any zeros around.

Reese was back up with the motor home, doing guard duty alongside the useless Jones. Reese was pissed about it, too, but Murdo wouldn't have minded being up there on the hill instead of heading down into this fucked-up town. One thing was for sure: Murdo wasn't letting Reese and Ace do anything together. He didn't trust them. Murdo stood beside Estevez, searching town with the binoculars. His confidence that they had found Hawkstone's regional HQ was shaken by the fact that there was nobody around, no guards on the road into town. There were no men on the roofs. There was nobody moving around down by the hotel, where he expected his people would have bunked up. They liked the best, did the Hawkstone brass. It looked like a comfortable hotel.

Amy's heart was slamming so hard she thought her ribs might come loose. Potter was where Danny had gone to look for Kelley. Danny came back alone, so no Kelley in Potter. That wasn't a good sign. The inch of dust and sand over the street wasn't a good sign either. The dark traffic lights, also not a good sign. The shrunken bodies lying in the gutters? Not good either.

Murdo had frog-marched them all out of the motor home at the top of the hill. He said they were going to walk, because he didn't trust them to behave. That meant nothing. Rather, he didn't have the guts to tell them they were bait. Murdo looked sick. His face was waxy. Amy thought it was raw fear she was seeing, because Murdo had been so very certain things were going to go his way in Potter. Now it appeared they might not.

There was a huge train loaded with stuff at the station, but it was covered in dust. It had been there a while. If that was Murdo's headquarters, things might not be one hundred percent awesome in Hawkstone's command structure. That is, unless Hawkstone was in the habit of abandoning its command posts.

A whirling dust devil made its way through downtown.

Amy studied Main Street as she approached it. There were bodies lying on the ground. They could be zombies, or just dead bodies. She looked up at the vultures circling high overhead. There were crows in the trees.

It was Troy Huppert who persuaded the rest of the men to let Danny go alone. He was the kind of man who kept in the background unless something needed doing. Troy liked Danny. He liked her a lot. While she was away on her adventures he'd tried to figure out how he was going to take some role as a leader—and never got the hang of it. Too many alpha males in their group. It was a relief to have Danny back, the unstoppable alpha female. But now he understood something about her: She was going to do what she was going to do, and they would get by somehow whether she lived or died.

Here she was, telling them she wanted to take her new car for a spin. She was surrounded by wrecked cars and a wrecked world, one hand chopped apart, beat all to hell, the customized police car idling at the open gates, and saying she was going into town *alone.* Topper and Ernie started arguing right away, the others jumped in next, and you couldn't hear yourself think. They were all fired up to get down to Potter and make some noise. This was their fight, too. Danny was trying to explain what she had in mind. They weren't listening. Finally Troy did a sharp two-finger whistle.

"Let the lady explain herself," he said. It worked. He so seldom pressed his will on the group, he had leverage just by the novelty of it. Danny nodded her appreciation.

"Listen up because there's not much time," Danny said. "I been going solo for a while now and I figured out it's a pretty good way to get things started. It's not a good way to get things finished."

"She *can* be taught," Patrick muttered. Danny was unconsciously massaging her primitive steel hand protector. "Potter is full of the undead. These Hawkstone assholes are taking our friends there. They used Patrick as bait before, and I think that's what they're going to do with everybody else in Potter. That means they're not so sure Potter is a happening town anymore. The way I see it, they'll just keep sacrificing people until they hook up with their command unit. That means this is an ongoing situation."

She looked around at the men, appraising them. Troy tried to imagine what Danny saw: Don, the plump older man, was starting to look like a tough guy, hands greasy, face suntanned. Patrick, with his busted face, looked like toughest guy there. He probably was. The rest were looking pretty fit and capable, too. What had once been a random collection of isolated, scared individuals was now a team, after a fashion. And they were getting stronger, not weaker. Troy thought they might possibly get through this thing together. He hoped Danny felt the same way.

Wulf, on lookout up above on the butte, broke into Troy's contemplations with a raucous shout: "You better move your ass, Sheriff, they're coming!"

All eyes returned to Danny. Troy's heart was racing. He wanted to get moving. He'd do whatever it took.

"If we mount an assault," Danny continued, "they will fuck us up royally. There is a twenty-mil cannon on that M-eleven-seventeen. There is a Ma Deuce on the Humvee—that's a .50 caliber Browning. They got all kinds of armament. And they're expecting trouble. What I got in mind is to use the zeros in town to our advantage, right? I won't be alone. I'm going to have an undead army at my back. For that, I gotta work solo."

"No you fuckin' don't," Topper reasoned.

"Just listen," Danny said. "I'm an expert by now. If I get killed, you all follow these boys and catch 'em at the next stop. But I'm not going to get killed."

"Oh, really?" Patrick said, in his most arch tone of voice. "How do you know that?"

"'Cause I can't fuckin' die," Danny said, and seventy seconds later she was spray-painting a message down at the intersection.

Then she was accelerating her bizarre machine down Ore Creek Highway to Potter, opening up a long lead on the convoy still rumbling along the road that led from Boscombe Field. Somehow, what Danny had said was frightening to Troy. It silenced the arguments. In a time when death was no longer final, immortality didn't seem far-fetched. But what chilled him to the core was the way she said it. With regret.

In fact, Danny could *absolutely* die. That thought was uppermost in her mind. She saw the Hawkstone convoy at the crest of the hill into town, and she knew showtime was about to begin. The problem was, as far as she could tell, she had captured the only zero in town. The desert around Potter was swarming with them, but the city had been cleared out. Without zombies, she had absolutely no idea what to do.

When she had told her guys back at the junkyard she was going to have her own army of the undead, it sounded crazy—but she felt like a snake charmer by now. She knew what to do, and what she could get away with. The men understood that. If they came along with her, somebody was going to get jumped on or bitten and then the whole scheme would fall apart. This was Danny's show, and hers alone.

But now, sitting in the interceptor in an alley with a view of the hill and Main Street, she was starting to panic.

Where the hell were the zeros? It had never occurred to her the place would be free of the undead. She had taken it for granted they would be here. That was always the fatal mistake: taking anything for granted. She should be grateful the place wasn't swarming with walking corpses, and yet they had become part of her world. She *needed* them.

Danny watched the convoy stop, and saw the Hawkstone mercenaries shoving the civilians out of the White Whale. She saw her friends begin the march down the hill into town, hands raised, like prisoners of war.

She briefly lost sight of the ASV and the Humvee. They were among the buildings of town, now, moving in and out of view, creeping along behind the hostages. Danny was positioned among the low, wood-framed buildings on the hill that rolled down through Potter and ended in the steep embankment above the train station.

She decided that plan B was going to be plan A without the possibility of her own personal survival. That would have to do. In a few moments, the hostages would cross the end of the alley that opened on to Main Street. She would let them pass. Then the ASV would roll by. She would let that pass. When the Humvee reached the end of the alley, she was going to charge.

With any luck, she wouldn't break her neck on impact, and the attack would draw the attention—and the fire—of the ASV crew. At that point, with the guns pointing in the opposite direction, the hostages were going to have to scatter and run for it. Danny expected they wouldn't need coaching. Patrick and the rest would come get them later on. Danny was sure her men weren't far behind, probably waiting on the other side of the hill to see how things went down. By that time, the Hawkstone boys would be long gone. At least Danny would have the satisfaction of killing one of them, if she hit the Humvee squarely in the driver's side door.

Danny's good hand was slick with sweat on the wheel of the interceptor. By now, the mercenaries would be able to see the decoy she'd set up—the decoy that required a street full of zombies. It would give them something to wonder about. But it was no longer part of the plan.

Murdo told Parker to stop. He was up in the turret with Estevez, suffocating from the man's rank armpit smell. The women, led by the veterinarian, stood in the street ahead of the ASV. The hotel was off to the right, on a steep embankment with the train station below it, the rest of town to the left, on a hill. There was a park up there, dying from lack of irrigation. Rows of shitty brick and clapboard buildings. This was a two-story town at best. It was all mud-colored from the dust and sand. There were bodies on the ground, but they didn't look like zeros. They were bird-eaten and stiff. There was no sign of a Hawkstone welcoming party. Nothing. The town was deserted.

Except up ahead, halfway down Main Street in front of the hotel, there was a police car. Or what used to be a police car. It had some kind of frame built around it and wire mesh over all the windows, and a massive timber fender that made the front end look like a siege weapon. The roof lights were flashing red, white, and blue. Even two hundred yards away, Murdo could see the silhouette of the driver inside. Wearing one of those campaign hats. Whoever this lone-wolf cop was, they had about ten seconds to get the fuck out of town.

Then Parker said, "Radio for you, boss."

"Tell him to get the fuck out of the way."

"It ain't a him, Murdo."

A trickle of premonitory alarm ran down Murdo's back. He climbed awkwardly down inside the ASV and jacked himself into the passenger seat, from which he could see the cop car up ahead through the narrow fore window. The civilian women were starting to put their hands down, looking around, looking back at the ASV. He thought of telling Estevez to shoot one of them, to keep the rest in line, but he didn't think Estevez would be able to stop at one. Instead, Murdo took up the radio handset.

"Police band," Parker said.

"This is the unit commander," Murdo said into the microphone.

"Let them go," a voice said. Low, dry, and cold, but a woman's voice. Murdo had heard that voice before. An iron fist clenched itself around his heart.

My fucking God, he thought. *Back from the dead.*

"I guess we didn't finish you off," Murdo said, trying for a jaunty tone of voice. He wanted to get a little patronizing chuckle in there, but it came out as a kind of click in the back of his throat. He swallowed. His mouth was dry. She couldn't possibly still be alive.

"Let them go and I let you live," the voice said. Murdo found himself studying the grotesque vehicle down the street. Was it wired up with explosives? Suicide bomb? Was there a rocket launcher on the back? He couldn't see anything. He cut his eyes up around the rooftops. Could be a trap. Could be that sniper was still around.

"Quit bluffing with us, bitch," Murdo said. He was letting his nerves get away from him. He was sitting inside an impregnable steel fortress. Even rockets wouldn't be effective against the mighty M1117. Even a car bomb. Somebody might pick off Estevez up in the turret, but Murdo was untouchable.

"Get on the horn to Backup One," Murdo called up to Estevez. "Tell them to look for a sniper. Tell them to light up anything that moves."

Estevez relayed the message on his satellite radio. Ace and Flamingo were back in the Humvee; with Flamingo on the heavy machine gun, Murdo had a further tactical advantage. Anybody who exposed him- or herself to attack the ASV would have to face annihilation from the Humvee.

"You got ten seconds," the woman on the radio said.

She has balls, Murdo thought.

At least one aspect of her plan worked like a charm. Danny had watched the women troop past the alley entrance. Amy was out front. Danny's heart heated up at the sight of her, maybe the last sight she'd have. Then the ASV went past, its huge wheels turning slowly. Nobody saw her. They wouldn't. She had thrown a couple of hotel bedspreads over the roof of the interceptor and parked it in the shade of a carport, well up the alley; it was only another abandoned vehicle in a town full of them. This interceptor was the one she had parked on the scenic outlook during her first foray into Potter, leaving it behind in favor of the Mustang. Nobody had molested the vehicle in the interim; it slept beneath the blue tarpaulin, dreaming of high-speed chases. It was a damn good car. Almost—but not quite—a pity to destroy it.

A few seconds after the ASV, the Hummer crept into view. And stopped—three-quarters of its length exposed to the alley. The driver's door was dead center of the intersection.

There was a man up on the machine gun, and a man at the wheel. Danny could see their faces. She could see their mouths moving. She watched as the gunner spoke on his walkie-talkie. So they were, of course, strategizing their next move, while Murdo, the boss, kept her on the radio. She was using the radio in *her* car, but of course, Murdo didn't know that. Danny had to time this thing right.

If she waited too long, Murdo would instruct his man on the cannon to blast the customized police special apart, which would mean firing right over the heads of the women hostages, or possibly through them. If Danny attacked too soon, they might still have the advantage of adrenaline, and get a bead on her. She was delaying only long enough for them to become accustomed to the situation, letting them focus their attention ahead, put their machines into neutral gear, maybe even switch off the motors.

The decoy was turning out to be useful, after all. Murdo thought he was talking to the figure inside the custom special, the one wearing the Smokey hat. He couldn't possibly know it was a living corpse, handcuffed to the steering wheel.

The idea was to crush the Humvee's driver, then shoot the gunner before he could bring the .50 caliber machine gun around. If she could still move after that, Danny was going to draw fire from the ASV. The women were going to escape. She was in the groove now, like a sniper with the target in her sights, finger compressing the trigger, a couple of foot-pounds of pressure away from making the shot with the target completely unawares.

And then a new variable entered the situation.

As one, the crows rose up.

Amy saw it at the same moment. All over town, the crows started clacking and cawing and flapped into the air. Survivors, those birds. They would be the dominant species someday. When Amy saw them take flight, she knew the danger was no longer from the cannon mounted on the rolling castle behind her. It was somewhere out there in town, not far away, coming closer. Possibly all around them. Where were the undead? She knew the place ought to be swarming, and yet she and her fellow survivors were the only bipeds standing.

The vehicles had stopped behind them, and Tattoo-Face had told them to stop, so they did, but now they were just standing around like idiots, out in the open. They were staring at the strange police car. It looked like some squat, prehistoric swamp creature, snouted like an alligator.

At first, Amy thought it was some crazy local yokel playing *Road Warrior* to pass the time of day. Then she thought, *Maybe it's Danny.* But the figure inside the car, although difficult to make out behind the wire mesh and steel pipe, didn't move like Danny. It almost appeared to be struggling. Besides, Danny was dead.

"Hey, guys?" Amy said, keeping her back to the ASV and her eyes on the custom police special.

"Yeah." It was Becky who answered, but the other women stopped whispering among themselves.

"Couple of things," Amy went on. "First thing, we got this cop in front of us and Turdo behind us, so I think there might be some shooting. Don't move—" She added this when she heard feet scuffling in the dirt on the pavement. "Don't do anything sudden."

It was important she keep her voice level and even, so nobody panicked, but they needed to do what she said.

"What I think we better get ready to do is run both ways, okay? Side to side. If you run down the middle of the street they'll get you. And everybody scatter. Go a different way. We can get out of sight in a jiffy if we go left and right behind these buildings."

"When do we run?" a voice hissed. It was Linda Maas. She was clutching Michelle and Jimmy James to her bosom, frightening them even further.

"I'm not done," Amy said. "There's another thing. See those crows? They fly away when there's zombies around."

"They just did," said Pfeiffer, her voice cracking with fear.

"Yes they did," Amy continued, her tone as level as she could muster. "Crows just love to do that. So *when* you run, don't run off anywhere you can't get out of. Okay? Just get away from these bad guys behind us. If I were you I'd double back the way we came in."

It felt as if they had been standing in the street for a long time. In reality it was under a minute since Murdo had called the procession to a halt. But with every second that passed, they got closer to something happening. The crows told Amy that. Even if the shooting never started, something else was going to happen. The shooting, however, was sure to begin—and soon.

"Amy?" It was Michelle. So far Amy had kept her feelings out of the situation. It was a simple matter of survival, like trying to get control of a car that was skidding on ice. When Michelle spoke, it added a personal element. She was reminded there were kids in the backseat of the skidding car. Amy took a breath. So little time left.

"Yeah."

"Should me and Jimmy James go the same way or should we scatter?"

"You two scatter in the same direction."

"Thanks."

"Don't mention it." Amy thought she might choke up, if the girl didn't stop talking. Although Amy was facing the wrong way to see anybody except the odd shape of the cop inside the custom car, she could picture

Michelle, her scabby knees, the blue hair with the pale roots starting to show.

The crows reached altitude and circled over town, the vultures above them, wheeling in the upper atmosphere. Any second now.

"Amy?" It was Becky again.

"You guys ready?" Amy was tensing to run, although she hadn't altered her posture.

"Hang on, Amy. Uh . . . Who's that?"

Amy looked over her shoulder. Becky was holding her friend by the shoulder; Amy couldn't remember the friend's name. She was pointing off toward the hotel. Amy followed her line of sight. She saw it, too. There was someone watching them from the parking lot of the hotel, crouched behind a minivan. Amy looked around again at the silent town. There was someone else hiding up there in the park. A couple of people. Watching, motionless, hunkered down among the dead bushes.

"There," said Linda Maas. Amy looked where she was pointing. Beneath one of the dust-coated cars on Main Street beyond the police cruiser, the dark shape of a pair of feet was visible. There were others, too. The scene looked empty at a glance, but they were far from alone. Amy wondered who they were, and why they were taking this risk.

"Don't point," she said. "Don't let Turdo know they're here."

"There's something weird about them," Jimmy James said, in his small, flute voice. Amy saw it, too. They all saw it.

It crossed Amy's mind that things might have gone from bad to infinitely worse.

Inside the ASV, Murdo was sweating and angry. There was always some fucking thing. He made an executive decision.

"You know what?" he said. "Fuck it. Estevez, open fire."

Danny glanced at the crows fluttering up in the air. *A murder of crows,* she remembered. *A muster of storks, a parliament of owls.* Amy had taught her those terms. *A swarm of zeros.*

She couldn't tell which way the threat was coming from; the crows lacked discipline. They took to the air without direction. Which could also mean the threat came from everywhere. In practical terms, what this meant for Danny was she was out of time. She reached her good hand to the ignition key, preparing to twist it and fire up the engine. The men in the

Humvee were looking anywhere but her position. She could make the distance down the alley in only a few seconds. This was her chance.

Just as Danny's fingers flexed to turn the key, she saw motion on the edge of her vision. She flicked her eyes to the rearview mirror, looking back along the alley. There was a human shape in the doorway opposite, staring at her. Hidden in the shadow, crouching down, still and intent. Its lard-colored eyes were fixed upon Danny. Its shrunken fingers were reaching out. *Hunters,* Danny thought. *Almost got me, you fucker.* She didn't know it, but she was growling.

Then she heard the 20mm cannon rattle into action. *Too late,* the voice said. In the same instant, Danny fired the ignition, stomped on the gas, and the Impala sprang forward, the engine's ungoverned two hundred horsepower devouring the length of the alley. Her ears rang with the machine-made thunder of the cannon. *Too late.*

The driver of the Humvee twisted his head around and saw the interceptor roaring toward him. The noise of the big gun had masked the sound of the motor; it was the motion that caught his attention. Danny could see his blue eyes widen, black brows flying up, then his shoulder twisted as he reached for the starter switch. *Too late.*

The gunner up above was already swinging the .50 caliber machine gun around, but he had a full two-hundred-degree turn to make before the muzzle came to bear on her. *Too late.*

The interceptor hit the Humvee with the force of a wrecking ball. Acceleration had raised the nose of the police car up several inches, but it still lacked the height required to clear the heavy chassis of the target. The impact, however, was of such power that the engine block of the interceptor was driven into the Humvee's front door, buckling the panel into the driver's position. The entire machine was thrust sideways five feet across Main Street, tires barking.

Danny was wearing her seatbelt when she struck the larger machine. One-twenty-fifth of a second after impact, both front airbags were fully deployed. The interceptor's nose collapsed according to its design, crumpling like an accordion around the engine. Danny was hurled forward, then backward against her seat. The interceptor filled with cornstarch dust from the airbag. Small objects flew around the cabin. Danny had meticulously cleared whatever she could find from the front of the interceptor that might turn into a projectile, but there was always something. Loose change and paperclips. Every pane of glass in the interceptor shattered, bursting apart into sparkling crumbs. Danny's arms flailed helplessly on impact, human muscle incapable of resisting the G forces generated by a sudden stop. Her hook-hand slammed into the dashboard. The steering wheel bent. The interceptor came to a halt, puking gasoline and antifreeze from its guts.

Danny's advantage was surprise. She knew what was coming. It was going to be another debilitating hammer blow to her abused body, of course. But she had made what preparations she could. Her mind blinked on and off for a few moments after the crash, but then she was present again, looking up past the flaccid caul of the airbag and the empty windshield frame, at the side of the Humvee. There was blood on the remaining glass in that vehicle, and the gunner was slumping down inside the cabin, clutching his broken face. She hadn't wasted her chance.

Then the pain from her crippled hand came roaring up, and for a few seconds Danny thought she wasn't going to be able to do anything else. The pain turned her entire side into fire and blue light, screaming. Every severed nerve in her knuckles awoke and cried out. Danny gasped, her eyes rolling, and writhed against the seatbelt. Then the wave of pain became a steady hammering, and she was back in action.

The door was jammed tight. She got the belt off and crawled out of the empty window frame. Danny's legs wouldn't hold her, but she was going to have to get around behind the vehicles, because the 20mm cannon up ahead would be coming around at any moment. She used the Impala for support and staggered behind it, reaching her shotgun out of the backseat. It was in working order. *Time to get ill,* as the saying went. Danny could feel the steel sleeve over her amputation filling with hot liquid, certainly blood.

And then she remembered the zero. The hunters were in town. Despite everything happening in front, she was going to have to watch her back. Her feet were responding again, so she made it around behind the Humvee. She was about to commit to her next move when it came at her, talons outstretched.

Amy heard the whine of the cannon powering up. They all knew the sound, from the demonstration they had received back at the airfield. She didn't have to say anything. Whoever the watchers hiding in the shadows were, it was time to get moving. The women scattered. Because she was facing the wrong way, Amy didn't get a chance to see if anybody but herself survived the initial explosion of cannonfire. She took a single thigh-stretching step, then threw herself headlong at the building to her left. There was no sound except the pounding of the cannon. She felt the projectiles tearing her apart, but they weren't. She was still alive. She threw herself forward again and hit something hard. It was the wall of the building. She scrambled around the corner, got to her feet, and began to run.

There was someone else beside her, and someone behind. Who they were, or how many, she did not know. Then the watchers that had been hidden all around them emerged from concealment, teeth bared, arms outstretched. Amy saw them for what they were, and her fear took wing.

If time had slowed around Danny when she charged the Humvee, now it was accelerating. Things were happening at a furious pace, events flashing before her eyes in staccato bursts. Danny stabbed the zero in the face as it reached for her, its momentum jamming her crude weapon into its head until the hilt grated against its eye socket. She pulled the spear tip out, kicked the creature back, and shot it.

When the 20mm had opened fire, less than a minute before, a strange kind of emptiness had come. With the sound of the cannon came the end of Amy, the end of old ties. Danny had come back for them, and this was her penance. She had only to complete her task, as much of it as she could before she was herself cut down or torn to pieces. Then they would have to get by without her. She would die before she was done. There was an inevitability to that. None of this was articulated in her mind. She thought only two words: *too late.* They encompassed all the rest.

The cannon had stopped firing after a single burst. They would know something was happening behind them now. Danny fired the shotgun twice into the Humvee. She didn't waste time aiming, but held the weapon over her head through the tailgate and pumped the trigger. Two of the undead swarmed into the cab of the Humvee as Danny got away from it, and there was the ASV ahead of her with white gunsmoke drifting away in the sunlight.

The periods of transition from place to place seemed not to occur. Danny was here, and then there, where the next thing would happen. Another of the hunting undead was behind her. She turned and fired, and the thing was thrown off its feet. Danny shoved her back against the nearest wall, then ran forward. Up past the Humvee, the ASV's cannon was swiveling around in the turret. She had to get close, below the maximum depression of the barrel. All the deserts she'd ever fought in were blending together now, all the enemies. They were all thin shadows, flickering beneath a bright endless sun.

Murdo saw the dragon's beard of cannonfire leap out over his head at the civilians, who were already scattering in every direction. The boom of the gun was deafening, a blanket of noise. One of the women, the dumpy one who cried all the time, spun and fell with her arm blown off at the shoulder. The rest were gone in a few strides. The tracers streaked down the length of Main Street, then caught the customized police cruiser. The lights on the roof exploded, red and blue plastic and shivers of chrome. The roof itself buckled and rippled with the impacts. Estevez was an artist. Chunks flew out of the tubular frame. He concentrated fire on the driver's side and the occupant exploded. Estevez released the firing grips.

There was a problem. The blood spilling out of the police car was black, not red. And now there were gunshots. Everything was happening too fast.

"Behind us," Murdo said, and Parker switched on the rearview camera. Just in time to see the dead sheriff rushing at them with a shotgun.

Parker threw the machine into reverse and powered it backward. The aft camera revealed a scene of carnage that had been masked by the roar of the cannon: The Humvee had been slammed into by a *second* police cruiser. Murdo understood in an instant. They'd been decoyed. They had stopped where she wanted them to stop, at the intervals she had expected, just like well-trained men. And then she fucked them up.

It didn't look, from the bouncing, chaotic camera picture, as if anyone else was moving around back there. The sheriff was there in the middle of the street, and then she dropped, and the M1117 rushed over her. Parker slammed backward into the Humvee, pushing it into the wall of the building beside it.

"That's how," Murdo said, offering a high-five to Parker. Then he looked out the front porthole and saw the sheriff getting back on her feet. With the M1117's eighteen inches of ground clearance, all she had to do was lie down.

She was making fools out of them. And now Murdo saw the game. The whole thing was clear. The sheriff had friends with her, a bunch of Arabs it looked like, dark people with white teeth. Except she was running from them, shooting at them. They were after her.

"Oh, fuck," Parker said.

They were zeros, and they were *running.* Loping along like apes, but *fast.*

Estevez opened fire with the cannon and half a dozen of the things flew apart. In the distance the rose bushes in the park shivered and spat leaves as the rounds flew through them. The fountain in the middle of the park disintegrated. Craters appeared across the landscape, from which leaped columns of earth. Murdo had lost track of the sheriff now. She was the one. They had to stop her, above all. But she seemed to have disappeared.

"Reload me!" Estevez shouted.

Then the battered wreck of the custom police cruiser on Main Street shuddered to life. A gleaming hook tore out the remains of the windshield. The sheriff was inside it, and she was going to charge them.

Amy ran for her life.

"This way," a voice said, and because it was in her left ear, she went left. There was a black rectangle. She ran inside and slammed into something and fell. There was a *bang* and darkness. They were inside a building. One of the things hit the other side of the door and started hammering on the wood.

Hands grabbed Amy and pulled her to her feet and now they were running again, almost dancing, between the objects inside the building. Storerooms and narrow corridors. It smelled of must and mildew. Then a large room with timbers overhead, dark, a million chairs and tables, tinware and cabinets. It was an antique shop, unlit except for a patch of sun on the floor that fell through the dust-clotted picture window on Main Street.

Michelle and Jimmy James were with her, running ahead of her in the shop. Amy ran after them, then hesitated—because she saw a strange vision through the window. The children were exhorting her to hurry up. But Amy had this vision to contend with.

It was Danny out there on Main Street, Danny with a shotgun, falling, and then the massive war vehicle went straight over her and crashed into something beyond where she could see. The next thing she saw was Danny on her feet again. Amy didn't understand. It was a vision, that was all. A door crashed open elsewhere in the building, and Amy followed the children through an opening on the other side.

Danny couldn't believe her luck when the police custom's engine started. The gunner had concentrated his fire on the upper half of the vehicle; the powerplant was intact. A couple of rounds had hit the cable-bound railroad ties on the front but hadn't punched anything vital. The roof, however, looked like a big rumpled piece of metallic lace; the pillars that supported it were battered out of recognition. The interior was soaked in zombie guts and stank, but it wasn't the worst Danny had been through.

Blood was flowing down her elbow from inside the steel amputation guard on her left hand. The spear point was bent. She had almost stabbed herself with it while clambering into the vehicle. No need to release the handcuffs with which she had bound the broken-legged zombie to the steering wheel: its arms were still cuffed in place, but the rest of the thing was gone. With her good hand Danny fired the shotgun twice, cleaning a couple of the fast zeros off the roof: They were prying at the metal, trying to get in.

She sank the accelerator to the floor and the machine responded, picking up speed. The M1117 Guardian rolled forward, like a maddened bull accepting the challenge of a matador. Its millwheel-sized tires churned the dust as it sped up. The distance between the vehicles was around two hundred meters. Danny had a loose idea of what she wanted to do. The hotel flashed away behind her on her left. Then the parking lot where she'd found the Mustang. A hunter-zero threw itself at her vehicle, and one of the custom overriders that projected from the railroad tie fender sank into its bony chest. The thing snapped its jaws, struggled, and was sucked under the wheels. Danny lost no speed, gathering momentum. Now the ASV was advancing fast, blotting out the sky like a battleship from her low perspective. The embankment alongside the hotel whipped past Danny next, with its ornamental steps down to the railroad station. Danny almost felt she was flying. In a few moments they would collide.

"*Run her the fuck down,*" Murdo shouted, hysterical with rage. Parker gunned the engine and the ASV surged forward toward the chewed-up carcass of the ugly police machine.

"Reload me!" Estevez shouted again.

"Hang on, bitch," Murdo shouted back. "We're playing fuckin' *chicken*!"

Estevez came down out of the tower and grabbed a couple of handholds. He couldn't see forward from his position, but Murdo was making it perfectly clear what was happening. "Run her the fuck down. She dodges, you go the same fuckin' way. This is the end game. She can't fucking *touch* us up here!"

The distance was closing. The cruiser moved out of the shadow of the hotel, then it was out in the open, revving hard along Main Street with the panoramic view of the supply train down below. When this was over, Murdo was going to power that train up and drive it to Colorado, if he could. They would join up with Base HQ there. One thing he goddamn well wasn't going to do was stay here with zombies that could run and hunt. Then he ran out of thoughts and braced himself, because impact was only seconds away.

Amy followed the siblings through what seemed to be a private residence attached to the antique shop, itself a warren of junk and old, broken things, but there was a cookstove and a wall phone and a few little islands of normal life in there. They held each other's hands to navigate the clutter. Behind them the hunters were crashing through the showroom, smashing things, knocking over furniture as they made the straightest course possible for the source of the prey smell.

The humans emerged, blinded by the sunlight after their brief journey through wooden caverns, on an alley. There was an awning overhead. At the end of the alley was a bloody mass of wreckage where a Humvee and a police car were tangled together, both stuck halfway into the side of the brick building opposite. Amy had to decide which way to run. Main Street was chaos, but wide open. The alley was narrow and the things could trap them there. She heard a voice. It was Becky, at the far end of the alley at the top of the hill, waving. Then she ran. Amy tightened her grip on the children's hands and ran as fast as she could, towing them up the hill, braving the long, cluttered alleyway where anything could be waiting.

Behind them glass broke. A door banged open. The hunters were close behind them. Now all they could do was run, and hope they ran faster than the undead. Somewhere down the hill, there was a tremendous crash, the bright sound of metal crushing metal, and then a series of earth-shaking noises followed. Amy was hardly aware of this. All she heard was the pulse pounding in her ears, the slapping shoes and the gasping breath of the children beside her.

When the sheriff yanked the wheel of the police car, it was the last possible instant. Too late to save her, Murdo knew. *Too late.* Parker, shouting in triumph, spun the wheel of the ASV at the same time, keeping the police special in his sights—and in that instant Murdo saw what she had done. The sheriff had tricked them.

Danny threw the wheel over. She could see into the cockpit of the ASV, time moving at impossible speed but every fleeting impression as vivid as pictures hung on a wall: crows in the blue sky above, brown-leaved trees. The massive grille of the ASV filling the passenger side windows of her vehicle. The nose of the police custom looking out over the trainyard. Then the door was open, and Danny was tumbling through the air. She heard an almighty impact, but happened to be facing the ground when it happened. She hit the embankment and rolled, the chrome guard on her hand stump flew off, and she tucked the wounded limb in her belly and kept on rolling.

When Danny came to a stop she was sprawled on her back on the chipped concrete train platform. Ten yards away, the ASV was completing its second barrel-roll down the embankment. It landed upside-down, squarely on its roof, the turret jammed into the buckled cement like some apocalyptic electrical appliance plugged into the earth. The astonishing thing was, the machine appeared to be undamaged. It had rolled twice in twenty vertical feet down the steep embankment, and yet looked very much like all that was required was a tow truck to get it upright again, and it could roll away intact.

Danny hoped the fuckers inside were dead, but she couldn't count on that. And they weren't trapped. The thing had hatches and doors all over it. Danny had to get to a weapon, fast, before they could emerge.

She stood up, and if she'd been in a better frame of mind she would have been pleased at the discovery that her limbs were mostly still working. She had thrown herself out of a speeding car and was pretty much uninjured. Except for her hand-stump, which was in trouble. The pain from that was so gigantic it was like the sound of a jackhammer: The ears went deaf from it. Her nerves were deaf from the shouting in her arm. Danny limped away down the platform, heading for the stairs.

Then she saw them. Three hunters, peering down over the embankment. They were watching her.

Two more appeared, one of them creeping forward onto the embankment in full view. They were getting bolder. Danny heard rustling in the bushes where the embankment became hillside again. It was time to move fast.

Danny decided she didn't want to go back up to Main Street after all. She ran across the platform for the dusty train, closed herself in one of the passenger cars, crouched as low as she could, and ran to the far end of the car, then slipped out the opposite door on the desert side.

She climbed down to the ground. Then she limped along the tracks as fast as her aching limbs would take her, until Potter was out of view around a long, geometric curve in the tracks that skirted the knee of a hulking rock formation. After a while she was tired and light-headed.

She had made some distance, she thought. Danny sat down between the scorching hot rails, a small dark shape in the flat white salt of the desert. She let her finger-stumps dribble blood on the iron of the rail. It sizzled and evaporated into little rusty coins with dark edges. The sun heliographed cryptic messages on the backs of her eyeballs. *Did what I could,* she thought.

Then she fell over on her side and was still.

7

Murdo was the only one left alive. Estevez's skull was crushed; Parker's head was twisted almost back-to-front. Murdo found it ironic that Parker's enormous neck had failed him. They were all in a jumble in the upside-down cockpit of the ASV. Murdo's rage was gone; now he was only afraid. He didn't know how Ace or Reese or Flamingo were doing, but maybe they were okay. He needed some help. Still, his luck was holding up pretty well. He had some bruises, a couple of cuts, sure. But he had survived. He was the survivor of all survivors, was Murdo.

He reached down for the toggles that opened the roof hatch—now a floor hatch in the inverted vehicle. Something banged on the hull outside the ASV. Murdo shifted his weight and looked out the small front window. And his blood turned to snow. Outside there were four of the quick undead, the hunters he'd seen. They were right there, trying to figure out a way into the ASV. Murdo panicked. Bone-tipped fingers scratched at the bulletproof glass, digging along the edge of the panels. Could they get in through the turret? He drew his sidearm and crawled back to look, banging his knees. He had to crawl over Estevez's stinking corpse. There was daylight under there, but the turret opening was jammed right into the pavement. He was safe inside the ASV. He sat and waited. Time stopped going by. It waited with him. He listened to the claws scratching at the hull.

There were more of them now, expressionless faces looking in with their lipless beaver teeth. They wanted him. They couldn't have him. He was secure inside his castle.

But Parker might come back to life. Murdo hadn't thought of that. Estevez was thoroughly dead, because his brains were showing. But Parker could maybe reanimate. Maybe.

Murdo put his pistol to Parker's head and fired. The noise was sharp as a spike. Blood and brain matter sprayed all over everything. He should have planned it better. Murdo settled back again. He would wait. It was getting hotter and hotter inside the ASV, but he would wait.

Hawkstone would send people back to look for them, eventually. He could drink his own urine. Even eat Estevez jerky, if he had to. Stay alive. Survive and thrive.

There were dozens of the things outside now. They were scrambling all over the exterior of the ASV, but they couldn't find a way in. So many of them were on the hull that the whole vehicle shifted slightly, its equilibrium changing. The turret grated loudly on the concrete. Slender, leathery fingers slipped through the spaces where there was a gap between turret and pavement. The light flickered as their shadows fell around the plugged-up opening. They were exploring. Murdo didn't think they could dig their way in. He'd shoot them if they tried it, and if he ran out of bullets he'd crush their skulls.

He was fine. He could wait.

He crouched there in the dim, stifling cockpit, his knees drawn up, trying not to look at the wizened, hungry faces that crowded the windows, the bony fingers groping around the edges of the turret.

He would wait forever, if he had to.

8

Wulf shot Reese.

The Hawkstone mercenary had been perched on the roof of the RV, watching the progress of his comrades through binoculars. He had no idea that Danny's entire squad of hardened survivors was behind him, watching him in turn from vantage points up the hill. Gunfire erupted down in Potter, and Reese picked up his AR-15 rifle. He put the scope to his eye, searching for targets. Wulf figured Danny had enough going on without additional cross-fire from above. So he tucked the beloved Winchester under his hairy cheek and shot Reese through the pelvis. The man dropped and rolled off the roof of the motor home, thudding flat on the pavement. He tried to crawl under the machine. Wulf shot him again, but Reese was still moving.

"You're losing your touch, old-timer," Topper remarked.

"You in some kind of fuckin' hurry?" Wulf retorted. "I'm just taking my time."

They found Jones asleep in the back of the White Whale. Wulf was all for skinning him alive. "He's almost human," Patrick protested. "This isn't his fault."

Patrick convinced the others to let Jones live. Jones would certainly have died, if not for Wulf's deliberate approach to mortally crippling Reese. Even Topper, who wanted revenge with an all-consuming thirst, was taken aback by that.

Once Jones was bound up on the floor, the men fired up the engine and took the motor home through town, searching for survivors. The undead hunters seemed to have gone away, although the crows were still aloft.

Eventually they found Amy and Michelle, Jimmy James and Becky (clutching the very quiet baby). They were hiding in a fuel storage shed where presumably the stink of kerosene was sufficient to conceal their presence. Once safe inside the Whale, Becky confessed she was prepared to strangle the baby if he had made any noise while they were hiding. Then she wept and squeezed him and woke the baby up. When they motored back up to the crest of the hill, Maria came running out of a small house with a concrete Virgin Mary out front; she had fled there from her own hiding place while the rest of them were searching for survivors in town.

That was everybody there was. Pfeiffer and the others were gone, presumably butchered.

Of Danny Adelman there was no sign.

Patrick couldn't bear the idea of leaving town without knowing. He wanted to look with their big telescope, to search all of Potter door-to-door.

"That's bullshit and you know it," Topper said. "Whole new ballgame. There are fast zombies out there, smart as coyotes. We don't fuck with that."

"Let's at least get up on the hill and see what we can see," Patrick said.

"It's open ground," Troy observed. "Let's do what Patrick says. If those things try to get after us, we'll see 'em coming and we'll split."

They agreed to delay for twenty minutes. Wulf and Patrick climbed up on the roof of the RV and watched. Wulf was looking for zombies. Patrick was looking for Danny.

They sat up there, baking in the sun, for the better part of half an hour, squinting through telescope and rifle sight.

"I see some of them things down there," Wulf said, breaking the silence. "Down by the train station."

"Is Danny—" Patrick said.

"Well I can't read their fuckin' nametags from here," Wulf explained. Then, after another pause, "No, she ain't. It's zeros. They're trying to get into that big old personnel carrier. It's upside-down. Fuckers must still be alive inside it. Guess that's why we had town to ourselves—they got themselves a box lunch."

Another ten minutes went by. It was time to pull out, but Patrick begged two more minutes. Wulf was getting agitated. He stank like a polecat in heat.

"I can't see 'em anywhere *else*, man."

"So what," Patrick said, disappointment giving way to anger.

"The enemy you can't see is the enemy that kills you," Wulf said.

"Oh."

"That ain't good," Wulf added.

Patrick was so patently uninterested that Wulf started looking all around them, making a production of it, so it would be obvious they were about to be ambushed on all sides. Then he stopped—having seen something for real—and his big, bowed shoulders locked tight. Patrick saw the change in him.

"*Are* they ambushing us?" he whispered, suddenly frightened.

"Somebody's down there. Gimme that." Wulf handed Patrick his rifle and took the telescope.

He sighted it out into the white, featureless plain of the desert, along the shore of which ran the railway.

"How the fuck do you focus this thing . . . I got it, get your hands off." Wulf went silent, then emitted a long, wet whistle, watching the desert through the eyepiece.

"Well, goddamn. I found your girlfriend."

9

All I ever do is wake up hurting, Danny thought. And then she woke up.

PART FIVE
THEREAFTER

1

The convoy rolled out every morning at first light. They shared watches in the nights, keeping to the wide-open places where there was no cover for stalking and creeping and slinking up. The White Whale took center position, with a tail of whatever vehicles they'd picked up along the way straggling out behind, sometimes joining the convoy for a few miles before turning off on their unknown errands, sometimes tagging along for days. A few stayed. Out front were the riders, the men on their rumbling bikes. A dangerous way to travel, but they were the eyes and ears. They could smell things, too, and darted like bees into the promising flowers to see if there was nectar to be had: big-box stores with cracked parking lots from which weeds and bushes were beginning to rise. Downtowns of lost villages. Sometimes long roads that left the main ways and disappeared into mountains or valleys, where small populations of men could still be found, living in ways their ancestors would have understood. Close to the land. No longer the top of the food chain.

In the lead of the convoy, before even the bikers, was the interceptor. It was the third and best of them so far. They had the construction of the exoskeleton sorted out. It was rigid but didn't add too much weight. The front fender was a wedge of steel with teeth cut into its leading edge; this caught the zeros and pulled them under the vehicle rather than throwing them up over the hood. Frames strung with piano wire protected the windows.

Sheriff Adelman rode up there in the interceptor. Sometimes she would take a passenger, Patrick or Doctor Amy or one of the other long-timers, but often she drove on alone, the wind rustling the choppy red hair beneath her Smokey hat. She seemed to have an inexhaustible supply of those hats.

The convoy foraged to survive. There was so much unconsumed stuff out there in the countryside, food and supplies and needed things all embalmed in preservatives, bound in plastic and vacuum packs and cans and packets, hermetically sealed so it stayed good for damn near ever, regardless of the "use by" date on the bottom. Those dates were slipping behind them now. You could get laid for a piece of fruit. Fresh things were best, but Adelman had her rules. You rode with her, you lived by them. They didn't touch orchards or crops, unless they were clearly abandoned. *Thou shalt not fuck up anybody else.* Sometimes they bartered with the brave souls who stayed put to grow things. In addition, they didn't kill unless killed at, as some put it. They didn't take what wasn't offered—whether it was sex or a jar of pickles. These weren't complicated rules. If you broke them, you got left behind. A fate worse than death.

There were troubles all over the land. It was like the Old West. Some folks took wild. They drove around raiding the fastnesses people had built up against the zeros. No matter how clever the monsters got, they were never as cunning or dangerous as men. Men could light fires and build ladders. They could throw grappling hooks and wield knives; they could pretend to be scared, beg for help, then slaughter the men and rape the women dead.

The undead were getting smarter, but they couldn't think the way men could. Tools were unknown to them, and language. They formed packs, hunting and feeding together and killing the slow, stupid zeros if they found them. They didn't breed. There were no alpha males or queens. They were all the same, eating machines that knew how to encircle and rush their prey and nothing more. Eventually their clothes rotted off. The ones that fed often, didn't decay. The ones that fell on lean times withered. If they withered enough, the dull spark that animated them went out and they died for good.

Their numbers were legion.

Dying was complicated. But the rules for dying were simple. You had a choice. If you wanted to, you could live out your life to its last natural moment. After, when you opened your undead eyes, they shot you in the head. Or, if you knew your time was coming, you could have somebody shoot you while you were still alive. It was called "sending you back." Being asked to do the shooting was considered a great honor. Sheriff Adelman got asked to send a lot of folks back. She never did. Nothing personal to the dying, of course. They didn't take it hard. The third way to die, which took a certain amount of chutzpah, was to shoot yourself. They called that "warrior style." You got extra points for shooting yourself.

2

Five months after the crisis began, the world was different. It was greener. Mankind's stiff-arm distance from other forms of life had been relaxed. Small trees and grass and flowers grew through the cracks in the ocean of asphalt laid down by an ambitious species without a long-term plan. Animals roamed freely, their keen senses adapted to keeping them away from the undead. The skies were blue again over the cities. Great skylines of architecture had been blunted down, felled by fire and warmaking, these sand-castle ruins subsequently flattened by epic rains that came that first winter. An earthquake—probably the Big One, except nobody measured it—sank San Francisco halfway into the bay. Men saw the cities fall, but did not care. Fewer places for death to lie in wait.

Nobody knew how many living human beings were left. The rest of the world was once more out of reach, a frightening place where mariners touched the fringes of land, then sailed on. There were stories of everywhere and news from nowhere. There was no internet, no telephone. Satellite communications were mostly lost: The ground systems required to track and maintain orbits had gone offline, and attempts to restore them failed because the satellites were lost in the sky. Many of those had already fallen.

Some said China was almost intact and planning to invade the globe. The Living Death was of Chinese manufacture. That's why you never saw Chinese zeros. Others said the disease had come from the mass graves in Haiti, extracted by Nazi extremists planning to raise the Fourth Reich. Some said the American government had come up with the plague as a way to reinstate its crumbling empire. It was all bullshit and conjecture, idle talk to fill the hours of wakefulness before the sun came up.

The zeros seemed to have reached their zenith. Their evolution peaked with the discovery that window glass could be broken with a stone. Had they continued to improve their intelligence and skill, had they been able to think, mankind would already have been extinct. Everyone agreed with that.

Now mankind was engaged in a game of keep-away. If men could stop getting eaten for long enough, the zeros would rot away. The difficulty was men kept getting eaten. The monsters remained prosperous, after their fashion. They felt no cold in winter, unless they froze, in which case they were finished; sometimes in the snow season men would find ghouls in nests, hundreds strong, huddled in stinking cellars where the things waited out the storms like huge, wingless bats. Their survival strategies seemed based on instincts dead for a million years in mortal men. They endured no pain, no fear, felt nothing but insatiable hunger; their self-interest extended only as far as the feast. They did not need to think.

Men, meanwhile, had begun thinking again in earnest.

Danny's Tribe moved slowly across the country. They weren't going anywhere in particular—the idea was simply to keep on going. They stayed sometimes in a promising place for a week at a time, then traveled on; once they spent a month near the cracked and overflowing Hoover Dam. There was always something to move their band along. The zeros would get thicker in the area, or the survivors would hear rumors of an army of men coming, cannibals that styled themselves after the undead, or destroyers, or zealots.

The zealots angered Danny the most. The destroyers were hordes of nihilistic gangs that wrecked and killed and burned because, in their estimation, what was left of the world was trash anyway. They engaged the zeros in pitched battles and helped feed their numbers, suffering bites and infections that left the dying scattered along the roads. When Danny found them, they would be taken in and cared for until it was time to make The Choice. The rest wandered off to die, and came back ravening.

The zealots believed the world was *supposed* to be like this. It was their beloved End Times, and the hand of God was upon the land. They grew strong on their heady brand of magic, writing new chapters to append to the old Bible, full of portents and signs. They had rules, too, but their rules were arcane and punitive and cruel. Danny would find their victims nailed to crosses or burned at the stake. The living flocked to these preachers of death, who seemed to flourish more, the worse things got. Danny might not have resented them if it was not for their insistence that joy and pleasure were abominations, as if God would relent only when the last smile was wiped from the last child's lips. Most of them didn't even allow music. The ones who did favored dirges and laments. Danny's Tribe, now a hundred strong most times, had their own little Woodstock nearly every Friday night, if there weren't zombies around. Music was all they had left: Art, movies, books—these things were artifacts that required carrying and preserving. Music you could conjure up from nothing, like fire.

The latest of her working hypotheses had yielded two organizing principles toward which Danny moved her Tribe.

The first was a safe place. Safety was a far more transient thing than it appeared. Even the mightiest fortress would fall. So they moved along, and found places that were safe for a while. But the place where the undead couldn't prosper—that place eluded them. Danny was sure there were tropical islands like that. She imagined Hawaii must be nice, by now. But they were in the American West. So far they'd never made it east of Kansas. The zeros were just too thick. Survivors said the Eastern Seaboard was an unrelieved nightmare.

The second desirable outcome, from Danny's standpoint, was to find a cure. There were people of science working on it here and there, when they weren't fleeing for their lives. The virus that caused zombiism was known. It had a number. Some said it was surely a virus engineered to do what it did, a combination of this and that until a perfectly lethal sickness was invented, not only deadly but wicked. It was said that the virus was part mosquito, for the sense of smell, part Hanta Virus for its ability to amplify so rapidly through the host. Other things. Rabies. Eye of newt. It didn't matter.

So far there was no cure, and no vaccine to immunize the living. Some people were born immune. Others carried the sickness inside them but did not sicken. Some got bitten, sickened, and survived. They were so few.

In the spring Danny's Tribe picked up the trail of a larger band of people, run with fairness according to homesteaders who encountered them in the occasional fortified settlements they passed. The larger band, calling themselves the Rovers, had their own set of rules, and ran things along military lines. Discipline was tight but it wasn't arbitrary. They were doing pretty well, folks said. Danny had a theory that groups could get too large for travel. She kept her band capped around one hundred individuals, simply because beyond that she didn't recognize everybody. It got harder to gauge the merit of individuals. Cliques formed. Little knots of people started coming up with their own plans and rules, which inevitably ran at cross-purposes to the larger group. And it got harder to coordinate self-defense.

Sure enough, as they got closer to the Rovers, who moved more slowly due to sheer mass of numbers, the funeral pyres got taller. The Rovers were decent about it, it seemed to Danny. They burned the undead in one pile and their dead in another; most traveling bands left the undead where they lay, which poisoned the water supply and fouled the air. And the Rovers left behind memorials. It was usually a piece of sheet metal with the names of the dead scribed into it, laid over the ashes and held down with stones.

As Danny's convoy crept closer to the larger party, day by mile, the pyres of the burned undead got smaller, and the pyres of the newly dead got bigger. Danny had taken to reading the lists of names scratched into the memorials. She didn't know about zombies in China, but people of every race and creed were still dying. Vehicles full of good supplies were often left behind. Danny found herself drinking more—she'd gotten it under control since the events at Potter, nerves buffered by routine, but the tension was getting to her.

The funeral pyres showed up most often in the derelict towns the Tribe passed through. Towns were deadly. The bigger, the more dangerous. People wandered away from the group. Got greedy and went looting. Found a nest of the undead and got bit. If their numbers were strong enough the silent, undead hunters would surround a foraging party and there would be a battle.

One day they came upon a pyre of the dead around which the undead had been left where they fell, burned in place with hasty splashes of gasoline. Several vehicles had been left behind in what looked like a defensive ring. The list of the dead was written on a piece of cardboard held down with a brick. Danny read the list and wept and nobody knew why. Most of them had never seen her respond with grief to anything.

"Will you find a nail or something and scratch these names onto a piece of metal?" she asked Topper, when he rode up to see what was happening.

He and Ernie took care of the job, and wondered about it. They didn't spend as much time with Danny these days—she seemed to have her own world around her, and besides, they had women of their own, now. It was a shock to see her grieving.

Two days later they found a service center in the plains, a little cluster of hotel, diner, truck stop, and bus station. The place had been looted long before, but still served as a waypoint; the names of different bands that had traveled that way were painted on the side of the motel. There were zeros strewn around. The remains hadn't been dealt with at all. Blood on the pavement. The human dead were heaped up and hastily set fire to. The remains, not ashes but roasted flesh, were still warm when the Tribe rolled in. They had their own difficulties with the zeros in that area, and lost a few people. Danny thought the proximity to the larger band put them at risk: the more of the living, the more of the undead. But they traveled on. There was no memorial in that place, and the dead went nameless.

Danny asked Amy to ride with her that day.

"What's eating you?" Amy asked, as the miles rolled slowly beneath them. And then: "So to speak."

"Remember Barry Davis?"

"No. Was he the Davises' kid?"

"Jesus, Amy."

"Well?"

"Yes he was the Davises' kid. I mean anybody named Davis is the Davises' kid. But he was *that* kid of *those* Davises. He was going steady with Kelley."

"I didn't know that," Amy said.

She had delivered a baby earlier that week, her first time with a human infant, and the thing was still alive. She only hoped the parents didn't blame her for how ugly it was. But the parents weren't exactly supermodels. Still, in the animal world, all babies are born beautiful. With humans it was obviously different.

"He's dead," Danny said, obviously expecting Amy would grasp the significance of that. She didn't. After Amy was silent a while, Danny explained.

"Barry Davis was Kelley's boyfriend. Her *real* one, not all the imaginary ones I thought she had. He's in The Note. They left Forest Peak together the morning everything went to shit."

"No way."

"Yes way."

They drove in silence for a while.

"Do you like that guy in the old Toyota—the one who makes the guitars?" Danny said.

"He's okay," Amy replied.

The silence wore on.

"Remember that place where we found the ashes marked with cardboard?" Danny said, after a while.

"Yeah. You cried."

Amy saw where Danny was going with the Barry Davis thing, and she didn't want to get into it. Danny had put her Kelley period behind her, although she still kept the filthy, tattered note in a plastic bag next to her heart. She was looking to the future again, even if she had no personal plans. The Tribe gave her something to do, something to perpetuate. If Danny got thinking about the past, she was going to end up crazy and alone again.

"The thing is," Danny said, "there was a Barry Davis on that list back there."

"It's not an unusual name," Amy protested. "If he was like Barry Hashimoto maybe. Or Mogambo Davis."

"Still."

It would explain why Danny was allowing the convoy to get closer to the Rovers, rather than falling back, as was her custom. She had found out the hard way that traveling bands of men don't mingle well. They're glad to meet, but once the drink flows, they're quick to fight. They mix up whose mate is whose. They have trouble coordinating night watches, and someone gets carried off in the night and their bones are never found. But now she was pushing to catch up, if anything. Danny had been urging them to pack their gear and get rolling much earlier than usual, and she rode herd longer into the afternoons.

She and Amy passed the rest of the day's travel quietly, as old friends will. Both of them were thoughtful.

The next day, they saw smoke.

3

They were somewhere in the Dakotas. The winter was coming: Danny thought they should probably head south before too long. Traveling was slower than ever, what with bridge collapses and little trees growing right in the middle of the interstates. If it got cold too soon—and the weather was wholly unpredictable now—they'd be stuck in some place living like Eskimos until spring.

She had been pushing to get close to the Rovers. She wanted to have a talk with their leaders, although perhaps as a solo envoy of her people, to save mixing with the larger band. They were obviously in disarray and she didn't know how desperate they were. They might decide her orderly baggage train was just what they needed to put themselves right.

Whatever plans she had made to that effect went out the armored window of her cruiser when she saw the smoke. It was a fire out in the prairie, the black smoke rising up against a gray, featureless sky that left the world without shadows. Her first instinct was to accelerate and catch up with the action, but she had people to take care of. She called a halt by the roadside. Recon was called for. Although this duty generally fell to the bikers, this time she wanted to join in. Topper and a big, scar-faced man called Pike elected to come along. Topper had lost a lot of weight. There were no more heavy people in this world. He looked pretty good, for an ugly bastard. Pike, on the other hand, made ugly an art form. As always when she rode out, Danny put Amy in charge. You never knew.

"What's happening?"

It was Patrick, come up from the middle of the column. He had weathered into his broken face, and he was tough as brass. He had a boyfriend, a guy from Philly who had walked and fought a thousand miles before he ran into the convoy. People called him "Beowulf," because his story sounded like something from Norse mythology. He'd killed hundreds of zombies, entirely with hand weapons. Patrick had become very centered with him, more emotionally self-sufficient.

Danny shook her head. "Old business."

"You still think—"

"Who knows," Danny said. But her eyes were on the horizon. She thought she knew.

"Remember we're here," Patrick said. "You're not alone."

They drove down the interstate at refreshing speed, not having to keep slow for the White Whale and the overloaded campers that made up the heart of the convoy. Danny kept her windows down and felt the freezing air blowing around her. It was that kind of weather: warm enough until the air started moving. Old thoughts Danny had buried in shallow graves were coming up. She banished their ghosts. Just go and see. Just go and see.

It was a city, not just a town. One of those places that sprang up around a missile installation in the far end of nowhere, all built at the same time, with an Army base and a high school and somewhere to buy groceries. Then it grew and some kind of industry came along and the place thrived for a while, same as all such towns, with good suburbs and low-rent neighborhoods, competing schools, white frame churches that stuck up like stalagmites. Then the downturn came and the place shriveled until it was half-empty at best. Then the dead rose up, and now the city was empty altogether.

They stopped at the only high place around, an overpass on the interstate where a local farm road passed beneath. Pike's motorcycle was a "rat bike," a monstrous, rusting piece of ironwork with scythe blades on the wheel hubs and ape-hanger handlebars, a scrap-metal beast. Topper rode a stock '75 Harley boattail he'd liberated from an abandoned garage. They swapped a pair of binoculars back and forth.

Nothing moved but the flames, so they followed the smoke. The heart of the city was on fire. On the outskirts of town they found burning vehicles and signs of recent combat. Brass cartridges and incongruously colorful plastic shotgun casings were strewn around street corners where pitched battles had been waged. Vivid gore stood out in contrast to the drab masonry and faded tar. There were trails of blood, as if the pavement had been swabbed with blood-soaked mops. The bloody stains led toward the inner city, not away from it.

Danny called off the search after only a few blocks. Whatever had happened here, it was only hours past. It looked like two competing nomadic groups had clashed; the tells of the fighting did not bear any resemblance to the pattern of zero assaults. This had been a two-sided confrontation lasting at least several minutes—the conflict had clearly been pressed from street to street. The undead didn't fight, they attacked. Lightly armed, Danny and her two companions were not going to profit from a chance encounter with either of the competing sides.

As they made their way out of the city, they saw zombie blood. It was spattered on the ground and on the walls of desolate buildings. The fallen undead had been dragged away, as well. With that, Danny was familiar: It was the mark of the Rovers. Why, then, were those bodies dragged in the opposite direction from the red-blooded corpses of the recently alive? She and her companions followed the drag marks to where the black blood formed pools, after which the signs ended. The zombie remains had probably been loaded into a vehicle. Now that she had her back to the fire in the city, Danny could see a blurred finger of smoke rising from a suburb to the east. She consulted with Topper and Pike on whether they should pursue the matter, and the men said yes, because they could hear the urgency in Danny's voice.

"Got nowhere else to be," Topper said.

They came to a broad, concrete plaza overlooked by a jolly sheet-metal clown: It was the entrance to a small amusement park. The plaza was surrounded by acres of parking. It was hard to imagine the place doing much business even in the best of times, but during the summer it might have been something to do with a boring Saturday. The parking lot was forested with lighting standards on which various comic characters were mounted: The lion was 3A, the monkey in a hat was 5G, and so forth. Beyond the entrance gates were ticket booths and turnstiles, and beyond those, a mock-cowboy town with Victorian shop fronts, a saloon, and a carousel. Beyond the imitation town were thrill rides as still and faded as dried flowers, and at the far end of the park a couple of skeletal roller coasters hunched their spines. Opposite the amusement park was a shopping center. On the unobstructed sides, there were views to the south that took in miles of featureless grassland, and to the north was the city.

The pyre of corpses had been hastily arranged in the center of the plaza directly in front of the gate of the amusement park, where ornamental shrubbery had once spelled the name of the place, but was long dead and now illegible.

When Danny, Topper, and Pike rode up to the crackling heap of corpses, they saw a Volkswagen microbus parked not far from the blaze. The windows of the bus were reinforced with barbed wire stapled to bolted-on wooden uprights. There was a woman sitting in the open side door, her head hanging. She held a pistol in her hand, loosely, drooping toward the ground, the way in an easier time she might have held a telephone handset after receiving bad news. When the woman heard the motors approaching, she turned her head to listen; at length, she looked up.

Danny climbed out of the cruiser. The men stayed back. There was electricity in the air. Pike had it in mind to ask what was up, but thought better of it when Topper gave a single, curt shake of his head. *This might be a good time for a moment of silence.*

There are no coincidences, Harlan had once told Danny; it's only the odds coming due. Danny walked toward the woman in the bus, and felt as if her legs had turned to new-fallen snow. They didn't feel substantial enough to hold her off the ground, but they kept moving, and she kept getting closer, and then they met.

"I got your note," Danny said.

The men left them and went back to the convoy to deliver the news: the sheriff would be away for a few days. She was fine, she was dandy, in fact. But she had some family business to take care of. Sure, she'd catch up. Meanwhile, the doctor was in charge. Most folks didn't know the significance of this intelligence. Amy wanted to go to them right away, but Topper insisted. Danny had been very clear on the point. There was something new in that city. It was a trap. Something so dangerous they weren't going anywhere near. The sheriff would catch up with them. When had she failed to come back?

Danny got Kelley into the cruiser with difficulty. She had great facility living with one functional hand now, and the builders in the Tribe had an informal competition going for who could invent the most useful replacement for her severed fingers. Normally she wore an ordinary glove. But lugging a person who couldn't support her own weight, that took two hands. With Kelley arranged in the front seat, Danny got out of that cursed city. She headed south, because that's where the nearest road went.

"I got bit," Kelley said. It was the first time she'd spoken.

"Yeah, I see," Danny said. "I'm sorry." She meant far more than *sorry about the bite*.

Kelley nodded. She was tired. "Not your fault," she said, and meant far more, too.

Danny's mind was whirling. There was so much to say, so many things jumbled in her head. She wanted to hear more of that familiar voice coming from the thin, strong woman who looked so much like the girl who had run away, but was also someone else—someone entirely her own.

"It's good to see you," Kelley said, as they drove along the narrow two-lane road away from town. The tall grass on either side of them, pale and yellow, had been crops, in past years. Now it was prairie again. Genetically modified corn couldn't compete with sturdy grass.

"Do you mind if I don't explain?" Kelley continued. "What happened back in Forest Peak, I mean."

"Just talk about what you want," Danny said. "It's all past now." Grief was pulling her chest apart and cramming it into her throat.

Kelley smiled a little. "Let's skip the ancient history, then. You need to know what happened back there in town. They're smart, Danny. And fast."

"Yeah," Danny said. "Like wolves."

"No—like men," Kelley said. She had to stop for breath. There was a strip of gingham fabric bound around Kelley's wrist. It was bleeding through, right where a wristwatch should be. Her skin already had the pallor of the infected, as if she were turning slowly into limestone.

"Like men," she said again. "They *shot* at us, Danny. They came after us with weapons . . . and they could talk."

"They weren't zeros, then. They were cannibals."

"Not with black *blood*." Danny heard in Kelley's reply the old, exasperated tone of voice she'd heard so many times before. Big sister, why don't you listen? Danny remembered trying to convince Magnussen of the more able zombies, back during her stint in San Francisco, and how frustrated she became when that woman wouldn't listen. She understood part of what it was like to be Kelley. The recognition fell into place in a moment, without articulate thought.

"I believe you," Danny said. "I'm listening." These were words her sister had wanted to hear for many years of her short life. Kelley continued, pausing now and then for breath, sinking slowly.

"They're like us, Danny. We never saw anything like it. They got us good. Killed a bunch of people. A few days back—"

"I know," Danny said. "I saw the marker."

Kelley nodded. "It was horrible. You gotta get away from the cities, Danny. This is new. It's made another evolution. A quantum leap. We're in a whole new kind of trouble."

She paused, then smiled and focused her glassy eyes on Danny. "You are, anyway. My troubles—You know. I'm almost out of troubles."

As they drove, Kelley told Danny more about the attack, the dynamics of it. It was important, but Danny didn't care. She would use the information later. Now she was concentrating on the sound of her sister's voice. Memorizing it, the way she memorized The Note.

She had to remember this, all of this, because it was all she was going to get. Kelley told her then about how she had been bitten in the midst of hand-to-hand combat with the undead, and she remarked on the irony of Danny's timing. Not that things wouldn't have happened the way they did, anyway.

"You could make up 'what if' scenarios all day long and it would never make any difference," Kelley said, and paused for breath. "There's only what is," she concluded.

Despite her aching heart, Danny smiled. She had spent the better part of a year making up "what if" scenarios. Her sister, meanwhile, had become philosophical in her old age.

They came to a farmhouse set back a little way from the road behind a couple of fields. Danny didn't bother with recon. She pulled up in the yard and helped Kelley out of the car and Kelley used the shotgun as a crutch while Danny broke in through the front door. The house had the stagnant atmosphere of abandonment. If there were zeros here, they would be dealt with.

For now, she made a fire in the dining room fireplace, breaking the chairs into kindling. Kelley sat in a dingy green velvet wing chair Danny dragged in from the living room. Danny put some bottled water to Kelley's lips, and her sister drank some and the rest ran down her chin. There was nothing else to do. Kelley rested her head against one of the wings.

"You know the choice about dying," Kelley said. "I decided to show I had the stones to do it myself. But when the others left me there, I couldn't. Five minutes before you showed up, I was trying to talk myself into it. Had the gun to my head. I think I could do it now, though."

"Do I bore you that bad?" Danny said, aiming for a joke. It evaporated in the air.

"You're pretty famous," Kelley said. "People have heard of you. I tell 'em I'm your sister. They say you dressed up in black leather and fought the zeros at the Battle of the Bay, and got a lot of people out of San Francisco."

Danny didn't want to hurt her sister's feelings—she could hear the pride in the thin, faint voice. She bent the corners of her mouth up as if smiling.

"They say you're the one that warned them the zeros were evolving," Kelley added. "People escaped by sea."

So maybe some of them had gotten out, after all, Danny thought. The history was garbled, but none of that mattered. Danny knew her exploits got around, but it was only bull to keep the darkness at bay. If a few lives got saved, that was something real. Kelley fell silent and still. Danny was frightened.

"Kelley?"

"What."

"Don't stop talking."

"I'm gonna have to. You know that."

"Until then."

Danny's sinuses ached. Her eyeballs felt too big for their sockets. This wasn't the same as the grief she had felt when their parents died. It was bigger, something connected to the passage of such tempestuous time. She was twice the age now. There was so much more to be atoned for.

"Maybe you're immune," she said. Kelley lifted her good hand an inch above the arm of the chair, the closest she could get to a dismissive gesture.

"Don't go there."

"So," Danny said, trying to think of what they needed to catch up on before they parted ways. "Uh, you had the same boyfriend this whole time. Barry. Did you guys—I mean were you in love?"

"Nah. It was good to know somebody, though."

"And this whole time you traveled with the Rovers?"

"After they formed up. We were with some people before that. You know, just fighting and staying awake. I'm so tired now. I could really sleep."

"Sleep later," Danny said.

Kelley didn't answer. Danny felt the panic come back. She was kneeling in front of Kelley, now, watching. The gun was in Kelley's lap. It slipped and Danny tried to catch it, but with her left hand. The gun bounced off her truncated palm and hit the floor. Kelley opened her eyes again.

"Danny?" she said.

"I'm right here," Danny said. Kelley's eyes drifted around and found her.

"It's getting dark."

"I'm right here with you."

It was afternoon. The sun came through the windows at a low angle, reaching from the front of the house into the back, the light creamy with dust motes. It would be getting dark soon, but Kelley was staring into a different kind of darkness.

There were so many things Danny wanted to say, but as always, when it mattered, she couldn't figure out how to assemble the words. She held Kelley's unbitten hand in her own hand and tried to squeeze some warmth into the icy fingers. All she wanted was a single sentence to come together so she could say everything she felt to Kelley, some way to express her gratitude and sorrow and love. Her mind was racing. She had to think of the words. All her skill at coming up with plans and stratagems on the fly, reacting like lightning no matter what happened, and here she couldn't come up with a simple statement that folded all the important things up into a small bundle Kelley could take with her when she went away. Then it occurred to her. It was so obvious she hadn't thought of it.

"I love you," she said.

But Kelley was already gone.

Danny picked up the gun. She felt for a pulse. There was none. No breath escaped the lips. Kelley was dead, and the thought, always present, hit Danny with new force because at last it was true. Danny fell back on her haunches and looked up at her sister's corpse, face slack, head tipped into the corner of the chair as if Kelley had only fallen asleep in the car with her head against the backseat window, the way she often did when she was a small girl. She had fallen asleep like that when they drove down to the go-kart place in the flatlands for Kelley's birthday. She had graduated to the front seat by then. Danny wished she could take her sister somewhere again. She wished everything, more wishes than fishes, more wishes than stars, as their mother had said, an eternity ago in a different world. The wishes collapsed into tears and Danny fell forward and sobbed in her sister's lap, a lifetime of scalding, unshed tears pouring from her eyes.

But there was no time for grieving anymore. It was that kind of world. Danny scrubbed her face on her sleeve, smearing the wet from her eyes and nose. The first of the three choices had already passed; Kelley lived until she died. Danny could shoot her sister's corpse in the head while she was still in the brief, blessed death-between, or she could wait until reanimation.

Danny thought it would be best if she pulled the trigger on the lifeless shell, rather than executing the alien, deadly thing her sister would become. It was time. She cocked the gun with her stump-hand and looked up once more at her sister.

Too late, said the voice in Danny's head.

Always too late.

The second choice had also passed. That leaden look had come to the flesh. The undead eyes opened, murky and dull. They wandered, then located Danny and fixed upon her. Danny raised the pistol and placed it up under her sister's chin. Kelley's slate-gray lips parted.

And spoke.

"I'm still me," she whispered.

ACKNOWLEDGMENTS

Nobody writes alone. I owe many thanks to many people. Here are a few of them.

My editor, Ed Schlesinger, is an easy one. He makes me think I know what I'm doing. My wife, Corinne Marrinan, who knows the difference between the weeds and the wanted is just a matter of care. The Aged Crone—you know who you are. Rich Procter. Steven Iammarino. J.M. Finholt. My many writer friends, who make writing seem almost respectable. Assorted members of the LAPD and LVPD. The professional firefighters of Altadena, California. The rest of you I'll thank in person.

Finally, no work in the realm of zombies can exist without the pioneering efforts of the prophet George Romero, who warned us: we spend our lives and treasure fearing the *other*, when the enemy, after all, is ourselves.